Emma Martin is 36 and married with three chil...   e,
William and Amara. After giving up her career in sales to
care for her three children she now writes from her home in
the rolling hills of North Yorkshire, *Racy!*, is her debut
novel and she sincerely hopes you enjoy it. Should you wish
to contact her she would be delighted to hear from you at
info@emma-martin.com, alternatively, please feel free to
visit her website at www.emma-martin.com

Best wishes,

Emma Martin

Racy!

Matador
9 De Montfort Mews
Leicester LE1 7FW, UK
Tel: (+44) 116 255 9311 / 9312
Email: books@troubador.co.uk
Web: www.troubador.co.uk/matador

This is a work of fiction. Characters, companies and locations are either the product of the author's
imagination or, if real, used fictitiously without any intent to describe their actual environment.

ISBN:
Paperback: 978 1848760 622
Hardback: 978 1848760 639

Design of Cover: Andy Newton, Designworks, Easingwold.
Photography for front cover- Mark Kensett photography.

A Cataloguing-in-Publication (CIP) catalogue record for this book is available from the
British Library.

Typeset in 11pt Stempel Garamond by Troubador Publishing Ltd, Leicester, UK
Printed in the UK by TJ International Ltd, Padstow, Cornwall, UK

Matador is an imprint of Troubador Publishing Ltd

Acknowledgments

In the time it has taken me to write this book I am fully aware that, if I had put the lonely sometimes disheartening hours into 'a real job', my husband and my family would have certainly seen vast monetary reward. As it is, they have as yet seen nothing aside from an enormous overdraft and a medley of alternating mood swings. Regardless of whom I was impersonating at the time, I was the individual everyone had to accept was their wife, mother, daughter, sister or friend. To that end and without doubt, my first acknowledgement must go to my family and my friends. Thanks for everything and I love you.

In addition there were experts who took the time to meet with me and share their mines of knowledge and expertise, these include, Johnathon Walford-Carol QC, Howell and Hudson veterinary surgeons in Easingwold, Sarah Todd editor, Michael Naughton former jockey and race horse trainer, Nigel and Kim Tinkler race horse trainers in Malton, North Yorkshire and Simon Waudby of Waudby Farms, Flawith. Again, you gave up what little time you had to help me, from the bottom of my heart, thank you.

To all the people who have encouraged me to fulfil my

dream of publishing this book (you all know who you are), you have no idea what your support and encouragement has done to help me through the long, silent nights I have spent endlessly tapping away at my laptop. You are as much a part of seeing the book in print as I am. When I have sold a million copies I will buy you all a drink!

Every person in the above list means so much. However, there is one person who has given her heart and soul into this book and has never asked for a single thing in return. She has worked hours on end, pondering, deliberating, correcting and advising and above anyone else has encouraged me to continue in what, without her, could have seemed to be a pointless task. Vida Townson, I have to say you are a lady who is loyal, true, and so brilliantly focused. Thank you, thank you, thank you for the laughs, the tears and the honesty that you have ladled out from your bucket sized heart. I could never have done it all without you.

Finally, on reading other acknowledgement pages I have never understood why you the reader goes without being mentioned. Having worked so hard in the hope that one day this book may be a success I would like to give a final huge felt thanks to the reader of this very novel. It is only your enjoyment and, hopefully, your recommendation of the book to others that will enable my dream of becoming a bestselling author to become possible. I hope you enjoy reading it as much as I enjoyed writing it.

Chapter One

CHARLES LANCASTER-BARON soothed his black Bentley Continental to a halt at the red traffic lights where a teenage girl stood on the pavement waiting to cross. She glanced at Charles once and then, unable to resist another look, her young demure eyes lifted for a second time and shyly appraised his breathtaking good looks.

Like a hummingbird at flower blossom, the denim mini skirt she wore hovered at the top of her young supple thigh exposing perfectly formed, long, tanned legs. From the corner of his eye he saw his brother Hugo, sitting next to him in the passenger seat, strain to get a better view of her as she crossed the road. Charles felt his nonchalance rise; he had had his fill of women for one day.

It now seemed like days ago since the good-time girls that had lain naked at the brothers' sides had been forced to leave. He glanced at the Breitling clock on the burr walnut dashboard; it was almost surreal that in fact it had only been a matter of hours. The power of the vodka and cocaine frenzy that, at the time, had made him feel invincible had been no match for the strength of the shock.

At four a.m. he had received a sombre phone call from his mother informing him that his trusted friend, Gerard Santé, son and heir of one of the world's most prestigious racing stables had been killed in a car crash. The news had forced the joyful effects of the drink and drugs to come to an abrupt halt and had trapped him into realising that, even for him, life really was a mortal gift.

The lights turned to green. With his mother Kitty in the back and his brother by his side their journey towards Chelmsley Manor continued.

Chelmsley was a village in the midst of North Yorkshire that perched happily within the prestigious area of the Howardian Hills. It sat proudly, possessing a picture postcard beauty that allowed every household within it to hold an almost regal postcode. It was dusted with romantic sandstone cottages that sat side by side, their façades coloured by the sporadic creep of coloured rose bushes, their prettiness remaining unaffected by the elegant grandeur of rectories and halls that hovered grandly above them. Chelmsley's appeal was boosted by a host of family run amenities, incorporating fine antique shops, expensive boutiques and delicatessens with windows that were so amply packed with the refinements of locally reared meats, home produced baking and locally churned cheeses that you could almost see the original bowed sash windows greedily swell. Without doubt, Chelmsley attracted and captivated even the most discerning clientele, with all of them unable to resist peering through the colourful window displays as they meandered upon the cobbles of the swirling village streets.

Today however was a different story, the usual hustle and bustle of village life had almost been brought to a standstill. Irrespective of his privileged upbringing, Gerard Santé had been unbelievably popular, radiating warmth and compassion to everyone who had associated with him. Solemnly the locals of the village left flowers and messages outside the wrought iron electric gates of the village Manor House.

Unable to restrain from showing their respects Charles, Hugo and their mother Kitty were the first to arrive at Chelmsley Manor. Charles parked upon the elegant gravel driveway, turned off the contended throb of the V8 engine, and then shared his 'Mint Ice' breath freshener spray with Hugo.

Hugo and Charles could actually have passed for twins. Both were incredibly handsome, Hugo possibly less so than Charles, but nevertheless, their dirty blonde hair and large saucer blue eyes never failed to attract female attention. With only eighteen months between them, Charles being the eldest, they had always done everything together, failing to see why last night's sex should call for a compromise.

Before getting out of the car Charles checked himself in the vanity mirror. He ran his fingers through his hair, wishing that he had found the time to visit the hairdressers yesterday; it was too long and far too informal to befit the sombre discussions of today. He strained his eyes open wide to try and ascertain how many little red veins were mapping their way around his eyeballs, and wondered guiltily how many people at the solemn gathering would view them as a tell-tale sign of last night's antics. He studied the rest of his face, taking pride in the fact that having not had any sleep *and* the shock of Gerard's death to contend with, he still felt he looked incredibly attractive.

Charles was right, he was incredibly good-looking. His tousled blonde hair ran in wispy lengths around his sculptured face and roguishly tickled the edge of his collar, and a blonde feathering fringe bridged striking blue eyes that smoked sexily beneath. It was impossible to tell whether it was his alluring eyes that could captivate a woman in a glance, his manly nose, slightly crooked from past heroism on the rugby field, or the strength of his physique that offered him as irresistible. Whatever it was, every one of his cool, aloof characteristics signified the immaculate portrayal of fine breeding, and captured, with astounding elegance, sheer superiority.

"Is there any chance of somebody letting me out of this bloody vehicle?"

The crisp cultured voice of his mother, exasperated in the back seat, reminded Charles that this morning was not a time to preen and self appraise. He duly closed the mirror.

"Coming, Mother," he responded with breezing sarcasm. "Put that out Hugo!" He barked at his brother sitting by his side, pointing to the cigarette clamped between his sibling's shaking fingers. Hugo rolled his eyes, took one last enormous draw followed by a deep, lingering inhalation then stubbed it out into the car's immaculate ashtray. Charles shot his brother a look of despair before helping his mother from the backseat.

Gracefully she steadied herself against the car and took a moment to straighten her black cashmere coat-dress and gently swept the palm of her hand against her newly set hair. Her wise blue eyes, swamped with sadness and reflection looked up to the sunlight and glinted like crystals as the tears welled inside.

"This is one hell of a sorry business," she whispered.

Her sons, sensing her sadness and sharing her sentiments, each took an arm and began to slowly help her to the door.

"I can manage!" she snapped pulling her arms from their caring grip. "I may be seventy-seven but I am perfectly capable of walking to a door for goodness sakes!" She forged ahead, planting her walking stick heavily into the ground as she strode.

The brothers looked at each other and smiled fondly at her zest and determination for life. With her back turned, her sons took a second opportunity to spray another burst of breath freshener into their mouths.

They followed their mother's steps toward the Manor, and tentatively rang the traditional brass bell that hung alongside the gigantic old oak door.

The morning sun shone proudly against the crisscross network of ivy that crept its way against the soft stone walls of the Santé's mansion, its bottle green harvest twisted and turned, lovingly cocooning the numerous tall elongated windows that spread across the manor's face.

The estate held a hushed privacy. Only an impatient kick to a stable door broke the refinery of its peace. Charles looked through the grand archway which adjoined the house. It boldly beckoned its visitors to observe the traditional cobbled courtyard, the Santé's stabling for over sixty racehorses. Charles noticed their arrival had sought the interest of only a few of its inhabitants. Their heads peered over the doors and hung sombrely in their direction. Charles wondered if their despondent expression was a sign that they too had been informed of the sobering news. Their ears twitched to the sound of the clock-tower above signalling another passing hour. Charles glanced up at the golden clock face that rested upon the pinnacle of strong, powerful, sandstone shoulders. It was eleven a.m., as Charles heard the door unbolt. He knew, the mornings' time would be eternally carved in his mind.

James Santé stood in the doorway and on seeing the Lancaster-Baron family his face warmed slightly, but unlike the gigantic proportions of the vast oak door, his stance portrayed a vulnerable fragility.

The history between the two families had been firmly cemented many years ago; Kitty, Charles and Hugo were as good as family. Kitty had been Gerard's godmother and he had known Charles and Hugo all their lives and both had been good friends to Gerard. In addition, for many years James had been a loyal friend with the boys' father, Charles Baron senior, before he too had tragically died in a car crash when Charles and Hugo were only teenagers. From that time he had treated the boys as if they were his own sons, although he had to admit, Charles had always held special sentiment.

"Thanks for coming," James nodded quietly, standing to one side allowing them to walk through the door.

Kitty embraced him and kissed either side of his cheeks. The familiarity of Kitty's presence and her reassuring squeeze immediately sank into the depths of his grief, and for a brief moment he felt comforted from the pain.

Looking back at her beautiful face, he could see she was unable to talk, the loss of her godson Gerard had unlocked a strong emotional connection to her own personal memories of death and the sentiment was too much to bear. Silently she walked towards Victoria Santé.

Charles and Hugo shook James's hand firmly,

"I'm so sorry, James," Charles said quietly.

Victoria Santé had been watching the greetings in rigid silence. Kitty's presence was immensely reassuring, like the sight of a lighthouse to a dinghy in a sea storm, her strength and wisdom always a beacon of welcome light. Kitty walked toward her with arms outstretched,

"Victoria," she whispered soothingly, "I am so, so sorry." She hoisted her shoulders, realising that her failing emotions would be of no use at all to her friends.

"Right Victoria," she stated with conviction, "you must have others attending today, I'll go into the kitchen and sort out the china."

"Thank you," said Victoria. "The glasses are in the display cabinet in the dining room for those who prefer something stronger," she added.

Kitty span round in disbelief, "What, you mean? Alcohol?"

Victoria nodded, acknowledging Kitty's alarm with a faint smile.

"You are never going to serve them alcohol are you?"

"For those who want it, yes." Victoria managed a small laugh, fully aware of Kitty's disagreement with alcohol being served at even the most relaxing of gatherings. Hugo and Charles looked at each other in the hope that the Santé's would not relent with their initial proposal.

"Whatever you see fit," Kitty said casually making her way back toward the kitchen. "There really is no accounting for the demons of alcohol when mixed with emotion," she added over her shoulder.

With relief, Charles and Hugo led Victoria back into the drawing room and took their seats, allowing James and Victoria to recount, to the last detail, receiving the news of their son's death.

As the morning wore on more people arrived to briefly show their respects to Gerard's parents, that was, with the exception of Francesca Montford. She had forgotten this was a time to comfort others, turning up on the back of her grieving daughter Paris' invitation. The Santé family had thought it only right to include Paris, knowing that she had been casually dating Gerard for some time.

Charles glanced over to Paris. She looked terrible. Not that she had ever been blessed with beauty, but it was clear by her timid mannerisms and her shaking body that she was heartbroken by Gerard's death.

Francesca Montford, on the other hand, took the visit as a devious opportunity to view as much of the mansion as she possibly could. Charles and the rest of the party could see her visibly craning her long neck around any of the open doors that she passed, continually "helping" to deliver glasses back to the kitchen, and quickly "nipping to the lavatory" at any given opportunity. With the exception of asking Mrs Santé to show her around – which even Francesca sensed would be inappropriate – she was pleased with how much of the house she'd managed to see in the first half hour of her visit. She was about to tell Paris she thought it time they leave when the next visitor to arrive made her want to stay a while longer.

Frankie DeMario walked into the room, a wealthy and

formidable man by anybody's standards. He was also father to the world ranking jockey Luca DeMario, which only added to the family's prestige. Quietly he sat down in a free chair, nodding at familiar faces. Dressed immaculately, he wore a tailored navy blue suit, a stark white shirt   complemented by a silk gold and navy Italian tie, all of which coordinated flawlessly Francesca decided, taking in every last detail of his attire. *Now, they really have got money* she thought. Moving closer to Paris for the first time since they arrived she whispered in her ear, "Do you know how he made all his money?"

Paris resisted the urge to scream at her mother and instead turned her back, treating her comment with utter disdain. Her mother didn't notice the rebuff and continued.

"You know rumour has it that he has been involved in the mafia," she hissed knowingly to the back of her daughter's head. "Didn't Gerard ever mention him to you? After all he may have known. I believe Gerard trained his horses didn't he?"

"I'm going to the loo," Paris snapped.

Francesca continued to try and catch Frankie DeMario's eye. She wanted him to notice her, she was desperate to say hello, how welcome it was that her daughter had become involved in such circles. Francesca had been delighted when Paris had started to date Gerard,

"At last! The past torture of trying to find the money for those bloody school fees has been worth it after all," she remembered saying, going on to urge: "These are the right social circles for you to be mixing in Paris."

Francesca's shoulders submerged beneath her black Jaeger jacket, what a shame he had to die, the high hopes she had had for a county wedding had been dashed. She continued to stare at Frankie and her imagination started to run away with her. All she could think about was Paris and Luca DeMario, the son and heir to Frankie DeMario's grand fortune, and imagine, one of the world's top jockeys as a son-in-law...

Paris returned to the drawing room and let out a chesty bark like cough, hastily awakening Francesca from her idyllic dream. She looked across and observed her daughter's chubby red face; she was beginning to resemble a pig Francesca thought. Her eyes were starting to swell up due to her erratic emotional outbursts, all of which were so unnecessary as far as Francesca was concerned, so much so, she was wondering if her daughter was vying for attention. Francesca felt further incensed when she noticed several stray dog hairs on Paris's black trousers. *Those bloody mongrels she works with,* Francesca berated internally, controlling her urge to dive across the floor to pick them off. *Unlike me* she mused, *that girl has no finesse. How could I even think of her moving up a scale to Luca DeMario?* She arched an immaculately lined eye-brow; *after all, it's a mystery how she managed to bag Gerard.*

Charles started to feel a little edgy. He was badly in need of another drink and a good eight hours sleep. He stood up and walked out of the room, his mother followed him.

"What is that vulgar DeMario man doing here?" she whispered. Charles gave her a perplexed smile.

"What do you mean, vulgar?" he asked.

"All that brash display of wealth, it's like your car, ridiculously vulgar" she spat, dusting off some invisible spots from her dress. "Remember what I have always said to you two."

"Yes, yes mother I know Mon…." Charles was about to continue but his mother cut him dead.

"Money talks," she hushed quietly, "but, wealth whispers." She took an exasperated deep breath before adding into her son's ear,

"Always remember that my dear and you won't go far wrong."

Charles shook his head and walked towards the kitchen to get himself a second drink. On his return to the drawing room he studied a photograph upon the Steinway piano of Rebecca, Gerard's sister. A twinge of excitement hit the pit of his stomach as he thought of her coming home. His only hope was that she would be alone and not with the half-wit Piers she had blown him out for all those years ago.

He overheard Frankie De Mario strike up a conversation with Hugo about share prices. Charles suspected that Frankie owned most of the horses on the Santé's yard, he may be vulgar in his mother's eyes but he was certainly a very wealthy man with a keen eye for a good thoroughbred. He bought them more as a hobby and placed them in training yards not just around the country but around the world. Charles looked on and wondered with intrigue the source from which his wealth had amassed.

James Santé walked into the room and gave Frankie the glass of water he had asked for. In a thick Italian accent he spoke softly to James.

"If there is anything the DeMario family can do or help you with then we will be only too glad." He hung his head, glancing briefly at his diamond studded Rolex watch on his wrist. "I must apologise for my short stay, James, but I am afraid I am due in Paris in ninety minutes time for a meeting, I will have to leave very soon."

James replied his understanding and thanked him for coming.

"Don't mention it; Gerard was a very good boy," Frankie told him.

"How are you getting to Paris?" James asked.

Frankie lowered his voice trying hard not to be overheard. "My private jet, the flight takes only forty-five minutes, it will enable me to get home again by this evening" he answered before discreetly making his way towards the door.

I could do with some of that private jet business Charles thought.

On returning into the room after accompanying Frankie DeMario to his awaiting car, James saw Charles examining one of the many photographs of Rebecca that sat in the window. James remembered the happy days that Charles and his daughter had spent together, his lips tightened, *that was before the uncouth no-hoper Piers had turned up and ruined everything*. No daughter of his was supposed to fall for a womanising, two-timing letch like that. He had willed it not to last and did everything he could to break it up but, sadly, all his efforts had been in vain. She had emigrated to Kentucky with him and consequently he had not seen her for six years. She was determined and pigheaded, but hell, how he missed her. He needed her so much.

Sensing Charles felt the same way he walked over to him and placed a re-assuring hand on his shoulder.

"When is Rebecca coming home?" Charles asked softly.

"She arrives in the morning," James answered immediately feeling the heavy shove of apprehension rise within his chest. "Would you join me in a large scotch?" he asked Charles.

Charles was relieved. A stiff drink was exactly what he needed. So too was Rebecca Santé.

In Kentucky, Rebecca was ready to leave. Hoping that Piers had calmed down, cautiously she walked towards him.

"Look Piers, you know it would be impossible to come with me," she said, pleadingly putting a hand on his shoulder. "I haven't seen them myself for years. There will be the funeral to organise and I don't know what kind of state the business will be in. There will be enough to sort out without having the additional stress of you and daddy at each other's throats."

"Look, just go will you!" he shouted. "You've shown me where your priorities lie. Just fuck off." He looked down at the floor.

Once again Rebecca tried to extend her hand for him to hold.

"GO!" he shouted. "Piss off to your Daddy!" he mimicked.

Her bright green eyes grew cold; she certainly wasn't going to be told again.

"Piers," she shouted back in retaliation, "I can't believe you have spoken to me like this, today of all days. I'm going now; I will speak to you later." Her fizz of bright auburn curls spun in the air as she turned on her heels.

She slammed the front door and stamped towards her waiting taxi, throwing herself and her bag onto the backseat.

"To the airport," she ordered curtly. "The first-class terminal."

The driver, trying hard not to react to her patronising tone, looked in the rear view mirror. He had driven many of her sorts in this car before; he could tell by her upturned nose, her designer clothes and her whole demeanour what she was about. He had to admit though she was very pretty and a good figure too, slim and petite. But god, those eyes of hers looked angry. *What the hell would somebody like her have to get angry about?* He asked in private irritation. *People like her don't have a worry in the world.* His thoughts returned to his own problems, *lucky bitch* he concluded looking at her one last time in the mirror.

Rebecca Santé stared out of the window and watched her home of the past six years slip from her view. She felt far from lucky. The fact that her wonderful brother had died meant to her nothing could get any worse. Today was the worst day of her life. However, what she didn't realise was that it could get worse, *and* it would. Going back to England would prove it.

Chapter Two

KITTY LANCASTER-BARON stirred in her bed as she heard the door of her bedroom gently creek open. Distantly she became aware of Mary, her trusted housekeeper of twenty-five years, creeping across the room with habitual delicacy to deliver her morning tea.

"Morning Mrs L.B," she whispered placing the solid silver tray and tea service upon her bedside table.

"Good Morning Mary," Kitty replied sleepily.

Carefully Mary began to prepare her tea, just the way Kitty liked it. Sugar lumps in first, two of them, uncompromisingly brown, the already warmed china cup filled half way with Earl Grey followed by a tiny splash of skimmed milk.

Kitty lay still for a few seconds, staring up at the ceiling before making any attempts to move. Hearing the sound of Mary's cheerful hum as she collected her mistress' dressing gown and slippers, Kitty eased herself, slowly, up the bed. Each movement caused enormous discomfort to her limbs. Mary rushed to help her.

"No, no, I'm fine thank you," Kitty scorned. "Will you pull my curtains back please Mary?"

Mary immediately obliged allowing Kitty, once Mary's back was turned, to hoist herself in the bed with a quick, giant burst of effort. The pain on exertion caught her breath.

The morning light poured into her vast bedroom and Kitty felt relieved to notice the weather was miserable.

"Well at least it's a dull day. I detest it when the sun shines for a funeral. Good weather makes one feel happier about life." She reached for her teacup. "There's nothing to feel happy about when someone is about to be buried or burned and you are never going to see them again." She shuddered and took a sip of tea. "I hate bloody funerals with a passion." A dark cast of morbid memories urged her to continue. "I know it's against my Christian beliefs to be so utterly traumatised by them, you are supposed to take solace that the good Lord above will take care of the deceased, but," she took a deep breath and shook her head, "it's the poor souls that are left behind to hold the fort. For them, death is nothing but a heartbreakingly beastly burden."

Mary heard the dogs barking frantically outside. She looked out of the window and saw the milkman trying to release his jacket from the playful jaws of Darcy, one of the black Labradors.

"Darcy has captured the milkman," Mary laughed. "I'd better go and rescue him; I'll be back in a minute."

Kitty was left to contemplate her words alone. Propped up by feather-down pillows, she sat upright in her bed and felt unable to cast the sombre subject of death from her mind. Her first experience of death had been her father's and to this day she still felt the ache of his passing.

Her father had been her life and she her father's. Her mother had become infatuated with an Australian artist when Kitty was only two years old; as a result she had walked out of the family home and emigrated to Australia. From that moment on, father and daughter had become inseparable.

Kitty, being an only child, had enjoyed a life of unstoppable love and laughter with her father. Their bond had been unbreakable. She remembered with fondness the days and hours he spent behind her whilst she nervously wobbled her way around the courtyard, trying to master riding a bike and remembered the hollers of delight as he cheered and whooped with pride on the day she had managed a full circuit unaided. A year later his paternal pride had been emulated when she gained her first clear round on the pony he had bought her for Christmas. For six whole months previously he had patiently set up practice fences for her at home, never tiring of running beside the pony, willing it to take her safely over them and never, ever becoming bad tempered at her occasional lack of courage in pulling the pony up before she even reached the fence. She remembered the new suit he had bought to take her to school on her very first day and the note she had found inside her school bag at lunch time telling her how much he loved her. She recounted the fury in his eyes when she informed him of a fellow classmate who had bullied her and forced her to hand over the new Cartier pen he had brought her back from a business trip. Immediately he had pounded into school and raged to the teacher and the girl herself about what action he would take if it happened again. Needless to say, from that day forward she was left alone.

He had been a lawyer, and a brilliant one at that, believing that hard work dedication and integrity to all would always bring success, and he was right. His flourishing career had begun with one law practice in the centre of affluent Harrogate and, to his credit, throughout the years he built up a company that spanned several continents. 'Lancaster Law International' was one of the most respected law firms in the world and remained so to this day. Kitty was grateful that her father's name lived on in the world and not just in the private confinements of her heart.

Kitty heard spots of rain tap against her bedroom window; she stared out, and watched the drops dribble like large teardrops down the pane. They appeared to remind her with insistence of the day her father had died in her arms following a long- suffering battle with cancer.

As a result, at the tender age of twenty-three, she had been the sole beneficiary of the seventy million pound legacy he had built. Along with it came the family home, a Tudor mansion named Cedars Hall, located three winding miles out of Chelmsley.

Cedars Hall remained her most treasured possession and her appreciation was clearly evident both inside and out.

Kitty craned her neck to look outside. She saw the rolling stretch of perfectly manicured lawns, all encased, just as she had planned, by the grand elegance of topiary bushes. She adored the wisteria arches and the sandstone path that led her under them. It guided her past the abundantly stocked flower beds which, when in season, romantically showered the grounds with displays of roses, delphiniums and the relaxing scent of thoughtfully scattered lavender bushes. She had spent hours appreciating her gardens and took great pleasure from witnessing the change in their offerings as the seasons passed.

The inside of the house had been cosseted by just as much of her attention. A breathtaking combination of fine original antiquities graced the entirety of every room, allowing a true sense of Tudor history to seep effortlessly into every molecule of the air. Solid arches of oak timbers swept through the rooms and hallways, their darkness unable to dwell due to the detail of the finely carved angels and cherubs that coasted across them, and the ceilings, also graced with magnificent cornices and enriched with ornamental carvings and quatrefoils. The vast drawing room, a favourite room for Kitty, boasted a proud stone fireplace with a depth large enough to accommodate a hog-roast and above it the Lancaster and the Baron coats of arms.

In the winter Kitty would request the fires to be lit whereupon some thirty pear logs, glowing in alliance with the panelled walls and permeating their sweet welcoming perfume would greet the room's guests. The stone flagged floors, laid by hand centuries before, were warmed with antique tapestry rugs though not one of them could disguise the echo of each stride taken against them. With each reverberation of the footstep, the sound lingered in the shadowy hallways and rooms, purposefully reminding the newcomer of the many other steps that had been taken across it over the centuries.

The walls, marred by the reluctant ache of ageing cracks, were alleviated by a host of original oil paintings and grandfather clocks that sprawled affluently against the surfacing hardships. Kitty's favourite picture hung before her every evening and every morning in the privacy of her bedroom. She looked at it now and remembered with clarity the day she received it. It had been a gift from her father on her twenty- first birthday, a vast painting by John F Herring, of a bay filly. According to dealers, it now had a worth of over a quarter of a million pounds, but for Kitty, the monetary value was insignificant. Like everything else that had a connection to her accumulation of wealth, none of it had a real meaning, or indeed, could ever be a replacement to the importance of love and relationships.

For Kitty, it was not the history of the passing eras within her home that soothed her soul, it was the eternal memories she held close to her heart. Memories of a happy childhood with her father and the happy years with her husband, all of them she cherished, and refused with the passing of time to allow them to fade. As the years had passed every atom of laughter, every heartfelt conversation, and indeed, every tear, had long been engrained and had delicately soaked, like intermittent lashings of brandy quenching a Christmas cake, into every fabric and facet of the house.

She thought about the rest of the vast inheritance and subconsciously her face hardened, for that had been nothing but an overriding burden. Her thoughts softened as she thought of Charles Snr, her wonderful, ever faithful husband. His death had been the second blow. Not only had she had to face life without him when he died, but he too, had not died without passing on even more responsibility. Accountability for their two sons had been transferred to her alone; it had been a troublesome time for the two boys who had only been teenagers at the time. Yes, she confirmed silently, she was right; death brought nothing but a beastly burden.

Her reflection was brought to an abrupt halt when Mary walked back into the room.

"Now, where were we?" she asked cheerfully. Kitty, agitated temporarily by Mary's cheerful demeanour, retorted sharply.

"We were just about to choose some morbid attire from my wardrobe; I have a funeral to attend." She felt her bones creak as she edged her slim legs out of the bed. *Will the pain ever subside?* she wondered.

Julia Smith stepped onto the pavement and felt utter relief to have escaped from the house. The thought of working as a live-in housekeeper for a woman like that filled her with dread. No matter how much she wanted to better her life, there were only so many sacrifices she was willing to make, and being a glorified slave was not one of them. She recounted the woman's words,

"I want the pathway that leads up to the door scrubbing once a week. And the steps? It goes without saying, they need to be scrubbed daily….." The orders continued to roll steadily, "Oh! And the toilet? Here look" she rummaged in the cleaning basket "This toothbrush needs to be used under the rim" she held up a pink toothbrush with bristles that were flattened from systematic abuse.

"Do you work?" Julia had asked politely. Observing the lady's eyebrows rise to the ceiling in horror she knew the question had been a mistake.

"Goodness! No!" She had gasped, "I do charity."

Julia glanced at her watch, having cut the interview short she hoped she might just catch the earlier bus back to York. For the past two weeks the weather had presented long days of warm spring sunshine but now it had turned, blowing a cold blustering wind, offering nothing more than the gloom of cynical grey skies and from it, relentless drizzle.

Julia pulled the belt of her second hand black mackintosh tight around her slim waist and began to quicken her pace in the hope it would initiate some warmth. Stealing her thoughts away from the dull weather and her downbeat experience at the interview she took in her surroundings.

She was disappointed the interview had not gone better; she would love to live in a village like Chelmsley. She was struck by the charm of the cottages; she watched the chimney pots choke back into life due to the unexpected decline of the weather, her eyes following the winding and crooked pavements. All of them she decided could only lead to places where, mingled with the smell of freshly baked bread, lazy chats would transpire. She thought of her home surroundings and grimaced at the thought of what a wrong turn on those paths could lead to.

She continued to walk, refusing to allow her dream of one day living in such a village with a family of her own to leave her mind, until, a stream of bright yellow tape and a crowd of people surrounding the village church prevented her from continuing.

Intrigued, she stood alongside the gathering and watched intently from the pavement as formal black cars and limousines swooped up to the church gates and stopped to allow their passengers to disembark. Ladies in long black fur coats and huge conspicuous designer sunglasses hastily made their way up the church path. Trotting at their sides were uniformed men holding umbrellas in a determined bid to protect the mastery of their chic hairstyles from the rain. Businessmen in pinstriped suits swarmed the previously deserted church path and chatted in small tight knit groups before gravely walking towards the service. The guests continued to stream up the path, the swelling of the church interior was such that late arrivals were forced to stand outside. Julia felt as though she was being disrespectful standing with the many other ordinary laymen that now lined the streets to witness a stranger's funeral, she looked around for a route to escape, but found she was hindered by an ever increasing crowd. She felt her stomach jolt when a selection of pressmen anxious to report on the event began to barge their way through the crowds.

Suddenly, a late arrival caused a stir of excitement between the reporters. A young handsome man sprang athletically from the back of his chauffeur-driven car. His black eyes, moody and wild, scanned the bustling reporters before continuing towards the church gates.

Julia, now watching guiltily with a keen interest heard a shocked voice whisper.

"Fuckin 'ell, it's Luca DeMario."

Barely a second elapsed before Julia had been shoved forcefully and thrown almost to her knees whilst the amateur photographer, eager to make it in the world of journalism began to take photographs of the superstar's arrival.

"What the hell do you think you are doing?" an angry voice shouted.

Julia felt a firm hand grasp her arm and pull her to her feet. She stood and stared into his eyes.

"Are you okay?" he asked. Agitation stirred upon his face.

She continued to stare into the eyes, they were the deepest, darkest brown, indeed almost black, they were stranger's eyes, yet something encouraged her to delve beneath. Unable to speak, she nodded helplessly and longed for the invisible thread that had just fused their eyes to remain forever in place. Slowly he released her arm from his protective grip and stared at the reporter. A look of hatred and disdain filled his eyes. Resisting the temptation to air his views he turned and walked up the church path.

Shaken, yet silently thrilled by her experience, Julia felt compelled to ask an old lady at her side whose funeral she was actually witnessing.

"D' ya not know luv?" the woman croaked unhappily. "It's Gerard Santé, a lovely chap 'e was that." The woman turned away and gazed down the street, she was eager to observe every detail of the man's passing. The sound that followed the lady's words forced every witness to follow suit.

The slow distant clatter of horses' hooves hushed the awaiting crowd and cast almost ghostlike reverberations across the silent damp air. Some eager spectators shuffled to the pavement side to gain a clearer view.

A sharp twist of irony sealed the day. In contrast to the speeding red Ferrari Gerard had been killed in, the four black Friesians adhered to a respectful harmonised pace. With every step they made, a shroud of restfulness permeated every soul present. As the horse-drawn hearse came into Julia's view she immediately became engulfed with emotion at the sight of the elegant, yet sobering, epitome of funeral tradition.

The powerful Friesian stallions' muscles were so well defined they bulged and rippled beneath arduously groomed black glossy coats. Standing erect and proud between alert pricked ears were black pluming feathers, accentuating the horses' already gargantuan stance. Their backs, the size of dining tables, were blanketed by a black shroud that was appeased slightly by soft golden stitching along their edge and a huge golden cross that boldly crowned the centre. Two horsemen in mourning coats and top hats sat upon the seat that pulled the glass carriage where Gerard's coffin lay within. Respectful of their duties, their faces remained motionless and their eyes fixed in resolute focus on the road ahead.

Despite the drivers' professional detachment, the uninvited audience, now swelling along the pavements, became immersed in their personal uprising of emotion. So courteous and dignified were the horses' languid steps, the atmosphere around the spectators appeared to change. The air was filled with a noble calm, whereby each person present felt strangely soothed by an almighty presence, the feeling that something much greater than life itself was in attendance. The onlookers, transfixed yet internally alight by their unique experience felt their mortal souls carried and eased by an invisible promise.

The coffin bearers climbed from their seats and tipped their top hats in respect before opening the doors of the finely etched glass carriage. Additional coffin bearers appeared and carefully they lifted Gerard's coffin onto their shoulders steadying themselves before they began to walk.

Julia felt a pain strike her throat and her tears heat her eyes as she thought about her own mother and the undeniable fragility of life. Slowly, with professional grace and unified steps they inched their way up the church path. The crowd outside the church door tipped their heads and dispersed into two lines, allowing the procession to walk through. As the coffin was ushered out of sight through the church doors, Julia felt tears fall down her face. Not only had painful harboured memories been stirred, but an inexplicable feeling engulfed her. Today was to be a turning point in her life. As yet, this young mysterious beauty had no idea why.

Inside the church, the congregation stood to their feet as the coffin appeared, and following its path were Gerard's chief mourners, James, Victoria and Rebecca Santé.

Charles, sitting between his mother and Hugo, turned and for the first time in six years his eyes fixated on Rebecca, though only for the briefest of seconds. Impatiently he looked past her, searching for the unwelcome presence of Piers. Charles felt relief engulf him; he was nowhere to be seen. Charles was free to look back at Rebecca. Even the eighteen-strong professional choir who began to sing Delibe's *Dome Epais* with skin tingling clarity could not dissuade his stare.

She wore an elegant black hat that draped a fine veil across her face and Charles could see her green eyes stare with wounding at her brother's coffin ahead. Charles noticed she looked pale and tired which accentuated the girl-like translucence of her skin and vulnerability. Her fiery auburn hair was tied neatly in a pony tail with a black ribbon and fell in an organised bundle down her slim back. Without noticing his presence, Rebecca walked past Charles down the aisle. His eyes scanned her body.

He loved the way her black tailored trousers eased their way down her long slim legs and effortlessly caressed her sexy pert ass; she walked with class, held an undeniable dignity, women like her were hard to find and he knew his life had never been the same since the day she had left.

Kitty stared down at the order of service she held in her hands. The thick expensive card was filled with pictures of Gerard, all of them picturing him looking happy, youthful and carefree. Although the choir was singing beautifully she noticed that there were more hymns ahead. F Schubert's *Ave Maria, Lord of all Hopefulness* and quite out of tradition, GF Handel's *Hallelujah Chorus* was to be sung when the coffin left the church. Not only that, but all the songs were to be interrupted with an assortment of readings and speeches from various guests, and then of course, the service by the Bishop.

She could barely believe it, this was the order of her godson's funeral. She looked around the packed church, proud that her godson had touched so many people's lives. She noticed the many tear-stained and sorrowful faces that stared ahead and pondered fleetingly if her own son's would warrant the same grief should they have been unfortunate enough to trade places. Casting the ghastly thought aside, the memories she held of Gerard growing up tumbled through her mind. Her eyes bathed in salty tears tried to make sense of his untimely death. She stared up to the enormous arch of the stained glass window ahead of her. Somehow, the morbid weather outside had managed to muster the strength to illuminate the beauty of the image within. The painful crucifixion of Christ held centre stage amid a medley of vivid colours. She examined the pained expression, immortalised across the face of Virgin Mary as she pleaded helplessly on her knees beneath her son's torturous cross. Her eyes cast upon Victoria Santé. How merciless life must feel to have a child taken from you. She felt a sympathetic stab of pain rive across her heart at the thought of how her dear friend must be feeling.

Staring back at the simplistic yet profound sentiment of religion etched across the window, she felt angered at the over the top ceremony that was about to ensue. She began to calculate in her mind the cost of such an extravagant display. She glanced back to the exuberant order of service and an unstoppable crackle of irritation rose within her.

"Amor est vitae essential," she found herself whispering aloud.

Having had Latin shoved down his throat from an early age of his public school upbringing, Charles managed to decipher the meaning of the phrase, 'love is the meaning of life'.

Charles managed to ignore her, angered, although not surprised by her disgruntlement.

His rising frustration was diverted when Rebecca stood to speak at the pulpit. Her voice held a dignity and strength, but her pain, to those that knew her well, was plainly evident.

"The music played today may not be that for a traditional funeral, however, I, and my parents feel it only right that Gerard be remembered for what made him the wonderful person that he was. My brother…."

Charles was whisked away by a melting furnace of adoration, finding it impossible to distil her words. He stared at her longingly. His stare flickered as a woman, also dressed in a black trouser suit and plastered in a thick layer of make-up stood up with her young son to take him outside. He remembered, three years ago having sex with her in a hot tub after a hard day on the hunting field. That was what his life had consisted of since Rebecca had left – sex with easy riders. He glanced at her husband and felt puzzled, slightly amused that a man could marry such a woman. The woman glanced at Charles and smiled with a brief longing before tip-toeing out of the church. Charles turned his attention back to Rebecca.

"And that is why we are now very grateful to Sicily Lowery, our chief soloist; she is going to sing *Ave Maria*, another one of Gerard's favourite hymns."

The congregation sat in silence as the woman's voice mesmerised them with her undeniable talent. The high gabled rooftop of the church avidly harboured every note, allowing the acoustics to linger with skin tingling clarity.

Hugo turned to Charles and whispered, "No wonder this is Gerard's favourite song, I remember 'aving Maria as well, she was a bloody good sort to 'ave." A reflective smile adorned Hugo's face whilst listening to the remaining memoirs of his friends' life.

Charles contemplated the reason for their attendance. It all seemed surreal that a good friend, the same age as him was lying inside that coffin. He was dead. No longer able to laugh or smile, no longer able to love, and worst of all, no longer able to fulfil his greatest desires, whatever they were.

Charles felt a torrent of fear overtake him. If he were to die tomorrow what would his passing bring with it? He thought of his mother learning in disbelief the news of his failing finances, he thought of Rebecca never knowing the extent to which he loved her, and worst still he thought of his father's last words.

"Look after the family as I have done," he had asked.

He had made a promise to his father that indeed he would, but so far, his promise had escaped priority. His heart began to pound just as it always did when he thought of his father and the cruel unachievable request that had been asked of his teenage son. Unable to distil the remainder of the service, he was relieved when the guests began to walk outside.

Slowly, Charles walked down the church path with Hugo and his mother. Kitty looked aged, yet stunningly glamorous in a floor length black velvet cape that was cosseted at its edges with black mink fur. Kitty placed her ivory walking stick delicately to the ground, another one of her treasured possessions, a present from her husband Charles senior, brought back from an African shooting trip he had attended many years ago. She touched her large black hat with her gloved hand, checking it remained in place. It was large and romanticised by a gown of soft black lace, its necessary camouflage only allowing her vivid strike of fuscia lipstick to burst through.

Mother and her two sons walked down the path in silence, each one of them sheltering their own private thoughts and emotions. Kitty was the first to speak.

"You know," she sighed, "it is so funny when we look around and see how different we all are."

Charles immediately sensed the cantankerous sentiment of her tone and stiffened.

"My father would have turned in his grave if I should have squandered his hard earned money on his passing," she continued, unable to suppress her thoughts. "And, so would your father," she insisted.

Charles annoyed once again at her opinionated obsession with money turned in anger.

"No mother you are wrong," he bit. "*You* would have turned in *your* grave. For God's sake, woman!" He stood to face her, his blue eyes as cold as frosted ice. "You have more money than the whole of this congregation put together but your bloody life has been consumed with guarding the lot." His frank outburst had shocked even himself. "Can you not conceal your fanatical obsession for one day?"

Hugo was stunned. His mother stared back at him; a look of pounding thunder stiffened her face.

"How dare you?" she whispered chillingly. "How dare you?" she repeated before walking away with Hugo at her side.

Charles stood alone, overcome with regret for his words and for Gerard's short life. *My life too could all be over tomorrow*, he thought in alarm.

Charles was blatantly aware that his cold words towards his mother had burst out as an antidote to his own personal disappointment. At present, he was living a chaotic, deceitful lie. In that instant he decided his time for procrastinating was over. The time had come to turn his life around.

Chapter Three

JULIA SMITH walked swiftly along the street, trying hard to rid the stench of last night's burning rubber from her nostrils. It was probably someone's car tyres – set alight for no reason whatsoever, some neighbouring half-wits on a mission to amuse their tiny minds. She breathed deeply, willing the smell to subside then turned around, briefly glancing at the camp behind her. The camp's activity continued to thrive, all intermingled with the latest 4x4 vehicles and a selection of caravans. She gave a deep sigh. As usual, dissatisfaction reigned. She felt as though she was stagnating in a life that didn't belong to her. Everyday she tried so hard to share the same passion the others felt for the "freedom" of the gypsy life, but as each day passed her urge to leave the camp and achieve something with her life grew stronger.

She turned her back and continued to walk towards the City Centre, away from the gypsy camp in which she lived.

This feeling of utter frustration was a normal emotion for Julia, especially since her mother had died and strangely, this feeling had only intensified since she had witnessed the funeral in Chelmsley.

Tanned, tall and voluptuous, she walked swiftly down the street. Her Levi hipster jeans showed off her perfectly flat stomach and the white T- shirt she teamed them with, a recent purchase from her favourite charity shop highlighted her Mediterranean dark treacle skin. Her T-shirt was too small rather than trendily cropped and sat gently underneath her pert breasts that jiggled freely as she walked. Unable to foresee the weather but with predicated storms ahead, she played it safe and slung her simple black mackintosh over her handbag.

There was no particular reason for her trip into York. She didn't have any money to spend, but she enjoyed looking around the city on a Saturday afternoon, if nothing else, it was interesting just people watching. Needless to say she always went alone.

She did most things alone, feeling that the simplistic monotony of gypsy life simply bored her. Every night they did the same things and the night before had been a prime example. Having been for a walk she made her way back to her family's caravan where a group of gypsy camp dwellers sat around a large fire, they joked and talked with one another, taking comfort from the conversation and the fireside warmth. The gentle flicker of the firelight shone against their faces, highlighting the weather torn wrinkles that spanned across their faces with each line paying homage to their rugged outdoor existence. She smiled but walked past the group, taking herself quietly inside the caravan. Once inside, in sheer frustration, she threw herself onto her hard lumpy bunk and tuned into radio four in a bid to drown out her feeling of being a misfit.

Her trips into the city centre fuelled her aspirations for a better life. Visiting the shops gave her an opportunity to live out her very own fantasy; it was her means of escape, her chance to become someone else.

Walking along the crooked pavements within the historic strength of the city walls Julia was awe struck by the designer shops that lay at either side of her. She felt as though they were beckoning her to enter, with the doorways like chattering mouths, calling her name to go inside.

Why me? She wondered. *Why am I stuck with the slummy gypsy life?* She stared at the manikins in the windows, all of them dressed with impeccable taste and each one resuscitated to life with the bold strike of the new season's colours. In her modesty, she failed to realise how the outfits would exemplify her beauty, for now as she stared back at them, her frustration that she could never afford them only encouraged her feeling of discontent.

A colourful poster in one of the shop windows caught her eye, she walked toward it. It was advertising the first meeting of the season at York Racecourse, encouraging shoppers to go inside and buy an outfit to wear for the races. Julia instantly connected the poster to Gerard Santé's funeral before allowing her mind to wander on to happier thoughts. What an opportunity to meet new people. People would be there who might actually have something interesting to talk about. Her mind dashed from one thought to another as it dreamt of being a part of the glamour of it all – drinking iced Pimm's, or possibly, if she was lucky, even champagne. She imagined herself chatting endlessly with other punters about the form and watching the finely tuned thoroughbreds as they jogged around the paddock.

A faint smile of contemplation adorned her lips, the sport of Kings; it would all be a brand new world. A world she so wanted to be a part of.

Looking at the display advert in closer detail she realised that the first date of the exclusive May meeting was only a matter of days away. What kind of clothes could she possibly have within her second-hand wardrobe that would suit such a day? The smartest outfit she had was a white floating summer dress. Her father told her she looked like a fashion model in it, but she cast the thought aside, he hadn't noticed the straying hemline. Not that a straying hemline would affect the kind of racing day her family were used to. They frequented the silver ring where they spent the day happily swilling beer and brawling, she knew they would find it amusing just to hear that she wanted to go into the "posh, snobby end" of the racecourse. Her father wouldn't understand why she would want to do that when she could "mix with her own kind" on a cheap ticket – or nip over the fence for that matter as the day wore on. She cringed at the mere thought of that, it was not the day out she was looking for. Her thoughts continued to roll until movement in the shop window awakened her from her trance. She looked up and noticed that a sales assistant inside the boutique, struck by Julia's beauty, was looking back at her and smiling warmly.

Julia's face reddened and though she smiled back at the assistant, hastily, she turned and crossed the road.

There was a jeweller's across the street, she hovered in its doorway and peered in at the magnificent window display. As she was looking, a couple with a little baby lying asleep in its pram stood at the side of her.

"Go on choose some diamond earrings," she heard the man tell his wife.

"They're expensive," the woman hesitated.

"And you're worth it," the man answered sincerely.

How wonderful that he should be so kind and appreciative Julia thought. The man leaned over to kiss his wife on the lips and in that instant Julia's appreciation for his kind sentiments were overshadowed.

She didn't know where it had come from but the cruel awakening of a dark, morbid memory reappeared in her mind; she put her hand to her nose, trying to rid the ghastly smell of his breath that screeched up her nostrils and intensified the nauseous detail of her childhood trauma.

She had been a girl of thirteen years old when her uncle had asked her to have a look at a lame pony he had tethered nearby. Within seconds of her being cruelly enticed to a quiet spot away from prying eyes he grabbed her by the hair and threw her to the ground. He smothered her bewildered and terrified screams with his dirty stinking hands and yanked down her pants. He rammed himself hard inside her, wheezing breathlessly as his tar ridden lungs struggled to cope with the exertion, finally his forceful thrusts subsided. He zipped up his trousers and told her if she ever told anyone about it he would make sure she ended up the same way as her mother – dead. He then let out a haunting laugh at the sight of her lying bleeding on the floor whilst she grappled shakily to pull up her torn pants.

With a twisted toothless grin he forced his manky stale breath against her cheek and whispered, "Remember, oh snobby one, I 'ad you first." Like the coward he was, he turned and fled.

Her haunting memory remained as sharp as ever, and now, as her hands trembled against her mouth, she was cruelly struck by the worst experience of all – her mother's murder. She shook her head and looked back into the shop window. Her eyes raced to look at everything, anything, in a desperate need to distract her thoughts from more detail. As her eyes searched they fixed upon an enormous pearl ring that was perched inside an oyster shell, it was this pearl that reminded Julia of much happier times.

"The world is your oyster," her mother would to say to Julia as a little girl. "Climb every mountain whilst you get the chance, my dear, for one day the mountains might crumble. Never live your life with regret."

In that instant she made a decision that she was sure her mother would approve of, she was going to go to the races. She turned around and her eyes met for the second time with the outfits on display in the shop window.

She had to change her life, and the race meet in York would just be the start of it. She took two deep breaths before walking over the street towards the boutique, the persuasive beckoning of an unknown world was far too much to resist.

Julia walked inside and instantly felt consumed by the smell of superior quality that lay still in the air. She had never been into a shop like this in her life and the feeling of privilege, just to be looking at the rich decadence of the fabrics, lifted her mood.

She was the sole customer inside, but a man at the far end of the store was arranging outfits from a hoard of rails. He turned briefly.

"I'll be over in a minute Madam," he assured before resuming his work.

His casual manner suited Julia; it allowed her the time to appreciate fully the disbelieving comforts that the shop had to offer. Cream leather sofas invited customers to sit and rest, a coffee percolator with china cups and saucers sat by the sofa's side and a pile of magazines covered the table in front and, as she walked around, she almost giggled to feel her feet practically bounce against the thick pile of the golden carpet.

She reached up and touched a black and ivory satin blouse, its stark print was heavy yet tasteful, her fingers gently caressed the material and instantaneously she felt its melting warmth against the soft skin of her hands. Mesmerised, she slowly repeated the sequence with several outfits, gently building up the confidence to peruse some of the price tags whilst fantasising of becoming their proud owner. The designer labels and astronomical price tags that dangled besides snaking security tags may as well have been in a foreign language. One or two of the names seemed familiar from the long out-of-print and dog-eared magazines she enjoyed flicking through.

"Good morning, do you need any help, madam?"

The man startled Julia, a glinting badge against his impeccable navy suit caught her attention and she noticed the title of Manager engraved across it.

"No, I don't think so," she stumbled, "I'm just browsing for an outfit for a very special occasion."

"Is it a formal occasion, madam?" he offered.

"Erm." She ran her fingers nervously through her long mahogany hair and awkwardly glanced back at him with innocent dark eyes, then smiled apprehensively. "I'm going to the races," Julia said quietly. "I've been invited."

John Holmes, the newly appointed shop manager, had just fallen in love with the most beautiful woman he had ever seen. He stood silently in front of her for seconds, imagining how he would feel if he was the lucky man attached to her arm for the day.

"Well, in that case come with me," he said quickly composing himself. "You will need to see our brand new deliveries; they are just in this morning." He turned to Julia exhibiting slight embarrassment. "Things are a bit disorganised, we have just changed suppliers and there seems to have been a few teething problems with deliveries. These outfits should have been in weeks ago. It's a shame; we could have sold them three times over if they had been in on time. They are perfect for the races."

Julia, fully aware that her sense for decorum had been slashed, dropped her bag and mackintosh to the ground and simply gasped.

"Wow!" she shrieked with wide excited eyes pulling one outfit after another free from the rails. "They are absolutely stunning!"

He watched the magnetism of her young fresh face lurch into the life of a wondrous child's. Her eyes laughed and danced as they stared at the outfits and he wondered, longingly, who would be the lucky bearer of her company.

"Like I say, they are new in today," he repeated, feeling her excitement to be contagious.

Without warning the shop darkened as the sky outside became shrouded with stormy rain clouds and instantly John Holmes became infatuated with the idea of being alone with this exquisite woman on a stormy evening. He could hear the fire crackle beside them as the sky above rumbled between bolts of cracking lightening and could feel his fingers glide across her soft young skin.

"I'll like to try this one, and that one, oh and definitely this one."

Her excited voice roused him from his lustrous daydream and he felt his fingers eagerly tingle as though he really had touched her skin. Her arms were now weighted with a collection of outfits, too many to count. He smiled at her childlike eagerness and graciously showed her to the changing room.

"Its looks as though there is a storm brewing," he managed, trying hard to distract attention from his lewd thoughts.

"Mmmm," Julia replied, struggling to pick up her bag and coat before following on behind.

He showed her in and was relieved to scrape the curtain closed; he needed some time to collect himself before he could see her again.

Julia stood in the plush changing room and, as the curtain was pulled behind her, a loud rumble of thunder greeted her entry. The air cast a thick muggy stillness in the room, one that she could feel threaten an enormous downpour. Suddenly feeling hot, she began to take off her clothes.

Moments later, she sat on the chair in only her pants. She ran her toes through the thick pile of the golden carpet and gently allowed her fingers to glide across the cold, glamorous, glint of the glass designer chair she sat upon. She wallowed for only seconds in the opulence and luxury, realising it was the only taste of either she had ever experienced. She looked back at the jaw-dropping outfits that hung in front of her and felt reality deflate her. What chance did she have of owning them? She reached out and touched the first outfit that had caught her eye, a halter neck ivory dress and felt her fingers bump sedately against the hand stitched embroidery and ivory pearlescent sequins that adorned its bust-line. She couldn't resist, regardless of whether she could afford it or not, she just felt compelled to try it on.

Within minutes she was in it and Julia stared in astonishment at her reflection; it was a reflection she could hardly recognise. The ivory halter neck straps tantalised the onlooker by the seductive exhibit of her soft, dark treacle shoulders. Julia turned an inch at a time and watched as the beads and sequins embellishing her bust flashed and glinted in the shops light. She swept her hands against the remarkably soft material that melted against her slim curving torso and watched its hemline fall gracefully to just above her knee. She span round in disbelief, the dress had transformed her into a beautiful woman and for the first time, drenched in the innocent sensuality of this dress, she felt like one. Her face was flushed with excitement and her breaths were shallow and fast in response to seeing herself. She felt fantastic, then again, like a balloon that had popped, she felt her pleasure wane. No matter how good she looked she could never afford it. She looked at the demoralising price tag and the numbers £2300 flashed back at her. She flopped against the chair. That was all the price tag was to her, numbers, in monetary terms, just impossible to afford.

She heard large drops of rain plop coldly against the window outside, then she sat upright, realising that potentially, the weather, combined with the fact that these dresses had not yet been introduced to the security tags were possibly the ingredients that could allow her dreams to come alive. She hurriedly unzipped the dress. She had a plan.

With trembling hands, she removed the remaining outfits from the hangers and dropped them carelessly upon the flamboyant dressing room chair. Then, wearing only her pants, she hid her body behind the silk drape of the curtain and felt the cool material brush across her skin, then, ensuring she was concealed, she beckoned the manager for assistance.

Without delay, like a dog to its master's whistle, John Holmes stood in the changing area. He took a sharp intake of breath as his eyes surveyed the naked goddess standing behind the curtain. His mind tortured him, goading him that only a thin slither of a material stood in between him and her body, he felt his passion stir.

"I have finished trying on the clothes and although they are fantastic I rather feel I would like a second opinion. I am going to bring a friend in later to see what she thinks. Could you put these to one side for me please?"

A long golden arm appeared with outfits that dangled from her hand. Silently he traced its origin, allowing his eyes to lead him to a soft naked shoulder and then wrestle with his mind's agony of not taking her here and now. He reached out to retrieve the hoard of outfits and his persisting eyes wandered again. They were stunned as they caught another electrifying glimpse of the honey glowing flesh that made up her taught curving waist. He blushed ashamedly and quickly grabbed the outfits.

"I'll get dressed and will be out in a minute," Julia called.

Lost for words he walked back into the shop.

A second crack of thunder rumbled loudly, she wondered if it was warning her to relinquish her plan, she ignored it, the dress would be hers. Swiftly, she stepped back into the ivory dress that she had purposely left behind and zipped it up, all the while trying to disregard the ferocity of her pounding heart. She heard voices come into the shop and she almost screamed in fright whilst she pulled on her jeans, first one leg then the other. With deep stuffs, she pushed the dress into the waistband of the jeans before finally and breathlessly pulling on her top and reaching for her mackintosh. The heavens outside crashed open with torrents of rain and Julia was so relieved they had, she needed to be completely covered. She fastened the last button of her mackintosh, tied the belt so tight she could hardly breathe and looked back at herself in the mirror for a trace of suspicion.

Her nerves began to heatedly bubble and with it beads of perspiration began to spring upon her forehead as she grew hotter and hotter. Feeling ashamed, she slumped down on the chair, closed her eyes and willed herself to face her fear and walk back through the shop. Random thoughts began to dissuade her plan, throwing a series of 'what if' scenarios through her anxious mind. What if her actions had been recorded on CCTV within the changing room? Her eyes searched for a camera against the walls and ceiling. What if they asked to search her before she left? What if they found the outfit and then called the police? Julia's terror intensified at every question she posed. She couldn't turn back now, she desperately wanted to attend the races and this dress was perfect. Surely she could be forgiven for wanting to feel truly special for once? With a burst of boldness her clammy shaking hands picked up her handbag and walked out of the changing room.

John Holmes was now out of sight and Julia saw that at the other side of the room, the original shop assistant had replaced him, she stood behind the desk with the door to freedom wide open by her side. When she had initially entered the boutique she couldn't recall it looking so large, now, with her heart banging nervously against her chest, Julia began the arduous journey towards the exit.

As she walked she smiled at the lady who was now staring straight at her then panicked at the assistant's un-flickering response. *Why is she not smiling at me? After all, she smiled at me through the window before; she knows what I'm up to...* Julia continued to walk straight for the door. The damned thing looked to be a million miles away. Her nerves sprinkled sharp glassy splinters of angst through her body, immobilising her throat and casting a heavy numbness that filled her legs. She forced her stride but faltered again when she read the prominent sign that hung above the door,

CCTV in operation, shoplifters will be prosecuted.

She imagined the horror of being arrested by the police, but the smell of the torrential rain and its offer of freedom encouraged her to continue. *I've nearly made it* she thought. *I've nearly done it* she internally encouraged. Just as one foot stepped against the mat at the door, the sound of the assistant's voice rooted her to the spot.

"Excuse me, madam!" she heard the woman's voice shout behind her. She wondered fleetingly whether to run. She couldn't turn around.

"Errr, madam," the lady repeated.

Her voice rang shrilly in Julia's ears. Maybe now was the time she should throw herself to the ground and plead with the shop assistant to let her go amid cries of apologies? Instead she remained still with concrete legs that felt unable to move an inch.

"Is this yours? I think you've dropped it."

Julia turned stiffly to see the woman was holding the scruffy leather band that she had used to tie up her hair. Relief sank through her body.

"Yes, it is mine – thank you very much." She quickly grabbed it, masking her temptation to laugh with the effects of relief. It amazed Julia how her voice had remained so collected when her innards seemed so close to collapse. She took it from the lady's hand and walked out of the shop.

John Holmes, watched her leave his boutique from an upstairs window, he would have liked to have personally wished her farewell but was afraid he would find it impossible to harbour the strongest attraction he had ever felt.

"She is the most beautiful girl I have ever seen in my entire life," he told himself. "I just have to see her again."

The determined rain drops poured against Julia's face but brought with them nothing but exhilaration and excitement. She quickened her pace, barely able to believe she had made it. As she turned the corner, she ran. For the time being, freedom was most definitely hers.

Chapter Four

LUCA DEMARIO sat at the twelve-seater table in the kitchen of his family home. The steamed fish his mother had served him looked soggy and extremely unappetising on his plate. He daren't tell her how hungry he was; already he could see her from the corner of his eye shaking her head in frustration that she had to serve him it at all. Given a moment's notice he knew it would be her pleasure to cook a large homemade pasta dish swimming in a thick creamy sauce, and being a lover of fine food, it would also be his pleasure to eat it. However, it was times like this he had to remind himself why – to be one of the world's highest ranking jockeys – he made the sacrifices he did. Luca pushed the fish around the plate with his fork before eating it slowly; it would be the last thing he would be eating until tomorrow evening.

Maria DeMario watched her son eat his fish and tried to suppress the scowl she felt creeping onto her face. She worried about the low calorie diet he stuck to religiously, and simultaneously, it broke her heart she couldn't cook for him. Diets and fasting were not something a traditional Italian mother and wife could come to terms with, especially when Luca did it to take away what god had given him – a broad muscular physique. However, through experience she knew better than to mention it, like her son had often told her, it was all part of his career. She turned up the volume to *Il Divo*, her favourite CD and sung unashamedly at the top of her voice whilst preparing dinner for the remainder of the family.

She was a small woman, generously plump, with large curving hips that swayed involuntarily as she trotted around her sumptuous home – both factors, that unlike most women, Maria viewed as assets, a clear hallmark of success for her love of cookery and her passion for good food.

Her lustrous black hair was so thick that every morning she was forced to scrape it back from her face into the confines of a French knot but by lunchtime, with so many chores to complete, it would be straining at the tucks and wrestling to break free. Frankie often told her how much he loved to see her hair off her face, explaining to her bashful giggles that it gave him the opportunity to see the whole of her pretty face, which to him, had never changed since the day they had met.

Her hips now swayed purposefully as she became transfixed by the electrifying atmosphere that *Il Divo* transmitted throughout the kitchen. She engrossed herself in their powerful voices and intermittently threw her arms high into the air as she joined them in reaching their crescendo, throwing the odd extra mushroom and additional clove of garlic into the pan as she did so. Indeed, her kitchen was her sanctuary, and the perfect place for enjoying a lively concerto.

As far as Maria DeMario was concerned she was living her dream. When she had married Frankie thirty-eight years ago at the tender age of twenty, she had never thought that one day she would have the opportunity to choose a handmade designer kitchen. But ten years ago when they moved into their dream home that was exactly what she was able to do.

The thirty foot kitchen was bathed in ivory and the blinking sparkle of pure gold leaf upon many of the furnishings. Boasting prime position in the centre of the room was an island that appeared to almost float against the glass like gleam of the polished marble floor, like a vast galaxy, it had been a worthy assistant for baking, mixing and storage since its day of instalment. However, Maria's absolute favourite was her made-to-order triple Aga oven, it sat neatly in a bespoke ivory tiled alcove at the far side of the room, and barely ever got the opportunity to rest. She often baked in the evening, her tendency illuminated by two original Venetian crystal chandeliers that hung at either end of the room. In Maria's eyes, her work was her family and looking after them all was a pure joy, the fact that she was surrounded by utter luxury was a secondary bonus.

Luca began to flick through a magazine which had been newly delivered that morning, though he barely took in its contents. His hectic schedule over the next couple of days took precedence in his thoughts.

Thomas Markington, his agent, had booked him various rides at race meets around the country, it would involve a lot of travelling in car and helicopter to and fro, but keeping up his spirits was York races in two days time. York was one of his favourite racecourses, a place that always held a special passion for him.

Having had the privilege to travel the length and breadth of the United Kingdom to race, York racecourse remained unique. Often he would have his father's helicopter fly him in. When ascending, he would look down and the pit of his stomach would become captured by a mixture of nerves and excitement. He could almost hear the good cheer raised by the authentic Yorkshire racing crowd as they poured through the various entrances, moving with the same gusto as champagne foam escaping from a magnums' neck. They never failed to attend, attracted by the never ending supply of top quality racing continually offered there. Their spirit and knowledge was ever present with words of advising encouragement prior to a race and rip roaring congratulatory toasts when he had finished with a win. It was the warm sincerity of these punters that managed to strip the sport of its historic infusion of snobbery and stuffiness and, at York racecourse in particular, the sound of infectious laughter along with the enthusiastic popping of corks was never far away. York racecourse had played host to some of the most memorable meets of his career and to this day it was a place that always made him proud to be a part of the sport. He smiled and felt energised at the thought of returning in a couple of days for the first May meet of the season.

He heard the voices of his twin sisters Emma and Sofia, their footsteps hammered down the vast stairway.

"Why the hell do you want to call him?" he heard Sofia ask Emma.

"Why shouldn't I?" Emma answered sharply. "Maybe he's lost my number."

"Yeah, right," Sofia answered doubtfully.

Their conversation ended as they barged into the kitchen. Luca looked up at Emma.

"Call who?" he asked protectively.

Emma screwed her face to her brother's intrusion and ignored his question, aware that the suggestion of contacting Charles Lancaster-Baron would be fuelling an unwelcome lecture from her elder brother. The two sisters sailed over to their mother who was chopping a selection of vegetables and each grabbed a few straying peppers. Munching avidly they began to argue as usual as to who would be wearing which outfit for the York meet.

They, like all the girls he knew, had to start having a military parade of all their clothes at least ten days before any event. Their hoards of outfits would be exhumed from their wardrobe and every designer shop in the area would be hounded and preyed upon until the prefect look had been created. Luca turned the pages of the magazine he had been viewing.

"Can you believe this, you lot?" Luca beckoned to his mother and sisters. He turned the magazine to show the article he had spotted. It was a well known magazine featuring a shot of him, taken the week before, whilst racing at Ascot .

The women moved closer to peer over his shoulder at the picture. It was showing him in his racing jodhpurs after winning a race, a huge red circle had been drawn by the editors around his crotch, the caption read, "Luca DeMario proves the ladies are not only interested in the package of success!"

The picture's aim was quite clearly to illustrate the fact that Luca was well endowed. An anonymous group of glamorous female race-goers were in the background of the shot pointing and smiling at his generous bulge so clearly evident through his tight jodhpurs.

"I just can't believe that women talk like that, they amaze me." He shook his head in disbelief.

His mother followed suit, tutting uncontrollably for what seemed to be minutes before reacting.

"Those English a gals, no manners," she declared teasingly with an

Italian accent so thick it could be spread on toast. "They are all the same, you keep away from a them," she continued. "When you take a holiday from a your'a racin', Mama will take you to Italia where the good gals are, and then I find you a real'a lady!" Her eyes widened and danced in excitement as she imagined the collection of sumptuous Italian girls wanting to take up the honour of becoming Mrs DeMario.

His sisters joined Luca in laughing at her remarks.

"Mama," he said lovingly as Maria swept up his plate to place it in the dishwasher, "I don't need you to find me a wife. I will find one myself when I am good and ready."

"Hmmm," she snapped, "with girls like that around I need to find you a bodyguard, not a wife."

She fondly ruffled his hair. She was so proud of him. He inherited all his attributes from his father. He was confident and charming, but it was his typically Italian incredibly handsome looks that were an instantaneous hit with everyone. At 5'6" he was slightly taller than most of the other flat jockeys. His height and his naturally broad physique were factors that forced him to accept that a strict diet had to be adhered to, for his racing weight had to be kept down to the minimum.

Mrs DeMario knew she had bred a real man, good-looking, exceptional manners, hard working and more importantly, he was honest. What else would a woman look for in a man? He was an incredible catch for any girl.

The two sisters began to argue again. The whole family knew it would continue until they entered York racecourse.

"No, I'm wearing the Gucci dress, Sofia; you said you were wearing that purple Prada suit."

"It's not purple you philistine, it's blueberry," Sofia snapped.

The sound of their father's footsteps echoing down the marble hallway postponed the girls' bickering, summoning Sofia to run to greet him. She flung her arms around him excitedly.

"Pappa, hello, how did your business trip go?" She barely listened to his answer. "You know Pappa, I really love you, you know that don't you?" She let out a giggle as a look of amused distrust entered her father's eyes.

"Well," she continued, "I really need to look good for York races, and you know," she paused, exaggerating a pet lip that sprouted from her mouth, "I haven't got a thing to wear," before snuggling up to her father's ear and adding, "I don't know how it has happened but my allowance has just disappeared, I telephoned the bank and it has all gone. Will you top it up, Pappa? I desperately need to go shopping. It is the York meet after all, I love it there, I really need to look right, the best in fact." She sneaked a sideways glance at her sister Emma. "Please, please," she continued in a puppy like whine.

With a defeated smile on his face he nodded.

"Yes, I'll top it up, in the meantime." He reached into his pocket, "Here." He handed Sofia a folded bundle of fifty pound notes. She didn't stick around, she ran off gleefully shouting a hoard of "Thank-you's" over her shoulder.

Her sister then appeared at the table. Unfortunately for Emma he was furious with her. He had received a call on his mobile on the way home informing him that Emma had slept with Charles Lancaster-Baron one night the previous week. Frankie had fumed internally all the way home; he really thought he was something, that little shit. Frankie silently vowed, by hook or by crook, he would seek revenge. In the meantime he was ashamed that his daughter had such little self-respect. Abruptly he handed her the same amount of cash he had given to Sofia.

Emma put the abruptness down to her being second in line and skipped away after her sister.

Luca shouted after them, "At nineteen years old you should not be relying on your father for money!"

"We don't care who gives us money, if you're offering that's fine!" Emma shouted back down the stairs.

Frankie ignored their reply and turned to Luca.

"How did Gerard Santé's funeral go? You remembered to pass on my condolences didn't you?" he asked.

"Yeah, I did, it was terribly sad." He shook his head. "I've never been to a funeral of someone my own age before; it really brought it home to me."

Their conversation was interrupted by the phone ringing. Luca bent down to pick up his overnight bag to put it in the car. His mother passed him the phone

"It's for you Luca, it's Thomas."

Luca screwed up his face but took the receiver from her hand.

"Hi Thomas, How are you?" He listened for a short while before saying: "Look I'm about to set off for Windsor now, I'll speak to you about it later but I really don't think so. You know how that kind of shit drives me mad, let's talk about it tomorrow. Take care, Thomas, I'll call you after the racing."

Luca's mother could tell he was agitated after the conversation. "What's the problem?" she asked

"Oh these bloody agents, you employ them to take away the hassle from your life only to find they still pester you for the same things everyone else does," explained Luca. "He wanted to know if I would attend a television interview." He sighed, "He knows full well I hate all that kind of crap. Sometimes I just think I pay him a fortune so he can piss me off!" He slammed his bag onto the table and kissed his mother and father on both cheeks before turning to walk out of the house.

"I wouldn't be too quick to dismiss the idea," his mother urged. "It could be Parkinson. Oh Parky, you can not beat him, I adore that man. Bellissimo! Bellissimo!" Mrs DeMario crooned at the top of her voice continuing to finish the dinner.

"Mama, Parky has retired," Luca laughed.

"Oh, nonsense, he would come back to interview you in a flash," she sighed "He's such a wonderful man!"

Luca ignored her comments with a shake of his head and turned to walk out of the door, his father followed him out.

"Don't let them get to you, just do your job and do it well. You do right to say no. Keep yourself to yourself." He placed his spade like hand on his son's back. "Listen, you can go in the helicopter if you prefer. If I call him now, the pilot can be back in an hour or so."

Frankie was worried about his son driving when he was wound up; he didn't like the thought of him being alone in the car with no one to talk things over with. His mother, unable to resist, also came outside to share in the farewell conversation.

"No, it's okay. I'd prefer to drive thanks," he answered. "The long drive will do me good. I will be calm when I get there." He played with some of the gravel nervously with his shoe before adding, "Try and come to the York meeting, it would be great to see you there."

Looking up he noticed his mothers' face freeze.

His father sidetracked the conversation with the subject of Lucas's car. "You should have asked your mother to give that car a wash! You can't drive around in a car plastered in mud."

Luca laughed as his mother gave her husband a playful swipe with the tea towel she held in her hand. Eager to regain his own space, Luca got into his Mercedes SL, holding a hand out of the window in farewell to his parents. He drove away, down the long sweeping drive and through the enormous electric gates that fenced the DeMario family off from the rest of the world.

Maria DeMario hung back from her husband's retreat into the house. With her son's suggestion of Frankie attending York racecourse, the thought weighed heavy on her mind. Many years had passed since the events in North Yorkshire had almost shattered their lives, and those events were the only reason they had moved here to Cheshire. Privately, her roving thoughts crept into a far away place.

Chapter Five

"WHAT AM I going to do without him? I can't believe it." Paris felt her voice rise and fall in uncontrollable waves. "And, I can't believe you are insisting I go racing today, you are a heartless bitch!" Paris screamed at her mother from the corner of her bedroom where she sat crumpled upon the floor.

She felt completely helpless. Her legs and arms felt as heavy as iron, only the incessant shaking confirmed any life. The stark reality of Gerard's death was sinking in, one, slow, painful blow at a time. Gerard Santé had been her friend as well as her lover, the only one of either she had ever truly had. Her mother responded to her outburst.

"Look, Paris, you must pull yourself together." She continued in her usual dismissive manner, "You cannot let this ruin the rest of your life, it is not worth it." She began to raise her voice as the reality of what she was about to say took a hold of her. "You will learn as you go through life that all kinds of trials and tribulations have to be faced. There are times when the reality of having to deal with a situation you hate will hit you hard." She took a deep breath through her nose whilst simultaneously screwing up her eyes in desperation "BUT, you and you alone have to get up and get on with it." She spat, "Now get up off the floor and get this outfit on I have chosen for you." Her mother threw the clothes onto her bed and slammed the bedroom door as she left the room.

Francesca huffed in frustration as she stamped into the bathroom and promptly bolted the door.

"There's no talking to that girl," she hissed to herself. "She needs a kick up the…" She stopped herself, she didn't want to get angry and feel stressed whilst getting ready. She recalled a conversation she had had only yesterday.

"She thinks I don't care. I am as disappointed as anyone that Gerard has bloody well died," she had explained to her husband Bill. "What hope has she got now?" she had added. "I mean, unless a miracle occurs and Paris starts to lose some weight and get a transformation in the make over department she will be batting from a very sticky wicket indeed."

Mrs Montford prided herself on the fact that she was a realist. There was no point beating around the bush or trying to fluff up the facts in a grave situation, the truth had to be realised and dealt with.

She heard her husband coming up the stairs.

"Leave me in peace!" she shouted through the door.

She didn't want to be disturbed. With rushed strokes she began to brush her new firming and lifting mask to her face and neck. She wanted to get her money's worth, silence and privacy was the only answer.

Paris felt internal anger gush through her body like a mighty ocean wave. How could Gerard have left her? He had no idea how it felt to be alone, but, he had known how lonely she felt, she had told him on many occasions. Didn't he understand that, now he had gone, those feelings were only going to manifest themselves? Especially with the crude and cold level of support she got from her mother. *How can my own mother not care how I feel?* The questions continued to roll in her head, she tried to dispel them but couldn't. In anger, she kicked the wastepaper basket that sat near her feet; it rolled across the floor, spewing its innards in a haphazard trail across the room. Paris thought that the disorganised scatterings resembled a pretty accurate picture of the whole of her life.

Mr Montford went into his daughter's room. Crouching down he squeezed himself up beside her. Gently he placed his arm on her shoulder and waited until her sobbing breaths had subsided slightly.

He knew only too well what his wife's opinion of the situation was and he was quite honestly disgusted by it. However, he was not surprised. As he held his heartbroken daughter in his arms he marvelled at the difference between the two women.

In this family, mother and daughter lived in two separate worlds. Francesca was attractive and slim and worked hard at being so. Every day for years she had worked out at the gym, abstaining from fattening food and had shopped until she dropped for the best make up and outfits that money could buy.

Paris on the other hand placed all the emphasis in her life on love, family and friends. She didn't care for the hierarchical ranks bestowed upon social backgrounds and education, instead preferring genuine people that were good fun and friendly.

"Why is it always the loveliest people that are hurting in life?" He hadn't realised he had spoken aloud until Paris prized herself away from his tight embrace. She wiped away some tears.

"I don't know but I wouldn't wish this pain on my worst enemy if I had one," she whispered. "How am I going to live without him?" Her voice was breaking up as her emotion fought to escape. "He was the only person I have ever met that I felt I had something in common with." She banged her clenched fists on the side of her head. "Together we were the only ones that could see right through that ridiculous two-cheeked pucker they all give out at the races and polo." Through her snivels she gave out an empty laugh. "We used to laugh at how empty hearted and false all these people were."

Her father held her closer as she opened up her heart.

"Most people only hung around him because of what he had. I could hear them sometimes, Oooh that's Gerard Santé over there, he's loaded." She began to sob again. "But I didn't want him for that." She looked into her fathers eyes as though trying to convince him of her honesty. "I loved him Dad for who he was. He was my wonderful, wonderful friend I am going to miss him so much."

Again, she broke down and sobbed into his arms. He could feel the magnitude of her pain and loss, he wished there was something he could do to take it away from her, but there wasn't. All he could do was hold her. Some fifteen minutes went by before she spoke again.

"I've been thinking," she added as she wiped more tears from her cheeks, "I am going to go today, Gerard would want me to." She tried to take some deep breaths so she could continue. "He was such a good friend to me, I feel I want to be around the people that knew him and cared for him as I did." She looked down into her lap. "I think it will help me." She bit her lip hard and tried to regain control of her crowded emotions. Slowly she got up from the floor, her legs felt shaky and nausea was setting in. She walked over to her dressing table and began to brush her hair. Her father gently kissed her on her forehead and walked quietly out of the room.

When her father left the room she sat on her bed. God, she loved her Dad so much. He was the kindest man she had ever met; she felt a deep affinity towards him. Her thoughts turned to her mother; in anger she began to brush her hair furiously with small tough strokes. *How will my life interest my mother now Gerard's dead?* Her thoughts appalled her as to why she sought her mother's approval in the first place. Everything that her mother stood for was alien to her, but the last few months had been the only time her mother had shown any interest in her life. She knew that now Gerard had died that would all end, Paris held no purpose now, not even to her mother.

She slipped on her shoes, she chose the comfortable option, she didn't want anything else to hurt today. Paris let out a deep sigh, she couldn't help feeling as though she was going to be alone for the rest of her life, or was she? She ran her hand over her stomach, the nausea was getting worse. She was now one week late with her second period and felt overwrought with fear that on top of everything else she could be pregnant. She had mentioned that she had missed one period only the week before to Gerard. He had laughed and gently dismissed the idea.

"Nah, surely not, my lovely little pea. Men like me were not made to be fathers!" he had joked.

She had laughed with him, thinking he was probably referring to the fact that he was really quite irresponsible in many ways, especially in terms of business and money. She was quite sure, though, when it came to love and people, being a father was exactly what he had been brought into the world for.

Paris looked in the mirror; she was as ready as she was ever going to be. She walked out of her bedroom and downstairs.

"What the hell do you look like? I'm not walking around with you looking like that Paris. This is after all York. You will stand out like a sore thumb, you look like a tramp." Mrs Montford was quite furious. "Are you just doing this for attention now?"

"For God's sake, Francesca!" Bill snapped as he walked into the hallway from the kitchen.

She ignored his comments and continued, "You haven't even put so much as a splash of make up on, and your hair looks like you've just got out of bed and you've got those god-awful stinking dog hairs all over you." She threw her arms up in the air in disbelief. "Paris! Get a bloody grip of yourself, you need a hat and..."

"I'd rather have my clothes *covered* in dog hairs than have *even one* of yours on me you evil witch!" Paris screamed. She pushed passed her father and ran upstairs in torrents of tears.

"Why the hell does she walk those blasted dogs?" Francesca bellowed. "I wouldn't care, but their stinking bloody hair gets dragged into my house which is exactly the reason I don't have them."

Bill, standing at the bottom of the stairs, remained quiet, aware that animal hairs alone were not the reason Francesca wouldn't have house pets. Genuine gifts of nature were as far removed from Francesca's life as were the disastrous consequences of world poverty.

She stamped over to her favourite antique decanter and poured herself a stiff gin and tonic, adding the ice and the lemon, but omitting the tonic.

The decanter had been a wedding present from her mother. Each time she used it she felt a huge appreciation for quality. She shook her head, *my mother would turn in her grave if she saw the rag and bone daughter and husband I'd ended up with, though to be fair to her* she thought, *she did warn me.*

She took an enormous slug and almost drained half the glass. She winced as the strength of the gin hit her throat. Aside from the wine she had drunk in the bathroom, this was the first spirit of the day and on first introduction spirits always stung.

Mrs Montford's family had been moderately well off in past generations, although Francesca tried to elevate her status by having people believe their family tree and heritage had aristocratic connections.

In fact, the reality of the situation was that one of her distant relatives had briefly worked as a servant for a member of the Royal Family. One evening she had got extremely drunk on the dregs of vintage port that had been left over from a banquet. That royal banquet had turned into a feast of her very own when the personal footman to one of the princes had taken a shine to her. Three months later, with morning sickness firmly in place, she was promptly dismissed with a glowing reference. Francesca tried not to dwell on the truth, only internally and very occasionally would she think of the commonalities between her and her 'Regal' Grandmother.

Unfortunately she too had consumed a few too many champagnes on the evening of a local Hunt Ball. Francesca had been twenty one and searching desperately for a wealthy socialite husband. As she was staggering and informing passers by in the marquee she thought she was going to be sick, a kind young man had led her outside. The fresh air had awakened her senses but unfortunately it had also awakened her passion. The surprised, yet agreeable gentleman responded receptively.

She hardly remembered the act itself but from that moment this pest of a man never left her alone. He followed her, phoned her, he would not be rebuffed no matter how nasty she was. Some three months later she was grateful for his persistence when she realised, with grave disappointment, that she was pregnant. Bill Montford, ever the gentleman, immediately did the honourable thing and proposed.

Begrudgingly she accepted, knowing it was the only hope she had to uphold the 'family name'. She consoled herself night after night prior to the wedding. Telling herself that she could marry him now, then, later, when something better came along she could ditch this no hoper as quickly as she had found him. Her parents were thoroughly disappointed, especially her mother.

"You are certainly marrying beneath yourself, Francesca," her mother would say in the weeks leading up to the wedding. "I mean, his name speaks volumes. Who on earth wants to answer to Bill and not William?"

Francesca had tried to make him answer to William but he had been adamant. In the end she had given up in the hope she wouldn't have to last too long before she found someone else.

Twenty-three years had passed, and as the years had dragged by she had taken solace with possibility of her daughter upholding the family name. She hoped she would amount to something so that she could at least have something to be proud of. She shook her head at how wrong she had been.

As she took a another massive slug of gin from her glass she caught a glimpse of her husband from the corner of her eye and snarled, "You make sure you keep out of my way today, just keep sat down and keep yourself to yourself. I don't want you embarrassing me when I'm talking to someone."

The familiar sound of her mobile rang from her handbag. Bill had never seen that bag before, another purchase he presumed, his heart sank. As she shuffled her hand inside to get the phone, two pieces of paper fell out at Bill's feet.

Barging by him she answered the call. "Are they really?" she sniggered venomously. "That's the second time he's gone bankrupt in the last ten years." She laughed out loud and lit a cigarette at the other side of the sitting room. "I thought something was wrong last week when I saw Lydia, she looked ghastly and had piled on the weight. No wonder, hey?" She shot a bitter look over in Bill's direction, who wants to be with a man who can't afford you?"

Bill had heard enough. Shaking his head behind his wife's stern back he bent down to pick up the stray pieces of paper that had fallen to the floor. He walked out of the room to try and eradicate the conversation from his earshot and place the paper in the dustbin. Her drivel continued, "I wonder where her children will go to school now? It will be impossible for them to afford…"

He closed the kitchen door behind him and noticed that the papers he was about to throw away were in fact receipts. He unravelled them and stared in horror, how could she do this? The receipt totalled £2600 and included three items, a handbag, a pair of shoes and a dress. He was motionless yet couldn't take his eyes off the figures. He opened the drawer in the kitchen and rifled out the number for telephone banking. As the recorded voice on the other end of the phone led him through the instructions it wasn't long before his bank balance was revealed. As usual they were in the red, but this time it was worse, they had insufficient funds to meet the mortgage payment due to go out tomorrow.

His mouth began to dry and his shirt began to constrict around his neck, he needed to speak to an operator and quickly. Frantically pressing the buttons that would get him through, he tapped his polished shoe against the slate tiled floor. The line began to ring, he knew one of the operators would pick up soon, he felt like a criminal; he needed to ask for more money. He heard the operator's voice.

"Hello, this is Sarah speaking, how may I help you?" The voice paused and waited for a reply.

"Hello?" the voice returned.

He heard Paris's footsteps thudding down the stairs. This was one conversation she shouldn't hear, especially not today.

"Errr, sorry," he said to the lady trying to locate him on the other end of the phone, "I dialled the wrong number." Bill cut off the call and walked slowly with his hands in his pockets towards the bottom of the stairs. Paris stood before him having changed into a dress her mother had bought her; her eyes were still red and swollen.

"You look beautiful, really beautiful." he repeated softly. He smiled tenderly and offered Paris his arm to link into her own. She smiled gratefully and together they began to walk towards the door.

Francesca finished her telephone conversation and also made her way towards the door. She was wearing a canary yellow dress suit with a huge black hat and black accessories to match. Like all her skirts, this was no exception, she had instructed her seamstress to take it up an extra inch. To her credit, for her forty-four years, she had a figure that any young girl would have been proud of – Long, brown and firm legs with a neat waist and bust to match. The only problem was she seemed to enjoy showing her assets off a little more than others and all her outfits appeared to be just that little bit too risqué for her age. Her dress or skirt was always that inch too short and the top was always just an inch too low, completely cheapening the expense of the outfit.

Bill never uttered a word; the fear of being buried under their expensive patio which they were still paying off was all too real. As they walked to the car he wondered if that was a better option than a life of debt. Through gritted teeth he forced a compliment about the outfit that had just cost him a default on their mortgage.

"You look lovely, darling," he said

She responded only by closing her eyes on him and looking away. Francesca was visibly swaying now; with her, gin always had an instant effect.

"I don't feel comfortable at all," gasped Paris as she tugged hard on her dress across her ample breasts, "it's about three sizes too small, I look like a complete and utter half wit in it and as fat as a pig to boot."

Francesca tried hard to speak in a soothing tone. "Well, don't expect to look as good as me when you don't do anything to help yourself, you should visit the gym and eat less..."

"Do you not know when to stop?" Bill interrupted. He activated the central locking on the car and opened the doors for the ladies to get in. Francesca had great trouble getting her foot onto the side step of the Range Rover and slipped many times before managing to swing herself into it. She crossed her legs then sat in silence.

For all her faults, there was no disputing the fact she was still beautiful. He glanced at her long legs; her skirt had ridden up and gave a full length view of her lean muscular thigh. Yes, she had lines around her face, but that was a part of any woman's aging. There were times when he watched her talking to others. He noticed the lines softly accentuating her deep blue eyes, but softness was not an attribute shown to him. When she spoke to him the only emotion to surface was bitterness, he knew it was a look that was cemented and set, born out of sheer frustration and resentment at being married to him. Over the years he had tried hard to please her, however, the harder he tried the further away she had moved his goal posts. "I knew I should have brought a flask of drink with me, fancy having to sit in this."

Bill looked ahead and saw the traffic was beginning to queue and they were still eight miles from the course. Francesca opened the vanity mirror and checked her heavily made up face.

"All my clothes will be creased to buggery by the time we make it to the racecourse," she tutted in disgust. "You know most people now are hiring helicopters so that they can avoid these terrible situations. I don't blame them either, this is such an inconvenience."

Bill panicked at the thought of her comment being a genuine suggestion. He began to hum indiscriminately in the hope that someone would change the subject.

"You really are something!" Paris blurted out. "Somebody has died who I loved so much and all you can fucking harp on about is the fact that you are stuck in traffic."

"Paris," Bill said, "don't talk to your mother like that, especially using that language."

"Well somebody has to; she thinks she can discount everybody else around her. I've had enough of it and if you ask me you should be at your limit too."

Oh I'm at my limits alright, he thought. He wondered how he was going to sort out the problem with the bank tomorrow. What a nightmare, he would be a laughing stock. How could a trained banker, retired only five years ago, be in this mess?

"Oh do shut up you two," Francesca replied. She watched as a large prestigious Mercedes car tried to edge its way into the traffic on their left hand side. The gentleman driving looked suave and sophisticated. His members' badge was pinned neatly onto his navy blue jacket. She liked navy blue, it looked very smart and had a timeless elegance attached to it. She glanced at Bill's black suit; it did not have the same appeal. As the Mercedes edged nearer she was able to get a good look at the lady sat next to him. Francesca presumed she was his wife; she sat motionless looking straight ahead. Francesca wondered if her statuesque disposition was because she was at pains to talk to her husband or due to the fact that her hat was so large it inhibited movement. Francesca recognised the enormous red creation. She had seen it in 'Higgins,' one of the finest boutiques in the area. It had been seven hundred and fifty pounds. Francesca had toyed with the idea of buying it but had been distracted by an evening dress. She regretted her decision now, the woman looked truly dazzling. *She's done well for herself*, Francesca thought, *her husband looks like a good catch*.

Paris quietly placed her hand on her stomach. What would she do if she was pregnant? She would take a test tomorrow, if it was positive she would think of a solution then. Gerard had spoken highly of his sister Rebecca. Paris had heard she had returned home now and wondered if she might talk to her. With that thought in mind she felt slightly calmer at the possibility of not being completely alone.

Chapter Six

REBECCA SANTÉ sat at her antique mahogany dressing table with the pretence of getting ready for the races. Instead, distracted by her surroundings, she stared with loving familiarity at her bedroom suite, feeling grateful that nothing had changed within it since the day she had left.

Her favourite grand four-poster bed, a 16th birthday present from her godfather Colonel Immanuel Rohl, sat majestically against one wall. She examined the beauty of the finely carved posts, rich with the autumnal glow of French mahogany, and the gold tapestry fabric that fell in romantic drapes against the rolling wooden posts. Against the opposite wall was a broad wooden fireplace, riddled with carvings and history and which harboured a large arching fire-grate. She remembered with fondness the nights she spent as a child huddled up against it in her armchair as it spat and crackled away the crispness of the winter air, its golden glow, warming into life the paintings of hunting scenes. Not that they needed any help, they hung imposingly against the luxurious fabric wallpaper with portrayals, so vivid, that quite often she found herself convinced she was galloping in the hunting field among them.

She loved this room and indeed the whole house, but the ever distant memory of Gerard not being present in the bedroom next door invaded her contentment. She ached for the sound of *Guns and*

Roses, it had been played so annoyingly loud at times that they had fallen out, but now, as the silence remained, a painful emptiness pervaded the air and his sister's mood.

She heard one of the racehorses whinny in the distance and the sound instantly ignited an inner awakening that consumed her, as though a life compass had guided her back to her roots, allowing her blood to once again pump freely. Her blood was true Santé blood, alive at the prospect of training horses. However, her enthusiasm was overshadowed by concern, aware that her trip to England was only a temporary measure, and in addition, marred by the fact that her fathers health had certainly deteriorated since she had last seen him.

She had been shocked on first seeing her father at the airport. The good life wrinkles that had once sat laughingly around his eyes had gone, in their place sat deep furrowed tram lines that sliced across his handsome face, a face that now looked drawn and tired. As their eyes met, the worry and torment that had blighted her thoughts of meeting had disintegrated. Both father and daughter had cast aside their pain and resentment of the last six years and fallen into the security of a rocking embrace. Rebecca squeezed her arms around his shoulders, searching for the vigour and strength that had always been present, but they had also been replaced, fractionalised by staggering weight-loss and crowded by an unspoken neediness and dependency.

Rebecca had then turned to her mother. As ever, her appearance was flawless, she wore a blue checked trouser suit, and beneath, a white shirt with starched, immaculately pressed, upturned collars that protected a delicate string of pearls. Her mother hugged her tightly and the smell of her old familiar perfume elevated into Rebecca's nostrils. The smell soothed her and rejuvenated feelings of family security that had long since cooled. Her father took her bag, an emotional mixture of grief and gratitude cementing their unity as they placed their arms around each other and walked toward the car.

Rebecca jumped up from the dressing table chair on hearing a second whinny that was accompanied by the sound of clattering hooves gracing the yard. She leant out of the window to the courtyard below and watched the stable lads, laughing jovially as they led a selection of two-year-olds to be exercised on the horse walker. The aroma of warm horse coats and the clattering sound of scraping shovels and forks busily mucking out the stables lingered in the air. She watched the lads, their jodhpurs soiled with horse sweat and saddle soap and realised that for her, their task was completely irresistible. Darting from the window, she exhumed a pair of old jeans and a T shirt from a drawer and hurriedly changed into them. Then flying out of her room, she raced down the stairway, sliding on some wellingtons in the boot room before running outside to the stables.

The pool of thirty five stables doors in the courtyard were open, airing the newly banked boxes and the horse-rugs lay neatly over the doors. She heard the splashing of water and looked across to see Caroline, employed by Rebecca nine years ago when she was only fifteen, scrubbing out the feed buckets.

"Hello Rebecca," said Caroline with a maturity Rebecca barely recognised.

"Hi! How are you Caroline?" Rebecca walked toward her smiling.

"Fine thanks, Rebecca." Her face furrowed in concern. "How are you?"

"Well," she shrugged with a slight grimace, "you know." She paused. "How are you getting on this morning?" She asked, promptly changing the subject.

"We have more or less done for the morning, we just have three stables to do before the second lot come back from morning exercise, and Midnight Minstrel and Sun Commander are already at York."

"David's gone with them has he?" Rebecca asked.

Caroline's face reddened. "Mmmmm," she answered turning her face.

Rebecca didn't notice Caroline's awkwardness. "Great! Well done! You have a good routine still in place I see," Rebecca said inspecting the immaculate yard.

Caroline laughed, "Well what do you expect? I was trained by the best." Her face sank to the floor. "Well, no disrespect to Gerard, he was brilliant too."

"Here pass me the buckets I'll put them away, and, which stables are left to be mucked out?"

She hesitated. "They are the last three over there." Then she added quickly, "But don't worry, I will do them in a minute."

"Nonsense!" Rebecca answered, striding ahead replacing the buckets inside the feed room. "We'll do them together; it won't take us a minute." She grabbed a fork and spade and placed them inside the wheelbarrow, with rapid tenacious strides she made her way over to the few remaining bolted doors.

With history repeating itself Caroline stumbled after her, struggling to keep up. Rebecca unbolted the door and gave a shocked intake of breath with the sight of David Donnelly's naked backside bobbing up and down like a spring hare upon a new recruit. The sight stopped her dead in her tracks.

"David!" she screamed in embarrassment before slamming the door shut again.

Caroline held her head in her hands, aware that her first vocation as guard for David, the head lad, and Mel a new stable girl, had not gone very well. He would kill her for this.

Rebecca heard the humiliated rustle and whisperings of two people trying to redress. Seconds later a red-faced David Donnelly and a stable girl she had never met before skulked out of the stable with David still tucking his T shirt into his jodhpurs.

"Morning Rebecca," he muttered "I didn't expect to see you this morning."

"Clearly!" Rebecca answered crossly.

His green Irish eyes danced with mischief and charm "I can't believe it's your first day back and already I've been caught with my trousers down!"

His wit only served to increase Rebecca's anger, she moved closer to him, "Listen David, let's get one thing straight." Her tone was cold and dangerously low. "Don't you think for one minute you can get round me with the silver luck of an Irish tongue." She raised one eyebrow. "There is work to be done around here, and as far as I'm concerned, as head lad, you should have been with those horses at York two hours ago. I don't give a shit what you do in your free time just make sure that your personal life never, ever, interferes with *my* time again. Do you understand me?"

He looked down to the floor. "Yes, Rebecca."

"Good. Now get going to that racetrack, and when you get there. WORK!"

Like a soldier responding to his officer's command, David turned on his heels and walked away.

"And, who have we got here then?" Rebecca turned to the girl who had not yet looked up to meet her eye.

"Mel," she answered timidly.

"Pleased to meet you, Mel." Rebecca held out her hand, Mel was about to take it but Rebecca pulled it away. "On second thoughts, let's keep our introduction as formal as possible; I don't know where that hand of yours has been." She followed with a stony silence. "Did Gerard employ you?"

"Yes, Rebecca." Mel answered, "He employed me a week last Tuesday."

"Today has not been a good start for you as far as I'm concerned, Mel. You will not be paid for today, I pay people to work, not to shag one another senseless. Hopefully you will work doubly hard tomorrow and regain your status on my pay roll." Mel nodded. "Right that's settled then." Rebecca said in a lighter tone, "Right girls, there are three stables that need mucking out there; I'll now have to get ready to face the racing fraternity."

She walked away to leave them to it, but aware that the girls were watching her, she turned around. "Oh Caroline, just for the record, don't lie to me again." Rebecca didn't wait for a response; instead she walked back to the house.

The yards apprentice stable jockey, Tim Harland, had heard everything from the next door stable and peered his head out to glance at her small tight ass as she walked away. God she was fit.

"Her arse beats Gerard's any day!" he joked quietly to the girls.

"Nothing else does," Mel huffed flatly.

James Santé looked out of the large patio doors onto the huge balcony that stretched from his bedroom and realised that nothing gave him greater comfort than seeing Rebecca around the yard. James knew his daughter was a natural business and horsewoman, just like his mother Elizabeth. Without his mother this yard wouldn't be here, she had been the one that had created the business and its outstanding reputation; she had had the guts of a rhino. She had been disgraced when she had become pregnant with James and was completely disowned by everyone, including her family who were trainers themselves. It was then she decided she would go it alone. The racing world didn't know what had hit them. By the time James was eighteen years old she was ranked as one of the top three trainers in the country. Rebecca he knew was made from the exact same mould as his mother.

Victoria Santé, his adorable, faithful wife walked into the bedroom and slipped an arm around her husbands' waist.

"Thank God she's back," James said. Victoria nodded in response. "She's an incredible girl that one and there's one thing for sure. We're not going to let her go this time. Rebecca, by hook or by crook, has to take over the training licence to this yard. We have to go through Gerard's death together." He clenched his fist trying to ease the pain before they broke down and sobbed onto each other's shoulder.

Charles and Hugo Lancaster-Baron were cruising home in the Bentley after another wild night out. Their hair was jutting out in wild unruly patches and their unwashed faces were beginning to shadow with the faint appearance of straining stubble. Charles could still taste the stale after effects of loose women and French champagne.

"I feel ill," he droned to his brother.

He rubbed the hard square of his sandpapered chin and thought about the day ahead. It was 12 'o' clock in the afternoon and they were going to go home to get changed and then do it all over again at the races. Charles felt a little apprehensive about setting foot out of the house today; a niggling feeling that he had done something unwise caused his instincts to harass him.

He had slept with Emma DeMario for a second night, usually that was un-heard of for Charles but he just wanted to give her one last blast. He couldn't resist, she was such a horny little piece, however he was all too mindful she was not someone to fool around with. Charles had always taken risks but messing with a DeMario daughter when you had no interest in her was really gambling on a large scale. The thought of marrying her for her money had crossed his mind, seriously relishing what he would do with all that money. It was serious wealth, he concluded, maybe even too much for him to squander. Or was there? Charles was acutely aware that the conclusions and judgements people made about a family's wealth could be wildly exaggerated. He closed his mind to his internal contemplation about marriage to Emma realising he was wasting his efforts; Emma DeMario was certainly not marriage material.

Charles' thoughts moved on to his own family's wealth. It was supposed common knowledge and frequently written about in the "Sunday Times Rich List" that Charles and Hugo were the most eligible bachelors in England and worth millions. This publicity, combined with Hugo's exceptional earnings as a stockbroker in the City and Charles' standing as a professional gambler and private commission agent, saw their image soaring. To Charles, if he didn't relish the exposure so much, it would all be laughable.

What people failed to realise was that this worth was tied up in watertight trusts, funds, properties, and obviously, if, God forbid, their mother died, then a vast amount would come from 'Lancaster Law International.' That money would be arriving in the future. Then his heart flipped as fast as a silver coin when he thought about his present.

Such were the state of his current financial affairs that Fabel Atkinson, his accountant, had been forced to call and urgent meeting with him.

"Don't mention this to anyone will you, Fabel," he had asked whilst he ran his eyes over the figures that screamed 'deficit' before him.

His accountant, Fabel Atkinson, knew exactly who he was referring to. "I have no intention of mentioning this to Kitty, Charles. I know your mother would be more than unsympathetic but you must seriously think about settling down now with this spending. You are a fortunate chap; you have the rental income from thirty seven properties your father left you. That is more than most people of your age." Fabel's thick black wiry eyebrow lowered as he scoured Charles' face for a response. Disappointed by the lack of reaction, he added, "Both your parents have worked hard for what they had, may I suggest you do the same."

This had been his parting shot before he stood and left the room. Charles was left alone, allowing the silence to confirm that he would rather die than send his family name into disrepute. Fabel was right, his parents had worked hard for the money they had, one of them at guarding it, the other at making it.

Their father had built a successful business in the polo industry. Breeding ponies for the Royals and the likes, training them and riding in matches all over the world that had ensured the family had seen the wonders of the globe three times over. They had met statesmen, royalty, and film stars, eaten in the finest restaurants in the world and slept in the world's most exclusive hotels, all before they could even walk. That luxury, which for so long he had taken for granted, had continued throughout his life, was he going to give it all up? Not a chance.

His fingers tapped sternly against the black leather steering wheel as he searched for a future hope. There was no doubt about it, he concluded swiftly, a project that would bring him money fast was the only answer to his prayers. His mind steered him to a second option. Rebecca Santé. She was one fine lady, beautiful, well bred and fucking minted to boot. Now she really was marriage material.

His stomach threw him a somersault at the thought of seeing her again today at York. The last six years without Rebecca in his life had made Charles realise just what a catch she was. Unfortunately it had been Gerard's death that had brought her home. *However*, Charles thought, *looking on the bright side, Gerard's death has awakened a second chance for me to win her back.* His eyes narrowed with the concentration of thought.

That is exactly what he would do, he would win her back. As his car cruised the two brothers towards their home, Charles silently considered the tactics he would use.

Three cars behind, the private detective hired to follow Charles increased his speed. The inconspicuous nature of the black Fiat ensured that the two brothers remained oblivious to its presence.

Chapter Seven

JULIA SMITH was making her way to the public toilets in the City Centre of York. Her eyes shifted nervously across the crowded streets, worried that somebody from the boutique might recognise her. She carried the dress under her arm in an old supermarket carrier bag, though the shoddiness of the outfit's transportation acted as a cunning guise. Since 'obtaining' it, Julia had treated her dress like pure treasure. Now, anticipation stormed her body that the day had actually arrived to wear it.

She entered the toilets. A lonesome toilet attendant sat in a small cramped box room, surrounded by mops, cleaning fluids and toilet rolls, her arm resting on an old sweeping brush as she flicked through a magazine on the counter. The woman, unable to conceal her discontent at yet another customer invading her privacy, curled her lip slightly before turning her attention back to her magazine.

Julia welcomed the attendant's snub; she, also, was too preoccupied for small talk. The stench of the toilet cubicles somehow managed to outweigh the sight of them, stale urine stalked the air, and the heat from the hot summer's day exacerbated the thick smell of excrement and grime. The walls bore the hostility of unpainted concrete, a few stained tiles sat rigidly around the washbasins, discoloured by the numerous washes of germ ridden hands. Julia, revolted by her dismal surroundings, screwed up her face as she hesitantly pushed at a cubicle door; reluctantly she peered in, nervous at what she might find.

It was alien to Julia how the woman could sit reading a magazine when there was so much work to be done around her. Feeling angered by the woman's disinterest she locked herself inside the cubicle, allowing privacy and the sight of the lavish ivory material peeping from the bag to resuscitate her excitement.

She gently lifted the designer outfit from the bag and watched as it filled the small cubical with elegance. The contrast of its beauty when compared with the grotty surroundings made Julia realise, getting changed hurriedly was not going to be an easy quest.

Determined not to touch even an inch of her infested surroundings she endured an unsteady balancing act, hopping on one leg whilst she undressed, standing on the carrier bag whilst she changed shoes and spraying as much perfume as she could across her body to prevent the heavy gag of the air from resting upon it. However, the haughtiness of her actions suddenly jabbed at her conscience, triggering her to feel like a dirty, stinking hypocrite.

She had spent her life feeling superior to the gypsy life, now her actions could be viewed as no better than that of a common criminal. She tried to reason her thoughts away. There was only this way, she told them, and she desperately needed to better her life and get out of this never ending trap. What else could she do? She took the carrier bag and placed it on top of the toilet seat. Holding the clothes she had changed from, she sat upon it.

She thought of her mother, allowing her kind warm face to appear in her mind. She had been a fine-looking woman, with a face that would have sat comfortably on the front cover of *Vogue* magazine. Her father had always told Julia that she was the image of her, but it was an elevation that Julia could never believe to be true. She closed her eyes and remembered her long dark hair, her large oval eyes, as dark and as warm as cinders with their sincerity surrounded by a feathering flash-dance of thick black lashes that swept up to her eyebrows. Julia could see her eyes were smiling, she tried to envisage her mouth, but already the picture was beginning to fade, she tried again to recall it but she couldn't, her mothers face had disappeared. Julia took a deep breath, *she is here with me,* she thought, *and she is willing me to go through with my plan.* She stood up and not daring to hesitate again, she stuffed the jeans and sweatshirt in which she had arrived back into the carrier bag and hid it with determined shoves behind the cistern. She would collect them on her return home in the evening. She had freed herself from the evidence of her double life, she took a deep breath and boldly smoothed the outfit against her body. She was ready to leave.

She unlocked the graffiti-ridden cubical door and listened to its menacing creek as she opened it. Nervously she peered out and thanked the heavens that there was nobody around, she was still alone.

She walked over to a small tarnished mirror that hung over the sink, but was unable to see her full length reflection, just a partial glimpse of her face and the halter neck straps that exposed her dark honeyed shoulders. Haphazardly she tousled her hair then looking back at her reflection one last time, concluding that, from the limited view the mirror offered, she felt satisfied with her appearance.

Concerned of the attendant's opinion regarding her sudden transformation, Julia guiltily edged her way towards the door, only to find her concern was met with relief. The woman, disregarding the adamant no smoking signs that surrounded her, was on her hands and knees dragging desperately on a cigarette and craftily blowing the smoke up an air vent that led outside. Her indiscretion allowed Julia to escape unnoticed.

Julia joined the swelling bustle of the city's streets and aided by the glorious day, she already felt fantastic. The sky was dusted with a flood of lazulite blue, its beauty and perfection only broken by giant bumping clouds that drifted lazily along the sky. Julia thought they looked like crumpled duvets from unmade beds and watched as the cool breeze lovingly carried them with it.

Julia, grateful for the chance to detoxify her lungs from the acrid stench in the toilets, gulped in the air with hungry breaths. It was bordering on lunchtime, causing hoards of workers to pour out of their stifled offices to grab a sandwich in their lunch hour. She looked at their pale ashen faces; they were in a rut just like she was. It consoled her to think she was taking action against her own situation, refusing to accept her lot. Her heart lurched as the thought crossed her mind that one of these workers could be from the boutique, they would recognise her outfit and call the police. Anxiously, she dodged her way through the crowds and hurried her pace in the direction of the racecourse.

As she neared her destination, other racing folk began to slowly join Julia's path. Groups of men all armed with the *Racing Post* under their arms walked together in small clusters. She overheard some of the men discussing the day's form and the chances of the horses that would be running. As she passed one group their discussion ceased, one gave out a cheeky whistle, placing his hand in his pocket he pulled out a bundle of notes that were secured with a diamond encrusted clip.

"Ere lav" he shouted in a cockney accent "I'll place aw me manney t'day that you are the best looking filly there".

Julia turned to see a smart short man with a shaven head; his aim was clearly to bolster the camaraderie shared between his group of friends.

Mmmmmm, not quite what I had in mind, she thought, but she was grateful for his compliment nevertheless.

"Thank you," she smiled and continued to walk ahead.

She heard the whispered tones from the men of "Beautiful." "Stannin." "Never seen nafin' like it."

Continuing to walk, she left their compliments behind her, allowing their presence to pose a new worry. The man's money being waved in the air reminded her that she did not have any at all. She had no idea how she was going to get into the racecourse itself let alone buy herself a drink. She was not going to let that dissuade her; after all, it didn't cost anything to look at the horses once she was in. She was certain that once she was there she would find a way. Her excited strides forged ahead.

Groups of girls were milling around the racecourse entrance. For some of them the prospect of dressing to impress had meant a compromise had to be made on the comfort stakes. They were quite visibly tottering uncomfortably in their high heels, trying their hardest to balance whilst simultaneously yanking down their skirts that were riding up with every step. Julia was aghast at the so-called competition, especially when she saw some of the girls quite blatantly, cramming their spilling breasts back into their ill-fitting bras and tops.

She watched as scores of men and women walked through the entrance to pay their admission fee. How could she get in? She heard a ticket tout walking up and down the entrance, shouting about discounted badges and holding them high in the air. As he passed her, she looked at him and smiled. He was about to talk to her when another race-goer tapped him on the shoulder whereupon an intense haggle over the cost of the badge ensued.

She turned her back on the lost opportunity and walked away finding herself instantly sidetracked by a large black limousine that had quietly swept up to the entrance. The driver got out and walked like a clockwork puppet to the passenger doors. He opened them and stood back, allowing his passengers to disembark. Julia was expecting to see a wealthy elderly couple appear but was surprised to see it was two girls, one brunette and one blonde, both of them in their twenties. The brunette spoke to the driver first.

"You don't need to pick us up again unless we call you. We will make our own arrangements thank you, Andrew."

"No problem, Miss DeMario," he replied whilst politely lifting his hat.

Julia felt astonished to hear the DeMario name for a second time. As the car oozed its way down the road the girls linked arms and began to walk towards the members' entrance. Three men came running across and began to snap photographs from the huge cameras draped around their necks.

"Quick, it's the DeMario twins!" one shouted.

"Shit!" Julia heard the dark haired girl say to her blonde friend, "I've dropped my bloody mobile."

As the brunette bent to pick up her phone the blonde pouted and smiled to the photographers surrounding her. With her mobile in hand and slipping it back in her bag, the brunette took up similar position for the cameras, failing to realise that her racing badge had fallen to the ground.

Julia's eyes focused on her opportunity and refused to let the metal badge, glinting in the sunlight, out of her sight.

"Smile, Sofia, smile Emma, let's have a great photo for *Country Life*." Another photographer bantered.

The two girls seemed to be happy to pose for a couple more minutes before continuing through the entrance gates. Julia waited until they were out of sight then seized the opportunity that had evaded everybody else's attention. Walking casually toward the badge she picked it up from the floor, turning quickly to check for witnesses, then, certain she was out of danger. She tied it securely to her bag.

Taking the girls' lead, she walked confidently through the owners' and trainers' entrance. A security guard, whose job it was to check arrivals' badges, stood by the door. When he saw Julia walk through he was mesmerised, there were some pretty girls here today, but this one was absolutely stunning. He beamed at her in delight as she passed him and she briefly held up her badge.

"Have a good days racing, madam," he said and passed her a racing programme.

"Thank you," she smiled and walked through the gates.

Well that is another hurdle over with, she told herself. She had to admit, she was really beginning to relish the obstacles that her new adventure presented.

"Anyway, don't you know who I am?" snapped the girl to a security guard at the champagne bar's entrance. "I've told you, I had my badge on a minute ago, I don't know where it is."

Julia decided to watch the horses in the paddock until the girls had gone. *"Don't you know who I am?"* Julia mimicked in her mind. *Who are these DeMario's anyway?* she wondered casually.

If she had asked the question aloud, any one of the punters around her would have informed her of the facts. Julia Smith was only ten minutes into her very first race-meet. Already she had crossed the DeMario line.

Chapter Eight

REBECCA arrived at York racecourse with only her father. Her mother, feeling unable to face the crowds, had stayed at home. The first race had only just finished, yet already in true York fashion the race-goers were in fine spirits. The weather was gloriously hot, with many of the suavely dressed punters taking refuge beneath the shade of numerous Veuve Cliquot umbrellas and quenching their thirst with vast quantities of refreshing Pimm's and chilled champagne.

When Rebecca and her father had embarked on their twenty-minute journey to the racecourse her head had been pounding. She wondered briefly if her headache had been brought on by the sudden responsibility and pressure that came with running the yard, but she hastily cast that notion aside. Running the Santé yard was a duty she had both missed and adored. On further reflection she thought it was more likely to have been Piers that had caused her angst. In fact, she decided, he had compounded her frustration by stubbornly ignoring her call when she had tried to phone him from the car. However, now entranced by the old familiar sights and memories of the race track, she felt her inner struggles slowly melt away.

Old friends that she hadn't seen for years came over and extended their heartfelt sympathies regarding her brother, they kissed and hugged her fondly and she could see they were all genuinely delighted to see her back in the realms of the racing circuit. The hardest part was hearing all the stories that people were eager to tell about Gerard so soon after his death. She listened politely, straining an awkward smile and camouflaging her ever conscious shield of protection towards her father. The last thing she wanted was for him to hear a story that would re-open the tender wounds of his fragile grief.

She turned and saw Charles edging his way through the crowd towards her.

"Rebecca, you look fantastic!" He kissed both her cheeks and stood back admiringly. "Really beautiful, in fact," he added, allowing his hand to rest upon her shoulder. "How are you feeling?" he asked sympathetically.

"Up and down," she admitted.

"That's understandable; I know how close you were. He was a tremendous friend to me and I will also miss him very much." He pulled a regretful face. "It was a pretty shit question to ask really wasn't it?"

The sincerity of his words touched Rebecca, making her feel instantly reassured and grateful he was not harbouring any bitterness for times gone by.

"No, not at all," she said reciprocating his affection by touching his arm. "I am grateful that you asked."

She marvelled at the change in his face and physique. Six years ago she had left behind a young boy, yet that boy had now transformed into a powerfully handsome man. Charles had been a great family friend to her and to Gerard for many years, and she had to admit the familiarity of his company felt undeniably reassuring.

"How long are you planning on staying?" he asked.

Rebecca turned quickly, checking her father was out of ear shot. "I don't know," she said, "it's a tough call. I'm just going to see how it goes, but there is so much to do on the yard."

Charles nodded. "I see you have two runners today, and both of them favourites." He winked playfully. "Do they take after their trainer in being on top form?"

Rebecca laughed. "How smooth, Charles!" she joked. "Sun

Commander is running in the second and he has a good chance, but Midnight Minstrel is so unpredictable." She screwed up her face. "The problem we've got is that there's only one jockey she seems to respect and that's Richard May, unfortunately he's been booked on a different mount." Her voice quietened. "Gerard obviously didn't book him soon enough." Charles saw the ache of sentiment crowd her eyes. "Anyway, we've had to get Martin O'Connell. He's a good jockey, but he's never ridden Midnight before." She shrugged. "We'll have to see how they get on."

Charles looked back at her in admiration, only a day back at the yard and already she was beginning to gain an understanding of each horse and their idiosyncrasies. She gave a professional wave to someone over Charles' shoulder before returning her attention back to him.

"I know the circumstances aren't the best, but I bet James is glad to see you back. I would say that every horse you have in that yard has a good chance now you're back," Charles complimented.

"Thank you, Charles," Rebecca replied with a broad smile.

"It's true; you're a natural trainer, the best in fact." He watched her furtively inflate with his words. "Look, there must be so many things you have to do whilst you're here; I want to help you however I can. How about we go out for a drink before you go back? You can let me know then what I could do."

Rebecca hesitated momentarily whilst a picture of Piers flashed through her mind.

"Yes, that would be great, though, like you said, there is so much to do on the yard, it's maybe a better solution for you to come round, we could all have a drink together couldn't we?" she suggested breezily. "Call me at home and we can arrange something." She looked over at her father; he was talking to a group of people and was reminded that her duty today was to be by his side.

"Will you excuse me, Charles? I'd better get back to Daddy," she said.

"Of course, I understand," he smiled warmly. "I think you are doing so well being here today." Again he placed a caring hand on her shoulder. "It must have taken a lot of strength."

"Thank you, Charles." She hesitated before adding, "for everything." She turned and sidestepped her way through the crowds towards her father.

Charles watched her every movement until she disappeared.

Julia had already surveyed the hubbub of the champagne bar, impressed but eager to explore more, she decided to take up the use of her elevated racing status and venture into the private bar for owners and trainers. Feeling confident, she flashed her badge at the security man on the door before breezing through.

It was packed with people, but feeling undaunted and aided by the feeling of euphoria from the day's experience, she confidently floated inside the room, sweeping a discarded glass of champagne from a table as she passed it.

Men and women were staring and turning in awe as she drifted past, all of them eager to obtain a second glimpse of her exquisite face and voluptuous body. It wasn't long before her pursuers, aided by the small quarters of the room, managed to hem her in surrounding her in pack-like formation and proceeding to bombard her with questions, flirtatious innuendos and champagne. For the first day in her entire life, Julia began to feel truly beautiful and with her new found confidence came an absolute certainty. This new world had been made exclusively for her.

Sitting on the horse in the stalls with a fixed, determined face, Luca DeMario focused only on the long stretch of green turf that lay ahead, habitually visualising his clear win with lengths to spare. The metal starting gates rattled ominously as other runners were led inside, Luca's horse pawed at the floor. This was his fifth and final race of the day, so far he had won three and been placed in one but, for Luca, this race held the greatest significance.

The horse he was riding was "The Italian Job". His father had bought the filly as a yearling at the Newmarket sales and over the past two years Luca had supervised the intricacies of her training. Today, he felt confident. The mare was at her optimum fitness, she had won on her debut outing at Newmarket four weeks ago, the ground was ideal for her at good to firm and Luca, too, felt positive vibes running through his veins. This mare was special, he felt it every time he sat on her back and now, determined to make his father proud, hoped the latter was watching.

He leant over and patted the side of the mare's neck but she shook her fiery head, obviously irritated by his touch. He soothed her with his calm controlling voice, though Luca himself felt the tension in the stalls. There were just two more horses to enter, he heard one of them clatter in but his avid focus forbade him to look. Luca pulled his racing goggles over his eyes and waited for the final horse.

Spiking nerves menacingly tormented his body as he willed the gates to open. The race was only six furlongs, a distance so short it was hard to rectify any mistakes should they occur. He knew from experience, these were races that could be won or lost in a split second.

The Italian Job began to prance apprehensively in the stall, impatience and nervous energy beating her brain. Luca sat further in his seat and bore his weight into the thin leather saddle, gripping his thighs against her muscular sides. A current of reassurance permeated through her shaking body and Luca felt her dance begin to calm. Luca knew this time they had was all important, the confinement of the stall, a swift reminder to both horse and jockey they were all each other had, a secret chamber of dependency and a time to build an unparalleled bond.

Midnight Minstrel on the far side stall began to rear in anticipation, Martin O' Connell, a top Irish jockey, was on board and gave the horse a crack with the racing whip;

"Get down ya fuckin' ijot," he yelled.

Good news, thought Luca, he knew it would have broken O' Connell's concentration.

Luca heard the counting call from the stewards, then, the stall gates smashed open like a slicing axe.

"And they're off!" came a cry from the loud-speaker.

Luca allowed his mare to settle among the field and felt her relax beneath him as she led him along at a smart pace. The runners and riders jostled eagerly for position with Luca and his mare remaining up front with the leaders of the field.

It was when Luca saw the fourth furlong mark that his experience took over and his strength and focus began to drive her on. The ground moved swiftly beneath them and he knew, with two horses galloping neck and neck at the side of him, it was their last chance to come through. With every morsel of strength and energy he had in his body he drove her on. His whole body shoved with giant thrusts against her neck and shoulders as he urged her to gather speed. She responded like a dream, and with every push he made, the full hearted mare gave him a little more in return and began to inch away from the group. He could hear the stampede of what seemed to be a thousand hooves behind him beat against the ground and was aware that the growing blows of his mare were intensifying with each galloping stride she took. Luca could see the winning post ahead but could hear the dangerous threat of thudding hooves closing in behind. She needed to exert herself more if they were to get across the line first. He couldn't look back; he continued to focus on the winning post. He grimaced in pain and for a second wondered if he could win the battle between body and mind. Somehow his sweat drenched body responded to its calling.

"I need more, fine lady!" he shouted through his own breathless gasps to his mare.

He raised his thick Italian leather whip and cracked the horse hard twice on its right side, her acceleration was immediate. He helped her by continuing to thrust his body hard against her and briefly she lost her footing and stumbled slightly, but it was too late to care. They had passed the finish line.

For the first time Luca glanced behind him and saw he had won with a length to spare. Again, like the week before at Ascot, he was the champion jockey of the day. He held out his arms with exhilaration and looked up at the stand in the vague hope he might see his father amongst the thousands of revellers now jumping and trickling out from the stands to collect their winnings.

As The Italian Job slowed her paces into a welcome canter, Luca bent his head down over the mare's shoulder and vomited violently. It was a usual occurrence from the pain of exertion, an incident that proved that not only horse but jockey too had been severely pushed to their limit.

Charles Lancaster-Baron threw down the programme and pen that had been clasped tightly in his hand throughout the race.

"Fucking greasy spick!" he spat venomously.

That meant that he had lost more money, favourites were a pain in the arse. He wished the asshole that had placed the bet for seventy five thousand pounds cash to win would drop dead. It had won at 4-1. This kind of shit was happening to him a lot recently, these losses were starting to cause a very serious problem.

His phone rang. He recognised the number, it was the punter wanting his money, and who could blame him? Charles had no idea at present where he was going to find it from. He diverted the call to the answer machine.

He grabbed a glass of champagne from a passing waitress within the box and wandered off to try and find Rebecca, at present his only consolation. As he made his way through the packed champagne bar Mrs Montford managed to grab his arm.

"Charles," she slurred, trying to steady herself against a random chair. She pulled him close to her alcohol-fuelled breath and began to whisper in his ear.

"I have to tell you," she giggled, "I dreamt about you last night. AND," she added, "you would be dreaming about me too if you knew what I did to you in it." She let out an enormous laugh to which everyone in the nearby vicinity responded to by staring in disgust. Charles saw Rebecca and discreetly beckoned her over. Smiling mischievously at Charles' company, Rebecca began to chat quite casually about the form.

"Oh I wanted to speak to you," slurred Mrs Montford. "Did you know that my daughter, Paris, and your brother Gerard were having it off for some time. She's mortified, absolutely mortified. I can't do a thing with the silly girl, she's bound to come pestering you at some stage." She stumbled slightly and clasped Rebecca's arm in an attempt to regain her balance. She turned her attentions once more to Charles. "I think you should come round and talk to her. I think if any man can sort a grieving girl out it would be you." She screwed up her eyes in a gesture of passion. "Oooh, you're a handsome bastard, and where's that brother of yours?" A hiccup threw her off her course, Rebecca took the opportunity of leading Charles away.

"God, she's a bloody nightmare!" Rebecca said half laughing.

"Tell me about it," he agreed.

Mr Montford politely shuffled past and tried to stand his wife up against the wall. With Paris close by he gave out his hand to Rebecca and her parents and expressed his sympathy. Paris began to open her mouth to speak but found all that appeared was a heartbroken sob, the incident was confirmation enough that both ladies in his life needed to be taken home.

"Piss off I'm not coming," Francesca told him.

Unable to face a scene, Bill and Paris left together, both aware it would be the early hours of the morning before Francesca would follow suit.

Bill Montford left the racecourse feeling slightly disappointed. He had been looking for Frankie DeMario but he had not emerged. He enjoyed listening and learning from his immense knowledge of horses and the racing world and greatly admired his success. Every time he spoke with him he seemed to find out about another type of business Frankie was involved in. When it came to money and business, Frankie was at the top. He was one of the few people Bill actually felt comfortable with; there were no airs or graces that were often seen with the majority of these people. Frankie was someone who had come from little means but had worked hard for everything he had. Bill admired him for the fact that he didn't pretend otherwise. Francesca always laughed when she saw Bill talking to Frankie, waiting until they got home she would refer to Bill as being one of Frankie's groupies.

"Why would a man like him be interested in befriending a pip-squeak like you?" she would snap degradingly.

Luca walked into the changing rooms after being weighed in. He began to strip off his sweaty mud splattered silks, heaving them over his head and across the engraved muscles on his stomach. He walked into the shower room to join his colleagues. As usual the jibing started. Shouting loudly one of the jockeys in the shower beckoned the others,

"Hey has anyone ever heard what happened to the donkey who rode the horse through the finishing line?"

"No what happened?" shouted another in response.

"I don't know either, let's ask him." He pointed at Luca's anatomy.

Luca smiled but didn't respond verbally, preferring to relive the day's races, retracing his horse's steps one by one, searching for internal advice on how he could improve his future performances. Overall he was happy with his efforts and decided that tonight he wanted to celebrate.

Even above the hubbub of the changing rooms he could hear the gathering crowds awaiting him outside. All of them would want photographs or an autograph, in some cases just to congratulate him. Whatever their request, he was happy to oblige. He walked to the mirror to check his appearance and thanked youth and extreme physical fitness that his feeling of exhaustion remained undetectable. His tawny eyes, like dark boiling bowls of French onion soup, stared back at him and the dark circles beneath, plainly evident only hours before, had disappeared with the rejuvenation of a steaming shower. He smoothed his hands across his stomach, straightening out the invisible creases of his white polo neck and patted the back pocket of his black Tommy Hilfiger jeans and felt the comforting bulge of the thick wedge of crisp British notes within.

Casually, with the evening sun beginning to set, Luca jogged down the steps to the predicted crowd. A swarm of race-goers surged toward him requesting his autograph, and large telescopic cameras, brought to life by his presence began to flash insistently. Answering their questions, thanking the punters for their kind words and obligingly transforming dog-eared betting slips into sentimental treasures with the simplicities of his signature, these genuine racing punters made him feel proud to be connected to them.

He then began to answer a bombardment of questions being thrown at him by the press. Swiftly losing patience, he made his escape.

"Now, if you will excuse me ladies and gentleman," he informed them with a second dazzling smile, "I am now going to the bar for a much needed drink."

He walked from the crowd with the sting of red-handed applause still continuing behind him. Luca felt ecstatic as he made his way into the owners' and trainers' bar. Again, raptures and applause filled the room as he entered. He thanked people for their congratulations as he walked passed, but his eyes scanned the heaving room as he searched for his father.

Sofia and Emma DeMario were examining a woman that they hadn't seen before. Whoever she was she had managed, annoyingly, to divert an awful lot of attention from them. Sofia continued staring at the mysterious beauty with envy then suddenly screeched when she spotted her missing badge.

"Hey!" she shouted, blatantly moving towards her, "That's my badge, where the hell did you get that from?"

The whole bar's frivolities began to quieten. Julia felt her shoulders lift as she cringed. She had let down her guard, too much champagne and complacency had left the stolen badge on display. Sofia stormed over to Julia and with angry, determined eyes she snatched it from her bag.

"What's the problem, Sofia?" Luca took hold of his sister's arm. "Just calm down, I'm sure there is a simple explanation for this."

Julia felt herself almost collapse with fear and shame when she saw that it was Luca DeMario, the man that had captured her stare so effortlessly outside the funeral. Her brain squirmed in embarrassment as she fought for an explanation, but as he looked back at her with his striking gaze, once again she found herself lost for words. She blushed violently, felt her legs drain of life and her hands begin to tremble.

Luca witnessed the fear that had pervaded Julia's mind; he looked at the badge again and like his sister, was convinced that is was indeed their family badge. He turned to his sister.

"This is a friend of mine, Sofia. Leave it now. Like I say, I'm sure there is a simple explanation." Luca thrust his head to one side and gestured for her to disappear.

Sofia was furious. Who was this girl who had taken all the attention away from her all day? Emma, who was already pissed off because Charles had ignored her, took Sofia's hand and pulled her out of the bar. Luca turned to Julia.

"Hello, Luca DeMario." He offered her a strong firm hand. "We met outside the church at Gerard Santé's funeral didn't we? It's a small world, hey?"

Julia held out her trembling hand. "Hi, I'm Julia," she managed.

She looked back into his eyes that now remained suspiciously still and serious. She interpreted his stern manner as a symbol of his disgust. Uneasily, she fumbled for an excuse.

"Erm, I need to get to the bar, I need a mineral water, I think I have had too much to drink." She laughed nervously, showing Luca a perfectly even set of white teeth. "I can explain the incident…."

Luca interrupted her. "There is no need, really, sometimes mix ups can happen." Luca didn't want to accentuate her embarrassment. *Who gave a stuff about a bloody badge anyway?* He liked her, he liked her a lot.

"I'll go to the bar for you," he offered.

Julia smiled. "Thank you," she said.

For a few uninterrupted seconds, just as they had outside the church, something within their eyes connected. It was a connection that sent a current of excitement through both of them.

Frankie DeMario rushed through the revellers outside to meet his son in the owners' and trainers' bar. On approach to the door he glanced casually through the window and, along with a sharp intake of breath, he was forced to do a double take.

His vision began to blur, he strained his eyes open, willing them to inform him they had played a sadistic trick. He looked away and back again, the image was still there. Taking his mobile from his jacket pocket he frantically dialled his driver.

"Come now!" he demanded. "Right now!" He stumbled to the gates.

Trembling in the back of his limousine, he poured himself a large neat whisky. There was a loose cannon in his life and he had to do something about it. His black eyes, immobilised by thoughts of sin, glared out of the window. This was a job that should have been done years ago.

Chapter Nine

PARIS stared at the results window of the clinical white stick that shook in her hand, with an indescribable panic and, hoping she had made a mistake, she re-examined the foolproof diagram on the packet. Once again, her innards emigrated to the soles of her feet. She was most definitely pregnant.

Sitting alone on the bathroom floor she tucked her knees under her chin and internally debated whether this meant the end of her life, or indeed, the beginning of it. Her mind began to put forward two sides to the argument, seemingly teasing her in haphazard waves with two life paths, and Paris, saturated by confusion, could see sense in both.

How the hell could she cope with a baby alone? Would she be capable of taking on such an enormous responsibility? What would she do? Where would she go? Would she live here with her parents and allow her mother's unhealthy thoughts and opinions to slowly seep into her baby's skin just as they had hers for years?

She pulled at the sleeve of the soft cashmere jumper that Gerard had lent to her whilst they had walked in the woods two weeks ago. Searching desperately for his comfort, she sniffed deeply into the woollen sleeve and another lonely jab scored at her heart, the once pungent smell of his Hugo Boss aftershave was fading fast. She looked back at the test results and wished she could say the same of the now vivid blue line that had settled across the results window.

She began to feel angry. Why the hell wasn't Gerard here to help her? Why couldn't she feel his arm around her as he softly comforted her? In fact, why was she alone at all? Her anger appeared to perpetuate the deathly silence that surrounded the house. There was nobody at home. Under duress, her father had been forced to take her mother to a garden party in the village, causing Paris to feel as lonely as she had ever done. She stood up and opened the bathroom window hoping that the noise of outdoor activity within the crescent would alleviate the suffocating boom of silence. She resumed her position on the floor.

At least, if she kept the baby, it would quell the continual ache and pain of loneliness. After all, this loneliness had been a feeling she had been forced to accept since childhood. She thought back to the school that her mother had forced her to attend, a private school that had the *"right image"* and the *"right people"* in which to associate with. They were people that were so insincere that Paris had loathed every one of them, with a passion. This unjust situation had exacerbated Paris' conclusion that she was indeed, a total misfit.

With sadness she inhaled deeply through her nose and slowly exhaled. If she did have the baby, then at least it would be something for her to love. Something that she could feel would be truly, wholly hers, something that only she could make decisions for, decisions that her mother would be well and truly outcast from taking involvement in. Her very own baby, she thought, taking on a positive slant. It would be her very own, nobody in the world could take the baby from her, she would be free to love it forever. What would her mother think? The question attacked her and immediately aborted her temporary optimism. How would she explain her daughter was a single mother to all her socialite friends? Her daughter would be an embarrassment to her, yet again.

Her eyes focused on a large candle sitting in a crystal surround by the bath, a small jug of aromatherapy oils stood at its side. She felt her mind convert into a venomous pit as the image of her selfish mother, relaxing in a sea of bubbles invaded her mind. Her eyes narrowed.

"How the fuck can anyone relax? Especially my fucking mother!" she screamed.

She ran over to the candle and threw it against the wall causing the crystal surround to smash into tiny coloured pieces and scatter like ocean shells across the bathroom floor. Paris burst into tears, clenching her fists in desperation.

Unable to cope with the claustrophobic silence in the house any longer, she ran downstairs, desperate to get out. Pulling her hair away from her angry tears she wrestled to get her feet into her shoes that were lying at the bottom of the stairs and stamped out of the door, banging it hard behind her. She needed to talk to someone, anyone who would listen. She had two friends with whom she was confident her secret was safe. She made her way over the road.

With trembling hands she searched for the keys in her trouser pocket and rattled the key inside the latch. The unmistakeable excitement of the two Dalmatians behind it as they danced and yelped made her realise that they, if no-one else, were eager to see her. She opened the door. Connor, the broader of the two dogs, wrestled to be the first to greet her, his lead was already trailing from his pink slavering mouth and behind him was Sadie, also trying to muscle in on the welcome. Two sets of tails applauded her arrival and enthusiastically whipped through the air in grateful slashes.

Paris reciprocated their welcome and sank to her knees, smiling as they licked her face, nuzzled her neck and pawed frantically at her arm. She responded to their appeal for affection and gently stroked their heads and kissed their faces. Then, feeling consumed by the force of her problem, she sank her head into their ever dependable soft sleek coats and sobbed.

Rebecca sat at the large hand-made dark oak desk in the office and looked in despair at the papers and documents that were strewn over every available surface. She was trying to make some order out of the chaotic filing and less than satisfactory office procedure that had been adopted by Gerard. She smiled, he had never been one for organisation, but then her shoulders slumped, Gerard could not be blamed for the unpaid invoice that sat in front of her now.

She read it for the fourth time, her mind still in denial that he was actually dead, but as the words began to sink in, an emotional chill rippled through her body.

She reached for the red cashmere blanket that rested on the window seat and placed it around her shoulders before sitting back at her desk. Gerard's funeral bill continued to stare back at her.

She wished Piers was here to support her, even though most of her time and thoughts were consumed by the yard, she had really missed him. Following a long conversation with him after she had returned from York races, he had promised her that he would be flying out the following night. However, having arrived at the airport with only six minutes to spare he had then realised he had forgotten his passport. That was now almost five days ago. Since then they had spoken every day and as each day had passed the tense atmosphere between them was beginning to fade, though, in Rebecca's heart she knew, if she and Piers were to have a future together, the fairest thing she could do was to return to Kentucky.

The thought made her feel so utterly torn. She loved the yard and she loved her parents. Being reunited with them had made her feel alive again and realise the intensity with which she had missed them. It was a hard situation, if only she could have Piers, *and* the yard and her family. Reality swallowed up her question in one dismissive lump; the two were like oil and water, impossible to mix. She had to accept that at some stage soon she would have to return to Kentucky.

Not wanting to dwell on any of it, she promptly signed the cheque and placed it in the envelope along with a compliment slip.

Her father's voice made her jump. She looked up and saw him standing in the doorway of her office, his voice sounded unusually distant. He stared at the vagrant papers that filled the entirety of the desk and silently commended her efforts.

"May I sit down?" he asked pointing to a chair next to hers.

"Yes of course," she said, easing his way in the chaos by pulling it towards him.

"Rebecca, I need to talk to you." He gently took her hand in his. "Rebecca, I want to talk to you, and until I have finished I don't want you to interrupt."

She nodded with a frown, feeling instantly disturbed at the sight of his trembling mouth and the tension within his voice.

"I love you Rebecca. I know that I have been stubborn and

pigheaded in the past but I love you so much." Emotion quivered in his throat. "I loved Gerard too." He held his breath and stared at the ceiling. "But, you know what? I never told him." His words hung in the air. "Can you imagine how I torture myself every minute of the day about that?"

She was about to intervene but her father held up his hand to prevent her interruption.

"Family life is the foundation on which every individual in the world bases his or her opinions. I want you to know Rebecca, I need you to come home; we need to be together so that I and your mother can show you just how wonderful our family can be. I want you to tell Piers to come too." He heaved out a rigid sigh. "I don't know whether he is right for you or not, but what I do know is, I have no right to judge either way. So come back and take over the yard, both of you, if you wish. You will have sole charge. I know you can do it and you will do it well, probably better than any other Santé has done before, maybe even including myself." He laughed at the unusual admission. "I respect you, Rebecca, and I need your help to build up that yard again." His voice dropped to even lower and softer tones. "No, that is not true, I do need you for that, but moreover I need you back in my life." Tears began to roll down his face and as they did he was forced into silence.

Rebecca had never heard her father speak so openly about his feelings. She stood and walked to him, locking her arms around his shoulders then sank her nose into his soft warm neck. The privacy of their intense emotion was startled into reality by the harsh ring of the doorbell.

"Who the hell is this?" she snivelled. She grabbed a tissue and, wiping her eyes and face, she tried to peer discreetly through the window to observe the visitor outside. She couldn't be sure; brushing down her jodhpurs she bent and kissed her father on his cheek.

"Thanks for that," she whispered. "We will talk later, but next time," she laughed softly, "when we have a drink with us!"

James made no attempt to see who was at the door, feeling he couldn't face a visitor no matter who it was. He stood from the chair and made his way back upstairs.

Rebecca walked to the door, checking her appearance in the mirror before she opened it.

"Hello Paris, this is a surprise." Rebecca concealed her frustration and welcomed Paris through the door.

"Yes, well I know it is," Paris snivelled. She continued to stand in the doorway. Now she was here she felt embarrassed to have arrived at all. In the awkward silence Rebecca studied her.

Her nose, having been wiped and rubbed so many times, shone like a glacé cherry, her hands rived and wrestled nervously with the tissue she had used to wipe away her tears, now frayed and soiled so badly it bore perfect resemblance to a thick dirty cobweb and her lips quivered with such ferocity it looked as though she was suffering from hyperthermia.

"Come in Paris," Rebecca encouraged. She did not feel like company at all, especially a hysterical stranger, but under these circumstances, she felt obliged. "It's not been an easy time for any of us has it, Paris?" Rebecca said sympathetically.

Paris shook her head in agreement and in the instant her feet met with the hallway carpet, she began to sob again.

"I really need to talk to you," Paris squeaked through her tears.

The enormity of the emotional display intensified Rebecca's own feeling of exhaustion. Also thinking of her father's emotional state, she explained quietly.

"Listen Paris, I can appreciate you're upset, but if you've come to talk about Gerard and his death …" she shook her head despairingly, "I don't think I can do it, not today. I'm hurting too, we all are." Rebecca added apprehensively looking up the stairs.

"I know that," Paris snapped, sensing another rejection heading her way "Don't worry; I know I have to cope with missing him on my own. To be blunt I'm here to tell you I'm pregnant, Gerard is the father." Her rambling words began to spill out in unstoppable momentum. "I can't believe it's happened, I'm desperately confused, I don't know whether to be happy or sad." She rubbed her face with her hands. "You are the first person I've told because, well, I don't know why, I just…" She began to sob uncontrollably and flopped into a perfectly upholstered armchair at the bottom of the stairs.

"Pregnant?" Rebecca's voice rose in shock. She threw her hands up to her face. "Are you sure? My god that's a bloody..." Her voice trailed, seeing the desperation in Paris' eyes flowing with torrents of tears. She crouched down next to her. "Don't worry, Paris, it will all be okay. There's nothing to cry about, it's a wonderful gift to be pregnant, please don't cry about it." With the soft reassurance of her words Rebecca gently ushered Paris into her office and closed the door.

Hearing some comforting words gave Paris some relief, feeling that, at last, someone was on her side. Her wet face and dripping nose somehow began to bury within Rebecca's shoulder and she felt the tears sink through her Joules shirt. Feeling vaguely eased by at last having a shoulder to cry on, Paris lifted her head.

"I don't want you to think I came round for anything. Err, I mean I know how a lot of people have viewed your family in the past as like a meal ticket because you're so rich. I want you to know, just like Gerard did, that that is not what I'm about. I just wanted to tell someone that was close to Gerard and feel like ..." She took out her ragged tissue and wiped her nose again, "well, like I was telling him, I suppose. I know he would have looked after me just like you have, so thanks for that." She looked at Rebecca pleadingly. "What do you think I should do?" she asked.

"Listen, Paris, with this situation you must do what *you* think is right. Think about yourself and what is right for you." She passed Paris a box of clean tissues. Paris, deciding she liked Rebecca, took one from the box and weakly wiped her face and eyes.

"Anyway, I don't want to take up any more of your time," Paris said, "I'm used to dealing with things on my own."

"Why don't you stay and have a drink to calm you down before you leave, a glass of water maybe?"

"No thanks," Paris insisted, already making her way to the front door. "I feel sick." She made a lurch for it and clumsily fell out. "Goodbye Rebecca," she mumbled over her shoulder.

Rebecca flopped into the armchair in the drawing room and rubbed her aching temples with her long slim fingers.

"Why her and not me?" she said in a tear-broken whisper. "Life just isn't fair," she whimpered.

Her mother stood in the doorway, torn apart to see her daughter upset.

"Is it Gerard, darling, are you okay?" Her voice was warm and gentle.

"I'm okay, Mummy, it's just a bad moment," Rebecca replied, momentarily surprised by another visitor. She wiped her tears with her hands. "Did you want something?" Rebecca asked looking up, trying hard to hide her pain.

Respecting her daughter's privacy she uneasily began to pass on the message.

"Well, it's just that Charles rang earlier. He asked if you would like to attend the injured jockeys' ball with him on Saturday evening. He had forgotten it was on, but said he thought you may enjoy it."

Rebecca was impressed with his timing, a chance to let her hair down was just what she needed, she didn't hesitate.

"Yes, definitely," she said nodding enthusiastically, "I'll go. Will you do me a favour though, Mum, and call him for me? Tell him I'm busy in the yard or something. I don't want to talk to him now. Tell him I'll call in the morning." Victoria nodded, then hesitated at the door.

"Erm, there's just one more thing, Piers called."

Rebecca swung her head to face her mother. "Yes? What did he say?" she asked.

Her mother hesitated again. "He can't come for another four or five days, he said something about work, I couldn't grasp it all, the line was terrible."

Rebecca sighed and examined her mobile. She had missed two of his calls. She fell silent.

Her mother left the room, taking her maternal concerns with her.

Chapter Ten

LUCA felt the plane making a gradual descent, drawing him to English soil and felt relieved he was nearly home. His day had been hectic. At 6 a.m. he had flown into Paris – a trip initiated by a wealthy owner and his trainer who had wanted to persuade him to become their full-time jockey. Although travelling the world and riding a string of top class thoroughbreds appealed, Luca was nevertheless aware that, in the long term, the flexibility he enjoyed at present, working freelance for a handful of well respected trainers would be compromised. The meeting, however, had not been in vain, he had picked up several new rides with world class horses and in addition, with ever retaining modesty, he felt it a compliment they had asked him.

His head fell against the rigid headrest of the economy flight he had chosen to board, a far cry from the sumptuous luxury of his family's private jet, but as that was not available until tomorrow, he had chosen a budget airline to return home in the same day.

If he was honest, his decision had been influenced by the burning desire to see Julia. It had been almost two weeks since they had first met at York races and in that time Luca and Julia had enjoyed meeting up most evenings. Their rendezvous had been accommodated by Luca inserting further travelling into his schedule, but even though he was exhausted, the indescribable magnetism that pulled him towards her enabled his extra efforts to seem painless.

In random recall, he thought about her now. There was no doubt about it, she was stunning, and charming with it. On every date she was so keen to ask, with genuine interest it appeared, about his racing career, how it had started and what the drawbacks were. She had encouraged him to share, to the finest detail, the joy he felt at the pinnacles of his successes. He could tell it wasn't contrived, he had seen more than enough insincerity from past girlfriends for alarm bells to strike immediately. No, with Julia it was different; he could see the interest and curiosity dance in her eyes as he talked of his work. He analysed her reserved ladylike demeanour and compared her to other girls he had met in the past. So many of them had been easy, all too willing to drop their knickers at the click of a finger. His face hardened as his sister Emma came to mind. His father had told him about her sleeping with Charles two days ago.

"You will have to watch out for your sister," he had said. "She is losing her self-respect. Watch her every move," he had thundered.

Luca agreed but was certain it was the amount of alcohol she consumed that led her to degrade herself so publicly. He was certain Julia would never behave like that.

Thankfully, like him, she was not a big drinker. Quite often she would sit with one drink all night, content to chat about all kinds of subject matters with most of their conversations brightened with her enormous flashing smile. These were the facts. From what he had seen, she was smart, she had self-respect, she was elegant and so, so god damned sexy. All this in a woman and yet every time he thought of her wonderful traits the habitual draw of wild uncertainty gripped him hard.

Despite all of her qualities, after leaving her and driving home, a nagging feeling that he couldn't quite put his finger on alerted him to a sense of danger. His instincts drove him to analyse every little thing she had said or done, and the questions that tortured his mind seemed at times inescapable. Was the reason he had never seen her home because she was married? Why, if she lived in York, did they always have to meet up outside the City? Why would someone as beautiful as her be single? Why did she quickly change the subject every time he asked about her home life? And why, at the end of each date, did she suddenly and so abruptly pull away from a goodnight kiss?

No matter which way he analysed and dissected all these questions, the answers to them never materialised and, more frustrating still, every time they parted company he found himself counting down the minutes until he would see her again. He could feel himself becoming captivated by her, times when she consumed his every thought and her gift, resting in the luggage rack above his head was a prime example. He hoped she liked it, goodness knows he had gone through the mill because of it. Anyway, he thought consolingly, that was a story he would save for her when they met later. From now until that time he had hoards of phone calls and a gruelling two hour exercise regime to focus on.

It was 8pm, Julia was anxious; she should have arrived at the hotel by now, Luca would be waiting. She sat upright in the back of the taxicab as it made its way through the thick of city centre Leeds.

Her dark hair lay straight against her white shirt and bordered her beautiful yet nervous face; edgily she brushed her hands against the soft denim of her Victoria Beckham jeans. She had been delighted to discover, when trying them in the shop, she had dropped a dress size and was now a size eight, but having scarcely eaten since meeting Luca due to the hyperactive butterflies in her stomach, she was hardly surprised. This whole situation bounced her in bungee jump proportions from the top, allowing her to feel that she had met the man of her dreams. Luca was funny, kind, focused *and* handsome. She completely relished every minute she spent with him. Then it would sadistically plunge her to the bottom again, reminding her she was a gypsy girl, associating with a man and a world of which she was so totally unworthy. In addition, it was her perpetual dishonesty that left her feeling like a complete and utter fake after each date. For Julia, this feeling did not sit well with her at all, yet, it was her mother, the woman that had guided her when she was a child and remained to this day constantly in her thoughts, that appeared to spur her on. Julia had a hunch she was leading her to a better place, she only wished that she was here to confirm that instinct in person.

Julia examined her outfit and hoped it would meet with Luca's approval. Her long slim legs melted into black knee length boots, with spiked heels that increased her height and snaking leg length by a further three inches. She worried that she would tower over Luca, bringing the humorous images of Nicole Kidman and her ex husband Tom Cruise to mind. Nevertheless, she felt reasonably confident in her attire, only the tags, still attached to the designer labels hampered her comfort as they continued to rub against her skin, an irritating reminder they were merely 'on loan'.

Like every other outfit she had bought especially for her meetings with Luca over the past two weeks, they would be returning to the shop the next day with the valid excuse of 'unsuitable', enabling her to receive an immediate refund.

Her large dark eyes, smouldered impatiently as she viewed her surroundings. Her second money-saving opportunity was around the corner on the left. The driver indicated to turn.

"Oh, could you stop here please at this supermarket," she said casually, "I just need to buy some cigarettes."

"No problem." The driver slowed to a stop outside "We're a dying breed now, us lot," said the driver, tapping on his packet of Lambert and Butler sitting in the ashtray, "especially since this bloody smoking ban. I can't even smoke in my own car now with it being a taxi. Bloody ludicrous!" he muttered.

"Yes, isn't it?" Julia smiled and got out.

Walking into the supermarket she made her way to the far side of the store where a second exit led out onto a different part of the street. Darting through the store she took it and made her way to the hotel.

She felt remorseful about the driver sat outside waiting for her to return. She had felt guilty about all of them over the last two weeks, but she didn't have a choice, where was she going to get a forty pound fare for a taxi? She checked the time and encouraged her footsteps to gather pace along the pavements.

Luca sat in the hotel, he had been sat waiting for Julia for twenty minutes and, as with everything else this lady threw at him, this was yet another unfamiliar experience. His gift to her sat at his feet in a proud paper bag and through the tissue paper he could see the fabulous glint of the red sequins shining back at him. When he had seen the dress on the mannequin in the window of the boutique there had been only one person he could see wearing it and that was Julia. At this moment, he realised the passionate impulse of his purchase was beginning to sour. Julia was obviously a very independent person and he wondered if she would be offended by him taking the initiative to buy it. Trepidation zigzagged through is mind whilst he thought of his second reason for buying it, he was attending the injured jockeys' ball on Saturday night and wanted to ask Julia if she would accompany him. He knew the dress would be perfect, that was, if she accepted his invitation *and* if she liked the dress.

For the tenth time since he had arrived he checked the time again on his Rolex and glanced out of the huge bay window that overlooked the street. There was no sign of her, he would have liked to call her to check she was okay, but surprisingly when he had asked for her number last week she had informed him she didn't have a mobile phone – another strange scenario.

Irritated, he walked over to the bag and roughly scooped it up, quickly making his way over to the concierge desk.

"Good evening, Mr DeMario!" A fresh-faced young man stood behind the counter.

"Good evening," Luca answered bluntly. "Will you look after this for me until I leave please?" He asked, handing the man the bag.

"Yes, of course." He hesitated, glancing over his shoulder and scanning reception before moving closer towards Luca, his voice turned to a whisper. "When I saw you come in I was hoping you would come over." He pushed a piece of crumpled paper toward Luca. "Is there any chance of your autograph on this piece of paper for my mum and my sister? You are their hero, you see." He cowered slightly beneath the formality of his uniform whilst he awaited Luca's response. "If my boss saw me doing this I would be sacked instantly."

Luca's moody expression didn't waiver, he took the piece of paper, signed it then coldly slid it back.

The young man looked down at the autograph. "Thanks very much!" He beamed with pride.

Luca nodded coolly, glanced at his watch again and began to make his way back to his table.

"Luca!" a voice shouted.

Luca turned to Julia's enthusiastic greeting and instantly felt his worries disintegrate. She looked striking.

"Hi!" she added, looking and sounding relieved to see him.

He held out his arms in relief, holding her for a second. "You look beautiful," he told her. Gently he guided her with his arm around her waist to his table. "I was worried about you," he admitted. "Are you alright?"

"I'm sorry, yes I'm fine," she said looking at her watch, "there had been some roadblocks and the taxi-driver ended up taking the wrong route," she lied.

Luca took off her jacket, their hands touched fleetingly. Luca looked quizzical. "Your hands feel so cold."

There had been quite a nip in the air for a May evening and fleeing from the taxi had forced her to experience it.

"Yes, I know." She paused "I walked a lot of the way, that's why I'm late. I couldn't stand the thought of sitting in his car any longer whilst he tried to fathom out the next short cut," Julia said, feeling guilty at how quickly and effortlessly lies were tripping off her tongue.

Luca laughed. "What would you like to drink?" he asked.

She was thirsty and would have loved to have ordered the simplicity of a large glass of coke but, looking around at the plush surroundings of the hotel, immediately felt compelled to order something more sophisticated.

"A white wine please."

"Have you any preference?" Luca asked passing her the wine list.

Alarmed at having to decipher the refinery of a list of wines, she quickly changed her mind.

"Actually, I'll just have a gin and tonic please," Julia added.

Luca beckoned the bartender's attention and with professional breeze she hurried over to their table. The waitress was a woman in her forties and extremely good looking, she had long dark hair that tumbled in giant twists and curls down to her chest and fabulous brown eyes that were lined with a thick score of dark eye pencil.

"Two gin and tonics please, and, one for yourself," he smiled.

"No thank you, not for me," she answered professionally. "Will you be eating in the hotel tonight, sir? If so, I can bring you this evening's dinner menu."

Luca turned to Julia to ascertain her thoughts but on seeing her expression, he fell silent.

She was morbidly transfixed by the waitress; he saw her eyes, wide like dinner plates move rapidly across the woman's face then waiver like a rattlesnake's neck in terror.

"Julia?" Luca quizzed "Julia? Are you okay?" He looked back at the waitress. "If you just get the drinks that will be fine for now, thanks." She nodded and walked away, leaving Luca and Julia alone.

"Bloody hell!" Julia said, trying to shake the apparition from her mind. "That was a really terrible experience." She felt comforted by the reassurance of Luca's arm around her shoulder.

"What happened?" Luca asked with a frown. "You looked like you had seen a ghost."

"I'm not sure I didn't," Julia answered truthfully with a compelling urge to explain. "That waitress reminded me with such clarity of my mum." She hung her head, feeling overwhelmed by disappointment that it hadn't been her.

Luca shuffled closer on his seat, grateful that at last Julia had mentioned something about her family life. "Oh? Does she look like that lady?" He urged

"She did." Julia answered quietly "But she's dead now."

"Oh no, that's terrible, I'm sorry." Luca said rubbing her back with his hand "Do you want to talk about it?"

Julia took a deep breath and exhaled with a strong blow. "I was a little girl when it happened," she answered distantly, "only nine in fact. She died in my arms."

Suddenly Luca felt the atmosphere surrounding them grow dismally thick and guiltily recalled his hasty misgivings regarding her elusive behaviour.

"You poor thing, what the hell happened?"

Her large eyes swooped upon him, their beauty postponed by a glacial bitterness; a morbid silence and a deep unrepentant stare persisted before she eventually answered.

"She was shot," Julia answered frankly.

A cold bluntness surrounded her three words and sent a chill down Luca's spine. His horrified eyes scurried frantically across her face in search of a sick joke but on seeing the desperate look on her face they ceased their search for comfort.

"Shit!" he managed faintly.

From the corner of his eye Luca noticed the waitress placing their drinks on a tray to bring to the table. He jumped up from his chair.

"Thank you, I'll get those for you," he informed the waitress as he rushed over to the bar.

She looked confused. "Are you sure, Mr DeMario?"

"Yes, perfectly thank you," he announced forcefully.

Luca walked back to the table, placed the drinks upon it and moved his chair nearer to Julia.

"Thank you, Luca," she told him with a lost look in her eye. "That was kind of you."

"Bloody hell, Julia, after what you've gone through, keeping her away is the least I can do," he answered blatantly. He watched her take a drink and remained silent; concerned she may not want to elaborate on further details.

Bizarrely with Luca by her side, Julia felt shrouded by a veil of protection and experienced a real desire, compelled, in fact, to unlock the painful memory from her mind. With his warm hand never slipping from her back, Luca listened to her story.

"We used to spend a lot of time together; she was a fantastic mother, the best. She worked in a hotel in the early mornings as a chamber maid, similar to this one actually," Julia said looking around. "She would go to work before I woke up in the morning so that her days and evenings were free to spend with me."

Luca recognised that was the kind of sacrifice his own mother would have made for her own children if she had had to.

"One evening," Julia continued, "we walked to a nearby meadow, a place we went often, to read books to one another under the shade of a tree. We had become so engrossed in one another's company that we stayed far too long. The evening drew in so quickly, it was dark as we were walking home. She was holding my hand and swinging my arm, looking down at me with that big glowing smile of hers." Tears began to swell in her eyes. "Suddenly, a car sped across the field, I couldn't see the colour, just its hazy outline, it screeched to a halt in front of us, I saw his face, then a black gloved hand." Her voice began to waiver and quiver with the weight of her words. "God, his face, that bloody face!" she recalled, placing her hands over her eyes. She threw her hands away and continued. "And then, bang! It was the loudest bang I have ever heard in my life." She put her elbows on the table and recovered her face with her hands. "That sound has never left me because after it, my mother was dead. She lay at my feet with blood spewing from her mouth. She was all I could see. When I looked back up again, her murderer and the car had vanished."

Luca sat speechless for a long time. He couldn't see her face, it was still hidden by her hands and her mass of shining hair, but he knew she was crying by the gentle shake of her shoulders.

He tenderly stroked the back of her hair. "Who the hell would do that?" Luca asked, feeling personally affected by the conversation, "And why?"

Julia was reluctant to tell Luca everything, she omitted talking of her roots and the fact that the murderer had been a presumed gypsy hater, instead she shrugged,

"Who knows why these maniacs do these things, all I know is that he got life." Her tone turned desperately cold and there was no mistaking the revenge that fuelled her words. "He's in prison and that is exactly where he belongs." With a determined bid to pull herself together she wiped the tears from her eyes and face.

The two of them sat in a stunned silence. Once again, Julia replayed the detail of her mother's murder in her mind whilst Luca looked intently at her face, feeling nothing but complete admiration for the strength she had shown. She was truly amazing and he should have never judged her detachment and reserve the way he had.

Julia took a sip of her drink then rubbed his hand that had rested on her leg "Come on," she encouraged, "have you got anything to talk about that will cheer me up?"

"Well," Luca said rubbing the side of his face as if trying to rid the sombre discussion from his own mind, "I think I might be able to cheer you up, but it depends on your answer to two questions."

"Go on," she urged with a timid smile.

"First question, are you doing anything on Saturday night?"

"No," she answered with a little giggle.

"Do you like the colour red?" he laughed.

"Yes," she answered, still smiling though looking baffled.

"In that case, if I'm not being too presumptuous, I think I may be able to help." He stood from his chair, "Will you wait here a second?" Julia nodded with an internal excitement that felt too much to bear.

Luca collected the bag from the concierge and walked back to the table.

"The thing is," Luca explained, "I am going to a ball on Saturday night in aid of one of the charities I work for, they've invited me to be guest speaker. I wondered if you would accompany me?" The stout carrier-bag rustled as he gripped it in trepidation of her answer.

Like a lottery winner recognising their six numbers had come up Julia gulped in disbelief and felt herself bubble in elation.

"Yes, yes, that would be great!" She blushed, secretly contemplating what she would wear. "Thank you for asking me," she added. She looked back at the bag with increasing interest,

"And this," he held up the bag "is something I bought for you today. I hope you're not offended." He twisted his face in awkwardness. "I just saw it and thought of you, and just for the record," he laughed, "acquiring it caused me a lot of hassle." He handed it over and Julia reached out for it, the intrigue almost amounted to torture, but Luca nervously snatched it back again. "But, if you don't like it, it's okay, I know you will have a wardrobe full of beautiful clothes. Oh God," he stammered, "I'm telling you what the bloody thing is now."

They both laughed as he handed her the bag. Slowly she peeled it open and pulled out the red dress with speechless fascination. The full-length dress graciously fell to the floor, allowing the millions of glorious sequins that adorned the whole dress to twinkle and sparkle against the hotel's lights.

"Luca!" she gasped. Her eyes were wide in disbelief, her mouth fell open utterly aghast.

"Do you like it?" he asked.

"Like it?" she giggled excitedly. "Luca, it is the most beautiful dress I have ever seen." She jumped up and kissed him hard on the lips. "Thank you so much," she added sincerely.

"You don't have to wear it on Saturday if you don't want to," he added casually

"Luca, you think I won't be wearing this on Saturday? I will be wearing this every day for the rest of my life!" she answered joyfully, but then her face turned serious, feeling guilty as to how much the dress must have cost. "Why did buying it cause you hassle?"

"Oh," he waved his hand dismissively into the air. Seeing Julia's obvious adoration for the dress made his anger seem so futile and distant. "It was just that I asked the taxi-driver who was taking me to the airport to wait outside the boutique whilst I ran in to get it. I handed him a bundle of money so that he knew I wasn't doing anything dishonest. Only to find that when I came out of the shop five minutes later the deceitful bastard had driven off with my money." He shook his head crossly "I really cannot abide dishonesty, it makes me sick. Doesn't it you?" he added.

Julia felt herself physically recoil. "Mmmmm," she strained. She held up the dress, feigning one last glance, and hid her guilt-ridden face behind it.

Luca drove home that night with a promise that Julia would call him the following day to finalise the arrangements for Saturday evening. Tonight, he realised, they had crossed a barrier and with a feeling of heart-sailing happiness he reasoned with his anxieties to subside. Julia was one of the most genuine girls he had ever met.

Frankie DeMario sat in his enormous drawing room alone. For the second night running he had drunk half a bottle of scotch, a habit which he had got himself out of years ago. He had a problem, a big one. He really didn't know whom he could turn to about this one. Sure, he knew his old acquaintances from his hometown in Italy would help, but he didn't want to have to go down that road if he could help it.

He stood from his chair and slowly took his glass into the kitchen. He was aware that Luca had not returned home yet.

"Bloody fool!" he muttered.

Under normal circumstances he would have told Luca to concentrate on his job and get home at night. Frankie knew first hand what kind of people were out there when money and fame were involved, it was a fathers' job to protect his son from these false spongers of the world.

But for once, Frankie had neither the time nor the inclination to get involved and for the moment he had to leave Luca to his own devices. Frankie DeMario had much more pressing matters on his mind.

Chapter Eleven

"DON'T DROP ME here, Bill," Francesca snapped as he put on his indicator and slowed the car. "This would be such an inconvenience," she continued, "I will have far too far to walk, I've told you, I'm going to Barkers and Browns, that's around the corner."

Bill, in full comprehension that Barkers and Brown was one of the most expensive department stores, gave an agitated sigh as he signalled to pull out.

"It's hardly far."

"Bill," she huffed, "I have my stilettos on".

"Well, why did you put them on if you can't walk in them, Francesca?" Francesca didn't answer.

"And, anyway," he continued, "why are you going to this place?"

"I've already told you why," she said raising her voice, "it's a bloody emergency; you are so unreasonable, Bill. I have already told you that nothing I have is suitable. I know why you are so annoyed, it's because you wanted me to drive here so that you could sit around home doing nothing." she threw her arms up in the air. "Look at all this traffic. How the hell could you expect me to drive in all this? I have no option but to come. You really have no idea what it is like, do you? Fancy expecting me to attend this evening's event without looking amazing." She stared at him in disbelief as the car ached the few extra yards through the mass of traffic.

"Francesca it is nothing to do with who drives here, I just don't want you to be spending more money. You already have hoards of dresses hanging in your dressing room." Bill looked in his mirror and pulled over again, this time three doors down from the department store.

"Oh, for God's sake!" she said as she rived at the door handle. "Money, money, money that is all you bloody well think about." She opened the car door, pulled out her handbag and slammed it shut behind her. Without a second glance to her husband she made her way toward the store. As her stiletto heels tapped against the crowded pavement, with a sense of relief that she had rid herself from Bill's miserable attitude her final words rang in her ears.

"Money, money, money!" she sang. *Oh yes!* she thought. *All the things I could do!*

On entering the store the usual burly security guard stood solemnly surveying all who entered.

"Good Morning Mrs Montford," he said with a harboured smile.

"Oh good morning, James," she trilled dancing past.

He had told her twice that his name was Jim, but she was sure he would much prefer her elevating his status to James. He had always made time to talk to her ever since she had seen a young girl in her twenties shoplifting. Being utterly disgusted by the thief's indiscretion she had immediately informed James of what she had witnessed. She had been "*utterly appalled*" by the young girl's actions and had given her some firm wise advice whilst they sat in the offices upstairs waiting for the police to arrive.

"My advice to you, young lady, is never touch what you clearly cannot afford." Adding condescendingly, "Stick to browsing in your 'everything for a pound shops,' my love, where your temptations will be limited."

Her lawful endeavours had seen a luxury hamper delivered to her door the following day from the store. Francesca being utterly delighted with the gift, yet to Bill's heartfelt disappointment, she had refused to shop anywhere else since.

The evening wear department was on the second floor so Francesca caught the elevator. As the stairs coasted up she noticed she was the only one on it and became surprised at how quiet the store was today. With privacy seemingly hers she thought it the perfect opportunity to apply a coat of her cherry plum lipstick. Taking out her Dior compact, courtesy of the encased mirror, she dreamily applied it and took the time to examine the remainder of her perfectly applied make up, but she became distracted, panic stricken in fact. A gigantic spot had appeared on her nose. She began to prod and poke at it, mystified as to how she could have missed it this morning and wondered whether she should return to the first floor and visit the cosmetic counter to purchase a concealer. With alarm she threw her lipstick back into her handbag and tried to ascertain how visible the spot was from a distance using the mirror that trailed the length of escalator along the wall.

"Watch out!" cried a woman who had got on the escalator seconds before. Francesca glanced ahead and became horrified; the elevator had only two steps to go before it sank into the floor. Panicking, she quickly tried to lift her feet to step off, but only one foot moved, the fashionably slim heel of her second foot had got wedged firmly in between the ridge of the step.

She shrieked, a group of casual shoppers turned as she called. She threw her bag and cosmetics to the ground ahead and with only seconds remaining she tried in desperate terror to grapple with her shoe. They were her only pair of Jimmy Choos, her horror heightened as the sharp hungry teeth of the elevator began to eat at their pointed toe.

"They are my Jimmy Choos!" she shrieked. "They cost me eight hundred pounds!"

The toe of her shoe jammed into the iron mouth causing the escalator to grind to a thudding halt, the entire stairway jolted.

"Aaaaaaaaagh!" she screamed. She lost her balance, she waved her arms at her side like an air traffic controller at Heathrow, trying desperately to keep her balance, her efforts were in vain, launching through the air she landed with a crippling thump and lay sprawled upon the floor in the form of a perfect crucifix, with the entire contents of her handbag lying scattered around her.

Francesca froze; her knee and her elbow throbbed. *Who the hell has seen this?* she wondered. She tried to ease herself up, inching her face from the ground and saw a Marilyn Monroe imprint of her lipstick scorched against the floor. *Oh dear God*, her thoughts fumed, *even childbirth wasn't as embarrassing as this.*

A fellow shopper ran to her aid.

"Are you alright, madam?" he asked, aiding her gently to her feet.

She didn't answer him; her eyes scanned her surroundings trying to ascertain just how big a captive audience she had claimed. The man began to gather up her belongings from the floor and placed them in her bag.

"That escalator is a bloody death trap!" she declared in a loud voice, returning to the scene to grapple with the lodged shoe. With one last forceful tug she managed to free it.

"Look what has happened to my shoe!" she bellowed showing a collection of scuffs and scratches to the gathering crowd. She continued to rant with blatant volume in the vague hope it would divert unwelcome ridicule from her. "That bloody thing could have killed me," she fumed. "Look at the damage to my shoe." Again she showed the interested parties her shoe, all of them nodding and agreeing sympathetically.

Tim Hill, the stores manager ran to the scene.

"Ah, Mrs Montford," he said, instantly remembering her from a few weeks previous recalling her complaint that her 'anti-aging' smoothie did not have sufficient beetroot juice in it. "What an earth has happened here then?" he asked.

"I want to speak to the Health and Safety Officer immediately," Francesca declared rigidly.

Tim Hill, sidled Francesca away and into the privacy of his office. He allowed her to rant for several minutes and superficially agreed with her complaints before placating her anger with store privileges and compensation. He saw her face beam at the prospect of having a personal shopper at her beck and call for the next six weeks and was further delighted by her free offer of luncheon with unlimited wine this afternoon. He also promised that any alterations that needed to be carried out on her dress for the evening would be promptly attended to whilst she had her lunch and would, of course, be free of charge.

Mrs Montford, rubbing her bruises, was just pleased that the embarrassing incident was behind her. She then trotted into the evening wear department and allowed herself not one, but two assistants to execute her mission. Already feeling rather superior as a result of the compensation she had been offered, the feeling heightened when she noticed that neither of the assistants had a particularly attractive look, with one of them being positively overweight. *What would they know about making an entrance at a ball?* With this in mind she felt she had to *thoroughly* explain what she was looking for.

"I want something that is truly spectacular!" she trilled. "Just to put you in the picture, I know you will never have been to such an event, the tickets alone are five hundred pounds per person," she informed them. "This occasion is a star-studded affair for the entire racing fraternity."

The two assistants made exasperated eye contact with one another and rolled their eyes to the ceiling. Mrs Montford, oblivious to their offence continued.

"Last year I wore a very understated dress, it was close fitting to show my figure but it was like a duck egg blue. When I arrived I realised it was not at all suitable, I was positively underdressed. That cannot happen this year. I want to pull out all the stops." She threw her arms in the air with enthusiasm at the colourful rails surrounding her. "Come on!" she encouraged, clapping her hands together. "Show me everything you've got, and remember, in this case, all that glitters certainly is gold!"

The two assistants obeyed orders and promptly began to scour through their stock.

"Why did it have to be that silly cow that fell?" one of the assistants whispered to her colleague.

"Ooooh! Now, this one is exactly the kind of thing I had in mind." Mrs Montford, distrusting of her passé helpers, had decided to take matters into her own hands and pulled a full length electric blue gown from the rail. The sumptuous satin fabric teased and shimmered in the light.

"Erm, yes," the slimmer assistant said, "but, I'm not sure it's your..." she hesitated, "What size are you, Mrs Montford?" she asked tentatively.

"I'm a perfect twelve," Francesca stated proudly. "Curves in all the right places," she trilled giving the larger lady a disparaging glance.

"Yes, I thought so," said the assistant, "only that dress is a ten."

"Oh, don't worry about that," Francesca replied confidently, "I can easily fit into a ten." She took the dress into the changing room "You carry on looking," she ordered over her shoulder. "I'll try this one on whilst I am waiting."

Ten minutes passed before the curtain slid open. The two assistants stared in disbelief.

"I love it!" Francesca puffed with a crimson face. "It is just what I had in mind," she announced with a forced smile.

It was obvious that Francesca could barely breathe; perspiration crowded her forehead, brought about by the obvious battle that had occurred behind the curtain. Concealing her breathlessness with a smile, she gasped her request.

"Could you do me up, please?" She pulled up her hair and turned around for the assistant to pull up the zip.

Behind her the two women looked at one another nervously. The dress was clearly too small and neither of them wanted to damage the material by forcing it together.

"I'm just wondering if we should try and order the size twelve for you, Mrs Montford, we could have it here for Monday," one of the assistants suggested.

"Nonsense," Francesca sneered. "Come on, zip it up," she insisted.

As the zip was forced up Francesca felt it tighten against her ribs and her waist, undeterred she studied her reflection in the mirror. Yes, she thought confidently, it was a perfect fit.

The assistant moved behind her. "You see, Mrs Montford, it is just slightly nipping you in the waist. You can see that from the way the fabric is pulling that it is slightly too…"

Francesca was incensed by the larger assistant's potential dissuasion. She was obviously burning with envy and having experienced the jealously of 'fatties' in the past, she cut the conversation dead.

"It fits like a glove, I will take it," she snapped before turning again. "Unzip me please," she asked coldly.

The assistants shrugged to one another. They were trained that the customer was always right, there was only so much a mere 'worker' could say or do, they did as she asked. As the zip slid down Francesca instantly felt the relief.

"I can take it right away," Francesca added. "It doesn't need altering at all, that's lucky for you all isn't it?" she said, falsifying a smile.

One of the assistants took it to the desk and rang it through the till; the second assistant began to carefully wrap it.

Francesca came out of the changing room and handed the girl her credit card.

"Thank you," the girl smiled. "That's five thousand pounds, please."

Francesca privately winced; she must remember to hide the receipt from Bill. The card was gently stroked through the machine and the three ladies waited for authorisation, but several seconds passed with no sign of response. Francesca tapped her fingers impatiently on the desk; she was so looking forward to her complimentary salad and wine. At last the machine beeped. The assistant read the screen.

"Oh dear," she said shyly, "there appears to be a problem with your card, Mrs Montford." She cleared her throat. "I'm afraid authorisation has been denied."

For the second time in the same morning she had been faced with embarrassment within the same store

"That's ludicrous," she frowned. "There's more money in this account than there is in your company's safe." She shook her head and frowned in a way that insinuated incompetence toward the girl.

"Try it again; I think you must have pressed the digits incorrectly."

The assistant blushed and was about to drag the card through the machine again when Francesca interjected.

"On second thoughts, don't bother, just use this one, I haven't got time for any more foolery in this store." She handed her the American Express card. The card that Bill had warned her that any balances put on this card would have to be paid off within the month and made her promise she would only use it in an emergency.

He is so lucky having a wife like me she internally appraised *many wives wouldn't take the slightest bit of notice of him, I however have kept my promise, there couldn't be a greater emergency than this.*

Charles slowed as he indicated to turn into the driveway of Cedars Hall. To his surprise, Dr White, his mother's doctor for nearly half a century, slowly and nervously crawled his way out onto the country road. Charles raised his hand in acknowledgement, but Dr White either didn't notice or was too busy inching the steering wheel anxiously through his aged gripping hands to reciprocate. *What was he doing here?* Charles thought. He made his way up the drive to check on his mother.

Their four black labs and Trent, the Border terrier, wrestled their way out of the stable in recognition of the sound of his car and gathered with expectancy around the driver's door. Charles, ignoring the dogs, made his way straight to the house, the dogs fondly wagging their tails, followed suit.

The house was silent but Charles knew his mother was home, the aroma of freshly brewed coffee filled the air.

"Mother!" he shouted, there was no response. "Mother!" he repeated up the stairs.

"Yes," a muffled voice responded, "I'm coming."

Charles heard the distinctive creak of his mother's bedroom floorboards then the gentle pad of her feet across the oak staircase. Charles looked up the stairs with a smile. She was wearing her floral housecoat, normal for this time of day; she usually took an afternoon nap around one. As she floated down the stairs, with a full face of perfectly applied make up, the mane of her housecoat trailed magnificently behind her. Charles noticed she looked unusually tense.

"I've just seen the doctor leave, Mother. Are you okay?"

"Goodness, yes of course I am," she replied kissing his cheek. "I was just going for my rest," she answered ignoring her son's reference to Dr White.

"What was Dr White doing here?"

"Oh," she shrugged, "he just popped by to ask me if I wanted to play bridge on Tuesday." She laughed walking to the kitchen "He was awfully embarrassed when he saw I was in my housecoat, you would have thought a doctor seventy years old would have seen it all by now, clearly he hasn't. Still, I suppose it indicates he has been mixing in the right circles."

Charles felt himself relax again; he worried about his mother's health and was becoming increasingly aware her energy levels were frequently beginning to flag.

"He shouldn't be driving, you know, he's starting to become a liability."

His mother was pouring him a coffee; she swung round in response, "What and you youngsters aren't?" she snapped handing him the coffee cup with a shaking hand.

Charles looked puzzled. "What do you mean?"

His mother was clearly agitated, crossly she folded the tea towels and laid them neatly upon the Aga stove. "You youngsters think that you have some kind of right of way passport to the world. That you can tread on anyone or anything that doesn't, in your book, serve a purpose. Doctor White has been an awfully good friend to me *and* your father throughout the years. He even delivered you and Hugo, he is honest and respectable and just because he doesn't care to drive like a mad man you want to write him off?" She shook her head in disdain and just because he doesn't care to drive like a mad man you want to write him off?" She shook her head in disdain "You need to show some respect for people Charles," she snapped.

Charles was surprised at her unprovoked outburst and tried to explain. "Mother, I was about to finish by saying if you needed to see Dr White I would be more than happy to take you to him, therefore saving him a journey. He looks nervous behind the wheel; it's hardly fair on the old chap."

Kitty felt tired. "I'm glad to hear that you have a regard for fairness, Charles, however, I have no wish to discuss the matter further, I am retiring for an hour. By the way, Mary has picked up your dry-cleaning. Your black tie attire for the evening is hanging in your room." She walked out of the kitchen.

"Are you definitely not coming tonight then, Mother?" he called out.

"At five hundred pounds a ticket I am damned sure I am not!" she snapped over her shoulder.

Kitty walked into her bedroom and sank onto the bed, staring up at the crooked beams along the ceiling, tears began to seep from her eyes a result of the secret pain that had welled in her heart and body for so long. She wept for a million reasons, and, certainly for the pain of losing her dear friend and husband. Where was he now when she needed him so badly? She needed his wise head to lead her through this problem.

Recollections of the first day they had met on the hunting field assembled in her mind. It had been a crisp October morning and when Charles senior cast his eyes upon her for the first time he told friends she would be the woman he would marry. Kitty Lancaster, he said had a sense of adventure that could only be associated with a wild mustang. He had recalled with clarity the dazzling intensity of her blue stormy eyes as she crossed the field at lightening speed. Her long blonde hair had been tamed into a ponytail with a black ribbon that bounced in the air like a fox's tail with every fence she charged her horse over. She was the only woman he had ever met that caressed the sweet offerings of freedom and courage with first class gusto. He decided to throw caution to the wind and gallop after her, when he eventually caught up, breathlessly he invited her to a friend's house for supper that evening.

They had shared pheasant crumble with fresh country vegetables, served with the warming grip of vintage port in front of a crackling fireside. From that day, with Charles senior already entranced by her beauty and Kitty, unable to resist his charm, the pair remained an item and within six months they were married.

When Charles had recited his vows that day, until the day he died, he had remained true to his word. He had adored and cherished her and had remained faithful and honest throughout, he would have given his life in protection of his family. With her tears still silently rolling down her cheeks she wondered insistently where it had all gone wrong.

Charles remained seated at the kitchen table. He wasn't surprised by his mothers' candour; he was used to her brutal honesty and blunt tongue. However, there was something about her reactions today that made him feel something was out of the ordinary. The five dogs that had continued to follow his every move with the faithful bond of their eyes, all pined for attention from beneath the table, intermittently nudging his hand, trying to force it upon their heads. Deep in thought and clearly anxious, Charles was interrupted by the Border terrier trying to jump up to his lap. Charles, irritated by its persistence, slapped it savagely around the head.

"Piss off you fucking thing!" he yelled.

The dog yelped and retreated with a cowered head to another room.

He stood from his chair and crept up the stairs, he felt he had to try to talk to his mother. Easing her bedroom door open he peered inside. She was sat on the window seat, looking out onto the formal arrangement of the gardens below. Sensing his presence she turned to look at him before looking back into the garden.

"I'm sorry for speaking to you like that, Charles; there really was no need for it," she admitted.

"What's the matter mother? And don't for Christ's sakes tell me nothing, I am not an idiot," he said.

He walked into her room and sat on the edge of her wrought-iron bed. She felt repelled to look at him, determined not to expose her pain. Still staring out of the window, she remained silent for a few seconds whilst she thought of her words.

"Gerard's death makes your father's seem like yesterday. It crucifies me when a good kind person dies. Every time, it makes me question my faith." She took a deep breath. "Why does he take all the good ones? But then it appears such a ridiculous question, because I know the answer. Sometimes," she gave a short laugh, "I feel envious of God that he is spending this time with my Charles. Never a day goes by that my heart doesn't yearn for him." Her voice lowered into a painful whisper. "Sometimes, I wish I was with him, there is nothing, nor anybody that can take his place."

Charles hated her words. They stabbed at his heart like a burning poker, forcing him again to remember his father's last words. His father's last request rang like funeral bells in his head. He felt his anger brew, he had lived with this intense pressure for the past twenty years, and he didn't know how much longer he could continue with the weight. How could he possibly take the place of the man his mother had worshipped like a God?

The thundering clatter of an engine outside infiltrated the silence within the room.

Kitty immediately jumped off the window seat. "What the bloody hell is that racket?" she shouted.

Charles ran towards her and stared out of the window. It was a helicopter, its silver pearlescent paint boastfully exposing a multitude of pastel colours in the sunlight. It landed in the garden and its engine fell silent.

Charles kept his admiration for the awesome machine to himself before being astonished to see that Hugo stepped out of the cockpit and began to walk towards the house with a huge grin fixed to his face. Kitty opened her bedroom window wide.

"What the devil are you doing?" she bellowed from her window.

"Ahhh! Glad to see you're home," Hugo replied laughing. "I've come over for the ball tonight. Only set off from London an hour ago," he said proudly. "What do you think of my new girl? She's really something isn't she?" he shouted pointing back to the awesome machine.

"I think you're the perfect match," snapped Kitty loudly. "*She* hasn't got any brains either." She banged the window shut then turned to Charles, "When are you two ever going to have anything real and honest in your lives?" she asked pointedly.

Charging through his mind like an army of uniformed soldiers began the vision of his meeting with his accountant regarding his financial decline, swiftly followed by the vision of his hot, rampant sex with Emma DeMario and numerous other women over past months. Just like the sex, his life was a casual lie.

Once again, his mother had succeeded in making him feel utterly guilty and thoroughly ashamed.

Chapter Twelve

GOLDSBOROUGH CRESCENT consisted of a cluster of six large detached houses about one mile out of Chelmsley village. They stood in a neat horseshoe formation and had been built in order to satisfy the discerning tastes of middle-class professionals.

As soon as they had appeared on the market, Francesca Montford, eager to investigate, had been the first to view the properties, and Bill, with painful reluctance, had been forced to accompany her. She had scampered through all six houses, meticulously comparing their every detail, trying to ascertain which one of the six held pole position, before standing in the road to face them all.

"These are truly prestigious properties, Mrs Montford," the estate agent told her, sensing her insatiable appetite to impress the outside world. "They have been built specifically with the aim of reaching out to individuals that are clearly used to the finer things in life, those people for whom luxury and comfort go hand in hand." He noticed her nose rising an inch higher with his every sentence. "You know, these are the kind of homes that are only within the reach of the higher echelon of house buyers." He cleared his throat, "The likes of your good self for example."

"You are so right," Francesca replied approvingly, glancing over each house again and paying particular appreciation to the white stone pillars that championed the front doors. "This crescent reminds me so much of a mini Belgravia in London," she had chirruped. "It takes me right back to my family roots," she added proudly.

Bill frowned. "But Francesca, none of your family *ever* lived in Belgravia."

Surreptitiously she jabbed Bill hard in the side, then smiled sweetly back at the estate agent. "They visited often," she confirmed boldly, returning her attention back to the houses before her.

The estate agent steered the conversation back to business. "You are the first to view the houses and therefore, if you are interested, for the next twenty minutes you have the pick of the crop," he informed them.

"Why only twenty minutes?" Francesca asked, feeling panic rise.

"I have another viewer turning up anytime," he replied.

Bill tried to conclude the meeting. "I think the wisest move would be to contemplate it over the next couple of days, that way..."

Francesca swiftly interrupted her husband. "Just out of interest," she asked casually, "what is the occupation of your next client?" Looking back at the surprise on the agent's face, she let out a sailing laugh. "It helps to get a feel for the likely neighbourhood prior to making a decision."

The estate agent somehow managed to mask his smile "He is a lawyer in Leeds."

"A lawyer indeed?" Mrs Montford failed to disguise her delight and allowed the information to instantly cement her decision. "I think we should have number six, not only has it got a larger garden but I love the red door, my mother always said that houses with red doors brought nothing but good luck."

As a result the deal was done and fifteen years later the Montford's still lived in Number Six, Goldsborough Crescent. However, it was only today that Francesca had felt truly blessed with her mother's superstition of good luck. Finally it appeared to have come into fruition.

"You're pregnant, Paris?" Francesca asked her daughter again. "Really?" The delight shone in her eyes as she stood beaming back at Paris who was curled up in the sitting room chair.

"Yes," Paris answered weakly looking baffled by her mother's enthusiasm.

Such was the gravity of the news that Francesca, for the first time since putting on her dress, felt free of its uncomfortable restriction. Her mind ran wildly, giving confidence and playing host to a multitude of dreamy scenarios. She made her way over to the drinks cabinet and poured herself a celebratory gin.

Paris watched her mother's cheerful face and wondered with increasing optimism if she had at last done something to obtain her approval.

"And you are sure it's Gerard's?" she asked over her shoulder.

"Francesca!" Bill chastised, standing in his dinner suit by the side of his daughter's chair. He already felt a paternal diffidence at being involved in this conversation and his wife's latest remark perpetuated the feeling he needed to protect his daughter. He placed a hand on her shoulder, a silent proposal that she ignore the question.

"Of course it's Gerard's!" Paris screeched across the room.

Francesca turned to face her husband and daughter "A genuine Santé baby!" she gasped, ignoring her daughter's upset. "You will need to get plenty of rest, Paris; you never know what opportunities could spring from this." She flinched, realising her private thoughts had already become air born.

"What the bloody hell are you talking about, opportunities?" Bill asked with disgust filling his voice.

Paris looked on and felt like an involuntary spectator to a stranger's dilemma. There was a cold insinuation wrapped around her mother's expression of 'opportunities' that made her feel as though she was about to become a pawn in a game. She looked up at her mother, still firing insults across the room at her husband, *If only you would love me for who I am.* She wondered whether the power of intense thought could actually travel to the dark dismal world of Francesca Montford's brain and out of the blue convert her into the kind, caring mother she had craved for a lifetime. She waited for only a matter of minutes and realised her hopes were futile.

"I'm going to bed, enjoy your ball." She told her parents with a cram of sarcasm. Getting up off the settee she walked from the room. Her parents were so engrossed in their argument that neither of them heard her.

Hugo and Charles looked magnificent. The pair of them stood side by side in the drawing room beneath the bold, historic statement of the Lancaster and the Baron coats of arms which hung in perfect centre above the monumental fireplace. Unintentionally they formed a quartet of symmetrical sophistication, and, on first glance, it proved hard to decipher which one of them looked the grander.

The brothers' stark white crisp bibs rejuvenated the tans they had acquired whilst visiting Cloisters back in March, their custom-made black dinner suits hoisted their already powerful six foot frames into omnipotent proportions, and the classic peck of their black silk tie's could have compelled *any* woman to rip them from their holdings and ravish every inch of their horny flesh beneath. With a supreme charisma that effortlessly filled the immense room, the handsome pair chatted casually whilst sipping approvingly on vintage Dom Perignon.

They were in high spirits, eager to get to the ball, but for the present moment both were content to be in one another's company, enjoying the amusing brotherly banter that fired to and fro like a tennis ball at the Wimbledon final.

Kitty had long since left Cedars Hall to attend a bridge night at a friend's house and since her departure, Hugo and Charles had enjoyed having a free reign within the idle drinks cabinet. As their finale, a crème de menthe shot sat on the mantle piece. Charles hoped that the lingering essence of peppermint would lie heavy on his breath mystifying any evidence of drink driving.

"Yes I suppose you are right to be careful," Hugo grinned. "After all, in this sleepy haven we're bound to be pulled up tonight."

"Why do you say that?" Charles asked looking concerned.

Hugo pulled his shirt from his trousers to reveal a dark rich tan that smothered his stomach.

"Well, look at my tan," he boasted, re-tucking the shirt into his trousers. "It's superb; the local constabulary will be perplexed and think that a darkie has moved into town, we'll be stopped straight away."

Hugo had also inherited the same sparkling blue eyes as both his mother and his brother, however, Hugo's were the only pair marred by the stresses of the City life. Deep rooted lines were beginning to appear around the corners of his eyes, each one signifying the pressure of the twenty-four hour responsibility of trading and, of course, the penance of regular sun drenched holidays.

Since his skiing holiday with Charles, his tan had been topped up twice with two holidays, one at Sandy Lane, Barbados and another, a freebie from a client, to Dubai. His dark blonde hair had been lightened by the sun and boasted intermittent flashes of baby blonde strands. Unlike the sensual tussling of Charles' hair, Hugo's was cut professionally short, a smart career move since his boss hated an unkempt appearance. It had also been his boss that had introduced him to the benefits of a daily exercise routine at the gym. Hugo had initially hated the regime but had found, in only a short time, his body had became tight and lean, but more importantly, his resilience and focus towards his daily pressures had magnified.

His tenacity and motivation for his work had paid off; yesterday alone he earned one hundred and ninety five thousand pounds. There was no doubt about it he enjoyed the money, he was already fortunately aware that wealth brought with it an extremity of bonuses, with fast women, fast cars and fast nights just being a few of them. However, he was also extremely conscious that this abandoned luxury did not give him the same kind of buzz as it used to. He stared outside and focused on his newly acquired helicopter that sat handsomely awaiting its pilot. When it had been delivered, his pulse had raced but as he looked at it now, only weeks after seeing it for sale, his neutral despondency had returned. He put his lack of enthusiasm down to exhaustion; he had been called into the office at three this morning and had not bothered going back to bed since. He needed a wake up call.

"I'm just going for a pee," Hugo informed his brother.

Locking the bathroom door behind him he unhooked the antique pewter mirror from the wall and carefully rested it on the floor. He laid out the white powder with caution and enticed it into two neat lines with his credit card, then using a rolled up fifty pound note, with one long deep breath he snorted the magic sherbet into his nostrils. Its effects were immediate; it gave him a sudden awakening that cruised him back to life. He wiped the mirror clean with his finger, rubbing the remnants into his gums then carefully he re-hung it. This stuff was a miracle cure he had decided some time ago, there was nothing like it in the world and he had a colleague's recommendation to thank for increasing his dose. His now regular indulgence had been born after complaining to his associate of feeling stressed and exhausted.

"Up the anti with the white stuff," his colleague had advised.

Taking his advice, Hugo's occasional fix had been increased to a twice a day hit, and as a result, he had seen his mental and physical capabilities soar. He checked his face in the mirror for the evidence of powder, rubbed hard against his nose, trying to free it from the burning sensation that gripped it, then, walked back into the drawing room.

"Who are you after screwing tonight then, Bro?" he asked Charles, flaunting a super sexy smile.

"Nobody," his brother snapped. "I'm a changed man," Charles added, draining his crème de menthe.

"Oh, no!" Hugo groaned. "Is this because Rebecca's home? She's already blown you out once; you're not going back for more are you?"

"Piss off!" Charles retaliated. "We all have to grow up sometime, you know."

"Oh well," Hugo shrugged, "that leaves more women for me."

"Come on, let's go and get Rebecca," Charles said taking off his dinner jacket and holding it over his shoulder.

They got into the car and each lit up a cigarette.

"How's business?" Hugo asked filling the car with the exhalation of his smoke.

"Shit, if I'm honest," Charles answered, lowering Hugo's window a couple of inches as an outlet for the smoke. "It would be alright if it wasn't for that Italian streak of piss, DeMario," he spat. "He's always the fucking favourite and it doesn't seem to matter what he's riding at the moment, he usually manages to win. Little dago bastard, he's costing me a fortune." Charles turned the ignition and appreciated the sound of the satisfied purr of his engine.

"The thing is about him," Hugo stated with ill-equipped confidence, "it's not that he's a good jockey so much, it's the class of horse he rides that sail him home every time. They need a shot of some slow down medicine" he joked.

On that note Charles' thoughts went into overdrive as his car crunched down the long stately drive of Cedars Hall.

Obscured by the density of a nearby wood, a car was parked and the driver within it had been waiting an eternity for movement. Utter relief dawned when he saw the brothers approach the road from the drive.

"Thank God for that," he grumbled, at long last starting his engine.

Chapter Thirteen

THE LOCATION offered the perfect setting for a summer ball. The venue was a traditional Queen Anne style manor set within hundreds of acres of rolling parkland and home to the Count and Countess of Yorkshire. The warm summer evening was so beautiful that the sky looked good enough to eat, like a huge glass bowl of Eton Mess, offering generous helpings of raspberry pink and romantically shaded with the biscuity breakings of ivory meringue cloud.

An assembly of waiters and waitresses dressed in black uniform and austere white aprons stood like emperor penguins with obediently fixed smiles that made their young faces ache. Each held large silver trays, brimming heavily with chilled flutes of bubbling champagne and tall glasses of Pimm's that were crammed with fresh fruit and newly picked mint. The flushed faced chefs in the kitchen were busy shouting and swearing at their underlings, though their culinary expertise clearly evident as the appetizing aroma of oriental hors d'oeuvres and canapés slowly filtered through the air.

Bill and Francesca Montford had arrived a little later than she had anticipated, delayed by Bill fussing and repeatedly checking on Paris before they left. A young man in a luminous safety jacket waved their Range Rover into the allotted space.

"Like I said," Bill seethed through gritted teeth as he followed the parking attendant's wave, "if you were to concentrate on what really matters in life, your daughter for example, instead of that bloody five thousand pound dress, we would all be a lot happier." He yanked at the handbrake. "What do you think you are doing anyway? We can't afford that kind of money for a dress. You still haven't told me how you paid for the bloody thing," he raged.

The worry tormented him. Finances were such now that he was having problems knowing just how they were going to pay for their next grocery delivery, at this rate he was going to have to get a job stacking shelves.

Francesca fumbled for an excuse. *How could I have been so stupid as to leave the tag on the bloody dress? And Paris hasn't helped this situation.* He had been shouting for the entire journey, Bill had thought his wife was purposely ignoring him, when in fact, whilst sitting, Francesca could barely breath in the dress, let alone talk. With every move she made the fear the delicate fabric might rip was an ever present threat. Inching her way out of the car with meticulous precision and once able to stand, she caught her breath and entered into conversation.

"Oh shut up now, Bill," she answered, gathering short bursts of air between words. "We are here to enjoy ourselves; I will make it up with Paris tomorrow. And anyway, you want me to look good don't you? Or do you want us to be the laughing stock?"

"I don't want to be here at all. The cost of these balls at five hundred pounds a crack are way out of our league, all this money you are spending is getting way out of hand."

"Yes, it probably is out of your league you pathetic little man. But remember," she said screwing up her eyes and pointing her finger directly into his face, "these kinds of parties have been a part of my family for centuries, if you can't afford me then maybe I should find someone who can."

Taking small, inhibited pigeon steps, and resembling a prisoner of the chain gang, she walked as quickly as she could towards the house. On reaching a waiter she swooped two glasses of champagne from his tray and drained one outright. She then turned to witness Rebecca Santé and the Lancaster-Baron brothers just arriving.

"Oh, Christ! Look at this bore, her dress must make you realise that this one was worth every penny," Francesca chided to her husband, looking over at Rebecca. "She's enough to make your tea curdle."

Rebecca wore a simple black halter neck dress that sat neatly on the slim calf of her legs. Most of the ladies, she noticed, were wearing full-length gowns, although she was in the mood to enjoy herself, she preferred the look of classic style to lavish glamour this evening.

Rebecca, along with Charles and Hugo, gravitated towards a small cluster of mutual friends. Sebastian Thompson, a sloppy mouthed red-faced heart consultant, with mousy hair that was visibly receding from his pronounced forehead, welcomed their arrival with an over-the-top bellow.

"Ah! The wonderful L-B brothers with the beautiful Ms Santé!" He struck Charles and Hugo firmly on their backs several times before planting a kiss on the side of Rebecca's cheek, leaving a visible snail trail of saliva across it. Disguising her abhorrence she idly wiped it away.

"I hear you're doing bloody well, my friend," Sebastian swanked loudly, turning to Hugo. "A pal of mine, he practices at The Portland, he says you're one of the best of the City's brokers now."

"Oh?" Hugo grinned. "That's good to hear, he's obviously not one of my clients then," he joked.

Sebastian continued, "When he started talking about the kind of figures you would be earning I was aghast. I said to the chap, good God, he's certainly come a long way since the days we spent jiggering on cream crackers at Eton!" He let out a loud thunderous guffaw that proved infectious to the rest of the party and onlookers.

"I hear you've just bought yourself a helicopter?"

Hugo nodded.

"You must fly it out to the pad I've just bought in St. Tropez, it's one hell of a place. I even prefer it to my lodge in Chamonix," he informed the group. "And," he said turning a quizzical eye to Charles, "what are you up to these days? Not trying to keep up with him I hope," he said pointing to Hugo.

Charles felt a gurgle of envy choke his throat. Oblivious to Charles' emotion, another friend turned towards him to interject.

"Ah yes, Charles, you remember staying at my place in Barbados about three years ago?" Charles nodded slightly.

"I told you I'd never sell, but you told me if I ever did I was to give you first refusal. Well, it's going on the market next week. If you are interested give me a call tomorrow and we'll have a chat."

Charles, remembering the conversation and the all consuming love for the suave luxurious villa, felt compelled to show interest.

"How much is it on for?" he asked confidently, concealing his heartbreak.

"The market is sodden at the moment, but I can't wait for it to ripen, unlike you lot." He gestured towards Hugo and Charles. "I need the cash for other investments. It's on for two and half mil, but if you were interested I would be willing to do a deal."

Charles felt crucified, internal embarrassment crawled around his body, something, for once, was out of his league.

"Great, thanks for letting me know. I'll call you tomorrow." He was grateful for the stunning distraction that attracted everyone's attention.

"Jesus! Would you feast your eyes on that beauty?" Hugo groaned having followed his brother's stare.

Walking gracefully towards the outdoor reception holding nervously onto Luca's arm was Julia. The gathering revellers turned and stared in awe, fascinated by her presence. The floor length red sequined gown rustled against her legs as she walked, catching the spotlights and the last of the suns rays casting a magical display of flickering fire. Her dark mahogany hair fell in large winding curls and sat peacefully on her slim tanned shoulders. The dark temptation of her eyes had been teased with a small application of mascara and the fullness of her young plump lips were accentuated with a simple, clear, shining gloss. Her eyes, enthralled by the magic of the venue, flickered and flashed in disbelief at the lavish colourful gowns, the scurrying waiters offering a never decreasing stockpile of champagne and food, in addition, the enormity of the marquee, its cruise ship proportions stood imposingly, waiting to receive the copious numbers of wealthy guests that now surrounded its entrance.

The jazz band, one of four bands hired to entertain the guests that evening, struck up their first tune. With a full spectrum of eyes upon Julia the band couldn't resist playing a song that contradicted their genre, and performed Chris de Burghs' Lady in Red. Luca laughed out loud and kissed her cheek. The incident caused Julia to feel so overwhelmed that an effervescent fizz of excitement bubbled in her chest. She felt euphoric as she reminded herself of the facts. Her arm was linked with Luca DeMario's, against her skin lay a dress that had previously only sparkled in her dreams, and surrounding her was utter extravagance, she felt so thrilled she thought she might burst.

Sensing a need for decorum she fought to collect herself, posing for photographs with Luca as the local press and a couple of national magazines moved in for their lucky chance but after the fourth photographer had made yet another request to, "Look this way and smile!" Julia excused herself to visit the powder room.

Luca followed her into the marquee and watched her walk across the room. He noticed her grace and exquisite style as she moved. She was tall and elegant; she held her head high and her effortless forthcoming smile, as always adorned her breath taking face. As she walked along, groups of people turned their heads to follow her path, all of them trying to get another glimpse of the unknown beauty.

"Wow!" Luca spoke out loud and shook his head in disbelief at the magical aura she possessed.

"She's some girl, you're a lucky man," Charles said, appearing by Luca's side.

Luca was baited by anger as he thought of his sister but before he could tell him to fuck off, Francesca squeezed in between the two men. She had been drinking heavily prior to arriving at the ball and the four glasses of champagne she had guzzled in the last ten minutes appeared to have warmed her spirit. She brushed her breasts across Charles' broad chest and rested them there, falsifying a 'well-to-do' voice she began to make general conversation, "What are you two handsome baggers talking about?" She took a Davidoff cigarette from her bag placed it in her gold cigarette holder and promptly lit up. The smoke drifted its way around the two men's faces and up Luca's nose. Luca wafted the straying smoke from his face and began to chat to another group of people by his side.

"They seem to have put on a good show this year, don't they?" Francesca continued oblivious to her intrusion.

"Yes," Charles answered abruptly, casually keeping his eye on Luca and looking around for Rebecca. Mrs Montford detected his attention was straying.

"Oh don't bother looking for miss prim and proper," Francesca snapped, beginning to draw away. "She'll be sitting having a cup of tea somewhere trying to get to grips with the news within her family."

"What news?" Charles, though bored of her company, felt the creep of vague interest.

"You mean you haven't heard?" She moved back into her familiar breast rubbing position "I thought Rebecca would have told you. Paris is pregnant to Gerard, apparently she told Rebecca the night before last." She took a deep draw on her cigarette. "It looks as though the Montford's and the Sante's are going to be seeing a lot of each other." She laughed out loud.

Charles restrained his surprise and he considered this to be the reason for Rebecca's reserved disposition this evening. Whatever, he decided this old trout deserved a reward for her free flowing information.

"What would you like to drink?" he asked, giving Francesca a dynamic smile. Getting her a drink was a chance to get out of her breast lock and prize himself away. He had another job to complete before he could relax.

"I'll have a gin and tonic, and, as we have something to commiserate, make it a large one, I hope she doesn't keep it," she hiccupped. "The last thing I need is to be a granny." She threw her head back and laughed. Charles turned his attention to the bar and Luca.

Julia had only been to the ladies and already she had been impressed. There had been hand moisturisers, hair spray, deodorant and perfume and even a lavatory assistant, this one being a whole lot friendlier that the one she remembered in York on race day.

Comparing the two events, Julia shuddered as she viewed Luca standing at the bar; he was so handsome, she was so lucky. Her spirits sank as she considered what he would think if he knew the awful truth about the *real* Julia Smith. She smiled nervously as he welcomed her back.

"Everything okay?" Luca asked her as he passed her champagne.

"Yes, I'm fine thank you," she said nodding her head.

One of the event organisers, an elderly gentleman, gently placed a hand on Luca's shoulder. "I'm sorry to interrupt, Mr DeMario, but we wondered if you could come over to the stage area to talk to us about the possible timings for your speech." The man pointed to the far side of the room.

Luca nodded hesitantly and then looked back at Julia.

"I'll be fine." Julia assured. "Go on, I'm sure I'll find someone to talk to."

"That's what I'm worried about," Luca answered in jest as he walked away.

Charles made his move.

"Hello, Julia," Charles said smoothly from behind her.

Julia turned to be faced with his stunning blue eyes.

"Hello," she answered; already flattered he had remembered her name.

"We met briefly at York races didn't we?" Charles smiled. Julia nodded feeling childishly speechless and spellbound by his infinite charisma.

"Luca has just been telling me all about how lucky he feels being partnered by such a beautiful woman," Charles lied, edging closer to her.

She felt flattered. "Really?" Julia's smile grew.

Charles heard the hope in her voice. He returned a charming smile and held her gaze. Nervously Julia took a sip of her champagne.

"Oh yes," he assured quietly, "he was saying how wonderful life is for him at the moment, at the pinnacle of his career, experiencing one win after another and to top it all, he has a wonderful glamorous lady like you by his side. He feels like he is on top of the world."

Charles' eyes twinkled as he raised his eyebrows suggestively. "And who can blame him?"

Julia found herself beaming at Charles for the second time and suddenly felt very hot. "Do you live locally, Charles?" she asked, desperately trying to change the subject and avert his eyes.

"On the outskirts of Chelmsley," Charles answered, delighted that he had managed to unnerve her so soon.

"Where are you and Luca staying tonight?"

The bluntness to his question took her breath and caused her face to flush. "Erm, we, well I..." She stopped talking and edgily pushed one side of her hair behind her ear. "I'm going home tonight."

Charles blew out an enormous breath. "That must be a bloody tough call for the poor bugger; I bet he never wants you to leave his side."

Julia laughed. "I find that hard to believe, we haven't being seeing each other that long," she admitted coyly.

"Well never mind, no doubt he'll have you all to himself at Ascot next week."

"Ascot?" Julia frowned, "Why Ascot?"

Charles closed his eyes and faked self deprecation "Oh no, I've done it again." Charles grabbed her hand. "Between you and I, Julia, Luca has told me he wanted you to watch him race at Ascot next week, but you being such a lady he didn't know how to ask you." He looked into her eyes with a pleading sincerity. "Please don't tell him I have mentioned this to you, he is such a gentleman he would sizzle with embarrassment."

Julia's mind was already waltzing into oblivion at the thought of Luca even contemplating inviting her to Ascot.

Charles sensed her mind was racing and continued. "The Ascot week is one of the most important events of the racing calendar, especially with the ranking that Luca is heading for at present, he will be nervous and looking for support. The fact that he wants you there by his side speaks for itself of how highly he regards you. But I guess that me uncovering his truths has just added to his pressures." He strained a guilty expression.

"Oh don't worry, Charles," Julia soothed. "I won't breathe a word."

"Thanks." He took a sip of his drink and looked back at her, waiting for the right opportunity. "So, do you think you will go then?"

"He hasn't even asked me yet," Julia laughed.

Charles looked over at Luca at the far end of the room, he was surrounded by young pretty girls all of them smiling and laughing with him in conversation. Charles inadvertently alerted Julia to the scene with a flick of his head.

"Why do you women always expect the men to do all the work, can you not see that us guys need some reassurance from time to time also? The trouble is for us, it's always the ones we don't want to give us it that do!" he laughed.

Julia looked at the group of girls bestowing Luca with oodles of attention and then allowed the sense of his words to sink in.

Charles lowered his voice. "If I were you I would take the bull by the horns and ask him if you can accompany him to the races. I am sure you will be delighted with his response."

"Charles! Charles!" The pair of them heard a voice call his name, they both turned to see it was Rebecca. "Come over here Charles, there is someone I would like you to meet," she shouted. Charles swiftly made his apologies and walked away, a successful smile covered his face.

Julia stood within the crowded room, feeling nervous and alone she thought about her selfishness. Luca had travelled to see her most nights after his gruelling work schedule, he had listened and sympathised with her heartache over her mother, he had accepted that she would be the one to call him, he had invited her here tonight and had even posed for photographs with her, and then – she ran her hands across the glamour of her exquisite dress – he had bought her the most fantastic outfit she had ever worn in her life. She was like Cinderella running on free time, and she was going to wait for him to invite her to Ascot next week? No way, she concluded. She looked back at the girls that swarmed Luca like bees to a honey pot; Charles was right – she needed to make a move.

The band began to play one of her favourite songs and she felt the urge to dance. Never taking her eyes off Luca she walked confidently across the room and sidled up to the group of people at Luca's side, his eyes poured with pleasure when he saw her and he instantly put his arm around her waist. The conversation in the group temporarily ceased as one by one each individual took in her allure.

"Luca darling, I'm sorry to interrupt," Julia said in a voice that was as soft and as warm as melting butter, "please would you dance with me?" She smiled apologetically at everyone that was involved in his circle. His face beamed with pride and adoration for Julia and he duly apologised to the envious circle and followed her onto the dance floor.

"Thanks for that," he beamed.

"For what?" Julia asked, giving him a mischievous smile.

"Well, two things first of all for rescuing me from that crowd, they wouldn't let me go. But more so for being with me, here, tonight," he smiled.

She flung her arms around his neck and pulled him close to her body. For a few idle seconds she rubbed her nose against his, stared longingly into his dark brown eyes and wondered if she would ever get to know what really lay behind them. However, she recognised that this moment had to be consumed with the present, her past was behind her, and her future lay ahead, tonight she had to deal with this instant. She drew her face closer to him and rested her lips against his. He squeezed her waist hard and as their kiss was sealed with the slow burn of passion they became oblivious to the paparazzi flashes that welcomed their union.

Moments later Luca rested his head on Julia's shoulder whilst their bodies swayed in harmony to the music.

"I have a proposition for you," Julia said. "I would love to come and watch you racing next week in Ascot, would that be possible?"

"Without a shadow of a doubt it is," he answered, keeping his head on her shoulder. "It means everything to me that you would like to attend."

Julia took a deep breath and shut her eyes tight in trepidation of her next question. "And, will you join me in the hotel the night before? I don't want you to think I am taking things too fast or anything," she said quickly, "I just love the thought of holding you all night and waking up with you in the morning," she explained earnestly.

Luca took his head off her shoulder and stared at Julia; he gently placed his forehead onto hers and looked into her eyes.

"It would be my pleasure, my ultimate pleasure to share an evening with you." Once again, they kissed, this time it was the creation of new love that permeated their lips.

The evening was blazing ahead with storming success, amid loud music, copious amounts of alcohol and loud belts of laughter filling the elaborately decked marquee.

Rebecca and Charles had been sitting with mutual friends for the majority of the evening. Charles had welcomed the security their ten friends had offered around the table, they had acted as a buffer, protecting him from a hoard of ex lays that were mingling freely within the party. His fear of pissing one of them off and one of them causing a drunken scene in front of Rebecca was heightened when Emma and Sofia DeMario walked in.

Having arrived purposefully late in the hope their entrance would be grand and that their absence would make certain hearts grow fonder, they stood and surveyed the scene of drunken revellers. Thankfully they didn't feel out of place as they too had been drinking heavily in the back of their father's limousine, entertained by the Scissor Sisters album.

Sofia, looking stunning in a black gown etched with a heavy drape of golden sequins that trailed along the hem and bust-line, pointed towards a table.

"Hey, Emma!" she snapped. "Look, there's Charles over there, that's Rebecca Santé he's with isn't it?"

Emma followed her sister's gaze and felt the eager stab of firing jealousy course through her veins, but before she could answer Sofia drew on another sighting.

"Oh my God, I don't bloody believe it!" she gasped. "Look there's Luca with the thieving bitch that stole my badge at the races."

"Shit!" Emma snapped indignantly, secretly relieved that the attention had been cast away from Charles' possible indiscretion. "Come on, let's go and see what's going on."

Grabbing her sister's hand, Emma pulled Sofia towards Luca and Julia. It was at this time the dignified evening began to lose its air of reserve.

Chapter Fourteen

LUCA, still on the dance-floor with Julia's head buried into his shoulder, struggled to remember a time when he felt happier. The band, having belted out a full spectrum of crowd-pleasing songs had temporarily toned down the tempo allowing everyone to regain their breath; this respite included the band members.

The lead guitarist, Jed, fondly known as 'Jedder the Bedder' due to the unscrupulous manner in which he treated women, was a cockney, with a long, wild flowing mane and a penis to match. For the first time in his career as a singer he had gotten quite a fright when he had the shirt ripped off his back during their rendition of Queen's *Don't stop me now*.

Francesca stood on the dance-floor and her drunken eyes and mind wallowed in his physique. She stared at the muscles that lined his torso like a redundant abacus and as his shirt hit the floor she was the first to pick it up. Her earlier concern as to the limitations of her dress had long since dissolved, so as a result, she pulled the button-less shirt around her shoulders and allowed her body to writhe in rhythmic thrusts to the music. It was only when Jedder the Bedder saw this crazy woman scrambling onto the stage that he realised his present rendition of, *Living on a Prayer* was for him, more appropriate than he had intended it to be.

Francesca suggestively rubbed herself against the half naked rock warrior and slurred unspeakable suggestions into his ear. Jed's band mates struggled to keep the act together whilst they concealed their laughter during his ordeal. He, however, had not quite seen the funny side. There was only one place for his beloved guitar and it was definitely not going anywhere near the areas she was referring.

Luca, oblivious to the display, languished in the feel of Julia's blanket of soft hair against his face, allowing the hazy smell of her perfume to gently fill the confines of their private bubble. As their bodies moved in harmony to the music, even his fingertips tingled each time they skimmed across the sensual softness of her skin.

Julia felt a harsh tap on her shoulder; she turned to see Sofia looking aggressively drunk.

"Is that your handbag?" she shouted. "I thought I might borrow it if you don't mind." She snatched Julia's bag from her shoulder.

Luca grabbed his sister's arm, "What the fuck are you doing?" he blasted.

"We could ask you the same thing" she retorted sharply. "Do you make a habit of dating thieves or is this just another one of your charitable donations?" She pointed to Julia with disdain.

Julia found the truth behind the words too much. Snatching her bag from Sofia's hand she turned to Luca with giant tears drowning her eyes,

"I'm going, Luca, thank you for a lovely evening." Julia ran from the marquee.

"You bitches," he spat, before running after her.

Sofia watched Luca leave and felt slightly remorseful, aware that her brother would make sure she paid for her actions. Emma, on the other hand, felt devoid of guilt, instead she focused her attentions and emotions on Charles. Burning with envy towards Rebecca Santé and the fact that Charles had still not left her side, she started to think of ways she could distract his attention. Suddenly, she began to smile.

The shadows flickering against the caverns of the marquee ricocheted against her face, heightening the dramatic rich etching of eye pencil that surrounded her dark brown eyes. Her multi-coloured halter neck dress swooped down to her ankles and caressed the feminine curves of her body that wriggled beneath with unapologetic sexuality. As the lights sporadically threw a storm of moody shadows and coloured light strobes across her, Emma DeMario shook a number of male attendees with a look that resembled Bridget Bardot, yet disinterested in their charms and objectives, she continued to dwell on Charles.

"Stop looking at him, Emma, he's an absolute bastard," Sofia yelled over the music.

Emma frowned defiantly, "What are you talking about? He's only talking to her."

"Yes, for now," she answered, rolling her eyes at her sister's dismissal. "Like I said, Emma, he's a bastard and always fucking will be."

"Shut up, Sofia, you're only bloody jealous."

"You know what? I don't pissing think so," Sofia barked. Stiffly, she turned and headed toward a crowd of friends.

With her mission unappeased, Emma found her way to Hugo; casually she tapped him on his shoulder, interrupting his heated judgment on the Labour government and their wrongful introduction of the hunting ban.

"The sooner the Conservatives get back in and sort this fucking mess out the better," he ranted unaware that the friend, to whom he was airing his views, was so drunk he resembled a nodding Churchill dog in the back-shelf of a car.

"Anyway," he continued, "I think Conservatives will get in with a land slide at the next election, Labour haven't got a chance next time around, I mean tell me who would vote for dicks that put the rights of foxes before the country's economy?" He turned to Emma. "Don't you agree, Emma?"

She nodded and beckoned him closer. "Hugo, I've just been outside and I think someone was trying to break into Charles' car. I've alerted security, but it was so dark I didn't want to venture nearer. Will you tell him to check it out?" she said convincingly.

"Shit!" Hugo immediately plonked his drink on the bar. "Thanks, Emma, I'll tell him now."

Emma's smile broadened whilst she watched him rush over to Charles. Turning on her heels, she quickly slipped outside.

Charles had noticed that Rebecca had been drinking heavily, her speech was beginning to slur and he remembered how in the past, excessive alcohol had caused her defences to crack. He filled her glass.

"I hope you don't mind me mentioning it, Rebecca, but I've heard on the grapevine that Paris is pregnant with Gerard's baby."

"Oh, great! The whole bloody world knows I suppose. That's the only bloody downside to this place – everyone knows your bloody business all the time." She picked up her glass of wine and Charles watched as her mouth chased the glass for several seconds before she managed to take a large wanton slug.

"No, Rebecca, that's not true, Paris told me in confidence knowing that you and I are good friends," Charles explained.

Rebecca's eyes tried to focus on him.

"Are we good friendsh, Charles?" she slurred. "I mean, you know I am with Piersh, don't you? I just want you and I to be good friends, is that ok with you?" She didn't wait for him to answer. "Anyway, you are a good friend and I need to tell you something." She moved her chair closer to his and reached for the bottle of wine.

"You know, I have been trying for a baby with Piers now for quite a few yearsh but nothing has happened." She filled her glass to the brim. "I know it shounds shelfish but when Paris told me she was pregnant I felt jealous." She took another large gulp, managing to drain half the glass. "All I yearn for is a baby that I can love and call my very own. Do you have a shigarette?" she snapped moodily.

"You don't smoke, Rebecca," Charles laughed.

"I do when I'm pished." She looked puzzled. "Or is it when I'm pished off? Anyway, I can't remember now, I just want one."

Charles handed her a cigarette and his lighter, Rebecca began to light it.

"You can't smoke in here," Charles reminded her, "you'll have to go outside."

Rebecca looked back at him in drunken disdain. "Bollocksh, I'll pay the fine." She replaced the cigarette back in her mouth and began to chase the lighter's flame.

Hugo approached the table and bent to quietly tell Charles about the car. Charles filled Rebecca's glass, excused himself then fled outside.

Leaving the sound of the band booming unrepentantly behind him he made his way towards the car park. The orange flame of outdoor torches warmed the dark hallows of the night with their shimmering flicker and their light escorted him towards his beloved car.

He looked across and saw the faint outline of a shadow, the detail was obscure but he was certain there was someone on his roof. He ran towards it, the element of danger or fear never entering his mind, but as he neared, he slowed, instantly exchanging his aggressive expression for one of all consuming lust.

On the roof of his car, completely naked, Emma DeMario danced to the distant rumblings of the band. Charles stopped dead in his tracks and the only sign that he appreciated the private show was the slow creep of a flirtatious smile. Casually, he lit a cigarette and coolly blew the smoke up towards the moon, the only other spectator that had free viewing on this flawless display.

Her naked body against the darkness looked virginally pale, self illuminating the perfect scorings of her flat stomach and curving waist. Like a serpentine she twisted and arched her body seductively, her long hair chaotically falling against her alluring face with every gyrating pulse her hips sexily bestowed. The erotic darkened circles of her nipples, erect in response to the pinch of the evenings air, wiggled temptingly before him and beckoned him to advance. Charles threw his cigarette on the grass and walked towards her, unable to resist the seductive hammering her body was willing upon his own. He stood beneath her, his passion alive and evidently hard, slowly, still looking up at her, he unbuckled his belt.

Watching him give in to temptation Emma smiled and slowly slid down the windscreen, stretching out her voluptuous body against the cold shining bonnet. Charles grabbed her legs and pulled her forcefully to the bonnets edge. Steaming with desire, she kissed him hard, her hot sultry breaths barely able to contain their kiss. The pulsation for sex crowded his body; unable to wait a moment longer he satisfied her desires with long powerful thrusts that forced her moans and screams of gratification to fill the still night air. As Charles pounded himself against the beauty before him he gained further pleasure in that, at last, he had christened his prize possession.

Fifteen minutes later, returning from the loo after freshening up Charles was back with Rebecca. She looked up blankly as he sat beside her, as if she had hardly noticed he had gone.

"Are you alright?" he asked.

"No," she answered bluntly, with an emotional undercurrent flooding her tone.

"It will all be ok, Rebecca," he said, gently rubbing her back. "Nature would never be so cruel as to leave you without a baby." He saw her shoulders begin to quiver.

"I mish Gerard too," she began to sob. "The thought of Parish having half of Gerard with her every day makes me jealous too, I'm a shelfish bitch aren't I, Charles?"

Comforting her with his broad arm, he kissed the top of her head and placed his dinner jacket around her shoulders. His eyes scanned the revellers for sight of Hugo.

The party was now in full flow, the dance floor was heaving with a sea of smiling shining faces throwing their arms and bodies around the floor in drunken, careless, disharmony to the band's late night throb. A flashing kaleidoscope of colours raced by his eyes as an assortment of sexy evening-gowns swayed towards the dance floor, the inebriated girls within them, firmly gripping bottles and flutes of Don Perignon as though their life depended on it. His life, he decided, depended on being able to leave this place with Rebecca without Emma DeMario noticing.

A table in the far corner of the room drew Charles' attention. A waiter delivered a tray of vodka shots and ten bottles of Cristal champagne to the grateful applause and whoops of its occupants and brought Hugo into view.

"Right, let's do the boat race, come on girls, choose your drink!" he shouted.

The girls surrounding him giggled and whooped as Hugo handed out their shooters. "When we've finished this lot," he enthused, pointing at the enormous stockpile of booze, "we'll have some more, and then, I'll take you all for a ride to London in my helicopter, we could all be in Stringfellows for three." He let out a booming laugh, the girls, impressed by his bombastic approach followed suit. "One, two three down them!" he shouted.

Charles watched his brother's antics and the sea of heads that jerked backwards to drain their glasses and fleetingly he thought about the dirty sex he had undertaken with Emma only minutes ago. "When are you two boys going to have something real in your life?" His mother's words collected in his mind and the torment of guilt began to resurrect. At present his life was nothing more than a tomb of deceit, with debt, lies, unscrupulous sex and the artificial sedatives of drink and drugs to keep him feeling alive.

He looked back at Rebecca, gazing obliviously onto the dance-floor and realised that the answer he had craved for so long was sitting right in front of him. Rebecca Santé was somebody his mother would term as 'real.' The pair of them shared a parallel background, they understood and were already familiar with the intricacies of one another's families and they shared mutual friends. Furthermore, he thought keenly, judging by her words she was ready to settle down, she had just stated she wanted children. He sat back on his chair and smoothed his finger against his chin. With her wealth, his debts would be dissolved. With that thought he stood from his chair.

"Come on, Rebecca," he said helping her to her feet, "Let me take you home." As he ushered her to his car he had already made up his mind, Piers was not right for her, but *he* most certainly was and with Piers away he had the perfect opportunity to prove it to her.

Rebecca sat in the car and held her breath trying to rid herself of the hiccups. Charles opened all the windows in the hope of getting some fresh air onto her face during the short drive home. He watched as her drunken head wobbled like a puppet, and felt amused by her evening of inebriated candour. He thought about her dilemma. A baby was indeed just what Rebecca needed and deserved, she would make an incredibly fine mother. Piers was a fool not to have acted upon her desires. He smiled remembering the saying, 'one man's loss is another man's gain.'

A plan began to materialise in his mind, his eyes narrowed whilst he contemplated in detail its likelihood of success. Tenderly his hand touched her knee.

"You would be a natural mother Rebecca, absolutely fantastic," he told her softly.

Rebecca let out another hiccup and tried to sit up in her seat. "Oh shit!" she slurred "Shtop the car, shtop the car!" she shouted.

Charles stopped two seconds too late and Rebecca promptly vomited all over Charles' ivory leather interior.

"Oh dear, I'm so shorry." Rebecca looked at him in shock and panic, fully aware of the love he had for his car, but seeing the devastation on his face made her giggle.

"It's okay," he answered coldly, "we're nearly home now. I'll clean it off when we get back."

By the time they had arrived home, Rebecca was beginning to sober up a little. Charles insisted that he clean the car immediately and went outside, while Rebecca put on some music in the drawing room and changed from her vomit- drenched dress into her dressing-gown. She made Charles a scotch and poured herself a mineral water.

Feeling ill from the stench, Charles walked in after scrubbing the car.

"Thanks for being such a good friend to me Charles," Rebecca said.

"I want to help you, Rebecca, with any problem you have. Come on, let's dance." He beckoned her over to him.

She walked over and sank her head into his dependable shoulders, swaying her body against his whilst Lionel Ritchie reminded Charles that Rebecca certainly was not only once, twice but three times a lady.

"I love you Rebecca, I really do."

"Charles, please don't."

The doorbell rang, they stared at each other and Rebecca glanced at the clock, it was past midnight. Who could be here at this time of night?

Mrs Santé walked into the room; with a worried look on her face she gave them both a grimaced smile.

"Rebecca" she said hesitantly, "it appears you have a visitor." She turned to the doorway of the drawing room.

Piers stood before them, with a thunderous look in his eye he held up a bottle of champagne.

Chapter Fifteen

REBECCA woke up at 6a.m. and heard her father standing on the landing outside her room complaining bitterly about the electric gates.

"We'll have to call the engineer out today. That's the second time they have opened obligingly, firstly Paris and now him," she heard him tell her mother.

Her head was spinning like a Catherine wheel. *Now him? What is he talking about?* She lay still, and willed her eyes to focus. Slowly, the events of the night before came seeping back to her muffled memory.

She remembered herself, in a short dressing gown, dancing softly in Charles' embrace, and then …

"Oh no!" she groaned as she remembered Piers turning up and the dreadful argument that had ensued. Inevitably, Rebecca had turned her embarrassment to a drunken conversation about motherhood.

"Oh Grrreat!" he had shouted. "Who the fuck do you think you are, throwing all this in my face the minute I walk through the door?"

"I am somebody that wants a fucking baby, Piers!" she had screamed uncontrollably. "Above all else, that is what I want," she continued, "and *you* can't give me one!" She fell on the floor sobbing in a drunken stupor.

"Great!" he had shouted throwing his arms into the air in despair. "Welcome home my *infertile* husband, Piers". These had been his last words before he stormed out of the house.

She rushed out of bed and pulled on some jodhpurs that were folded neatly in the drawer and quickly wrenched her arms through an old T-shirt, dashing past her parents still in deep discussion on the landing, she ran outside in a desperate attempt to find him.

Piers sat outside on the bench he had called home for the night. On hearing the back door opening he looked up to see Rebecca looking remorseful and pale.

"I'm sorry, Piers."

"What are you sorry for? All you've done is confirm my thoughts. I knew it would be a bloody nightmare if I came back here. It's just a recipe for complete disaster." His eyebrows were furrowed, his green eyes emblazoned in temper.

"Don't say that, Piers," she said. "It's all my fault, I was the nightmare not anyone or anything else." She sat down on the bench next to him and tried to reach out for his hand. He snatched it away.

"Don't you see, Rebecca? It doesn't matter whose fault it was, the facts cannot be ignored."

"What facts?" she asked, her aching head begging for the conversation to end.

"I made the effort to fly over here, against my better judgement, knowing that you were upset about Gerard, the IVF and Paris' baby. Do you know how hard it is for me to come here?" he asked pointedly. "Tell me, Rebecca," he continued without waiting for her reply, "how do you think I feel when Charles Lancaster-Baron is back in hot pursuit, trying desperately to get back in your knickers? Your mother and father, who hate me, are delighted to have you back in the fold, leaving me, once again the complete outcast. Oh yes! And let's not forget the crowning glory, you insult me within minutes by reminding me I'm infertile and insist that we either go for IVF here or we are over!" he shouted. "All in a matter of only weeks of being apart." He laughed savagely at the irony.

"Piers, that's not true, you're not the outcast. And probably what I told you last night came out completely wrong, I was pissed, I'm sorry." She moved closer to him. He stood up.

"So, in that case then, what you will be telling me is that we can go home, now together, forget about the IVF and leave all this behind us, yes?" he snapped pointing dismissively to the family home.

"Look," Rebecca paused to take a deep breath, "I know this is all hard for you, but we have all found it hard."

"Oh! It's the royal WE again is it?" he snapped.

"Please, Piers, stop it and listen to me. We have only just buried Gerard. It is impossible for me to leave Dad with the business at the moment. Surely you can understand that?" she pleaded.

"No," he shook his head, "not particularly, he managed before without you, he'll manage again. But, you still haven't answered me. What about this IVF you were demanding last night?" he urged forcefully.

"I can't talk to you about that now, Piers." Rebecca nodded to the car that had just parked up in the yard.

It was David, the head lad, and Mel joining the rest of the staff for morning feed and exercise. The horses neighed and kicked at their stable doors in appreciative recognition as the pair got out. David saw Rebecca talking to the stranger; it was 6.20am, who was here at this time of the morning?

"Is everything ok Rebecca?" David asked, giving Piers a suspicious glance.

"Oh, for fuck's sake! Even the fucking minions are at it now!" Piers stormed away and got into his hire car. He slammed the driver's door shut and before Rebecca could dissuade him otherwise he was racing down the drive.

"For future reference, David, that was Piers, my partner," Rebecca snapped before stamping into the house and slamming the door behind her.

James Santé had been watching and listening to the whole conversation from his bedroom window. He couldn't stand the thought of her leaving again. Aside from his wife, the only person he could think of that would feel the same was Charles. He was desperate for advice. He decided it was too early to call him now; he would wait a couple of hours.

Two hours later Charles was sitting at the dining table with his mother. The table had been set for three but Hugo, unsurprisingly, had not yet arrived home. Even though it was early in the morning, Kitty, as always, had dressed for breakfast.

The loose cerise pink blouse she had chosen emphasised the loveliness of her sapphire blue eyes, the high romantic ruffle of its chic neckline tickled the tip of the large diamond clusters she wore in her ears. Her navy calf-length skirt, felt comfortable and, unlike the last time she had worn it three months ago, had now ceased to dig into her waist. Her hair was immaculate, with high rolling blonde waves crowning her face; she had only loosely groomed it that morning, being reluctant to disturb the curls that Mary had worked so hard to put in place the day before. She looked over at her son as he ended his conversation on the phone.

"Don't worry, I'll sort it, James." Charles, being ever mindful of his mothers' presence, had listened with interest to James' one sided conversation.

"What was that about?" she asked helping herself to a thin slice of smoked salmon and a very small portion of scrambled eggs, her appetite, she noticed, was decreasing every day.

Charles shrugged casually, "Oh, it was James, he wondered if I could help with transport to Ascot next week for a couple of his stable lads."

He reached for a slice of wholemeal toast and attacked it ravenously with a determined crunch. Grabbing the Sunday Times he buried his head into the business section in the hope his mother was satisfied with his reply. She would be incensed if she knew the detail of James' conversation about his daughter. She had warned her friend years ago not to interfere between his daughter and Piers, but he hadn't paid the slightest bit of attention.

"Give the girl a free rein, James, let her make her own mistakes. If you don't you will drive her away." she had warned confidently. Kitty watched her son's bogus claims to read the paper. "How was your evening with Rebecca last night?" she asked.

Casually, Charles raised his head from the broadsheet. "Sorry?" he asked idly.

"Rebecca," she repeated, "how is she?" She stared across the table, the shrewdness in her eyes trapping his stare.

"Oh yes." He spoke quickly. "Rebecca, yes she was fine, obviously she has a lot on her mind at the moment, but she's doing well, overall." He smiled indifferently before returning to *The Times*.

"And what about Piers, is he over yet?" She held her hand in front of her and admired her diamond engagement ring that sat above the plain gold band of her wedding ring. The three large diamonds sparkled effortlessly in the sunlight.

"Yes, I believe he landed last night or early this morning, one of the two," he replied, this time keeping his eyes firmly fixed to the page.

"I hope they're happy," she said, still staring at her diamonds, though covertly glancing at him from the corner of her eye. "True love is such a blessing."

Charles did not respond. Kitty stared at her son's broad masculine shoulders and his strong handsome face. He was a man, and yet, her memories of his childhood were as vivid as if they were yesterday. She remembered his eyes as he sat on his dormitory bed, looking up at her like a puppy from a basket willing her to take him home.

"Don't worry Mrs Lancaster–Baron," the housemistress of Eton had assured, "he will be well looked after here. We promise you he will return to you a man."

She had cried solidly for the next two weeks and had prayed for him to have an accident on the rugby pitch that forced him to come home for recuperation. Her prayer was never answered. Instead, with each term that passed, her son's independence increased and simultaneously, the letters and calls she received from him reduced.

"They will be fine," her husband Charles had assured her when a few terms later she had had to face the whole drama again when Hugo was sent. "All boys have to go through it, I went, it made a man of me, and it certainly never did me any harm." *Had he been wrong?* she wondered.

Mary the housekeeper knocked on the dining room door before entering. "I have prepared lunch for your bridge friends, Mrs L.B." She smiled warmly, "I have made it for eight, is that right?"

Kitty smiled warmly toward her irreplaceable housekeeper and friend. "Yes, Mary, that's perfect, now you get home to your own family. You have done quite enough for a Sunday. Oh! And don't come in until lunchtime tomorrow. Take the morning off, I have a visitor tomorrow morning." Kitty saw Charles' head rise from the paper.

Mary said, "Oh thank you, that's very kind, there are a few jobs I would love to catch up on in town, those few extra hours will be much appreciated."

"That is my pleasure," Kitty replied. "Now go straight away before you see something else you want to do." Kitty smiled.

"Goodbye Mrs L.B. Goodbye Charles."

"Goodbye," they replied in unison.

"Who's coming tomorrow?" Charles asked with a quizzical look in his eyes.

"Hugh Stephenson, the solicitor, I'm thinking of selling some of our land so that I can spend the money on some new diamonds," she said.

She saw panic solidify in Charles' face.

"What?" he spluttered

"Oh, you seem a bit shocked, Charles. How could your mother possibly spend *your* inheritance? Was that the question drowning your mind?" she laughed.

"No, no, no," Charles shook his head vehemently, "I didn't mean it like that, you can do what you want with the money. It's yours."

"Oh that's kind of you to give me permission, but it's lucky for you I was only joking." She stood from the table and smiled mischievously. "If you two boys didn't spend so much on your vulgar contraptions," she said pointing to the helicopter parked in the grounds, "you wouldn't care what I did with the money." She walked over and placed a hand on his shoulder. "Remember, Charles, money talks, wealth whispers". He rolled his eyes at the worn saying.

Kitty left the room; she needed to make a call, in the privacy of her bedroom.

Two hours later, with still no sign of Hugo, Charles sat in his car outside the Montford's house. With the previous night's decisions firmly implanted and James Santé's words ringing in his ears, the time had come for business.

Chapter Sixteen

CHARLES looked round at the bleak austerity of Goldsborough Crescent and its meagre effort to replicate the image of wealth. It had been the only time Charles had ever frequented 'the estate,' having been fortunate enough to have never been in a situation grave enough to warrant the venture.

He could see the net curtains twitching at one of the Montfords' windows and could imagine that Francesca was burning with curiosity to know what had instigated his visit. He got out of the car and walked up to the brightly painted red door and grimaced slightly at the stark newly polished brass fittings that heightened the dwellings vulgarity. Just as he was about to knock, the door flew open.

"Charles, how wonderful to see you," crooned Mrs Montford before clearing her throat to pitch much huskier tones. "To what do we owe this pleasure?" she asked, arching a neat, pencilled eyebrow in anticipation. "Do come in." She smiled, but felt disappointed. Although she had managed to finish her housework she had not yet managed to clear away her cleaning paraphernalia.

Charles walked inside and immediately felt the smell of fresh polish and plug in air-fresheners assault his throat. He stared in disbelief at the clinical surroundings of the hallway. The tram lines left by the vacuum cleaner were newly engrained in the thick pile of the ivory carpet, a feather duster was perched on its head in the corner, its pink coronet of feathers lying ready for the next attack upon potentially concealed cobwebs, and a can of polish stood rigidly on a repro telephone table with a golden duster perched on its head. Charles thought how apt it was that Francesca's house should be so clean. His mother had always stated that housework was a pastime invented only by the bored middle classes, all of whom had an aching need to impress their frightful neighbours.

His eyes casually wandered, taking in the tacky distaste of the décor and felt haughtily amused by his surroundings. The straight contemporary lines of the furniture, every piece placed with strategic objective made every essence of the home feel cold. The black faux chandeliers hanging from the ceiling shuddered in inferior shame as his eyes fled past them, as though aware of Charles' daily contact with the real McCoy. Vibrant canvasses glared blatantly from the white impersonal walls, whilst glass wall lamps hanging over them waited patiently to illuminate them. The house reminded him of a private hospital, a place where MRSA would never survive.

Francesca watched his eyes fleetingly scour her home and felt gratified that, with the help of her interior designer, her four-week annual modernisation programme had recently been completed.

"I've come to see Paris if I may, is she around?" Charles was in no mood for flirtation.

Mrs Montford allowed her disappointment to surface. "Why in God's name do you want to speak to Paris?" she snapped.

Realising her comments were lacking in maternal warmth, she smiled falsely and hastily back-tracked.

"Well, it's just that the poor mite is a little under the weather at the moment, especially at this time of day. She doesn't usually get up for another hour or so, well at least ten anyway."

"Mum, I'm here." Simultaneously they both stared up to the top of the stairs. There crouched a pale, miserable-looking girl, swamped beneath a large oversized cardigan that hung over her denim jeans.

"I hope this isn't a bad time for you, Paris. I wondered if you could spare me a minute or two of your time." He walked to the foot of the stairs and stared up at Paris. She looked haunted, like a wild animal fixed in a trap.

Paris was taken aback, *why would Charles want a couple of minutes of my time?* She looked down at her mother who was also eager to learn the reason for Charles' visit.

Charles looked back at Francesca wondering how he was going to get Paris on her own. "Shall we go for a drive in the car?"

"Okay," she said sullenly. She wiped her face with the back of her bobbled cardigan and walked down the stairs.

Good God, Charles thought, *she isn't even going to get changed or wash her face, thank God for privacy glass.*

Minutes later, Mrs Montford, feeling rabidly envious, sneered her goodbyes as they walked out of the door.

"*What does he want with her?*" she whispered to herself in deep thought.

They drove for a short while before Charles pulled the car into a quiet lay-by. He switched off the engine and looked at her pale unhappy face.

"Paris, I hope you don't mind me coming to see you." Paris shook her head. Charles continued. "I heard last night that you are pregnant with Gerard's baby."

Paris nodded and hung her head in shame. Charles spoke softly, "Gerard was a good of friend of mine; we talked a lot about many things. He talked a lot about you to me, and he loved you very much. You know it would break his heart to see you so miserable, don't you?" He gently rubbed his hand against her arm in a friendly gesture.

"Did he really say he loved me, Charles? Really?" Her pleading eyes looked back at him, eagerly awaiting confirmation of his words.

"Yes, he did, he said you were a wonderful woman, Paris." He sounded sincere. "I know he would want you to be looked after, that is why I am here." Charles reassured himself, that part of the story was true. Gerard and Charles had been good friends, they had spent a lot of time chatting about old times and the future, including the vast family fortune he would one day inherit. The fact that Gerard hadn't really mentioned Paris was immaterial.

"What do you mean? Why are you here?" Paris asked.

"Well, I can only imagine how hard it must be for you to be faced with pregnancy at such a young age, especially when the father has died." He casually wrapped his arm around the back of her seat.

Paris nodded. "I don't know what to do; my head is all over the place, one minute I think I want to keep it the next I feel consumed with the idea of having an abortion." She was aware she was blurting out her feelings but felt grateful for having the opportunity to do so. There was only so much a daughter could tell her father. Charles nodded in understanding. "That's only natural, and only you can make the decision as to what you want to do. But, one thing I will say is that Gerard would not like to see you struggle and feel wretched. I know he would hate to see you keep the baby simply because you thought that was the right thing to do for him." He sighed sympathetically. "It's hard for us all, but we have to remember he's not here anymore."

"I know, I don't need reminding of that," she whimpered, her bottom lip beginning to quiver again.

"Look Paris, I'm going to tell you something now." He shuffled on his car seat making the pretence of moving closer towards her. "I am not a woman but I do know that any decision I make I have to have all the options in front of me before I make one." He placed his arm around her shoulder and looked into her eyes. "You see, you think at the moment you only have two options, keeping it and having that responsibility for the rest of your life, or getting rid of it. In fact, Paris, what I am here to tell you is that you have three."

Paris frowned. "Why? What's the third option?"

Charles paused, and then sighed as if this was that hardest thing to tell her. "This is not easy to say to you but I know Gerard would want me to be completely honest. You have to promise me that what I say now remains within the confines of this car." He looked back at her with an eagle stare.

Paris nodded, allowing Charles to continue.

"Rebecca cannot have children, she has tried very hard with her partner, Piers, but it seems her fate has been sealed and having a baby of her own is not an option. Her heart yearns for a baby and when she found out about your situation she thought this could be a way you could help each other."

The deep frown on Paris' face indicated further confusion.

"What I mean is," Charles continued, "if you were thinking of not having the baby, the Santés have offered to give you money for the baby and then they take custody." Charles waited for a reaction but Paris remained motionless. Charles, feeling uncomfortable with the silence, continued to elaborate. "They have told me to tell you they would pay a handsome price for the honour and privilege of still having a piece of Gerard around them."

Paris was stunned. Rebecca Santé wanted to buy her baby from her? Subconsciously she recognised that Charles was continuing to talk but every one of his words went unrecognised as she fell into a trance. Only his concluding sentence of, "So, what do you think?" managed to bring her round.

Her voice allowed the poison of her thoughts to escape. "You people make me sick. Take me home please." Paris stared out of the windscreen.

Charles tried to interject, "But, Paris ..."

"I said, take me home. NOW!" she said forcefully.

The short journey to Goldsborough Crescent was uncomfortable. Her anger was such it infiltrated the car with a stony silence. Paris got out of the car, slammed the car door and walked into the house without offering another word to Charles.

Charles crashed his fist hard against the steering wheel. He had moved too fast, she needed time and certainly persuasion. He chastised himself for making inaccurate presumptions regarding Paris; he had falsely believed she would be a replica of her money hungry mother. He sighed, reminding himself that all was not lost, now his second plan had to come into force.

His heart sank as he briefly considered the method he would have to use to accomplish his aim of ensuring Rebecca got this baby. He shuddered, revolted by his thoughts. He placed his foot on the accelerator of the car and felt its powerful engine surge. There was no time to dwell on that, he was on his way to the second meeting of the day. Having arranged to meet this next 'lady' away from prying eyes, especially from her sister's, Sofia DeMario was next on the list of accomplices.

Chapter Seventeen

REBECCA looked out of her office window; some of the horses, injured earlier in the season, were grazing contentedly in the lush summer paddocks with the final rays of the afternoon's sunshine resting soothingly upon their backs.

She had not heard from Piers since their argument that morning, but neither had she called him. She thought it more suitable to give him time to cool off and clear his head, perhaps then, he would see things her way. She looked at her Cartier watch; it was just past six in the evening. It had been almost twelve hours since their argument – time enough, she decided, for him to have seen sense. She decided to finish the last pile of essential paperwork and then she would give him a call. She heard her father shouting her.

"Rebecca! Rebecca!" he called. She opened her office door and saw her father standing at the bottom of the hallway.

"Come here, I've got something for you." He looked delighted. "Come on, come on! Hurry!" he hastened, beckoning her with sweeping hands.

He led her by the hand out into the courtyard. She saw several staff milling around a stable. Her father, still holding her hand, rushed her over to join the group. She peered over the stable door. A nervous prize yearling filly was dazedly standing in the stable with a pink ribbon hanging loosely around its neck.

"This is for you, my darling." Her Father held her face within his hands. "If it's okay with you I would like us to call it 'Rebecca's Pride'."

"Isn't she beautiful?" one of the stable girls commented with a broad smile. Rebecca was amazed, "Oh, Daddy, she's magnificent," she said. "Thank you!"

She flung her arms around her father's neck and squeezed him tightly.

His father told her with genuine certainty, "Like you, this horse will be a winner. You have done a great job for us, Rebecca, we don't know how we would get through this without you."

"Thank you! Thank you, Daddy!" Rebecca danced on the spot. "I am so excited!"

Her father beamed at his daughter's sheer delight. "Why don't you call Piers, let's all have a drink together?" He smiled, looking out onto the paddocks. "It's a glorious summer's evening. Let's enjoy each other's company."

Rebecca's heart swelled, her father really did just want to bury the past and start again. She wished Piers had been by her side to witness the authenticity in his voice.

"Yes, yes I will." Her eyes shone in appreciation. "I'll call him now."

Taking her mobile from her pocket she walked away from the small gathering to make the call in privacy. His mobile rang. He answered without a greeting, the only thing Rebecca could here was loud music and scant chattering in the background.

"Piers?" she asked, "Are you there?" She was becoming annoyed with the silence. "Are you in a bar?" she snapped.

Piers disconnected the call and walked outside to light a cigarette, he was not a habitual smoker but felt this situation was too much to resist a full-strength Marlboro. It would always be the same in that Santé' family, just impossible to get anywhere near any of them, especially when they were all together. He saw Rebecca's number flash up on his phone for the second time but again disconnected the call. He stamped on his cigarette and walked back inside the bar.

A dark glass mirror filled the back wall and attracted the last remnants of the day's sun to pour upon it, creating a moody ricochet of gold and bronze across the room. When he had arrived he was the only customer in the bar, but now, the Sunday evening's good weather had managed to attract a swelling of swanky customers through its doors. He sat at his table and took a sip of the champagne out of the fine cut crystal glass and scoured the room, drinking in the laughter and chatter that bounced off the walls.

"Hi!" A perky female voice caught his attention.

He glanced up to see a young woman in front of him. She must have been around nineteen years old with stunning dark looks that lay in striking contrast to the feminine ivory outfit she was wearing. He was instantly impressed by her elegance.

"Do I know you?" He asked with indifference.

She sensed his arrogance, liked it, and then briefly studied him. His dark curly hair lay ruffled against his dark imposing face and the sexy shade of stubble teased his plump dry lips into a subtle shade of red. He looked like a handsome rogue, fresh from the rugby field, she thought fleetingly.

"Yes, you know me," she laughed quietly, "but it was a few years ago since we were first introduced, I'm Sofia DeMario." She held out her hand and exposed two enormous diamond rings.

He held it for a moment longer than necessary, allowing himself to be captured by the warmth of her large magnetic eyes that were as dark as earth.

"You've changed slightly since the last time I saw you." His eyes caressed her body with blatant appreciation. "Can I get you a drink? I'm on Krug; would you care to join me?"

She hesitated, looking across at the group of friends with whom she'd arrived. Seeing they were all content, she shrugged her shoulders. "Sure, why not?"

She sat down at his table. Piers clicked his fingers to a passing waiter gesturing an order for another bottle before returning his attention to his guest.

The lights in the bar dimmed signalling that it was the beginning of the evening and time for the candles at the tables to be lit. A waiter flicked his lighter and ignited the candle to produce a golden flame. The romantic flicker of the candle triggered her dark Italian skin to glow alluringly. She pushed her black straight hair from her face and smiled, her hands caught his attention, her nails were long and flaunted a perfect French manicure. *How refreshing*, he thought, *unlike Rebecca's these will be free of horse shit.* The waiter arrived with their champagne.

"Shall I pour?" Sofia asked with a tempting smile.

God, she is fucking sexy! he thought. He nodded, feeling slightly concerned. Closing his eyes for a split second he prayed for the willpower to be strong enough to refuse the temptation of this lethal cocktail. He knew from experience that a sexy woman and lashings of alcohol burnt away common sense. He opened his eyes and loosened his shirt collar from around his neck.

"Cheers!" She passed him his glass.

"Cheers!" Piers replied, gently chinking her glass against his own. Momentarily their gaze imprisoned them both.

"What are you doing here anyway?" Sofia asked identifying a definite chemistry. "I mean, shouldn't you be with Rebecca?" Sofia wanted the question to sound casual, but intrigued as to his status, she felt compelled to ask.

Piers froze, his expression tipped stonily cold, informing Sofia she had made a mistake. "I will answer your first question," he replied dismissively. "What am I doing here? Well, quite simply I am here to enjoy myself" He topped up his champagne and paused as the bottle chinked against her glass. "I trust you are out for the same reason?"

"Yes I am," she laughed.

"Then I will fill your glass up as well," he joked, filling her glass to the rim with a froth of bubbles.

Having shared a further two bottles of Krug, Piers had enjoyed Sofia's company, they had laughed and talked endlessly, both of them surprised at the number of common acquaintances and friends they shared.

"What time is it?" Piers asked.

"Nine thirty," Sofia replied

"I'm starving," Piers said. "I haven't eaten a thing all day, I'm beginning to see double," he laughed. "Will you join me for some food? I know a fabulous bistro I used to frequent down Queen's Street. I don't know what it's like now but I would love to try it again." He winked at her playfully, now feeling positively drunk. "It used to have a wonderful hotel attached to it with the most enormous four poster rooms, once I almost drowned in one of the Jacuzzis when I fell asleep in it after too much champagne."

"Old habits die hard, I see," she answered, chinking her empty glass of champagne against his.

"Come on; let's see if it's still there," he suggested, steadying himself as he stood.

They sat alone in the warm cosy bistro; a banquet of seafood filled their table. Finding the fresh air from the walk enjoyable yet sobering, Piers ordered more champagne and the two of them began to share the tempting display of food. The Lobster Thermidor sat swimming in a melted sea of garlic butter. Piers took the initiative and fed Sofia one of the rich bite size chunks. She lent forward, all the while staring into his eyes, and gently she slid the food off his fork with her teeth, a small drizzle of the garlic butter oozing down her chin. Piers took his finger and followed the contours of her lips and chin and gently wiped the butter clean, slowly placing his finger in his mouth to suck away the remnants. Sofia felt the sexual permutation of his actions flood through her body. She wanted this man, and what Sofia DeMario wanted, she had to get.

Demurely she placed her elbows on the table, rested her face in the cups of her hands and looked at him across the candlelit table.

"Well, we've found that your bistro is still here." Her eyebrows raised in sultry anticipation. "What about those four-poster bedrooms?"

Piers smiled, and reached for his cigarettes. He lit one and casually reclined in his chair.

"You're not allowed to smoke in here," Sofia gasped. Piers shrugged. "Fuck them…"

Sofia laughed aloud at his confidence and smiled back at him as he stared at her across the table.

"You're fucking gorgeous, you know that don't you?" he asked, blowing his smoke in the air. He looked at her quizzically before adding, "And what would you say if I told you I had already booked a room?" His eyes narrowed as he played with the smoke in his mouth, blowing smoke rings towards her through the sex fuelled air.

"I would say that it would be a crying shame if a man like you went into that room without company," she smiled.

"I think you are absolutely right." He returned her smile. Then, stubbing out his cigarette onto his dinner plate he grabbed the bottle of champagne, took her hand and gently led her from the table.

They entered the room without words. She placed her opened bag on the bedside table and stared with anticipation at the finely carved four-poster bed. He walked closer and faced her, both of them remained silent neither one wishing to break the electric charge that surrounded them. Confidently he began to kiss her, slowly yet with meaning, gently holding her face within his hands before using the tender sway of his powerful body to ease her onto the bed. He lay on top of her, the entrapment of their locked eyes remained as their lips moved in unison with the intermittent horny flick of his tongue signalling his unquenchable desire. His thick manly fingers stroked her black hair that was splayed out behind her on the white cotton sheets. She felt a thrill of excitement ripple across her taut body as his hands explored her chest and roamed passionately beneath her white lace La Perla bra, her nipples were erect, yearning for him to take them in his mouth. He blew on them teasingly whilst his eyes explored every inch of her fantastic body. The delay was too much for her to bear she gave out a muffled distant moan, pleading with him to continue. Satisfying her pleas he licked around the dark hard edges of her nipples before taking one, then the other into the warm confines of his mouth. Gently he sucked and probed allowing his force to increase as her writhes of ecstasy grew stronger. His hands continued to explore. He unzipped her trousers to reveal a perfect landing strip of black velvet, he groaned adoringly, relishing the fact she had been out all evening without knickers.

With a feeling he was about to explode he slid her long firm legs apart and began to ravish her dampness with his mouth and tongue, kissing and licking until she twisted and arched herself beneath his face. She moaned, panted and writhed in pleasure, and just listening to her wanting made Piers realise he couldn't wait a second longer; he ached to be inside her. He slid up her body and she, with a wild, insatiable passion, yanked and tore at his shirt and trousers, sending a scattering of buttons across the room. Stripped naked, he stared into her eyes with a boldness that electrified her, then, powerfully, he plunged himself inside her. Sofia gasped in total satisfaction.

Chapter Eighteen

"MMMM. A good performance. Well done!" he purred. Charles Lancaster- Baron turned off the DVD and swivelled his chair around to face Sofia, he looked dangerously composed. He sat back in his chair and put his legs up on his hand- crafted oak desk, causing dried mud from his leather riding boots to fall onto the chaotic scattering of papers lying on top. His brilliant blue eyes shone with triumph, he stared at Sofia allowing a sinful smile to adorn his face.

"Your true vocation has been overlooked, you should have been an actress, you nearly had me fooled on that film." Slowly he rubbed his hands together in gloating satisfaction. "Now all we need to do is get this delivered." He tapped the DVD case on the desk.

Sofia felt exhausted. What little sleep she had managed to get had been numbed by the painful after effects of the champagne. Her head was banging and, unlike the evil perpetrator sitting in front of her, she felt traumatised by the set up.

"Please Charles, this wasn't a performance," she pleaded, "I really have fallen for him, please let's not give this to Rebecca." She placed her fingers on her throbbing temples trying desperately to think of a suitable solution. "Look, I don't care about her, it's Piers I care about. I don't want him to know that I slept with him as a set up." An idea entered her head. "I know!" She looked at him pleadingly. "I could have an affair with him and make him leave Rebecca, that way we will all be happy."

Charles saw the desperation in her eyes and began to laugh, making the sarcastic gesture of playing a violin.

"Oh you've turned into a romantic all of a sudden have you?" he laughed. "This is the best rendition of pride and prejudice I've ever seen!" Coldly he tore through the facts. "So, let's get this straight, then. You would rather that I showed your father footage of you having drug-fuelled sex whilst a load of drunken men look on?" He laughed out loud. "You know as well as I do that wouldn't be a good idea, he would disown you."

He took his feet off the desk, pushed his chair aggressively forwards and leant threateningly towards her. She could feel the warmth of his breath on her face as he spoke.

"And so would I if you were my daughter. I don't have the time to wait for a cheap little tart like you to get a real woman's husband to leave home." He reached across and gently nipped her chin, "Sorry," he added with a sarcastic smile.

Feeling as though her skin had been poisoned by his touch, Sofia quickly drew away. She knew there was no use tying to talk to him; blackmail and deceit were a common occurrence in his life. She had no choice but to go ahead with the appalling plan. She didn't want to disgust and shame her father and neither did she want her sister Emma to find out what this bastard had done the night he had drugged her drinks.

"How the fuck do you sleep at night, Charles?" Sofia asked coldly.

Charles laughed. "Come now, Sofia, both you *and* your sister know the answer to that one!"

Without saying another word she walked out of his home.

Charles held the recording close to his chest. This would surely pull Rebecca another step closer to him.

Two miles down the road an invisible intruder had witnessed the private conversation. The tape laboriously turned, mechanically unaware of the deceit and immorality that covered it.

Chapter Nineteen

AFTER ENDURING a one hour stint in the confines of his sauna in the hope of losing two pounds, Luca had showered, packed his bag for Ascot and then faced a second test to his fortitude, only this one made him more irritable than the first.

The smell of his mother's freshly baked bread and croissants drifted towards him in warm heavenly gallops, causing his hunger to increase with such vigour that he felt dizzy. Experience had taught him that if he ignored it, then in time the feeling would disappear. He continued to look for the *Racing Post*, rummaging through the kitchen cupboard where the last two days' papers were neatly concealed and tried to console his hunger with the promise of dinner with Julia later in the evening.

He was so looking forward to being with her tonight. However, there was a price to be paid for everything; he would have to set off early to get to Ascot, talks with the trainer, a brief walk of the course to check the ground conditions and a thorough appraisal of his competition, all needing to be completed before he could relax with her. They had discussed the ridiculous episode at the ball caused by his sisters. He was still furious with them, but though the incident had upset Julia it had never entered her mind to take it out on him. He was grateful for that and it emphasised further just what a special lady she was.

"What are you looking for?" his father asked.

"*The Racing Post*," Luca answered bluntly, hearing his father slicing a chunk of warm bread.

"Well, if you spent less time with the ladies and more time on your work, you just might have a better chance of finding it," Frankie advised with authority.

"You need plenty of fresh butter on that, Frankie," Maria told him, referring to the warm bread.

Luca felt his stomach groan in pain. "And what would you know about any women in my life?" he snapped, swinging round from the cupboard.

Frankie swerved the directness of his son's question. "You shouldn't be getting bogged down with girlfriends at this stage of your career," Frankie bit back. "A keen focus and hard work is the key. The only thing a woman will do is throw you off course."

Maria shot a look of indignation to her husband, "You take no notice of him," she told Luca whilst spreading the doorstep slices of bread with lashings of butter. "He's a romantic at heart. If you do have a girlfriend my son, you are welcome to bring her round here, take no notice of him."

"Talking of my hard work and focus," Luca responded sarcastically to his father, "The Italian Job is favourite tomorrow, are you coming to Ascot to watch her run?"

Two pairs of moody black eyes met across the kitchen.

"No, I doubt it," Frankie responded, quickly recognising he had had his fill of racecourses for the present. "If I don't make it, I will watch you from the television." Frankie bit into his warm hunk of bread, reminding Luca once again in stomach-hungry spasms his need for hard work and focus.

Luca couldn't stand the uninvited advice or the temptation of the food any longer. "I'm going now," he told his parents. "I'll see you in a couple of days."

He walked outside, packed his bag in the boot then turned for the driving door to see Sofia speeding up the drive like a maniac in her Porsche Carrera.

She screeched to a halt outside the DeMario mansion, slicing a throw of gravel into the air and then just sat, staring ahead. Now home, Sofia realised it had been adrenaline alone that had given her the strength to get here and that now, having reached her destination, she felt drained of everything. Only the burning hatred she harboured for Charles allowed her revengeful thoughts to roll.

Her brother watched Sofia remain stationary in the car and studied her pale sorrowful face, half buried beneath the enormity of her Dior sunglasses. He walked over to her.

"What's the matter, Sofia?" Luca asked protectively.

She shook her head, unable to find the words and so frightened of revealing the truth to her elder brother.

Luca reached into the window and lifted her sunglasses to reveal her vulnerable tear-stained eyes. Luca felt annoyed.

"Who has upset you, Sofia? You tell me now, because if you don't I will find out for myself."

Sofia knew her brother meant every word. "Oh Luca," she whimpered, "I need someone I can trust, I am in such a terrible mess." She took her sunglasses off and looked directly into his eyes. "I need to trust that you will not get angry with me." The usual fiery determination in her eyes had been replaced with a weighty pleading; it was a look that made Luca feel anxious.

"Come on, tell me, Sofia," he insisted.

"I did something terrible last night, I slept with a man that I know I shouldn't have done."

"Who?" Luca asked, secretly squirming at his sister's frank confession.

Sofia hung her head and began to cry "It was Piers, Rebecca Santé's boyfriend," she sobbed.

Luca's anger inflated. "What? You have got to be joking!" he shouted. "What the hell are you thinking of sleeping with another woman's man? Is nothing sacred to you? For fuck's sake, Sofia, I can't believe you!" In temper he hit the side of her car with the flat of his hand. "You should be ashamed of yourself, have you any idea how serious this is? It is unforgivable to be a part of that kind of shit. I don't know what has got into you at the moment. You caused a scene when you were pissed at the ball towards Julia, you sponge off Dad as though the world owes you a living and now you go and sleep with someone else's partner." He leant his head into the car. "Grow up, Sofia, whatever repercussions you get from this one, you deserve!"

Luca stamped away from her car and got into his Mercedes, without a second glance to his sister he sped down the drive.

Sofia sat alone in her car, she knew Charles was a complete bastard but, in the cold light of day, would he really carry out his threat and send Rebecca the footage?

It was just past twelve in the afternoon and Rebecca watched the performance of three of her horses that would be running at Ascot later in the week as they worked on the gallops. She was pleased with their progress and just hoped that the rain they had been experiencing down South would subside to allow the ground to firm. One of these horses in particular would have a better chance of being placed if it did.

"Lunch is ready!" she heard her mother call from the door. She turned to walk to the house and, passing the stables, she became distracted by the delicate rustle inside one of them. She peered over the top and then opened the stable door where her yearling stood. She walked over to stroke her.

"Rebecca's Pride," she whispered in her ear, "I bet you will be a real winner." She laughed as the yearling's nervous head nuzzled her hand, but the unfamiliar sound of a motorbike revving up to the house made her leave the stable to investigate.

"I'm looking for a Rebecca Santé," the rider informed her, making no attempt to take off his helmet.

"That's me," Rebecca told him with a look of confusion covering her face. He handed her a small package, "Will you sign here?" he asked, passing her a pad that highlighted the name and address of a courier service.

Rebecca signed the document, and then watched as the bike thundered its way down the drive. Rebecca looked down at the parcel, then back at the bike that was fast disappearing from sight. A strange feeling engulfed her.

Piers stirred, his mouth felt dry, his head like a bubbling cauldron. Sofia's face barged into his mind, followed swiftly by Rebecca's.

"Oh fuck!" he mumbled sinking his head under the duvet. He closed his eyes tight and moved his legs across the bed in physical search of his guest. The bed was empty, he was alone. *Thank God for that,* he thought. How would he have explained this morning that Rebecca, whom he hadn't wanted to talk about last night, was actually the love of his life?

A piece of paper had been placed on the pillow next to him; she had scribbled her mobile number on it. He smiled whilst reading the number, appreciating her sentiment, they had, after all, had fantastic sex. He scrunched up the note and threw it casually into the waste-paper basket.

Shuffling to the bathroom, holding his aching head, he turned on the shower and stepped in. Taking advantage of the complimentary shower gel, he soaped his aching muscles in the desperate hope that last night's secret would be washed away. As the water pounded against his head, he felt it clearing; he would make his way over to see Rebecca straight away, he decided. He felt desperate to see her. They would make amends, and he promised himself he would even show an interest in the yard.

He continued to scrub his body, as the torrents of dirty water were sucked into the gurgling plughole, comforted by the fact that his drunken sins, too, were rapidly being washed away.

Charles Lancaster-Baron felt exhilarated, the weather was fantastic, his roof was down and the force of the speedometer, clocking just over one hundred and twenty miles per hour along the M25, elevated his sense of freedom.

"Freedom!" he shouted joyfully to the gushing air that blew against his face.

Rebecca Santé was about to return onto the 'open market' and he would be the first to snap her up. Even if the payback for his efforts were not immediate, they would nevertheless transpire. Freedom was exactly how he could describe his feeling – with Rebecca by his side freedom from the stressful constraints he faced in his life was most definitely in sight.

His speed forced his blonde hair off his face and to twist like Medusa's snakes behind him; his blue cotton shirt coolly fluttered across his chest and beneath his black Gucci sunglasses, his eyes smiled cunningly.

Thirty minutes later Rebecca saw Piers heading up the drive in his car and the sight of him made her feel physically ill. Her legs shook, her arms trembled to her fingers and her water-drenched mouth threatened to vomit any moment.

"The bastard is actually here, he's had the audacity to turn up," she spat through gritted teeth.

A violent anger propelled her to storm from the house just as Piers was getting out of the car.

"I'm sorry, Rebecca," Piers said, holding out his arms to hold her.

"What?" she screeched. "Are you fucking insane?" Rebecca launched a savage attack and began to kick and punch him furiously. "How dare you?" she screamed. "You get away from me, do you understand? Get away from me, my family *and* my home!" She pushed him hard, forcing him to fall against the car.

Piers had never seen her in such a temper and neither had he seen the uncontrollable wild look in her eyes. He got into the car.

"That's it, you bastard. Fuck off!" Rebecca launched the DVD through the window. "And take your fucking sleazy life with you!" she screamed. "My father was right. I am too good for you." She launched for him again through the open window.

"Stay away from me, do you understand?" She yanked at his hair and scratched at his face. "Stay away, otherwise I will make sure you will regret it." She slammed the car door shut and, with breaths that heaved from her chest, she marched back into the house.

Piers slammed the car into reverse. The package had landed clumsily on the passenger seat. As the wheels of his car chased their way down the driveway he stared back at it in bewilderment.

Chapter Twenty

PIERS stood from the bed. He had only watched ten seconds of the film but he need watch no more, being the one that had been filmed, he already knew the exact details of what, and who for that matter, was to come.

He was angry, so angry that his venomous thoughts ripped through his body like the angry claws of a hunting hawk. He bit down hard on the inside of his cheek, but with masculine endurance he ignored the pain it induced. His breaths raced in shallow angry bites as he stormed over to the waste-paper bin, the same waste-paper bin that her telephone number had been discarded within earlier that morning.

"Fuck!" he yelled through gritted teeth, seeing that the bin had been refreshed with a clean liner. He kicked hard against a neighbouring chest of drawers and witnessed the bottom drawer fall from its castors and crash to the floor.

He fell back upon the bed and the irate pucker of his mouth sucked in the heated whistle of irony. After he had rebooked the same room as the night before, the chamber maid had cleaned away the filthy scribblings of Sofia DeMario's number. He buried his head in his hands, trying to eradicate the vulgar nightmare with the clench of darkness. Sofia DeMario was his nightmare and if it took him an eternity, he was going to find out exactly where she was and why she had instigated this shameful plan.

Sofia DeMario was also lying on her bed but, unlike her lover of the night before, she was at home, and her emotions were quite literally spilling all across her pillow. She sobbed endlessly, feeling her heart bleed with regret for her past actions; after all, it had been *her* past misconduct that had been the catalyst for the plan of assault – Charles Lancaster-Baron's plan of assault.

Just the mere thought of his name caused her hands to mould into tightly clenched fists, fists that gripped with such ferocity that her fingers turned white and the pinching dig of her nails almost penetrated the soft skin of her palms. She closed her eyes and willed for his name to be eradicated from her thoughts, only to be tormented again with Piers' handsome face and the blanket of lustful memories of the previous night. Her words to Charles had been the truth. In the short time she had spent with Piers, she knew she had fallen in love with him and that in itself was a torture she had to endure. Quite simply, he belonged to someone else and it was this fact, along with the sense that the dreadful mess she was in was about to get a whole lot worse, that allowed her unstoppable momentum of tears to continue to roll.

Thankfully, her brother was not facing the same misery. Having completed his arduous list of responsibilities, Luca arrived in the hotel and the head receptionist informed him that his guest had already arrived and was awaiting his arrival in their room, the Presidential Suite. His heart flipped over like a foaming surfing wave, he couldn't wait to see her. Declining all offers from the concierge to carry up his bags, entirely influenced by the need to be alone with her for the whole evening, he made his way in the lift to the top floor.

He knocked gently on the door before swiping his card through the lock. Apprehensively, he opened it and the vision he had dreamt of seeing all day came alive. Julia was here.

She was seated on the sofa and on hearing the door open, in a nervous flash, her head spun round to face him. For a brief second, against the sumptuous backdrop of the luxurious room, Luca noticed the fragility and vulnerability that swamped her eyes but once Luca's presence had registered, she allayed his concerns. As she sprang off the sofa and ran towards him her eyes were once again bursting with energy and life. She wrapped her arms around his shoulders, squeezed him tight and then let out an infectious laugh that filled the room.

"I am so pleased to see you," she told him excitedly with a wide smile. "You are earlier than you said you were going to be." She beamed ecstatically, "Just look at this room, Luca."

Luca watched her as she span round to face the room. She looked beautiful he thought privately, truly, truly, beautiful, like an Italian princess whose enthusiasm was born out of visiting England for the very first time.

Her dark hair fell in large billowing curls against a red cotton shirt, its chic tailoring nipped in her tiny waist and elegantly lay against the flat of her stomach before slim legged black trousers emphasised her long slender legs. Her feminine fingers pointed in appreciation towards the hoard of paintings and fine furnishings, whilst Luca, almost hypnotised by her pure organic beauty, continued to stare at her. Her sweeping eyelashes, emphasised demurely by a light coating of mascara, flitted hurriedly from one corner of the room to the other and encircled her gigantic dark brown eyes, her soft, dark, curving mouth smiled with the same sprightly transmission of a breaking sun and melted brilliantly against her Manuka honey complexion. He couldn't take his eyes off her; her breathtaking features combined with the casual vibrancy of her scarlet red shirt caused her to glow with a rich, possessing sensuality.

"And look in here," she gasped leading him by the hand to the bedroom.

The master king-size bed was festooned with a plush scarlet fabric, coordinating swags and tails draped fluently against the curtains, crowning the four enormous windows with a smug conceit. "Look at it all!" she continued to marvel, "And, I can't believe the size of that bed," she giggled in amazement, sitting on its edge bouncing playfully. "I've never seen anything like this in my entire life."

In the instant the words had escaped from her mouth she was filled with regret, the reference to her *real* life caused her to flush with embarrassment.

Luca sensed her shame and suddenly realised, for the first time that her humiliation derived from an unnecessary comparison of backgrounds. He sat next to her on the bed, unhesitant in his desire to reassure her.

"I don't care *where* we are, as long as I'm with you. That's why I had to rush; I couldn't wait to be with you. You are the first girl that has ever been able to ease my mind away from a big race like tomorrow's." He held her face in his hands and refused to allow her eyes to break from his stare.

"Well, you know what they say," Julia replied nervously, "There is a first time for everything," she smiled.

He continued to hold her stare. "I can assure you, the kind of feelings I have for you are definitely the first," he answered sincerely.

He neared his face to her lips and gave her a soft gentle kiss. As he did, Julia was swept away by the sensitivity of the moment. This was the nearest Luca had come to telling her he loved her.

The only sound in the room was their loving kiss, and at last, for the first time, they were truly alone. With a locked door behind them and not the slightest threat of interruption, Luca's mind began to hurl clear steamy images of their impending love- making into view. His raw masculine instincts encouraged and urged him to make love to every inch of her womanly flesh, and making passionate love to her here and now was the natural conclusion to the emotional intensity and lust that he held for her. His kiss became more adoring and his hands became braver in his search for sexual gratification. Julia responded zealously to his advances, her hands ran freely across his face and roamed excitedly through his hair, she wondered if he could feel her hammering heart as it pounded nervously against his chest. His hand slowly began to glide; his fingers found the flesh on her chest and the opening of her shirt femininely gaped, inviting him, with tempting folds, to explore beneath. With his hand only inches from her naked breast he allowed it to stray.

Julia suddenly froze; her eyes clamped tight in terror, and her kiss began to stiffen in its momentum as her morbid memories strangled her passion and rejuvenated her childhood fear. She could smell the perpetrator's stale breathe, she could see his sneering face, her legs and arms began to ache as she remembered the force with which he had held her down. Swiftly she drew away from Luca as nausea took a hold, she sat upright and straightened her hair with her trembling hands and looked down to her coiled up toes that she had curled in the nauseating tension.

"I'm sorry, Luca," she whimpered turning her head.

Luca broke away from her, allowing his sexual frustration to cool before he spoke. He stared back at her face; it was flushed with passion yet seemingly petrified of a force that was unknown to him. She looked like a young schoolgirl that was so totally afraid.

"Hey," he said in a caring whisper, opening his arms to beckon her to fall between them.

Hesitantly she drew nearer to him, realising that these outstretched arms would offer the security and protection she craved, even the possibility that their warmth could melt away the haunting apparition. Instantly she flopped in submission against his chest.

"Don't be sorry," Luca told her in a caring whisper, "I understand." He kissed the top of her head and really wished that he did.

Downstairs, the hotel bar was packed to the rafters with the following day's racing punters. They were jammed inside, ravishing the champagne, sharing tips, with some of the luckier ones taking the opportunity to ravish and share the young local girls that had turned up to take advantage of a free evening's booze.

Mrs Montford had managed to drink two bottles of Krug Champagne to herself, courtesy of Pierre, a small fat Frenchman who had flown in from Paris that morning especially for the Ascot meet. He had taken an avid shine to Francesca the minute he had set eyes on her. He, along with his dinner encrusted moustache, had followed her around all evening, foaming French obscenities discreetly into her ear that even Francesca had no wish to understand. Though his kindness in topping up her glass had initially been gratefully received, now she felt, it was high time they bid farewell.

"Listen you fat froggy fucker, piss off and chat up someone your own weight," she had slurred before staggering off to pastures new.

Sitting by Frankie DeMario's side at a nearby table, Bill watched as his wife 'in typical Francesca style' made drunken innuendos to a selection of men in the bar. Her behaviour grated upon him increasingly as the days and weeks wore on, especially now that Paris was expecting their first grandchild. He found it unbelievable that she would rather waste her time and her efforts on such meagre pursuits when the opportunity to revel in something so real stared at her every morning. He grew angry with himself, he was as bad as her he realised, *I am the bloody mug that has brought her here.* Bill poured another helping of whisky into his glass from the bottle on the table.

"I am in no mood for trips to the bar tonight." Frankie had told him an hour ago slamming the bottle down in the middle of the table. "Help yourself."

Bill noticed that Frankie's mood had not yet improved; his beady black eyes looked like hot barbeque coals, appearing to burn with rage as they scrutinised the corners and alcoves of the hotel bar, silently in search of his son.

Frankie knew Luca was staying here; it was with whom that was his main concern. The receptionists were doing their job well and remaining discreet, all they would tell him was that Luca DeMario had asked not to be disturbed. Frankie had persuaded himself not to call at the room unannounced nor to telephone, his son could be taking a genuine rest prior to his racing tomorrow. If this was the case and his son was taking his responsibilities seriously it was a pity, he reasoned, that the Santé's yard did not share a paralleled commitment.

David Donnelly, the head lad, having safely banked all tomorrow's runners in their stables, was now standing on the bar about to drunkenly dive into platted arms of several other colleagues. *That Rebecca Santé,* Frankie fumed, *she has got four horses of mine running tomorrow and she is allowing her staff a free reign the night before Royal Ascot?* He would call her, *she should be ashamed.*

Rebecca put Frankie DeMario's call onto answer machine; he was another caller she wanted to ignore. Piers had called her so many times and each time his name appeared on the window of her phone, her resolve to ignore him steadily grew.

"You were so right, Daddy," she offered stiffly, "I *am* too good for him."

"Without a shadow of a doubt, you are, that was all I tried to tell you all along," he answered.

James had to admit he felt complete relief; the offers he had made to share in Piers' company had been nothing more than pretence, suggested purely as a lever to anchor Rebecca back home. If there had been no other way to keep her here than to make forged peace with him, he would have done it, but now, there was neither the need nor the sanctimonious inclination, and for that, he thanked the Lord.

Restless and filled to the neckline with a stewing rage, she rose from the armchair and stood in front of her father in their sitting room.

"You know what?" she asked her father with a determined look in her eye. "When we get to Ascot tomorrow we are going to show *him* and the rest of the world just what we are made of, including that two-timing little shit! God, I'm going to show him!" she spat.

James Santé liked her style; she had true grit and dedication when it came to this yard, and that look in her eye, reminded him with such startling magnitude of his mother.

Rebecca ran to her room to throw some things in a bag, she would set off at four in the morning. Making allowances for her journey, she needed to be at Ascot for early morning checks and feed at six thirty, but first she wanted to call Charles. She already had high hopes, she wanted to organise a celebratory meal for tomorrow evening.

This time Charles diverted *her* call to answer machine. He had a job to do and it needed his full concentration and complete anonymity. He was not surprised that sitting, freezing to death in a beaten wreck of a car was not any fun. Both he and the ugly heap of a vehicle were perfectly obscured within a small clump of trees on the edge of the racecourse. It was a fifteen-year-old Escort, so not only was it well-disguised, it was also a car that nobody in their right mind would associate with him.

Straight ahead he could see the black silhouettes of the stables that housed the following day's athletes. To his right was the hotel, its numerous windows lit by the golden glow of lamplight. The faint muffles of its internal hubbub travelled towards him. He smiled shrewdly, thanks to his forethought, Luca DeMario was somewhere among those revellers, at least he was one obstacle banished from the equation. He turned his attention back to the security office.

As the darkness thickened upon the racecourse he could see the soft mono-cast shadows of the television flicker from the guard's window. It stood to reason that, with over a million pounds worth of horses stabled overnight, a security guard would be on site for the entirety of their stay. But soon that security guard would be leaving the confines of his office for ten minutes; then Charles would have his opportunity to strike. Within the main stand of the racecourse a meeting for the senior members of the Jockey Club was under way; once they had left, the guard would have to lock up.

His black leather gloves banged aggressively against the steering wheel whilst his steely jaw pulsated and twisted. He would have to wait, he told himself, patience he had heard was a virtue. So was retribution, he silently shot back.

Frankie continued to glare across at the Santé's drunken stable staff. "I think it is a crime," he told Bill "When people have so much money they lose sight of how they got it in the first place, there is no room for complacency in business. The Santé's should be here, keeping an eye on everything in their business." He looked at Bill, staring into space. "Don't you agree?" The strong liquor had gone to Bill's head, leaving massive scope for honesty. He angrily grabbed his glass. "Don't talk to me about money," he answered forcefully. "I am in no position at all to become complacent about it, money causes me nothing but anxiety." Bill rubbed his chest, already feeling the threat of heartburn just at the thought of his financial troubles.

"What do you mean?" Frankie asked, relieved to have the distraction of someone else's problems and filling their glasses for the umpteenth time.

Bill looked over at his drunken wife with utter exasperation. "She has broken me," he admitted. "I am in massive debt, she has broken us with her incessant spending and this insatiable need to try to keep up with people around her, yet I told her over and over it's just not possible, we can't keep up." He shook his head and Frankie observed Bill's unforgiving face as he watched his wife dance with a stranger. "There is nothing left," he told him honestly. "The only road I have to go down is bankruptcy." He shook his head. "Bankruptcy," he repeated solemnly, "at my age."

Frankie DeMario's eyes narrowed, causing his thick black brows to shadow his face as they met. Frankie sympathised, his gentlemen friend did not deserve such a fate. He would help him. Tomorrow, when they had both sobered, he would offer his condolences in a practical way.

Charles' senses prickled, he noticed signs of movement and the headlights of cars driving away from the racecourse and along the road leading into the centre of Ascot. The meeting, he concluded, had obviously ended. Suddenly the door of the security office opened illuminating a large expanse of grass upon the ground. The guard walked outside, locked the door of the office behind him, then he walked off with purposeful strides in the direction of the main stand, the silvery spray of his torchlight illuminating his path.

Charles fought for a second with the old weary door handle before the door sprang open with an unexpected jolt. The moonlight shone down and favoured his trail with the dim edge of a path; his gloved hand gripped his unlit torch, for now he could only allow the moon's goodwill and his years of familiarity to guide him against the uneven terrain across the course.

His heart was thudding in huge banging beats, Charles was charged with adrenaline and made small bursting sprints before stopping to duck against the grass, surveying his path for witnesses. With swift expertise he reached the stable block and crouched behind it, taking a few seconds to review his surroundings and safety. Slowly he edged from the shelter of the stable wall and read the horses' names written in thick black ink on the side of each stable. The clear words of "The Italian Job" at the far end of the block brought his search to an end.

Slowly he unbolted the stable door and walked inside. The horse lay resting, though, on seeing him, its flighty thoroughbred temperament drew it noisily with clattering insistence to its feet. She called out nervously in half whinny, looking for assurance from the approaching stranger.

"Sssssh, fine lady," Charles whispered, holding out a reassuring hand. "Ssssshh."

The leather gloves masking his hands slid their way across the mares coat in firm confident strokes. She calmed and blew warm nuzzling breaths at his jacket. Charles smiled, she could smell her bait. Walking over to the feed bucket in the corner of the stable, he pulled the small bag of racehorse nuts from his pocket and quickly emptied the packet of powder inside, mixing the feed thoroughly with his hands. The horse immediately took advantage of the unexpected supper and began to crunch on the meagre offering, licking the bucket clean with enthusiasm then nuzzling at Charles' pocket for a second helping.

"That's it my girl, you make sure you eat up, but more importantly you make sure you have a restful day tomorrow," he whispered. Looking back at the mare one last time he walked out of the stable and quietly bolted the door. His work was done.

Returning to his car and hearing only his feet brushing against the grass he took a giant breath of fresh air and felt proud, proud that he had the forethought to find a way to fight back. Many a man would have crumbled in the adversity he had recently faced, but not Charles, he was a Lancaster-Baron after all. Enjoying another victory and feeling as though the tide of fortune had changed in his favour, he sat in the obscurity of his car and lit up a well deserved cigarette.

However, in Charles' case, ignorance really was bliss. He was unaware of a man, not far away, who had secretly filmed *every* activity that had occurred on the racecourse that evening.

Chapter Twenty One

THE MORNING broke to the radio and television stations cheerfully informing their listeners around the country that today was the commencement of 'Royal Ascot'. The English weather excelled itself with a cloud free, clear blue sky that graced the sun with endless freedom to shine with blazing ferocity. The racecourse itself bragged in honourable silence, offering a never ending silken blanket of straight green turf that would have been fit for a game of royal croquet, and behind the scenes, scores of staff swept, polished, carried, lifted, arranged and cleaned the vast selection of bars, terraces, boxes and restaurants in nervous anticipation of the three days ahead.

In the car park, prior to the commencement of the first race, hoards of attendees took advantage of Ascot tradition and the weather with a picnic. The boots of their Range Rovers and Discoveries were opened as wide as hippo's mouths and inside them, out of their Fortnum and Mason hamper baskets, delicious salamis, soft rolls of pastrami ham, oak smoked salmon, olives and fresh crusty breads were exhumed. Some ate hungrily, welcoming the opportunity to line their stomachs, whilst others, mainly the ladies, could barely touch a thing with only the chill of the pink champagne having the capability to calm the froth of their excitement.

As the morning rolled on, the day's race goers steadily began to ooze through the gates. Scores of finely dressed ladies entering the course were encouraged by the strength of the heat to take off their exquisite custom-made jackets, yet they saw this as a welcome opportunity, the majority needing only the slightest excuse to exhibit more of their startling outfits.

Charles stood in the royal box, a privilege for a rare few and, for him, one that was handed down from his father who had bred numerous polo ponies for the royals in the past. Its enviable position brought with it a view of the entire racecourse. He stared at the streaming sea of colourful hats and outfits cascading through the entrance, all intermingled with the frequent bobbing and lifting of the traditional top hat by the gentlemen of the British aristocracy. It was a stunning sight, and one that only Royal Ascot, the epitome of English tradition, could bestow. Just watching the scene made Charles feel proud to be a part of it all, it was an event that had been a part of his life for as long as he could remember and he realised that it was his family's exceptional breeding that had endorsed his lifetime pass to such fineries. His head subconsciously rose with regal poise and he gave a conceited tug of satisfaction to the lapels of his long tailed jacket, then stood back for a second, allowing himself to take in every detail in a gesture of appreciation for today's experience. However, it wasn't long before his thoughts soured.

Charles stood alone, listening to the guffaws and the Sloaney chattering of the excited punters surrounding him. He heard their champagne corks popping and their crystal flutes chinking together in a fused harmony of celebration. He felt envious that they found this occasion a time for carefree nonchalance and remembered the time when he too had found it appropriate. Against their laughter he felt his nerves stiffen him into a rigid stance, reminding him that he was on the brink of losing the entirety of the inheritance that his father had left to him. He was going to claw it back, he told himself frankly. He was already taking risks to do so, enormous risks, and all these plans he had put in place were non-negotiable. Like a pan of simmering water he felt the pressure inside him was about to rise to the boil. His thoughts were diverted by the undiluted blare of the National Anthem and all heads turned toward the course to watch the royal procession travel by.

The string of open-topped carriages were filled with three

generations of the Royal Family, and all of them caused the usual stir of admiration within the crowd. The members of the royal box gracefully tipped their top hats from their heads and bowed respectfully to their queen as her carriage drifted past. She responded warmly, and along with the rest of her family, she waved and smiled in duty-bound honour to their adoring masses. Charles joined them in the hat tipping formalities before making his way to the Owners' and Trainers' bar, he needed a change of scenery.

He had only just entered the crowded bar when Rebecca, looking as confident and as self assured as ever, breezed inside. Their eyes met across the room and with swift expert appraisal Charles took in her attire to the very last detail. He was not surprised to see that Rebecca did not need to be reintroduced to the formalities of Ascot etiquette, her dress code was impeccable.

She was modestly covered in a soft lime satin suit and its fabric shimmered with the subtlety of a pearlescent voile, her outfit was simple, yet so incredibly chic. A fine bolero jacket covered her arms and her shoulders, its neckline, deep and sharp cut, added just a hint of glamour by spinning a ruffle straight down the centre that continued to run along the edge of her sleeve cuffs, then, this detail ended where it rested, upon the straight pencil style skirt that sat respectably at calf length. As she made her way through the crowd towards him he noticed her emerald eyes, their colour and life ignited by the shade of the outfit, her dark auburn curls twisted and spiralled across her shoulders and her small dainty mouth smiled briefly to familiar faces as she passed. She graced the room with a professionalism that just couldn't be ignored and, according to Charles, her appearance confirmed everything she was – a successful, capable lady, the type that like himself, had also enjoyed the privilege of being born into one of the wealthiest families in Britain. They were two of a kind and Charles felt proud she was heading his way. When at last she reached him, he held her proudly by the arm and kissed both cheeks.

"How are you Rebecca?" he asked, making the pretence of looking over her shoulder. "Is Piers not around?" It was a loaded question, and one he was eager to hear the answer to.

Nobody would have known the heartache she was feeling inside with the reply she gave. "No, he is not," she answered bluntly, "nor will he be." She looked back at him with a blaze in her eyes, "ever," she added with significance.

Charles looked puzzled. "Oh? Why's that?" he asked with a frown.

"This is a story I can only tell you when we have *both* got a drink." She rolled her eyes. "You are not going to *believe* this."

"It all sounds rather ominous," Charles responded. "What would you like to drink?"

"Champagne please," Rebecca answered with a forced smile. "There's a table over there, I'll go and grab it."

Charles nodded and turned to face the bar whilst he waited to be served. He had to concentrate hard and think about how he would react if he *really* didn't know what Rebecca was about to tell him.

Moments later, Charles walked back to the table with the drinks and sat down next to Rebecca. She immediately began, in a fast hushed whisper, to spill the events surrounding herself and Piers. In response, Charles' large blue eyes widened in disbelief and shock.

"I can't believe what you are telling me," he began. "How could he do such a thing to you? Who the hell filmed this filth?" he asked.

"I don't know," Rebecca said feeling her concealed pain trying to break free. "All I know is that it is definitely over."

"I don't blame you," Charles retorted, shaking his head. "What was the bloody fool playing at? Nobody in their right mind would treat you like that. Anyway, you do right to get rid of the stupid bastard, poor you." He sympathetically rubbed her back. "The whole world and his dog will know about his wrongdoings now." He filled their glasses with champagne. "The last thing in the world anybody wants is to be made a fool of in public," he added.

"Definitely," she answered quietly, "it's something I just could not bear." She hoisted her shoulders and her voice gathered strength. "There are some classy runners out there today," she said, examining her programme.

Indirectly Charles had been informed that the subject was now closed. He took a sip of his champagne and allowed his camouflaged feeling of satisfaction to gloat.

Luca DeMario crept out of the hotel suite early. As he was about to walk out of the door he couldn't resist having one last peak at Julia sleeping. She was truly awesome; her perfect face looked nothing but 'at home' with the sumptuous fabrics that surrounded her. Her breaths were soft and deep, she was so still and restful that it was clear, the privacy of her dreams were still bathing her mind. He hoped fleetingly that he would be a part of them before quietly closing the door behind him.

One hour later he was walking the course but, as ever, the sight of the other jockeys milling around the stewards and chatting to one another made Luca feel anxious. He scorned his nerves. It happened at every race meet; as soon as he witnessed the pre-race activity begin to liven, he felt his inner tension start to build. It was mind over matter, he told himself with routine insistence; he would pay his fears no credence. With sharp persistent strides he made his way over to the jockey's pavilion.

He walked to the changing rooms, and with an expression that emulated his father's, determined, strong and fixed, he only nodded his head in short recognition to his colleagues who were chatting amongst themselves, before he made his way into the sauna. He stripped off; wrapping a small towel around his waist and reluctantly opened the sauna door, instantly suffering the unrelenting heat that smothered his skin. Like the red line of a temperature gauge, he felt his blood began to heat; it pumped in wave like fathoms around his body before reaching its maximum levels and pushed into his head. He wanted to get out, but he knew that was not possible, he had to sit on the weighing scales in less than two hours time and he had to sweat out the small piece of fillet steak he had eaten for supper with Julia last night. He gritted his teeth, trying desperately hard to ignore the torturous symptoms. Reluctantly he inched himself down and forced his body to lie against the burning wooden slats. He closed his eyes and somehow his ability to focus on the day's racing began to surface.

Bill Montford answered the incoming call on his mobile phone. He hoped it might be Paris calling to let him know she was feeling okay. Unlike his wife, he had been worried for his daughter. It was

Frankie DeMario, and Bill blushed whilst recalling last night's fluid honesty regarding his finances.

"Good afternoon, Bill," Frankie reassured in a friendly tone, "I wanted to come over and see you but unfortunately I have been delayed in the Royal Enclosure. I want to know if you will come golfing with me the day after tomorrow to Ayr, there's something I want to talk to you about. Can you make it?"

Bill hesitated. He wondered what plans Francesca had for him and what her reaction would be if he accepted the invitation. He hesitated for a split second. "Yes, that would be my pleasure, Frankie," he chuckled down the phone. "Thanks, thank you very much for asking me." Bill answered with a schoolboy smile that expressed utter relief that Frankie's opinion of him had remained unchanged. They passed their final pleasantries and then Bill snapped his phone shut.

"Who was that on the phone?" Francesca asked.

"I've been invited out on Monday to play golf," he answered without looking at her.

"Well you can't go!" she barked. "I need driving to Wiltshire's boutique. I've already made the appointment to look for outfits for Ebor week at York. And we also need to go to the garden centre, the Broadmoors over the road have got a beautiful showing of rose beds, I think it's high time we increased our stocks." She begun to turn her back signalling an end to the conversation but intrigue saw the better of her. "Who was it supposed to be with anyway? You never go away golfing."

"Frankie DeMario has asked me," he replied.

She swung round her thin eyebrows rising in ecstatic delight. "Oh Bill! Well done!" she sang. "You must go, you must have managed to strike up quite a conversation with him last night, oh well done!" She immediately began to prune him, straightening his collars, patting them with her long painted fingernails picking any tiny flecks she could see off his suit jacket before continuing.

"Oh Bill you're not a bad chap at all, you've done a really good job. Where are you playing? Did he say?"

"Ayr," Bill answered dourly, sickened by her reaction.

"Oh my goodness!" Francesca stated throwing her hands to her delighted face. "I bet you'll be flying there in his private jet," she gasped in disbelief. "When we get back I must sort out your attire," she trilled. Francesca closed her eyes and looked up to the sky in prayer-like gratitude. "My husband is going to be golfing with one of the richest men in the country!" she crooned.

Bill didn't respond, shaking his head and, with loathing written all over his face, he walked away to examine the form of the entries in the paddock.

Frankie and Luca stood inside the enclosure, scrutinising the form of each horse as they were led in by the stable lads. Luca, having spent an hour in solitude focusing his mind, currently felt unperturbed by the competition, but although confident, his stomach still churned relentlessly. He wanted to win.

He had spotted Julia looking on with the rest of the punters from the railings of the paddock. As he looked across, her wide bright smile for him didn't register, nor did her breathtaking appearance. It was this concerted detachment to the outside world before a race that made Julia, and a whole host of other girls, simply swoon.

Luca and Frankie looked on as The Italian Job was led inside the paddock and both men immediately noticed a difference in her behaviour. Under normal circumstances she jogged and danced around with her ears pricked high, foaming at the mouth with excitement, it was a bursting zeal that always caused worry that her nerves would expend too much energy prior to the race. Today, to their surprise, she was different. Physically she was unchanged, her strong muscular physique rippled beneath her shining bay coat, her ears were pricked, her eyes and senses alert but both Frankie and Luca commented on how relaxed and calm she appeared. After a brief consultation between themselves, the mare was led into the middle of the paddock and with a leg up from the spade like hands of his father, Luca mounted. The horse had barely set out a stride before Luca frowned.

"She feels different," he told his father "it's as though she's lost her spirit, there's no pull from her."

The two men patted her neck and examined her head and her breaths, everything seemed in order.

Luca shrugged, "Maybe it's just that she's maturing and becoming focused at last!" Luca said in hope.

One of the Irish jockeys walking past the DeMario's to mount his horse overheard their conversation and stopped. "Or maybe," he interrupted sarcastically, "the 'orse just prefers to be left alone in its stable on a night, he's maybe just tankful you were out shagging your girlfriend last night instead of pestering its' arse." He laughed out loud and gave a mocking wink to Luca.

Frankie stared up at Luca with a fury that engulfed his eyes and then stormed out of the paddock.

Standing on the balcony of a friend's private box Charles Lancaster-Baron was able to see every expression on Luca's face through his binoculars. These binoculars were both lucky and sentimental. They had been passed on by his father, a token reminder of the shoots he used to attend in South Africa. His father had said to his shooting companion that, when an animal had been viewed down the exceptional lenses of these binoculars, it would be immediately hypnotised prior to it being shot, as if accepting its cruel fate and was waiting to fall to the ground.

His son remembered his words and viewed Luca and The Italian Job down the cylindrical hollows with a piercing stare. Every cell in Charles' body hoped that his father's hypothesis would prove itself today.

Chapter Twenty Two

THE HORSES and their jockeys lined up for the parade, a grand quintessential offering to the punters now crowding into the spectators' stands to witness the race of King George. In organised formation the runners and riders were requested to walk past the stands, allowing the punters a final appraisal of the form before placing their bets. It was a parade that each of the jockeys detested, a display that called for control and unwelcome interruption to the focus of their race, but more importantly it was the threat to the delicate physiology of their thoroughbreds that caused them most of their concern. They had to hold their strong horses back throughout it, as over exertion prior to the race harboured the threat of dehydration to each finely bred horse.

However, the background intricacies were of no interest to the majority of punters. To these spectators, as the jockeys and riders passed their stands, they conveyed a line of sumptuous brilliance. Brightly coloured flash-dancing silks covered the lithe athletic physiques of nervous jockeys within, their faces showing strain, yet masking expression, and beneath them, their world-class thoroughbreds with arduously groomed coats, glossed by the perilous excitement of sweat and foam. Their ears were pricked, aroused by enthusiastic applauding crowds, and their yanking heads, fighting to break free from the constraints of the bridle, yet ever controlled by the jockeys' sharp, masterful draw to their reins.

Luca gathered his racing armour and took in every detail of his peers and the apparently forbidding competition. He planned his position in the field, allowing himself the final two furlong mark before he would drive her home. His plan faltered slightly in his mind as unease for his mare grew, she still felt unusually quiet and reserved. With the parade over, they turned to canter down to the stalls. Despite his concerns, he refused to allow his observations to be construed as anything but positive, with The Italian Job appearing so focused, he had a better chance than ever to win, he was determined to give it his best shot.

Frankie stood in the Royal Enclosure watching every move his son and horse made through his binoculars. He watched as the horse entered the stall and thought back to the racing comments in the papers yesterday. He had purposely held the information from Luca, trying everything he could to divert his attention from reading the *Racing Post* for fear of heightening his son's tension. They had given a negative review of Luca's chances, stating, 'He is about to be found out, his talents exist only as a sprint jockey,' and 'up against the best jockeys in the world DeMario wouldn't stand a chance,' adding, 'The Italian Job exerts too much fizz prior to a race, we think it highly unlikely she will find the strength to quicken at the final two furlong mark'. Frankie viewed the two of them in the starting stalls, already they had been proved wrong with the mare remaining effortlessly calm. Could his son win the race? Only time would tell.

Luca was the first to be led in. The gates slammed shut behind him, rendering both horse and rider in solitary confinement. He sat motionless on a horse he could barely feel beneath him, a second horse was led in beside them but The Italian Job appeared oblivious to company. Luca exerted a gentle pressure against her with his legs in an effort to both reassure and remind his mare where she was, but again, although her ears were pricked and her breaths collected, she remained despondent to his encouragement. Luca nervously pulled down his goggles before fixing his stare on the turf ahead. The two horses, now stalled at either side of him, banged nervously against the stalls and pounded the ground with their dancing hooves as others were led in. A nervous tension leaked rapidly into the air and caused the final seconds to drag. Luca strained to hear the muffled countdown from one of the stewards about to release the stalls. Suddenly, the clattering release of the gates sprang open allowing the horses to leap out into freedom.

"And they're off!" The famous words echoed from the tannoys across the bursting racecourse, allowing the world-ranking jockeys and their horses to set off at a good pace.

Rebecca Santé and her father glanced over to Charles. He stood alone on the balcony only feet away, avidly watching every detail of the race. James saw the time as a welcome opportunity to talk with his daughter whilst their eyes watched the race from the big screen in front of them.

"You know Rebecca, you wouldn't go far wrong with a man like Charles, damned good stock he is, a true gent, he wouldn't dream of treating you the way Piers has done."

"Oh Daddy, please don't talk about my love life today, it is the last subject in the world I want to discuss. Can't we talk about something interesting?" She looked back at him, "Like how I am going to ensure our yard continues to flourish?" She hesitated, "That is, if you still want me to take over?" She pulled at his jacket giving him a flashback of the young childlike girl that used to accompany him to the races.

At last, she has returned, James thought with a smile. "Welcome back, Princess," he said and kissed her hard on her forehead.

Rebecca knew she had made the right decision; she and Piers were well and truly over and with that reality decided, there was nothing to pontificate. She glanced over to Charles with fondness. His binoculars were still fixed to his eyes; and she noticed his jaw was pulsating in agitated nips. A crescendo of cheering from across the box travelled like a Mexican wave and permeated the length and breadth of the racecourse, encouraging Rebecca to look back at the screen.

From the second furlong into the race the course challenged the horses with an uphill track that swept its way towards the finish line. Up to now Luca had managed to gain a respectable position in fourth place, and was now beginning to see some of his peers losing ground. They had just passed the three furlong mark and he was conscious he needed to quicken pace as he reached the second. They had both worked hard, retaining their place, now breathless and his body saturated in pain, Luca began to ride with every morsel of being he had left. They reached the second furlong and he felt a rush of adrenaline motivate him to ride harder as he neared the horse in front. He lifted his whip and thrashed it hard against his horse's rear, urging her to find the additional energy. He felt her tremendous body accelerate beneath him. Feeling her response and fuelled by excitement he lowered his head against her shoulder and roared, "Come on girl! Come on we can do it!" Again she responded to his call, Luca knew the winning post was inches away but he wouldn't look ahead, he struck his whip for a second time and again rode her for his life. He heard thundering hooves closing in behind and saw the image of a horse gathering pace alongside him. He shoved his clenched fists that were filled with mane and rein against her neck and pushed her along. An excited wind blew inside his silks as her pace persisted.

"Come on!" he roared.

They crossed the line. He had won. He felt tears of pride fill his eyes, only now was he conscious of the cheering and chaotic cries of the crowd as the race approached the finish line. Only one person appeared devoid of emotion.

Chapter Twenty Three

CHARLES stood, momentarily in silence, as the cold rush of panic infested his body. He suddenly felt the tight formalities of his shirt dig into his throat, choking him, restricting his breaths. Roughly he tugged on the neat knot of his constricting cravat, yanking it free and allowing it to fall. Frantically he fought through the crowds, oblivious to his destination, he didn't care where, he just wanted to be alone. His face was draining of life, his body mopped by a cold sweat that hungrily sucked at his cotton shirt, drawing it to his skin. He pushed silently through the people crowding his path, their faces hazy, their bodies huge, he stumbled through a doorway and was greeted by the searing heat of the summer sun that tormented him further, cruelly targeting his face as the perfect place to shine. His body slammed hard against a wall where he shook, before slowly, despairingly, he slid to his knees and sobbed.

In the winners enclosure Luca was being treated like a hero, punters, press and racing colleagues alike gathered proudly around him, aching to be the first to pat him on the back and congratulate him on his tremendous win. Amid shouts of, "Well done, you rode that horse with your life!" and, "Jesus, have you shown 'em!" Frankie DeMario made his way toward his son.

"Well done," Frankie offered, coolly rubbing The Italian Job's nose, "you rode well."

Standing by the mare's side, holding her reins and finding it impossible not to be drawn into the rush of the atmosphere, Luca beamed proudly towards his father.

"Thanks for being here to see it," Luca replied genuinely.

Julia was also unable to fight her excitement and, forgetting Luca's plea of the night before to keep a low profile, fought through the crowd and ran excitedly past the security guards and into the winners' enclosure. Overwhelmed by seeing his face, and her still breathless, sweat drenched Luca standing before her, she didn't hesitate in flinging her loving arms around him. The flashlights of the press lit up the enclosure like a lightening storm. Within seconds Frankie DeMario was pushed aside by a sea of cameramen and the couple were surrounded by a wolf like pack of paparazzi.

Frankie was unable to view the exhibition a moment longer. He angrily turned on his heels. As he walked away he felt fearful. He now had an additional problem, he was no fool; he could see that his son was in love.

Charles sat in the backseat of the Mercedes, the driver he had hired for the next twenty-four hours to drive him in supposed celebratory style around the bars and clubs took the strain of the roads. Charles was on his way home. He hated his life and indeed every bastard within it. For years he had been melting in a trap, a trap where money was your only escape, yet for the first time in generations, a member of the Lancaster-Baron line had none.

Luca had no idea where his father had disappeared to. It had been two hours since he had seen him. As he stood in the changing-rooms having been weighed in, showered and changed, he decided to call him on his mobile.

"Get rid of that girl, Luca," Frankie exploded.

"What are you talking about?" Luca asked

"That girl who came into the winners' enclosure and made a fool out of you with her public displays. With a girl like her your mind will never be on the job, she will force it to be on her. If you want to be champion jockey and hold the title you will do as I say, that woman will drive you to distraction. Not only is she an outsider to the family who won't have your best interests at heart, she is also not to be trusted. I can see it in her eyes. I'm your father, trust me, get fucking rid of her!" his father yelled.

Luca fought back. "Listen, I have put my heart and soul into this job and I will continue to do so, but I am not your little boy anymore. Don't even think you can control me, because I'm telling you now; I can do this without you. Do you understand? I can do it without you. Now fuck off and butt out!" he shouted and angrily cut off the call.

His fellow jockeys stood in silence and stared. One of them braved the potential consequences and took the opportunity of making a lonely quip.

"What's the matter mafia boy, has someone just sawn your mother into pieces? Fucking hell, it would take a fucking big chain saw to take that Mamma on!" They all laughed in unison.

Luca felt a second surge in his temper. He lurched forward and punched one of them hard in the face sending him crashing to the floor. Leaving his belongings behind, he stormed from the changing room, his father's words drowning his mind. He stormed his way over to the Owners' and Trainers' bar where he had arranged to meet Julia. They were going to get the hell out of here.

He stamped wildly across the racecourse grounds. *Why had his father spoken about her like that?* But he didn't know why he was surprised; his father had always been possessive of him where women were concerned. With the exception of Luca's mother, Frankie DeMario didn't have a lot of time or trust for women.

When Luca walked into the bar he noticed that Julia was hemmed in by the usual pack of sharking predators. They had better piss off now, he thought; he was in no mood for that shit.

When she saw Luca enter the bar, she bestowed her second public display of affection on him, hurling her arms around his neck and kissing him hard on his lips.

"I can't believe you won," she told him. "You were magnificent," she beamed. "And, you won even though we were together last night. That means we can now do it more often!" She laughed holding his face in between her hands. "Charles Lancaster –Baron is worth listening to, I'm glad he suggested it." She kissed him once again with zeal, but Luca broke away.

She looked back at his face, contorted with confusion. "What? What did you say?" he asked quietly.

Julia froze. Her eyes began to dart searchingly around Luca's face, desperate to seek a facet that suggested potential forgiveness. She felt her cheeks burn with an embarrassed nervous flush. In her momentary hesitation Luca read the answer in her eyes. His father was right. Though he responded to her quietly, his words escaped through the spitting anger of gritted teeth.

"You have allowed Charles Lancaster-Baron to advise you on our relationship?" He waited, she said nothing. "Julia, don't come near me again, do you understand? Just fuck off!"

Luca thundered out of the racecourse, leaving Julia standing helplessly alone and completely heartbroken.

Chapter Twenty Four

SO RELIEVED it was Sunday, her day to walk Zip a neighbour's rescued greyhound, Paris pulled on a worn sweatshirt and jeans, desperate to free herself from her mother's incessant empty chatter.

Francesca had been fussing around her father and his wardrobe all morning, ecstatic about the impending golf meeting between Bill and Frankie DeMario the following day. Intermittently she had wandered into Paris' bedroom, sidestepping with disdain across the mountains of strewn clothes crumpled on the floor.

"You should get this lot tidied up instead of moping around in bed," she had bitten, oblivious to Paris' unbearable wave of morning sickness. "It's ridiculous all this mess everywhere." Francesca looked across at her daughter, noticed the distant look in her eyes and realised she needed advice. "You know dear, motherhood is nothing but a strain on one's life. It's not a decision to take lightly; there are all kinds of problems associated with it. Breast-feeding, for one." She grimaced. "All that does is cause breasts to droop and look unappealing, on top of that your innards will never be the same again, and, in addition Paris, the *further* stretch marks you will gain to your body will do you no favours at all. You've already got them across your back," she cruelly reminded her daughter. Guardedly, looking over her shoulder, she raised an optimistic eyebrow and added, "Having said that, in my opinion, you could *potentially* be the luckiest single parent in the universe."

Paris poked her head from the confines of her crumpled duvet. The possibility of solace brought hope to her fragile voice. "Really? Why?" she asked.

Her mother scowled, genuinely amazed Paris had not yet grasped the huge potential this opportunity had to offer. "Well," she sighed, perching uncomfortably on the edge of her bed, "if you keep this child, you will always have a hold over the Santé's." She gave a glib shrug. "Since Gerard has died, naturally that hold will be on an emotional scale, but also," she smiled, finding it impossible to conceal her delight, "from a financial one. Whatever your needs for that baby in the future, they will feel compelled to assist, or at least you would think so." Her face temporarily hardened. "But, that plan is a little risky, one whereupon you are literally left holding the baby, also giving them the chance to pull rank at some stage, leaving you well and truly in the mire." Francesca paused for thought.

Paris, still lying beneath the duvet, stared in horror at her mother's meticulously cold dissection of the problem.

Francesca, looking anxious, peered over her shoulder for the second time to check her husband was nowhere in sight before edging closer to her daughter.

"In my view, Paris, to avoid all risks, you are better off taking the money that Charles says the Santé's will offer you to buy the baby. That way, you will have the best of both worlds, freedom from motherhood *and* money." Francesca remained indifferent to the pain on her daughter's pale, needy face.

"Oh for God's sake, Mother, don't remind me about that proposition," Paris pleaded. "I only told you about it because it sickened me. Stupidly I thought you would feel the same." Paris wrenched herself from her bed, then lowered her voice to a whisper, "And, don't mention it in the house, I really don't want Dad thinking terribly of the Santé's, they are Gerard's family after all."

Bill, standing outside Paris' bedroom door, felt utterly appalled. Moreover, he felt his hatred rise towards the two people encouraging his daughter to involve herself in such an unscrupulous act.

Feeling tired and emotional, Paris left the house, calling at the corner shop for her first lift. She bought two Mars bars, one for herself, and one for the baby. Even though the baby was invisible, its presence gave Paris a sense of appreciation that for the first time in her life she could devour both bars completely guilt free.

Collecting an enthusiastic Zip, who was fervently licking her lips after consuming the last piece of Mars bar that Paris had saved especially for her, the pair made their way towards Edding Woods. Paris loved the woods. She loved the way the arch of the branches romantically touched like embracing fingers across the pathways, as though cocooning its visitors into the confines of safety. The whole place embraced her with tranquillity; a place far removed from the turbulent realities of life that she was certain nature did not intend to create. Today, Edding Woods was just the place she needed to be. She made her way carefully along the uneven terrain of the grass verge that harboured her from the country road. She glanced up at the woodland trees and their breathtaking enormity, squinting as the morning's sunlight scorched her empty eyes. She wished she had the strength of this woodland furthermore, she wished she had their ever present lock of companionship, all these trees, she pondered, standing side by side, not one of them would have been as lonely as she.

A car approaching from behind gently popped her personal bubble of thoughts, protectively gripping Zip's collar, she stood to let it pass but looked up when she heard it slow to a halt. Her eyes suddenly grew cold, it was Charles.

Releasing her hold on Zip's collar and resisting the temptation to tell him to piss off, Paris increased her pace. Unperturbed by the rebuff, Charles lowered the passenger window and drove slowly alongside as she stamped her way to the entrance of the wood.

"Am I really that bad?" he asked with a smooth smile.

Paris ignored him, nervously continuing to walk and concentrating on stabilising her footing against the clumps of wild grass in her path.

"Where are you heading?" Charles persisted.

"Towards an escape from the falsehoods of life," Paris snapped.

"Sounds fantastic, just the place I need, can I join you?"

"You? Escape from a false life?" She gave a short sarcastic laugh. "It seems to me you wouldn't see an escape if it slammed you in the face, anyway," she added sharply. "Do whatever you want."

Concealing a triumphant grin, Charles drove on ahead and parked in a clearing a few hundreds yards up the road. He walked back along the grassy verge to meet her, temporarily scowling with irritation as he noticed the dewy watermarks that covered his new suede loafers. He looked up at Paris and the skeletal dog she was walking and wondered if today's hassle was worth the inconvenience of marred shoes.

Paris paid no attention to his presence and walked into the majestic clearing of the wood. Charles followed her and instantly became spellbound by childhood memories.

"God above!" he said, staring up at the thick canopy of trees that overlooked the soft fern pathway. "Edding Woods, I used to come here as a child." He marvelled, thinking of all the fun he and Hugo used to have here. "I just remember it looking huge, not half as magical as this." He stared across at the infinite pathway that swept through the cool, romantic arch of the trees and noticed the perfect strobes of light from the sun's rays, forcing themselves through the small gaps between the lush green leaves and flashing against the ground like soldiers' swords. His imagination ran riot and reignited thoughts of childhood play that had long been forgotten. "There's a lake about one mile down this path, Hugo and I would bike up here and then go fishing" Charles smiled in fond remembrance, enthusiasm gushed in his voice.

"I know there is, I come here often, Charles," Paris scorned. "It may surprise you, but some people come here even when they are adults." Her belittling words caused his smile to drown and, as she saw it disappear, Paris felt guilty; her criticism had been unfair. "Sorry," she added quietly.

Charles smiled apprehensively. "How often to you come here?" he asked

"About three times a week, depending on which dog I am walking and when, they just love it here, as I do." She tapped her hands against her trousers and knelt. "Come here. Zip," she beckoned.

Zip turned and took a treat from her hand as she unclipped the lead, but afraid of his freedom he anxiously retreated and hung his head low between Paris' legs.

Charles stared at the dog with contempt. *A greyhound,* he announced in his mind with disgust. He had never come into such close contact with a dog *renowned* for its association with the working classes. Its dusky coat quivered against rattling ribs and a knobbly arched back that looked ready to snap at any moment, *why the hell would anyone bother?* he thought.

Paris immediately knelt by the dog's side. "Oh you poor thing, Zip," she poured sympathetically, hugging the dog close to her chest; she looked up at Charles to explain. "You know, she was abandoned after being tortured because she didn't win any races, she was found with her legs tied together in a back yard with injuries so horrific the RSPCA officer said she wouldn't have lasted the night."

Paris kissed her face, stroking her coat from her head to her tail with a loving patience so kind that she reminded Charles of his own mother. He watched as Zip looked into her eyes in search of comfort.

"How could anyone do that to an animal?" Paris continued. "Look at her, she is so faithful and kind, it's written in her eyes." Paris' sympathy and repeated revelation brought tears to her eyes.

"Mmmm, she's really lovely," Charles lied. "Who does she belong to?"

"A neighbour, I walk a lot of dogs, I love them, plus," she stood up and began to walk with Zip following reluctantly behind, "it pays the bills, not that I have many." She looked at him and smiled. "I prefer the simple life."

For the first time Charles noticed the glisten of her eyes. He had never noticed before but they were blue, and surprisingly quite pretty, he thought.

"Your eyes are really pretty, Paris," he told her.

The surprise of the sudden compliment caught her breath, but not daring to acknowledge it, she continued to walk in a bid to conceal her blushing face.

"Do you think a baby will allow you a simple life?" Charles asked casually following on behind.

"I don't know what it will bring," Paris snapped, instantly remembering the solution Charles had offered "I know what a baby is supposed to bring into the world and that is love." She turned to face him, causing Zip, still following cautiously behind to bump into her legs. "How bad can that be? Isn't that what we are all here for?"

It was a pointed question, one that Charles did not expect; he wrestled for an appeasing response. "I guess so," he answered uncomfortably.

"That's the problem really isn't it, Charles? We all have to guess, regardless of creed, colour sect or breeding, life is one big guessing game." She took a deep breath, continuing her walk in slow thoughtful steps "The trouble with my pregnancy is that it's a human life, guessing as to what to do would be unthinkable. Coming here, you see, will help me with my decision."

"How will coming here help?" Charles asked, wishing he had brought his walking boots; his loafers were beginning to rub and were covered in pine needles.

"How can this place *not* aid a troubled mind?" she stated, pointing at the striking surroundings. "This is nature; nature has a way of pulling someone down to their roots and forcing them to think in simple terms about what they want out of life. The trouble is people these days seem to be so wrapped up in their tiny worlds they miss it all." She heard the overbearing immoral teachings of her mother in her mind, causing her emotion and frustrations to surface. "You're a prime example," she said turning to face Charles.

"Me? Why?" Charles laughed, amused by her forthright comment and hardly believing that this was Paris Montford, Francesca's daughter holding his attention.

"You are consumed like so many others with shit. Cars, houses, status and money, at the end of the day who gives a toss about that, what will it bring you when all is said and done? Look up at these magnificent trees." Her eyes travelled up to the proud pinnacle of trunks and branches that reached up to the sky. "If you're here for long enough they will modify your ego. Gerard used to say that, and he was right, they will even make an important man like you feel small. I'm sorry to tell you, but in comparison to nature, you are exactly that. Small."

Paris felt exhausted, her candid opinions had drained her. She walked to a fallen tree and perched on its edge. Charles was taken aback, though, he had to admit, also silently amused. Never could he have imagined that Paris Montford would emulate words and feelings of his own mother. He sat down beside her.

"I think your being a bit harsh on a fellow that only wanted to help you, Paris," Charles said softly. "Our lives may have their differences, but that doesn't stop me caring about your feelings."

Zip was sitting at Paris' feet. Grudgingly Charles bent to stroke his thin wiry coat marred by knobbles of protruding bone, and felt the grease from her unkempt hair soil his hands. Discreetly Charles rubbed his hand against the bark of the tree stump.

"Why do you want to help me, anyway?" Paris asked blatantly.

"Because I know that Gerard would want me to. Rebecca and her parents are too distraught to help you; their grief over Gerard's passing is as raw as yours. I must do what I feel is right. In this instance it is right that I make sure you are okay."

Paris stroked Zip, keeping her head down to hide the well of tears that were mounting in her eyes, hardly daring to believe that someone genuinely cared. The very mention of Gerard's name had instigated her feelings of loss all over again, causing her to wonder for the millionth time what he would advise her to do.

Charles noticed her chin quivering beneath her fiercely bitten lip; he reached for her face and turned it towards him, he looked into her eyes with totally sincerity.

"I'm sorry if you think I am intruding, but I am not going to go away, not until I know you are back on your feet again."

Paris couldn't hold it together any longer; she burst into tears barging her head into his shoulders. Charles held her, gently rubbing her back.

"There let it all out Paris, I'm your friend, I'm here for you, just like Gerard was."

"I'm sorry I was so rude to you," she sobbed. "I had no idea you were so kind." She lifted up her face to look at him and allowed his good looks to capture her, his eyes, his mouth, the tousles of his soft hair, he was gorgeous. She chastised herself for being gullible and believing the hateful rumours about him. "I feel so bad," she sniffed, failing to notice Charles grimace as she wiped her nose on the sleeve of her sweatshirt. "I should have known that if you were a friend of Gerard's you would be a good person."

Charles had a quick glance around the wood assuring himself of privacy, he didn't want anybody to witness him with a hysterical overweight girl at his side and a greyhound at his feet.

"You are sweet Paris," he told her.

"I don't feel I am, especially not at the moment, I feel like shit." She looked up at him, her eyes like a pleading child. "I actually feel sick and so desperately tired all the time, and, from one moment to the next I have no idea which emotion will surface. When will it all stop?"

"Look. Let me make a suggestion, why don't we go home and I will pick you up later. We'll go for a drink somewhere out of the way where nobody knows us. You can talk to me, shout at me or cry to me as much as you want." He pulled her hand and held it. "I want to help you," he said sincerely. The strike of his handsome face and the strength that poured from his dazzling eyes imprisoned every atom of her vulnerability. "I really do," he assured her.

Paris thought about the night she faced, alone in her room, dwelling on her grief and problems. Just the chance for company would be a bonus.

"Okay, I suppose so," she answered quickly. She reached for Zip's lead, anything to break away from his powerful stare, then thought wearily of the long walk home. "Can I ask a favour, though? Will you give Zip and I a lift home?"

Charles' eyes widened in horror at the prospect of a greyhound inside his immaculate car, he fought for an excuse. "Well the problem is I…."

"It's okay," Paris interrupted, sensing his hesitancy. "We'll walk back, it won't take long."

Remembering her words warning of the falsehoods of life, and still with a desperate need to win her round, Charles relented. "She'll have to sit on your knee," he said with a forced smile.

Half an hour later, Charles silently fumed as he drove along the winding roads with Paris and the stinking, flea-bitten greyhound perched on the back seat. Looking in his mirror at the unsightly scene behind him, Charles felt agitated at the thought of this evening's date. Based on this as an example, what the hell was tonight going to bring?

Chapter Twenty-Five

KITTY stared out of the drawing room window, looking way beyond her paddocks and taking in the magnificent blend of countryside views that surrounded her home. It was harvest time and each acre of Chelmsley's rich fertile land bustled with the monstrous chug of combine harvesters, tractors and trailers. She could see the matchstick proportions of the farmers in the distant fields, enthusiastically carrying out the tasks that would secure them another lucrative yield. Under normal circumstances, Kitty would have been enjoying the sights that this, her favourite agricultural event, would offer. She had always relished the simplicities of taking her horse and carriage out along the meandering country roads, allowing the golden treasures of nature's gifts, the sights, the smells and the sounds to soak into her every being. However, today, the sight twisted her thoughts.

"They are lucky enough to be reaping what they have sown," Kitty said distantly. She sighed, "If only I had been offered the same rewards." Her voice was swamped with a disappointing reflection; she turned, allowing Hugh Stephenson, her financial lawyer, to look into her eyes.

Having acted on her behalf for over twenty years, to him, her pain was clearly evident, although her tough, external mask remained cemented in place. She was an incredible lady and he held enormous respect for her – all the more reason why seeing her trapped by this unrelenting torment and pain tore him apart. He remained silent, acutely aware that there were no words which could even remotely pacify. On hearing a noise in the distance, Kitty nervously turned back to the window.

Having returned Paris and the decrepit greyhound back home, Charles swooped up the drive of Cedars Hall. His arrival was impressive; with the roof down the masculine superiority of his car crunched against the winding path of the gravelled driveway. Dark stylish sunglasses protected his eyes from the soft flicker of the afternoon sun which adoringly touched his gorgeous face, and the topiary bushes that lined the drive appeared to coyly giggle upon his arrival as the breeze tickled their inner branches. Within their paddocks, his well-bred hunters grazed contentedly and the historic Tudor mansion of Cedars Hall, the luxurious dwelling that he called home, stood grandly before him. Charles however, consumed and distracted by internal pressure, failed to notice any part of his good fortune.

His arrival was welcomed by more dogs. Fleetingly the well bred family Labradors offered a slight reprieve from his experience of the wretched greyhound. He got out of the car. The dogs crowded his path, suspiciously tracing the unfamiliar scent of another dog against his legs and excitedly fighting for affection, nuzzling his hands and legs with cold wet noses.

"Piss off!" he snarled. A harsh kick sent two of the dogs into a hasty retreat with a yelp, the others followed suit with their disappointed heads bowed low and their tails hanging heavily between their legs.

Kitty watched her son's malicious behaviour towards her beloved animals and felt personally offended by his attack upon them. She turned to her guest.

"Charles is back!" she said with urgency. Hastily she began to collect the strewn papers lying across the table. "I wasn't expecting him back so soon, we will pursue our conversation tomorrow," she said, stuffing the papers randomly into his briefcase. "I will come to your office in the morning," she whispered.

Kitty's panic was contagious. Hugh, a fine lawyer, normally of steely and unflappable disposition, felt his own anxiety rise as he heard Charles' footsteps nearing the drawing room. Frantically gathering up his pens, folders and papers he grappled with the locks of his briefcase in a fierce bid to protect the information within.

Charles walked into the room and glanced at the two nervous individuals sitting uncomfortably in front of him. Although they had succeeded in clearing the table they had not had the time to clear the air, it lay heavy with suspicion.

"Hello, Charles," Kitty said, "How are you?"

"I'm fine," he replied, looking at Hugh with question. Hugh stood up extending his hand.

"Good Afternoon, Charles," he smiled calmly. "Long time no see, how are things?"

"Great thanks, Hugh." Charles casually ran his fingers through his hair. "Are you here on business or pleasure?"

Kitty quickly interjected, "Oh, Hugh has kindly offered to have someone to check over my pensions and investments for me," she said, reaching for her china tea cup. "The market has been rather unstable of late, we were discussing our options."

Charles observed the slight tremble of the tea cup in her hand. "Are you alright Mother?" Charles asked with genuine concern out-shadowing suspicion.

"Yes," she laughed, "of course I am." Turning her back she gently slipped some papers into a file. "Why wouldn't I be?"

Hugh sat silently watching Kitty with admiration. She was the most resolute woman he knew. He stared in wonder at her grace and composure, only he and one other person had any idea of the pain she was going through. She stood with certainty before both men in the room, her hair as always styled in high swooping curls, her striking blue eyes still radiating the same wisdom and strength as the day he had met her, and their loveliness, as always, emphasised perfectly by her customary lashings of black mascara. Once again Hugh felt deeply saddened by her private trauma.

"Ok," Charles replied unsurely, "if you are sure everything is alright, I'm going for a shower."

"Right, Hugh was just leaving anyway," Kitty said. "Right then Hugh, if that's everything I'll see you to the door."

The indistinguishable conversation that followed would have sat comfortably on a cold knifes edge. Upstairs, leaning against the galleried landing, Charles strained to hear the hushed sharp whispers between his mother and her lawyer downstairs. Acutely aware his mother was harbouring a secret he became enveloped by an excruciating feeling of distrust and an unhealthy intrigue as to what his mother could be hiding from him. With quiet yet urgent steps he crept down the stairs, the unattended file she had left on the table beckoned him into the drawing room. Still hearing the muffled voices Charles rushed with pattering steps into the vast room and made a lunge for the file.

"What the hell do you think you are doing?" Kitty's voice angrily ricocheted across the room.

Charles jumped and swung round to face the sudden appearance of his mother. Her eyes were irate, her stance rigid.

"I was just looking for something," he answered.

"You were snooping, that is what you were doing." Her eyes narrowed. "What could you possibly be looking for in *my* own personal files?" She walked over to the file, grabbed it and held it against her delicate frame.

Charles winced in humiliation at her condescending manner. "Well, actually mother, I was looking for the documents you shiftily concealed on my arrival. It made me worried that you had a problem," he snapped.

"Oh, really, Charles? Isn't it a mother's job to worry about her son and not vice versa? Perhaps one's energy is better spent worrying about one's own affairs rather than the trivial happenings of your boring old mothers?" she sniffed. "Your concerns are unfounded, my dear. Those documents were simply written confirmation from Hugh that he was getting additional advice on my financial affairs. You know me," she smiled, "when it comes to financial matters I like to have all the I's dotted and T's crossed." She walked towards him and gently reached up to touch his face "Now come on," she advised, "that's quite enough worrying about your old mother." She stared into his eyes.

"But I am worried," he snapped. "Don't treat me like an idiot, Mother, I am not one"

"Mmmm," she answered, raising a quizzical eyebrow.

Charles shook his head in defeat. "I'm going for a shower."

He walked slowly upstairs; as the creaks in the wooden staircase orchestrated his ascent, the nagging feeling that something was wrong remained.

Kitty sat in her armchair, relieved that Charles had left the room; she held her head in her hands and sighed. She felt weak and tired, so tired the thought of walking upstairs for her afternoons rest filled her with dread. A fiery tear fell down the side of her face; this was a titanic journey, but one she had to face. She forced herself to stand, wiping the lonely tear with agitated strokes from her cheek.

"Come on Kitty," she said sternly, "stop feeling sorry for yourself and get a bloody grip." She tried to force her mind to summon the strength to motivate herself, but it was no use. Admitting defeat, she drew the curtains in the drawing room and lay upon the Chaise Longue. As she closed her eyes her troubled mind teased her with guilt, reminding her of past failures and the many aspects of her life she could improve upon should she have her chance again. A cascade of whirling thoughts and wishes continued, but none of them were strong enough to overpower her desire for rest. Minutes later her body's unrelenting call for sleep overtook her desire to dwell.

Eager to rid himself of the stench of greyhound and with a desperate yearning to see Rebecca, Charles was ready in only ten minutes. Wearing a white soft cotton shirt that hung casually over his dark denim jeans and his hair still damp he rushed down the stairs. Before leaving he checked the whereabouts of his mother and was surprised to find her sleeping in the drawing room; he stood by the door and watched her rest.

Her lips were emblazoned with her usual fuschia pink lipstick, her complexion was as soft and as flawless as ivory velvet, bearing no trace of a line or a wrinkle, only her eyelids closed by the seduction of sleep looked faintly creped and illustrated with delicacy the essence of ageing. He smiled at the thick coat of mascara that lengthened her lashes and emphasised the vivid blue eye shadow, a trademark she never failed to apply. She had always been the most glamorous mother a boy could have wished for, he felt proud, that even now, she remained so. Quietly he eased himself from the doorway and made his way outside to his car.

The dogs, faithfully forgetting the hurt he had caused them an hour before, jumped to their feet from under the kitchen table and followed him with wagging tails and adoration oozing from pools of soft brown eyes.

Parked in the courtyard was his mother's twenty-year-old Land Rover 90. He glanced through the window and smiled, amused by the out-dated switches and dashboard and the way in which the gear stick stood rigidly in the air like an old fashioned lollipop. He took in the refinements of his own car and became bemused that his mother had never tired of the old contraption and still adored it the way she did. He had tried on many occasions to persuade her to trade it in but each time she had refused, explaining she would feel a sense of betrayal towards it after the vehicle had served her so faithfully for two decades. He thought of her driving it and his concern for her grew, it was such a basic, aged vehicle and these days she was not a competent driver. He walked away and got into his car, briefly deliberating upon his mother's ailing health.

In the privacy of his car he called Dr White, his mother's doctor; he had given Charles his home number months ago in case of emergencies. Irritated at the sound of the answer machine, he left an abrupt message asking him to call him back, slowly recounting his mobile number, and confirming his call was most definitely confidential. He hung up and made his way to Rebecca's home.

"Have I got news for you!" Charles stated enthusiastically sitting down at the Santé's kitchen table ten minutes later.

Rebecca had followed him inside from the yard. Her hair was haphazardly tied back in a lopsided pony tail, strands of haylage and random crisps of wood shavings poked out from her auburn curls and her face looked flushed from a morning's hard work. She slipped off her quilted waistcoat, resting it on the back of the chair before pouring herself a glass of iced water from the fridge and drinking it in desperate thirsty gulps.

"Your news sounds intriguing," she said, pushing strands of hair from her face. "Would you like me to get you a drink before you start?" she asked with a smile.

Charles rubbed his aching temples and tactfully studied the slimness of her body, simultaneously wishing he could hold it whilst she rode on top of him with passionate bucking thrusts. "I don't want water that's for sure." Thoughts of his day, the greyhound, his mother and his date with Paris later helped him decide. "I think it will have to be a wine," he answered.

Rebecca reached for the wine from the fridge just as James and Victoria walked in.

"Charles has got something to tell us," Rebecca informed them cheerily. "God!" she fanned her face with her hand, "Is it just me or is it bloody hot in here?" she asked opening the windows and doors to allow the fresh air to cool the kitchen.

Her father laughed. "You can tell who the workers are around here." He nodded towards Rebecca proudly. James and Victoria, pleased to see Charles, greeted him fondly whilst Rebecca poured Charles his wine.

Rebecca sat next to him at the table. "Well, come on," she urged, nudging him with her elbow, "what have you got to tell us?"

Charles looked up at James and Victoria. "I think you two also better sit down for this one," he suggested. "I think you may be shocked, I know I was," he added.

Victoria and James pulled out two chairs and waited for him to begin.

"It's Paris Montford. She called me very early this morning asking me to visit her at her home. When I got there, she had the most unique proposition, she begged me to talk to the three of you, you see, her proposition affects you all…"

Chapter Twenty Six

UNPERTURBED by the three stunned faces staring back at him, Charles sat at the kitchen table with his tanned muscular arm casually, yet strategically, curled around the back of Rebecca's chair. Rebecca was the first to break the silence.

"She wants us to buy her baby?" She shrieked disbelievingly. "That's outrageous!"

"Poor Gerard," Victoria managed, keeping her tears at bay, "she's certainly not the girl I thought she was."

James, seething with anger, followed. "Well, as my mother used to say, what's bred in the bones comes out in the flesh." James rolled his eyes disparagingly, "Look at her mother."

"That's true enough," Charles offered sympathetically, though covertly recalling how different mother and daughter actually were.

The conversation between the four of them swayed to and fro like an unbalanced pendulum, lacing the air with an emotional concoction of confusion, anger, pity, and in Rebecca's case, masked enthusiasm. She smiled inwardly, imagining the feeling of holding a baby of her own. It may not be her baby, she reckoned privately, but it would be a Santé baby after all.

All the while, amid the discussion and his discreet advising comments, Charles continued to glance at the kitchen clock. He mustn't be late to collect Paris. Spending time with her was imperative, her thoughts also needed to be swayed.

For the past few days swaying thoughts had been an everyday occurrence within the DeMario household. The three siblings, each with a personal trunk of problems, trailed an omnipresent cast of cloudy moods through every room.

Emma was furious. She had called Charles several times and, after each brief conversation which he had abruptly cut short, he had promised to call her back later. But he had not. As a result she had locked herself sulkily in her bedroom suite and stood naked before her full length mirror, mistakenly blaming her voluptuous curves for failing to retain Charles' interest. Aggressively she squeezed the backs of her thighs in a bid to expose non-existent cellulite, finding fault in every conceivable blemish and chastising herself for being unable to resist her mother's homemade wares.

"I'll show that bastard!" she cursed determinedly. Throwing herself on the floor, she endured another set of two hundred sit ups.

Across the hallway in the bedroom suite opposite, Sofia's problems, heightened by an unremitting silence from Piers, appeared insurmountable. Even though she had left him her number, he had never been in touch and, considering the grave severity of the situation they were in, it was this alone that caused her mind to try to find answers within a huge feast of uncertainty. She had concluded that there were only two reasons why he hadn't called her, and which ever one of her deductions were in play, she lost.

Had Rebecca shown an understandable lack of restraint and taken him back? The thought of that filled her with jealousy and also dread. If that were the case, was the pair of them now planning their revenge on her, resulting in every detail of her misdemeanours being unfolded before the world, including her father and her brother? She shuddered in fright as to how her father would react. Her second assumption involved him hating her, despising her with a passion, and he was waiting for his anger to cool before he contacted her to unearth the truth. The thought of him contacting her appeased her slightly, she would give anything to talk to him, yet, at every conceivable angle, as she imagined their conversation, she felt trapped. She had lain on her bed questioning and verifying every possible scenario in which to explain the situation to Piers, but how could she explain to him that their lovemaking, which she now replayed over and over in her mind in a bid to rekindle the delights, had been a set up? And how would he believe that her feelings for him were genuine? Either way, because of Charles Lancaster-Baron she was backed into a corner, it was a claustrophobic corner that felt cold and unyielding.

For Luca, although his hectic schedule over the past week had thrown him many challenges, frequently travelling the length and breadth of the country facing several difficult rides a day, nothing had prepared him for the heavy empty vessel that had anchored in his stomach since his break up with Julia.

There were hours when his thoughts would ease him into believing that Julia was not the girl for him, not only had his father's instincts sensed it, but so had his own, many times. It was these feelings along with the fact she had been so easily persuaded by a bastard like Charles that temporarily settled his turbulent mind. Then, just as he felt he had mastered his judgment, his mind would then twist, like an elastoplast yanked savagely from an open wound, the pain would return, reminding him of the unique, breath-taking love he had lost.

Stepping out of the shower, he dried his body with the soft white towel his mother had hung on the warming rail. In the instant the soft cotton drifted across his body, that exact pain returned, forcing his thoughts to return to the night he and Julia had stayed in the hotel in Ascot, inducing bitter-sweet torrents of emotion to surface.

After he had reassured her about her sudden withdrawal from lovemaking, Julia had bathed in the Jacuzzi; he could hear her humming softly through the door and intermittently he would hear the water splash and imagine the haven of bubbles and water cocooning her miraculous body; he had ached to burst through the door, fighting avidly with the temptation of pulling her soaking body into his arms and making love to her against the cool marble floor. He had resisted, softening his frustration with the knowledge that Julia was special and that he would be seeing her again, many times, he hoped, and their chance for lovemaking would come soon enough.

He sat on the edge of his bed and closed his eyes, angered by the burning scorch of regret. Never would he have the chance to feel her warm soft skin against his own, never would he have the opportunity of making true love to the woman he adored, and worst of all, never again would he see her stunning face.

Unable to deal with his harsh reality he grasped his mobile lying on the bed. He had bought her a mobile whilst they had stayed in Ascot, and like so many times before, he dialled the first three digits of her number before swiftly turning it off. His father was right, she was better off out of his life for good; he had come too far in his career to be sidetracked by a naïve girlfriend. He threw the towel, the instigator of his troubled thoughts to the ground and with his body still damp began to wrestle with his clothes. But, his mind could not resist one last dig. What was she doing right now? Luca wondered exactly that and wished with all his heart that he knew.

Julia sat at her makeshift desk in the caravan and tried hard to finish the crossword she had started three hours ago. She tapped her pen in frustration as her mind, as always, drifted towards Luca. She yearned for him and missed him with an all-consuming passion, her thoughts never refraining from the torturous wonderings about what he was doing, and where he was. Only her portable television offered second rate compensation. After spending hours of her time re-tuning and patiently moving the portable aerial one inch at a time so she could watch Luca on the racing channel. She had then sat, watching Luca's every race, excited by his every win and glued to the screen with every personal interview, each one firing a medley of memories. She watched his mouth as he spoke and felt herself floating into his eyes as he laughed and searched desperately across the screen for the welcome sign that he missed her, there were none. Instead, on seeing his image, the power of her mind beckoned her into the land of cherished memories. She could smell the warm loving scent of his skin, she could feel the soft touch of his hands across her face, hear his kind tender words of affection in her ears and temporarily she would smile, believing with conviction he was with her. It would be the sounds she hated so much, outdoor camp life, her father's unapologetic snores or worse, the imaginary ring of the mobile Luca had bought her that would awaken her to the fact Luca was out of her life and would never call it again. At that time she would then contemplate a second question, was it the guilt or was it the misery that was worse?

Julia felt guilty about everything. For the deceitful way in which she had concealed her true identity from Luca because, ashamedly, she had been embarrassed about her family and their roots. Guilty for the way in which she had convinced herself she was superior to them all, causing her to search for a so-called 'better life.' And this so-called 'better life,' she thought bitterly, had driven her to steal and lie in order to live it.

Then there was the slow, painful tick of the misery. Misery because however guilty she felt, she wished so hard for those dishonest days involving her time with Luca to return. She would stare at the mobile that Luca had bought for her, willing it to ring, but would then reprimand herself for her optimism, recoiling at the heartbreaking realisation that Luca, his pockets aching with the swell of cash, would probably never remember handing it to her.

She looked out of her window and saw Coy, a girl from the camp, walking hand in hand with her new boyfriend whom she had met recently at Appleby Horse Fair. A broad proud grin was fixed to her face as the pair walked hand in hand across the camp. Julia had vowed she would never again turn her back on 'her' people. She stood from her desk, feeling a huge sense of envy toward Coy that she should have the capacity to be satisfied with her life. Slowly she walked out of her room, she wanted to meet Coy's boyfriend in a bid to try and rectify the wrongs her past thoughts had committed. However, just as she walked from her room, she turned to pick up her mobile. With a distant wish, she placed it in her pocket.

Charles had chosen a quiet bar some forty miles from Chelmsley in the hope he would not be recognised. He had endured a forty-five minute update from an exasperated Paris in the car concerning her mother fussing about Bill's golfing trip the following day. Now he felt relieved to be ordering himself a drink at the bar, mulling over what appeared to be an abhorrent suggestion that Frankie DeMario would even contemplate inviting Bill Montford on a golfing day. He walked back to Paris who was sitting at the table he had chosen within a quiet alcove. He placed the drinks on the table. Paris was still pulling uncomfortably at her jumper in an effort to both cool herself and cover the evident bulges that lay beneath.

Ignoring her apparent discomfort he smiled and sat beside her, inching himself along the seat until his arm purposefully rested against her own. With his touch and bodily warmth Paris felt her temperature rise further. Charles took his mobile from his pocket.

"I'm turning that off. I want to make sure we have no interruptions. By the way I sidestepped the orange juice you asked for, I thought you might like to join me with a wine, it won't do any harm at this early stage." He gestured his head towards her stomach and gave her a heart-stopping smile that heightened the tension of her nerves.

She returned the smile, grateful for the calming effects of alcohol and immediately took a sip. The close confines of the seating arrangements meant that Paris was wrapped in the masculine haze of Charles' fresh musky aftershave. He ran his fingers through his hair, freeing a giant waft of expensive shampoo into the air. He turned to look at her, his large dusky blue eyes capturing her own, then as he took a sip of his drink, her eyes timidly traced his face and stopped at the manly dimple on his chin as he looked back at her.

"Are you okay?" he asked soothingly. "I'm so glad to be with you tonight, Paris, thanks for coming."

Paris nodded and shuffled uncomfortably on the seat feeling aghast that Charles Lancaster-Baron would actually thank *her* for going out with *him*. Again, she pulled at her jumper and nervously blew cool air against her fringe that was now clamped to her sweating forehead. Feeling acutely uncomfortable, she took a second slug of wine.

She had come along believing that the change of scenery would do her good, now she wished she had stayed at home alone. Her writhing nerves unsettled her already turbulent emotions and sitting so close to Charles, confident, stunning, apparently caring and, even worse, focusing his attention purely on her, aggravated her awkwardness.

"Now, what's important for me, Paris, is that I know you are alright," Charles continued, sensing her unease. "Talk to me, Paris. Truthfully, how are you feeling?"

As her eyes sank into the radiance of his, she felt his warmth and understanding overwhelm her. Stunned by his good looks and at last having the opportunity to talk honestly, a rush of hysterical chatter and inescapable truths came bubbling to the surface.

"Well, to be honest, I feel as low as I ever have been in my life, I loved Gerard with all my heart and I miss him terribly. I know everyone does and I shouldn't just think of myself but I am..."

Charles interrupted her sensing she was about to sob, he immediately tried to contain the potential embarrassment.

"Hey," he said soothingly, "of course the grieving is worse for you. You and Gerard shared something special, very special; I told you last week he spoke about you often with such fondness." He gently rubbed her knee, willing her to continue.

Paris looked at him; once again she blushed as her mind silently registered his touch and his charismatic draw. She looked down towards the floor, her voice turning to a soft whisper.

"Thank you Charles, that's very kind of you. I just don't know where to turn or what to do. I so much want this baby to love and to cherish. My mum keeps telling me about all the negatives of being a parent, like the never-ending responsibility of parenthood. She comes out with utter rubbish like my tits going saggy. I'm not bothered about any of the physical problems, I mean look at me now." She pointed towards her body. "I'm hardly Kate Moss, I couldn't care less how I look that has never interested me." She shrugged and shook her aching head. "I just don't know if I'm ready and if I would be a good mother when it came." She began to snivel slightly but fought hard to keep the tears at bay. "After all, it's not as though I've had a good role model, is it?"

Paris fell silent in quiet contemplation; Charles allowed the silence to continue for a few seconds.

"I can understand why you are so upset and confused, Paris, but do you know what I think about the whole situation?" She nodded for him to continue.

"Knowing Gerard as I did, I know that he would hate the thought of you being burdened with his baby when you felt there were still plenty of things you wanted to do with your life." He stared at her intently. "Let's face it, he was a free spirit, he lived life to the full and encouraged everyone else to do the same. He would hate the thought of you keeping the baby for the sake of remembering the love you shared together." He placed his warm hand under her chin and turned her face, which was staring emotionally at the floor, towards him. "You will always remember that love and so will he, you don't need a screaming baby to remind you of what you had."

Paris began to cry and fought hard to contain the intense gasping wails within her chest.

"But, I feel lonely, Charles, really lonely. I feel as though, without him, I will have nothing real in my life, that's what keeps me holding on to the thought of keeping the baby." She looked away from him. "For once I will have something that is mine for keeps, but moreover something that is real." Her nose was running and tears were cascading down her red ruddy cheeks. Charles rummaged around in his pocket and quickly found his handkerchief and handed it to her. Stroking the side of her face and taking stray strands of her wet wispy hair between his fingers, he moved them out of her eyes.

"You know, what I'm going to say now may surprise or even shock you." There was a long pause before he spoke again. "You know when you were going out with Gerard and when I was around you both I didn't really pay much attention to you?"

"Yes," Paris nodded.

"It was because Gerard spent many evenings with me telling me how lucky he was to have you. He spoke of how genuine and warm you were and a complete contrast to all the other false gold diggers that float around. Those kinds of girls are ten a penny and can be found anywhere you go. You, however, are a completely different kind of lady, someone like you is so hard to find." His tone changed. "Paris?"

His forthcoming words, she could sense, were to hold meaning. She turned her face to him, her attention truly captured. Gently he smoothed one finger down her face, his touch felt so powerful that it sent a tremor of enchantment down her spine. Nervously she picked up her wine glass and drained it dry.

"Paris, I didn't speak to you because I was envious of what Gerard had found. I always have been, which is why I am here talking to you now. I know, as much as I shouldn't say these things, I can't contain myself or my feelings for you any longer. You see, this might surprise you, but I too am searching for something that is real."

Paris held her breath and for a brief second she felt her heart hold its pulse. Was he being cruel and about to tell her this was all a joke? She examined his eyes; they stared back intently, coolly awaiting a response.

"I can't sit here, Charles, I want you to take me home please." Her voice was faint; she stood and felt her legs almost give way.

Charles followed her to the car park outside, blipping the car door open with his remote. She quickly clambered inside. Once again Charles sat beside her.

"What's the matter?" he asked her quietly. "Do you not believe what I have said?"

Paris couldn't speak. She sank her head and watched her toes nervously twitch and tap in the foot-well of the car. Carefully, she tried to bring some order to the vault of pent up emotion and memories of Gerard, all overflowing carelessly into her mind. Charles gently lifted her head to face him.

"Talk to me, Paris, I promise you my words are real, tell me how you are feeling?" She looked at him and felt her warm tears spill down her cheeks.

"I think you are being dishonest to Gerard," she squeaked with words that hurt her throat. "I miss him so much!" She let out a cry but it was restrained by Charles' finger, he placed it tenderly across her lips.

"Sssshhhhhhhh," he soothed, leaning closer toward her. Paris could feel his warm breath on her face and smelt the fresh warming aroma of his red wine as he spoke.

"Don't cry, Paris."

Taking heed, she closed her eyes and tried to lock her tears inside. His voice was relaxing and caring, she felt him edge even closer.

"I am not trying to take Gerard's place," he assured, "I am just trying to be honest with you." He paused. "Tell me, Paris, tell me what you miss about him the most, tell me," he urged with a floating whisper.

As the questions registered, her mind began to unlock the memories of Gerard's kiss, she rested her head against the seat, closed her eyes and imagined his gentle touch against her skin. The vivid detail of her memories caused her heart to ache and to wish beyond anything else that his affection was real again.

With her eyes still closed and her imagination continuing to run free, only seconds later it did became real, only this time with a sensual pleasure much stronger than her memory of Gerard. Charles kissed her lips tenderly; she flinched in shock as his mouth met hers. There was an instant she wanted to withdraw; shamed by her traitorous thoughts of enjoyment, but it flitted as fast as her heart now pounded. His kisses smouldered against her lips and the touch of human flesh against her own ignited her like a firework. She felt alive, she could feel the blood flow back into her cheeks, she could hear her heart beating again and could feel her skin tingling with desire. Yes, she had been awakened, awakened by a passion too great to dismiss. She kissed him passionately, Charles was incredible and for this time he was hers, just like her beloved Gerard.

Chapter Twenty Seven

IT WAS MONDAY morning and Paris was woken by her mother asking, "Oh, Bill! Why does everything have to boil down to cost? Can you not see how I have gone out of my way to ensure you look the part today? Do you not realise that, if you fail to make the right impression, Frankie DeMario may never invite you again?"

"Francesca," she heard her father sigh from the bedroom next door, "a diamond money-clip is a complete waste of money, there is absolutely nothing wrong with my wallet. But, more importantly, I have no cash to clip into the bloody thing!"

Paris switched off from the remainder of the conversation, instead, becoming consumed by the memory of the previous night. Her stomach turned with excitement at the thought of the kiss and indeed the words Charles had spoken with such sincerity. She got up and made her way to the shower, remembering, yet trying to cast the promise that he would call her today to the back of her mind.

Frankie DeMario looked sophisticated yet casual in a pair of sand coloured trousers, a shirt with a faint gold pinstripe running through it and a formal blue blazer. He said his final goodbyes to his wife and daughter outside; Maria kissed him fondly on both cheeks shouting,

"Relax, and enjoy your day!" over her shoulder whilst fleeing hastily across the front drive towards Emma's Porsche. Emma refused to conceal her annoyance at having to sacrifice her visit to the gym and sauna and was impatiently revving the engine. With Luca having left ten minutes ago to drive to Epsom, and Sofia feigning illness, Emma had been given the unenviable and lengthy task of taking her mother shopping into Cheshire.

"Don't drive too fast," Frankie warned his daughter. "You are carrying precious cargo." He gestured toward his wife.

Emma tutted and rolled her eyes, skidding sandy gravel into the air as her foot slammed against the accelerator.

Today, feeling physically and mentally drained, Luca had chosen to utilise his driver. With a heavy heart he sat in the back seat of his father's Maybach and watched stretches of monotonous motorway quickly disappearing from his eyes as the car sped by. He felt thirsty but, ever conscious of his impending weigh-in, he chose a mineral water from the bar in the back and took only controlled sips from a crystal glass. During the trip he had taken numerous calls from various people whilst, in between, scrutinising DVD footage of his recent rides. He had only just finished one call when his mobile rang again. This time it was Thomas Markington. Luca answered.

"Luca, we have a problem, a fucking big problem," he barked with an unusually harsh edge to his voice.

"What?" Luca sat upright, sensing the urgency in Thomas' voice.

"The Italian Job was obviously drugs tested when you won at Ascot, it turns out the tests have returned." There was a pause while Thomas summoned the courage to say the following words, "Luca, they are positive."

"What the fuck are you talking about?" Luca yelled. "Nothing goes near that horse, what the fuck are they saying it's tested positive for?" His mind was racing.

"A.C.P. The doping drug, it dopes horses for short periods of time; it's just that she was given so much it was still in her system the next day, well, traces of it anyway."

His information was met with a tense silence whilst Luca tried to piece together his movements, hour by hour, leading up to the race. His mind chased for details and recollections and vividly remembered his mare behaving differently at the racecourse. His mind then stopped as it encountered two names – Julia and Charles. Luca spoke with venomous anger.

"The bastard!" Luca lurched to the edge of his seat. "Thomas, I have to get off this phone, I have a good idea which bastard has done this. I'll call you back." Luca hung up and, whilst dialling his father's number, he knew he had Julia's naïve honesty to thank for his rapid dissection of the crisis. He was also completely aware she had nothing to do with it. His father answered the call and, in chaotic outbursts of rage, Luca recounted the information to him.

"I think it's that bastard Charles Lancaster-Baron," he spat.

Frankie DeMario sat back in his chair remaining calm as he listened to his son's fury over the loud-speaker. The information made the expensive cigar and the Rose champagne he held in his hands taste all the sweeter. He waited until his son had finished his furious tirade before answering with a cold certainty.

"Don't you worry about Charles Lancaster-Baron, Luca," he advised knowingly. "Superficially, let's first play it the right way and call the police. In the meantime," he nodded assertively, "let me assure you, if it is him, his cards will be well and truly marked." Looking over at his three friends sitting in front of him he winked shrewdly at one in particular.

Bill Montford was astounded by the conversation he had been privy to, unable to believe that anyone, however arrogant, would be foolish enough to disregard the power of the DeMario's.

Bill's astonishment had begun that morning when limousines and uniformed chauffeurs had arrived at his home to deliver him safely to the airport. Now, he sat in ultimate comfort on Frankie's private jet on their way to one of the finest golf courses in the world, situated in Ayr. From the first moment the four men had boarded the aircraft Frankie began to talk business. Bill, feeling proud to be involved, soon realised that, if he was to place his trust in Frankie, there could be the opportunity to earn some serious money, alleviating all his financial concerns.

A small collection of conscientious staff were on board to meet their every need, champagne, scotch, and a full a la carte menu being offered to all Frankie's guests, of which today there were three. Every experience had left Bill wondering how one man could acquire such vast wealth. He didn't know exactly, but there was a certainty to one of his conclusions – he hadn't made it by allowing individuals to take advantage of him, and Charles Lancaster-Baron had done exactly that.

Bill recounted eavesdropping on Paris and Francesca's conversation about Charles' proposal of giving up the baby to the Santé's. He also knew there would be something sinister around the recent outings Charles had been keen to pursue with his vulnerable daughter, and internally fumed at the veil of lies he would be undoubtedly casting upon her.

He reclined his chair and rested his head on the cool Ivory leather seats. There was one thing he knew for certain: Charles Lancaster-Baron – he hated the pompous shit.

Chapter Twenty Eight

PARIS ended her call to Charles and stood motionless in her bedroom, they had arranged to meet later. Her face was flushed, and her eyes so wide with surprise that the muscles around her eyebrows twitched as they reached for the ceiling. She felt glued to the spot, recalling his voice across the line and recalling, in heart clattering detail, the kiss they had shared the night before. They had arranged to meet later and she wondered, guiltily, if he would kiss her again. The thought caused the previous flutter of butterflies in her stomach to develop into giant flapping eagles, turning her excitement into apprehension. She flopped into the armchair in the sitting room and contemplated cancelling their arrangement but, just as she was about to act, Leona Lewis, a previous X Factor champion, began to sing her earlier number one hit, 'A Moment Like This' on the radio. As Paris listened to the words, a sense of hope that miracles really do come true began to surface.

Charles turned off his mobile, realising there was a strong possibility Paris might call him back.

"I'm turning this off," he informed Rebecca casually. "The bloody thing has never stopped ringing all day, "and, anyway, I want to give *you* my full attention," he smiled.

Rebecca appreciated Charles' consideration, relieved there was one person in the room that had a true understanding of her personal dilemma.

"It seems inconceivable that anyone would even consider giving up their baby," she said softly, "but, do you really think she will go ahead with it?"

Charles picked up on the concealed hope behind her question. "I am the last person to comment on what is going on in a woman's mind," his eyes shifted quickly in aversion to her gaze, "but, all I can say is, I was as shocked as you are now, but, she seems adamant that is what she wants. She gave good reasons," he shrugged his shoulders gesturing a sense of logic towards the idea, "she needs the money, she feels too young for the responsibility, she knows how much you would adore the baby, and, to her credit, abhors the idea of a termination."

Rebecca flung her hands towards her mouth. "A termination?" she gasped. "We wouldn't want the thought to enter her head, would we?" she said, turning to her father for corroboration.

"No, no, that would be a crazy solution," he said, scratching his head.

"Well, that option would just be nonsensical, wouldn't it, Rebecca, given your desperate situation?" Charles said sympathetically. Her mother nodded. Charles gazed at Rebecca across the room and wished she knew how much he wanted her to have this child. She would need to have someone dependable around her when Paris handed over Gerard's baby, and with Piers out of the way, that would be when she would realise how much she needed him. His thoughts were broken.

"So, what happens now, then?" Rebecca hesitated, looking fleetingly to her mother and father, "Assuming we want to go ahead with it, that is."

"Well," Charles leant against the Aga, "the only thing she has asked is that you don't mention this to anyone, she wants the discussions to be solely carried out by myself at this early stage, with the finer detail sorted as we go on. Are you happy with that?"

"Yes, yes," Rebecca answered quickly. The telephone ringing in her office broke the discussion. "Excuse me," Rebecca said, standing from her chair. "I need to get that." She walked to her office with her mind dreamily imagining holding a new born baby; *at last* she thought *my greatest wish could soon be a reality*. If only the situation was as it should be. She had expected to hold her baby whilst Piers stood adoringly at her side. They would have been a family together and now, knowing he wouldn't be, made her miss him so much. She picked up the phone, it was Piers. She fought with the burning desire to tell him the news.

"Please Rebecca, listen to me," he pleaded.

This was not his first call. For days he had called her several times each day and in every conversation she had remained strong, but today, they both noticed her tone had softened.

Piers, sensing an opportunity continued to beg. "Can't you see this was a bloody set up?" he continued, his voice becoming stronger. "And when I find out who it is I will kill them," he spat.

His voice continued to churn through the line and Rebecca's thoughts began to drift. Rebecca felt confused at the mass of destruction surrounding her life. She sat in the carver chair, the distant conversation of Charles and her parents talking of actualising her dream drifted from the kitchen and into one ear, whilst Piers, continuing to convince her of his love for her drifted through the other. She doodled carelessly on that morning's 'to do' list and defiantly ignored its beckon of responsibility. She was missing Piers more than she could say. She wondered how different things would have been if she had listened to him and kept away from here. Back in Kentucky everything had been fantastic; it had just been the two of them with no interference from anyone. But she wanted interference; she wanted to share their love with a baby, what was so wrong in that? Charles understood, why couldn't he?

"Rebecca, I don't ever want anything or anyone coming between you and I," he had said whilst cradling her fondly in his arms one evening in Kentucky, "I never want to share you, even with a child," he had informed her.

She mocked the statement in her mind and simultaneously felt her temper rise. *That must have meant, unless something or someone has pert tits and is a size ten*, she thought bringing her emotional sentiment back down to earth.

"I'm going now, Piers. Goodbye." Abruptly she cut off the call and sat back in her chair looking around the room with indifference until her eyes rested upon a photograph of Gerard. Why did he have to die? Her eyes filled with a pool of grieving tears, she needed him now and knew, if nothing else, that Gerard would find something out of this mess to make her laugh. She grabbed a tissue and dabbed gently at her eyes. She had one consolation that made her heart warm. Gerard's baby was her consolation. She stood up from the chair and made her way back into the kitchen.

Piers, sensing a slight resolve in Rebecca's voice decided to visit her. His small hire car travelled along the road with the same accelerated speed as his temper. It was a straight one mile journey from his hotel and he felt nervous as he realised he was only minutes away.

Rebecca reoccupied her seat at the table. Charles and her parents were in deep conversation about Kitty. She listened intently, waiting patiently for the opportunity to steer the conversation gently back to Gerard's baby. Victoria looked concerned.

"I'm sorry to hear Kitty isn't one hundred per cent, Charles," she said caringly. "Is there anything we can do?"

"No, not at all," Charles answered, reminding him that Doctor White had still not returned his call. "I'll keep my eye on her, but thank you," he added. Victoria made a mental note to call Kitty and arrange a luncheon meeting.

"What does she think about the situation with Paris's pregnancy?" Rebecca asked, seizing her chance.

"Oh, Christ!" Charles was flabbergasted Rebecca had even asked. "I haven't mentioned a word of it to her, nor should anyone else," he insisted before dampening his tone. "She wouldn't understand," he added with a laugh. "Her thoughts and ideas are heavily engrained with the legalities of the world, it stems from her childhood. She would see the process of you buying Paris' baby as tantamount to infant retail." Charles, realising his mistake, rolled his eyes. "You know what she's like."

Rebecca looked hurt. "Well, I don't think we would be *buying* the baby, I would see it more that I was helping Paris out of a terrible situation, like you said before, she needs the money, and after all," she said convincingly, "it is Gerard's baby too, that means the baby is already ours anyway." Her green eyes flashed around the table in search of agreement but the conversation was brought to an abrupt halt by the sight of Piers leaning against the open door.

"Oh what a surprise," he announced arrogantly, "another Santé plot in the offing, is it?"

Piers felt incensed by the fact that Charles was there *again*, and to be faced with another example of the cold impenetrable wall the Santé family had always erected around them.

Rebecca felt her panic drown as she appraised the broad masculinity of his physique and the colours of his red and white Ralph Lauren rugby shirt which accentuated his swarthy complexion. Then she remembered the image of him in bed with Sofia, returning her emotions to jealousy and humiliation.

"There is no plot, Piers," Rebecca snapped sharply.

"Oh no of course not, Rebecca," Piers replied with sarcasm so thick it stuck to the walls. "In your family, buying a baby will be a standard day's work."

Charles looked across at Piers and, sensing he was annoyed, smirked blatantly with satisfaction.

"You don't know the full story, Piers," Rebecca answered abruptly. "When you do, I will discuss it with you."

"Oh that's good of you, when you're ready, let me know," he retorted, stepping inside the kitchen.

James stood from his chair and unable to bear being in the same room as the uninvited guest, he poured the remainder of his cup of coffee down the sink.

"Right," James announced, "I am going to look at that Range Rover that we are interested in, would you like to come, Victoria?" he asked his wife.

"Yes, yes," she stammered, rising to her feet, "We will leave you alone, we will be back soon."

"Oh, no, James, please don't leave on my account," Piers snapped. "What I am about to say I would like everybody to hear."

A wave of panic flooded through Rebecca. Was he here to inform them he was leaving for Kentucky? The thought of him leaving caused the week's hurt and anger at his betrayal to escape from her mind. Her father's interjection saved her from crying.

"You want to talk to me, do you?" James boomed raising his

eyebrows. "Well, go ahead Piers, I am intrigued as to what you would like to say." His words were followed with a brutal stare.

Piers, clearly uncomfortable, struggled through his burning anger to articulate what he had initially intended to say.

"There is no point in beating around the bush on this one." He took a deep breath and shuffled nervously from one foot to the other. "I realise I have done something that is so very wrong to your daughter, James. It is the worst mistake I have ever made in my entire life and I have come to formerly apologise to you for treating your daughter with such disrespect." He paused for a second. "I know you have never approved of my relationship with Rebecca and I know that you dislike me, but I want to do everything I can to show you how much I love your daughter and want to care for her." Piers walked slowly to Rebecca and placed a hesitant arm around her waist.

Predictably, on feeling his touch, Rebecca quivered internally and simultaneously, knowing him as she did, felt proud of Piers that he had had the courage to bear his soul in public.

Piers turned to Rebecca. "Rebecca, I am so sorry for what I have done and how I have hurt you, I ..." His words were broken in mid sentence.

James Santé walked close up to his face, his stare was menacing. "Don't you dare come here and expect your insincerities to be listened to. You are the pits," he spat, stabbing his finger into his chest. "You walk into our home begging for forgiveness after what you have done to my daughter! You are everything I ever thought you were and more. You know what?" he screwed up his hate fuelled eyes, "You said before that you knew I disliked you, well you are wrong, very wrong, you see, I fucking hate you!" he shouted. "My daughter doesn't need a low life bastard like you in her life." Degradingly his sickened eyes traced the length of Piers' body and back up again. "Your mother was a slut and your father, well," he threw up his arms, "he was nothing more than a mere peasant boy thieving for his living. You, it shows beyond a shadow of a doubt, are from the same stock."

"Daddy, stop!" Rebecca appealed. "Stop it!"

Her father continued, "Rebecca, you see, she has many, many

suitors that would love the opportunity of being with her, she doesn't need your kind treating her the way you have." He looked at Charles sitting at the table and his face brightened. "Oh! And what a surprise, there's my favourite right here." He placed an arm around Charles' shoulder and turned to Piers, laughing patronisingly. He stormed over to the fridge and grabbed a bottle of champagne and viciously tore at the foil neck.

"I tell you what," he announced to the table before him, "I have a great idea; lets all have a celebratory glass of champagne. What shall we toast?" he looked up at the ceiling feigning thought. "I know, let's celebrate new beginnings for Rebecca and," he walked over to Piers, "the fact that *you*," he prodded Piers aggressively in the chest, "are now leaving."

Piers caught sight of Charles goading him with a condescending smirk and felt his anger rip in fierce retaliation.

"Well, you know what, you decrepit old fool" he shouted at James, "I fucking hate you too. I wouldn't piss on you if you were on fire. You know something else?" This time Piers invaded James' space, sidling up to him with only inches between their faces. "You will fucking pay for the way you have just spoken to me." He paused and pointed into his face, "Big time. You will pay!" He barged out of the kitchen and slammed the door behind him.

Rebecca watched in silence as Piers thundered his way across the drive to his car. She concealed her emotion and realised that this situation delivered her to a crossroads but, whichever turn she took, there would be no going back. She had the chance to follow Piers now, to run after him and agree to his suggestion of them both returning to Kentucky. For a split second she contemplated the option but then felt her body sink further into her chair.

She stood and watched him leave, she had put him before her family and her home once before, she couldn't bear to go through it a second time, *and anyway,* she deciphered coldly, *I have a racing yard to control.*

Charles rose from his chair and walked over to the window where Rebecca stood. Remaining silent, he placed a protective arm of concern across her shoulder.

In the instant she felt him comfort her she harshly shrugged away his arm and looked back at him with an icy stare. "I don't need comfort, Charles; I just need to get on with my work." She walked over to the door and slid her feet inside her wellingtons, banging the door behind her.

"Who the bloody hell has left that bridle out?" Charles heard her bawl across the yard. "It's easy to see you lot don't fork out for this tack, get it cleaned and put away, NOW!"

Regardless of Rebecca's dreadful mood, Charles breathed a sigh of relief. He appeared to have completely eradicated one of the obstacles he had been facing. It was obvious, Piers was now out of Rebecca's life.

Chapter Twenty Nine

THE NEXT DAY, unable to get the argument with James Santé and the situation with Rebecca out of his mind, Piers still felt swamped by a foul, angry temper. However, he had this bad temper to thank for leading him at top speed toward his destination. His small hire car heaved with protestation along the motorway, but he ignored its discontent. Only last night had he managed to ascertain where the DeMario's lived from a drunken local in the hotel, and now, at last, he was on his way. He took long aggressive draws on a cigarette whilst he thought about the bitch he was about to see again, Sofia DeMario, daughter of the Mafiosi, he took another long angry draw of his cigarette. He recalled the drunken talk in the pub, rumours about her father, Frankie DeMario having connections with the Mafia. It made him wonder, if it was true, and when her father witnessed the anger he presently felt for his daughter, how long it would be before he was chopped into pieces by a chainsaw and hung to dry in the cellar like Parma ham. He battled with straying cigarette ash blowing around the car and realised he couldn't give a shit. He was livid. He couldn't give a shit what, or who she was, there wasn't a woman on earth that was going to turn his life upside down and get away with it, however much of a good shag she was. He needed all the facts, to know the exact truth before he, like Rebecca, felt able to turn his back on their life together.

A journey that would normally have taken one hour and a half actually took Piers and his overly exerted car fifty minutes. After stopping at a run-down service station and asking for more detailed directions he sat in his car outside the DeMario mansion with the hot engine creaking and cracking as it cooled.

Having made the journey in temper, Piers some hundred miles later, was disappointed and embarrassed to find he had calmed down. He had parked on a grass verge alongside the road and stared up at the clinical prison wall that surrounded and obscured any view of the house behind.

Nervously lighting up his seventh cigarette since his journey had begun, he got out of the car and wandered across to the solid wooden electric gates that separated the DeMario family from the rest of the world. He tried from every conceivable angle to peer through a forgiving crack or gap but the place was frostily hostile to inspection, with neither the bricks nor the wood in the gates relenting an inch. He looked up on hearing a robotic noise and noticed a security camera lens, protruding and swivelling with interest at the visitor below. He also noticed an entry intercom illuminated to the right of the electric gates. His finger hovered over the button but the recurring image of Parma ham forced him to hesitate. Having come this far, he reasoned, it would seem ludicrous to surrender now. He pressed the buzzer firmly and stood back to await a reply.

"Yes," a woman's voice coldly snapped. Piers shuffled edgily towards the intercom.

"Hello, I am looking for a lady by the name of Sofia DeMario."

"And?" Sofia sighed assuming it to be another reporter trying to bait information about the drugging of The Italian Job. Piers fell silent. "Who are you?" The voice asked.

"It's Piers, I'm a friend."

The intercom fell uncomfortably silent and the only sound that broke it was the mechanical zip of the surveillance camera with its lens zooming toward him. A second later the intercom crackled back to life.

"It is Sofia," her voice sounded crisp, "you'd better come in," she announced.

Piers watched as the iron gates of the mansion slowly inched open. Jumping into his car he cautiously drove through.

Like a bullfrog in a sauna Piers' eyes bulged at the sight before him. A formal drive lined with scatterings of clustered woodland paid homage to a variety of wild inhabitants. He watched as squirrels and rabbits jumped and scurried, birds flew from one sprawling oak tree to another and the pheasants, dressed suitably in the finery of bright cuffs and collars, strutted grandly among the private tranquillity of their surroundings. Like an ocean, the swell of green paddocks ran far into the distance. They were railed with wrought iron fences and offered security to some of the finest thoroughbreds in Europe, their tails swished against glass-like coats in an effort to expel the irritating twitch of inferior horsefly.

The drive totalled one mile in length and as he neared its end he took his foot off the accelerator, temporarily losing the notion to drive. As the DeMario's home came into view, Piers stared in utter astonishment.

A white mansion with a seamless palatial façade stretched magnificently across a backdrop of woods. The turreted roof boasted seven white broad chimney pots as their crowning glory. Beneath them, four rows of large oblong windows were spread in uniform intervals across the front of the house, and six audacious pillars, like white muscular forearms, appeared to hold the entire building in place, preventing it from crashing to its knees. Between them, twenty six ivory marble steps led the way to a gigantic double door entrance. Piers replaced his foot on the accelerator and slowly drove towards the mansion.

Nervously he ventured out of the car and was welcomed by a bronze statue that stood upon the immaculate front lawn; it was a ten foot figure of the Virgin Mary holding an ever flowing cup of love that cascaded torrents of silver water into a deep trough. The water smelt as fresh as a country spring and the magnificent power of its gushing fountain fanned the air.

The giant scrape of the entrance door unbolting and opening forced him to turn quickly and see Sofia standing in between the gigantic doorway. She was dressed in a pink velour tracksuit, its casual intent ignored by the adornment of hand- stitched crystals winding their way across the sleeves and legs. Her long black hair, as smooth as satin, fell down to her chest and her wide dark eyes, looking shameful yet appealing looked out to him. She stood, unable to speak, and watched as he neared the steps.

"Hello," Piers ventured unsurely.

"Hello," she said solemnly, "you had better come in."

Piers hesitated, his eyes lurked behind her as he wondered who else was at home.

"Nobody is in," she reassured him, sensing his trepidation. "I am alone."

"You're brave," he smiled, walking up the steps, but Sofia's sullenness continued.

"No," she replied, "I am just stupid."

Piers looked into her dark eyes and saw slow burning embers of remorse and sadness.

"Mmmmm," Piers nodded before shrugging, adding brightly, "But I am a big believer in guilty until proven innocent." He laughed, walking through the entrance. "So come on," he encouraged lightly, "let's get all this out of the way. Tell me your version of events."

She nodded, cautiously locking and bolting the door behind them.

"Come on, I'll make some coffee," she said leading him through the elaborate marble hallway to the kitchen.

"Not for me, thanks," Piers replied. "I'm allergic to coffee."

"Oh!" Sofia turned; their eyes locked.

"Well, I am if it's after eleven a.m. After that I need something that has a percentage etched along the side of the label," Piers laughed.

Sofia smiled for the first time, grateful for his blasé manner and began to feel, once again comfortable and at ease in his company. She poured chilled Chablis into two wine glasses that goldfish would be happy to call home and sat beside him at the kitchen table. Slowly, not knowing where to start, Sofia began to explain everything, ensuring the story in its entirety consisted of nothing but the truth.

"So, you see Piers?" Sofia explained feeling exhausted by the truths of her story and the amount of wine she had nervously drunk,

"I didn't mean for any of this to happen, and genuinely I …" she paused, sharing the final contents of their second bottle of wine between their two glasses.

"Go on," he encouraged.

"I really enjoyed, our…" she thought of their passionate sex "…our time together," she added quickly, "and I honestly never meant for you and Rebecca to break up."

"I might have known it was that bastard Lancaster-Baron," he fumed. "One day I will get my own back on that fucker. But," he took a deep breath then blew it out, signifying strained efforts, "it wasn't just this situation that caused Rebecca and me to split. The minute she left home alone to be with," he spat out his words, "that lot," he shook his head in bitterness as he thought of James Santé, "I knew that this would be the conclusion. I told her as much but," he shrugged, "she made her choice."

Sofia began to talk again, but to Piers the subject matter was irrelevant. Instead of listening he stared at her good looks, overflowing with the glamorous charm of Mediterranean mystique and such a welcoming contrast to Rebecca's frigid demure. In fact everything surrounding him now presented a sharp contrast to the Santé life. He examined and appreciated every detail of the spacious ivory elegance of the DeMario mansion, critically comparing it to the austere environment of Chelmsley Manor, crammed to the rafters with the conceited plunge of burr walnut and yew antiques. He loved it here. Despite its enormity, the place had a casual essence that simply flowed.

Hearing the continuing blur of her words he stared at her face and became struck by the excited dance of her inebriated eyes and the melting sensuality of her lightly glossed lips. He thought about the night they had shared and the details surrounding it. Like most, himself included, she had a closeted past but her confessions and the way in which she had communicated them had told him a lot about her. She was like a magic stick of rock one that had the ability to offer many different flavours and colours. She was a passionate woman with a bold streak of honesty running right through her middle; she was a woman who was daring though pensive and also young yet internally very strong.

Strength and passion, he mused. Qualities he adored in a woman. The only passion Rebecca held was for the four-legged variety that shat in a stable, and strength? Pah! There was a time he had thought Rebecca was strong. Externally she appeared so, but now, the only vision he had in his mind was a woman that cowered internally like a trembling kitten behind her father and the Santé name.

Feeling the relaxing effects of the alcohol sink down into private domains he moved himself closer to Sofia at the kitchen table. "That life for me is over now," Piers stated surely. "I have many new plans in mind."

"Oh, really?" Sofia answered.

"I want to get into the movie business," he laughed, playfully anchoring her head in his arm, "but I need some practice, and by the looks of your last film, so do you." Piers let out an enormous laugh.

"You cheeky sod!" Laughing, Sofia made a playful swipe towards him "Well if you want another showing, you are going to have to catch me first." She leapt hastily from the table accidentally catching her wine glass which smashed into pieces as it hit the marble floor. Ignoring the debris she continued to run towards her bedroom with Piers in hot pursuit, wildly stripping off his clothes and blindly throwing them behind him as he chased the delightful sound of her provocative screams.

Chapter Thirty

AS SHE WALKED out of the caravan door Julia glanced back at her mobile phone lying silently upon the bed. For the first time since their split, she left it, finally accepting its deathly torturous silence would never be resuscitated by the welcome tone of Luca's ring.

It was mid July and contrary to that morning's bright sunny weather forecast the sky held a muggy grey blanket of cloud within its grip. The air was humid and still, the atmosphere morbidly ghostlike, as though a collection of evil spirits above had clandestine plans for the minions below. She had only reached the corner of the road before she felt her stride slacken and her morning stroll, quickly lose its appeal.

She sat on a nearby bench and wondered why everywhere seemed so quiet. With the exception of the occasional car passing through, the roads were clear of the bursting traffic that usually filled them. Then she remembered it was Sunday, a time for families and loved ones to set off on a day's adventure together in relish of fresh terrain, the seaside, possibly a theme park or even a day at home. She imagined how it must feel to be a part of a family unit, to sit beside your husband in the car, both having the amusing task of trying to become au fait with the nonsensical rambling chatter of your child in the backseat.

To Julia it was a magical dream; a dream that she knew many

people out there at this very moment would be experiencing, *but would they be appreciating everything they had*? she wondered heavily.

There was only one person in the world that could have answered her dream and, through her foolish naivety, he now hated her. With that thought, just like the weather, she also began to feel gloomy. Apart from dozens of small birds taking ballet like steps across a telephone wire and causing it to tremble, her surroundings remained eerily still. It felt as though it was the lull before a storm. A large determined raindrop fell from the sky and burst onto Julia's cheek, she wiped it away, oblivious to the fact that the conclusion she had just made held a double-edged promise.

John Holmes had slowed his car almost to a stop about two hundred yards away. He was sure it was her; surely, he couldn't have been mistaken? He strained his eyes; her face was too unique; he could never forget those magnificent looks. His heart raced as he recalled the spellbinding effect she had had on him whilst in his boutique. He was desperate to talk to her again, to see that Hollywood pearly white smile and hear her awesome voice.

His thoughts became ugly; this thieving bitch had nearly cost him his job. He would be hearing her voice alright, only this time it would be at the police station. Determined her jaw dropping attributes were not going to get the better of him a second time, he reached for his mobile phone. Carefully he dialled the enquiries line and waited for an answer.

"Hello," he said, "can you put me through to York Police Station please?"

Luca felt as though he was only inches away from Julia but the fact he couldn't see or touch her had tormented him all day. He was at Doncaster, a stone's throw away from their past meeting place of Leeds and each time the tannoy at the racecourse had belted out the race meet's destination to the throngs of punters he had been drenched with a blizzard of private suffering. Despite this, his professional focus had not been impinged upon, having managed to urge four winners past the finishing post, but his attitude to his day's success had remained indifferent. He had relieved his driver from duty the night before, holding an unrealistic hope that Julia, living in the area, might attend the meet today. But now, with the day over, he realised his hopes had been overly optimistic.

He sat in his car, joining the long swirling queue of vehicles and watched the circus-like hysteria of race-goers leave the course. Jammed in the car park and feeling his impatience rise at the unmoving blockade, he scrolled the mass of missed calls on his mobile and wished that one of them had been Julia. His irritation at remaining stationary induced an urgency that made him realise, he just couldn't stand it any longer. Taking a deep breath and swallowing hard to rid the harboured knot of pride that had swelled and lodged in his throat, he called Julia's number.

Luca's clenched fist thudded impatiently against the steering wheel and his jaw began to pulse as his call continued to ring ….and ring. His mind cruelly began to envisage Julia purposefully ignoring his call, coldly sniggering at the fact she had eventually succeeded in causing him to cave in. The answer machine clicked in, surprising him with Julia's personal greeting. He listened intently to every syllable and vowel she pronounced and instantly felt the familiarity of her soft clear voice temporarily lift his dark mood. He heard the beep signalling him to leave a message, he paused trying to think of the right words but then, feeling his temper return, he cut off the call and threw the phone into the foot-well of the passenger seat.

The congestion of the vehicles ahead started to move into a slow crawl bringing his attention back to driving and at last, he noticed the four girls sitting in a ford escort cabriolet who had been avidly trying to break his concentration.

Despite the dull weather, overjoyed at seeing 'a star' for the first time in their lives, the four girls had dragged back the aged fabric roof of the car. Each was sporting tattoos and bleached blonde hair, and none of them were in the least bit troubled by the receipt of attention. The driver, laughing raucously with her passengers, kangaroo-hopped ahead of Luca in the queue, allowing one of her friends on the back seat, clearly fuelled with lashings of alcohol, to stand.

"Wey-hey, Luca!" the girl on the back seat screamed, "get a load of this!"

She jumped up and down on the back seat, blatantly lifting her top to expose her naked drooping breasts that flapped erratically like part deflated hot air balloons in the wind. Luca, embarrassed by the crude display, heard the distant applause of car horns and appreciative drunken jeers of other men passing by. Exasperated by the traffic and his new, yet unwelcome fans that had once again reminded him of Julia's demure manner, he rammed his car into reverse and made his way towards the second exit from the course.

Eventually he reached the road that offered links to a selection of motorway routes. Again, he thought about his meetings with Julia in the hotel in Leeds and saw a sign for the link road that would take him there. He didn't hesitate, he took the turning. Pulling over in the next lay-by he sent Julia a text message.

I am on my way to our usual hotel in Leeds. I would love to see you there, if you aren't there by 6 o'clock I will understand. L x

As he neared his destination, having still not heard from her, he began to feel uneasy and uptight. An aggravated sense told him she was not going to reply. Luca tried to overpower his pessimism. Even if she wasn't going to reply to his message, perhaps she would just turn up at the hotel? He hoped his assumption was correct and continued toward his destination.

Julia could hear the distant shouts from a mother on the camp behind her.

"There are police cars coming round this corner, they better not be anything to do with you, son!" she bellowed.

Julia, still sitting on the same bench, sighed with frustration. How different her life could have been if she had been lucky enough to be with Luca. She wondered what he would say if she were to call him and tell him how sorry she was for listening to Charles. She heard another voice, this time closer and unrecognisable.

"There she is!" the man shouted.

Julia turned. Two policemen walked swiftly towards her, placing their hats on their heads as they approached, initially concealed from view, a man behind them. A current of fear enveloped her body as she realised, it was the manager of the boutique.

"That's her!" John Holmes shouted. "That is the woman who stole the outfit from my store."

Her first instinct was to run, instead she froze. The officers began to ask her questions, her name, her address, her date of birth. Julia looked up at the bodies in front of her but only the formal scare of black police uniforms registered. A blast of adrenaline, too harsh for her body to deal with, caused her to tremble and her previously still, silent surroundings to spin. The officers' words whizzed around her head like a broth in a witch's cauldron.

"It may harm your defence if you do not mention when questioned anything..." The voice continued but Julia's ears, fiercely trying to protect her, managed to close the rest of the words out. Her hands were wrenched behind her back and her wrists enclosed within cold constraints of steel handcuffs. She was shoved into the backseat of the police car and as her hands trembled she tried to gain some relief from the pressure of her imprisoned arms and hands but each time she wrestled, the unforgiving grip of the handcuffs only intensified.

A roaring crack of thunder burst from the sky as the police car set off at speed. Terrified and alone Julia watched in horrified silence as the buildings and trees rushed by her eyes, everything obscured by the pelting rain that smothered the windows. As the car made its way to the station she closed her eyes and wished she had brought her mobile phone. The only person she knew that may be able to help her was Luca. For so many reasons, she needed him now more than she had needed anybody in her life.

An excited mob of reporters armed with cameras, notepads and huge cylindrical microphones gathered around the doorway as Julia was led into the station. A buzz of chaotic voices, the delight in their pitch unmasked, fired questions at her and the officers as they passed. Julia said nothing, continuing to look ahead, the intrusive din whirling torrentially in her head.

"Julia, what reaction are you expecting from Luca with regard to your arrest?" one reporter shouted from behind the crowd.

Julia's heart sank. What an embarrassment she had become to

him. Like hungry wanton chicks waiting to be fed, the reporters' mouths continued to open and close. Relief temporarily stroked her body as she was led to safety into the station.

Feeling absolutely terrified at her unfamiliar surroundings, Julia was led into a stark impersonal room that housed four chairs and a table. The chairs scraped sourly against the bare cold floor as the rooms occupants took to their seats. It was then that the formalities began.

Chapter Thirty One

LUCA was sitting at the same customary table as he and Julia had always frequented, but this time, instead of being captivated by Julia's company, her chair was empty. It was well past the six o'clock deadline he had set and like a yoyo he would jump up and stand before the large window that overlooked the streets, peering out in the hope he would see her running towards the hotel, before sitting back down again to take another one of the numerous calls flooding through. None of which were from Julia. The next person to call was Thomas Markington.

"Just to let you know you are splashed all over the ITN News *again*, but this time *you* are off the hook."

"What are you talking about, what's happened this time?" Luca asked agitated at the thought of more publicity.

"I've had press agents and reporters on the phones the last hour, asking if you've got a statement to make about your ex-girlfriend's arrest," he said.

Luca sat upright in his chair, turning his face to the wall to prevent his conversation being overheard.

"Are you talking about Julia?" he asked in hushed tones.

"Yes, the silly bitch, she's been out shoplifting or something, I can't get to grips with it properly, every time I try and catch the story the bastard phone rings again with another reporter."

Luca ignored the fury he felt at Thomas' flippant disregard for

Julia. Instead, feeling instantly protective of her, he prodded for further information.

"Where is she being held?" he snapped

"York Main Station I think, but…"

Luca interrupted him. "Listen, Thomas, I don't care what it takes, cancel whatever I have on for the time being, I don't care what you tell them, I don't care if they never hire me again, just do it." Luca then cut the call dead.

He threw some money onto the table for the two gin and tonics he had ordered, then grabbing his car keys he dashed out of the hotel's revolving doors, wishing to God he still had his driver. Turning on the ignition he programmed his car's navigation system to direct him through the winding city streets of Leeds towards York.

"I need the quickest route!" he blasted towards the impersonal equipment. He stamped on the accelerator, sending his tyres spinning and screeching across the road and causing a flurry of disapproving heads to turn and stare.

"Come round later, Paris," Charles suggested. "I'll call you when Mother has gone out."

Charles couldn't stand the thought of spending another evening at the Montford's. The clinical feel of the house with its straight edges and contemporary furniture made him feel he was unsuitably dressed and would be much better placed wearing a white coat with a badge that described him as 'lab technician'. However, despite the uncomfortable surroundings, Paris had surprised him again last night, this time reintroducing him to Scrabble – which she had won – and with, yet another warm loving kiss.

If he had been blindfold whilst the kiss had taken place and then been asked to identify which woman in a line up had been the benefactor, even Charles with all his experience could have easily been fooled. Never would he have believed that Paris would be capable of holding so much tenderness and passion beneath such an unflattering disguise.

Charles didn't know where his mother had gone. He had last seen her walking down the drive carrying a wicker basket with all the dogs at her heels. Being too far away to hear his shouts, she had continued to walk slowly away, with only the shrill lively colour of her pink headscarf showing any clear definition against the grey muggy day.

Armed with a steaming hot mug of Earl Grey tea, Charles sat on the worn squashy comforts of the settee in the snug and, turning on the television, caught the final summary of the day's news. He sat upright, his mind barely able to distil the full length picture of Julia smothering the screen. EX girlfriend of Luca DeMario? Shoplifting? Arrested? And more....A GYPSY GIRL??

He laughed out loud; the information sweetened all the more as he imagined the look of embarrassment that must be adorning Luca's smug face now. With a broad malicious grin covering his own face, he looked at the picture of Julia on the screen. It had been taken the night of the Injured Jockeys Ball. To the untrained eye the exquisite nature of her good looks staring back at the viewers must have seemed breathtaking. Charles however, was not surprised she had turned out to be a criminal. He had seen the vague outline of rough edges surrounding her that night, she was certainly a far cry from the smooth pearly finish that a well-bred lady like Rebecca possessed, for example.

His elated thoughts married the two situations; now, things really were all knitting together nicely, he mused. Piers had pissed off and it looked as though Luca had also been given a portion of his just deserts – problems that would certainly take his mind off racing for a while. Turning off the television and forgetting about his tea, he poured himself a glass of wine, deciding it was a much more refined way to celebrate. Then, possessed by a feeling he was at last travelling the road of triumph, he allowed himself an unusual reward, relaxation.

He reached for the latest edition of *Horse and Hound* that lay invitingly on the coffee table and began to flick through the contents, stopping with curiosity when he reached the section advertising 'Horses for Sale.' Attracting his interest was a hunter, a nine-year-old, seventeen-hand black gelding. The ad. explained that it had hunted with the Beaufort Hunt for the past four years. He examined the photograph. He noticed that the horse, just like himself, looked strong and had enormous presence, however so did the price. They wanted fifteen thousand pounds for it, stating that the first to see would buy.

Charles had promised himself and his accountant he would not be purchasing anything at all until he had sorted his existing financial mess, but the hunting season would be upon him and, being Master of the Hounds, he needed a decent animal that would stand the pace. Anyway, he sniffed, it wasn't as though fifteen thousand pounds was going to break the bank. Luca DeMario, the smart arsed shit had already done that. The temptation to respond to the ad. was halted when he heard his mother humming in the garden behind the snug. Her presence reminded him that Doctor White had still not returned his call and that, secondly, whilst she was outside, he wanted to look again for those suspicious documents she had been hiding from him.

Throwing the *Horse and Hound* back onto the coffee table he made his way to her personal office, the place where all her documents were held. On her writing bureau there was a message from Mary informing his mother that Doctor White had called during her sleep and he had asked if she would call him back. The phone was by its side. Charles picked it up and scrolled through the digital display, he noticed that his mother had already returned his call almost one hour ago.

With suspicion playing heavily on his mind he placed the phone back on the table and guiltily looked out of the window and checked his mother was still suitably distracted. Kitty was on her hands and knees, ridiculously fighting overgrown rhubarb with a blunt knife. Charles shook his head, he would ask questions later. Like an ally cat in the depths of the night, Charles quickly slinked his way to the far side of the room. With a burst of curiosity he grabbed at the drawer, it didn't move, he tried a second time with greater force, it rattled, but again it failed to open, she had locked it. His face tightened, what the hell was she hiding in there?

He walked around the side of the house; he had a troubled feeling, one that made him worried for his mother. Was she really alright? Charles stood back and momentarily watched his mother kneeling in the garden with all her dogs lying nearby. She was wearing an old red sweater which clashed disgracefully with her pink silk headscarf. Charles gave a small laugh to himself, her hair was protected, he thought, but her eccentricities were on blatant parade.

"Mother, what the hell are you doing?" Charles walked over, baffled though amused at the sight of her sawing at rhubarb stalks with an old kitchen knife.

Still wrestling, she looked up. "Charles, shut up!" she puffed breathlessly. "What does it look like I am doing? I am trying to cut this bloody rhubarb stalk," she gasped. "You know absolutely nothing about gardening, you twit!"

"Mother," he laughed, "even I know you don't cut them," he said, easing the knife from her hand, "you pull them!" He yanked a stalk gently from the ground and held it in front of her with a smile. "Maybe you should have asked for Mary's help? She would have done this for you."

He noticed the beads of perspiration that had appeared on his mother's forehead and the flush of her cheeks that blended so well with her sweater. "What are you doing it for anyway?" Charles asked, sitting down on the grass alongside her.

"One of the seniors in the village isn't feeling too well, his wife died a couple of months ago and he told Mary he misses her rhubarb crumble, so," she paused to catch her breath, "I have found a recipe and I am going to make him one."

Charles let out a boisterous laugh. "You? Make rhubarb crumble? You've never cooked in your life," he said continuing to snigger. "What are you trying to do, force him up to his wife before his time? You may be a strong woman, Mother, but please don't start trying to play God."

Large sporadic droplets of rain began to fall around them and a rumble of thunder warned of an impending storm. Kitty tried her hardest to look at Charles disapprovingly, but the rain, as though washing away her angst, calmed her temperament. Slowly, recognising the funny side to her offer of kindness, she also began to giggle. Her forehead, beaded with silver pinpricks of perspiration and rain, sparkled and her eyes, as warm as the Maldivian sea, found her son's. The growing intensity of their laughing stare ignited a spark of love within Charles that ran like a faint electric current down his spine.

"There's no harm in trying," she managed through deepened laughs.

As Kitty laughed she held out her hand to her son, a gesture of loving contact that she felt compelled to share. Charles reached out, and as their hands connected the laughter of both mother and son ceased and was instead replaced by a loving smile that saturated their eyes. They sat in silence, oblivious to the rain, drinking in their special moment. Something deep within Charles informed him to savour the moment and also to speak.

"I love you, Mother," he told her softly.

"I know you do, son," she answered, "and, I love you too."

These words had never been spoken between them for years, the poignancy of that moment would last an eternity for both of them.

Chapter Thirty Two

THE RADIO whistled out the latest news regarding Julia's arrest, attracting thousands of curious listeners across the country to turn up the volume. Frankie DeMario, shook his head in disgust. Unlike the rest of the radio's audience, he was not surprised. Abruptly, he turned the radio off, thanking God that his son's relationship with this tramp had ended.

A second man of large stature filled his armchair as he sat down with a mug of hot coffee; he turned on the television to await his habitual viewing of the lunchtime news. His large oval eyes, like honeycombed acorns, effortlessly upstaged the dark dusky contours of his strong rugged face and lifted the glower of his raven black hair. Cautiously sipping on his coffee, he awaited the headlines.

His senses waded through the latest news of European conventions, political reports and the uninteresting results of recent ballots. The news broadcast moved on, this time stirring emotion.

"Bastards!" he shouted at the screen, on seeing police arresting young students for breach of the peace at a demonstration. "Pick on someone your own size you fuckin' bullies!"

The news reporter continued with the broadcast. "And today, we have breaking news about the ex-girlfriend of leading jockey, Luca DeMario," she proudly announced. "A woman by the name of Julia Smith is reported to have been arrested this morning on suspicion of theft and is about to be questioned at York Police Station."

The man's thick black eyebrows frowned on hearing the name read out; shrugging off any connection he took a second sip of coffee.

"We join ITN's Susan Murphy with live coverage of her arrival at the Police Station in York this morning."

The hot drink splattered out of his mouth, spraying coffee around his unkempt caravan like a newly lit firework. He jumped up from his chair startled by the pictures on the screen.

"That's my fuckin' daughter!" he boomed.

Slamming down his chipped mug, he reached for his work boots and frantically scuffled to force his feet inside. With his shoelaces still untied, he stumbled out of the caravan. Already he was on his way to the police station.

The pelting rain had gathered ferocity and, as Luca's car screeched to a halt outside the station doors, it soaked a small group of inexperienced reporters with a tidal wave of water.

"He's here!" One of them bellowed, saturated though grateful to be relieved of the heel-kicking boredom.

The name of John Holmes was not a favourite among the apprentice journalists.

"Some people will do anything for a few quid," they had scorned, prior to Luca's arrival, but he was here now and they had to seize their chance. Like a pack of hyenas to the smell of fresh meat, the soaking wet clan descended on his car.

Luca's temper erupted. He yanked at the door handle and pushed the door savagely against the baiting pack.

"You sick bastards!" he yelled.

Despite his insults, eager to make a name for themselves, they continued with their pursuit, thrusting questions and innuendos towards him, relentlessly digging for further comment. Like a charging bull, he barged them angrily aside, focusing with determination on the station doors.

Three youths sat in Reception, all of them unfamiliar with the fineries of racing. They looked on in amusement at the interest the new addition to Reception had accrued.

Luca stormed over to the officer in Reception who was shielded by a pane of glass and mesh caging. "I want to see Julia Smith, please," Luca said aggressively, wiping the rain from his face.

The overweight sergeant sat behind the desk and continued to complete the paperwork in front of him, though he grinned flippantly.

"We've only just begun our line of questioning, sir, she'll be a while yet," he answered, refusing to look up.

"Has she got a solicitor in with her?" He thumped upon the desk. "I want everything to be halted until I instruct my own personal legal team to aid her."

"Fuckin' 'ell!" exclaimed one of the youths, "I could do with shagging you, it sounds as though you'd be the only twat able to get me ou' a this shit," he jibed to the amusement of his two hooded look-alikes sitting by his side.

Luca and the sergeant turned and glanced briefly at the youth, Luca sneered dismissively.

"I'm sorry, sir," the sergeant continued, this time giving him his full attention, "we can't interrupt an interview at this stage; we can assure you she has been made fully aware of her legal rights. She may be a while but, if you would care to take a seat and wait for her you are welcome." The sergeant pointed to a group of chairs near the doors.

Hesitantly Luca sat down among the hooded youths, the overflowing waste paper bins and the graffiti-ridden walls. Luca lent forward in his seat and let out a groan, as though nearing submission, his face collapsed into the palms of his hands. It was one of the hoodies that brought the next visitor to Luca's attention.

"Jesus, this chav means business!" he laughed, straining his neck to see out of the doorway.

Luca didn't turn, but from outside heard the distant sounds of a loud irate voice.

"Get out of the way you set of filthy bastards!" The man blasted. "You leave my daughter alone, do you hear me?"

As the voice neared, Luca's agitation increased. The doors swung open and a man, broad in stature and nearing six foot three, stood motionless in reception. Even the rain dripping rapidly off his face gave the impression that the drops dare not stay. Black engine oil trailed down one leg of his jeans and his navy rugby shirt, also filthy, strained against the muscles of his arms that were hanging aggressively inches from his sides. With the almighty maturity of a thousand-year-old oak tree his strength and power filled his surrounding space, omitting words and motion; he glared towards the sergeant behind the desk.

The sergeant, recognising the new arrival groaned in reluctant anticipation. "Can I help you, Mr Smith?" he murmured.

"Yes you can," he thundered slowly. "I want my daughter, Julia Smith, out of 'ere now. Whatever you say she did, she didn't." He stabbed the counter with three unyielding fingers. "It's always the same with you lot, gypsy discrimination *again*, an 'ate campaign against us all, that's what's goin' on 'ere."

"Mmmm, right," the sergeant slowly nodded his head, privately appreciating the strength of the protective glass barrier.

Luca remained uneasily silent.

One of the youths still high from a previous fix was the only one who dared speak out.

"She's a popular girl this Julia Smith, it looks as though she 'as mates from all over the place."

Luca winced as the giant turned. First he glared at the youth and then he turned to Luca, his face toughened to hard, cold, rock.

"Oh it's you is it, you little shit?" he roared, taking what seemed to Luca giant steps towards him.

For the first time since arriving at the station Luca wished his own father was by his side. Luca looked up, afraid to make eye contact but simultaneously recognising all his options had ceased. He stood from the chair and stood before the man and modestly held out his hand. "Hello Mr, erm, Mr... Well, Julia's Dad," he laughed nervously. "We haven't met yet but I am..."

A giant muscular arm swung through the air and with a forceful thud smashed Luca straight between the eyes. The force of the blow caused Luca's brain to spin into star-flashing turmoil; he fell savagely to the floor, cracking his eye on a chair as he landed. The voice returned.

"The next time you want to take advantage of an innocent gypsy girl, Mr Superstar, knock on my fuckin' door first."

"Jees! Wicked shot!" one of the youths shrieked with excitement, laughing and clicking his fingers with consecutive rapid flicks of his hand.

Luca lay on the floor holding his face in his hands. Reporters seeing the scuffle and ignoring the restrictions to enter barged into reception and unashamedly began to click and flash through Luca's pain.

"What do ya think this is, a fuckin free for all?" the giant growled. "Do you want some 'an all?"

Antagonistically he neared the pack; hastily they backed away through the doors before running to report the incident to their news desks. Luca was saved further attack by a swarm of police officers surging through Reception.

"Mr Michael Smith, we are arresting you for assault." Breathlessly, they fought with the struggling prisoner. As they dragged him away to the cells, Luca called out from the floor.

"I don't want to press charges," he called after them.

"Damn fucking right you don't!" jeered one of the youths to the laughter of his friends.

Three tormenting hours had passed, and in that time Luca had managed to bathe his own wounds, refusing every offer from the station staff to get them professionally dressed at the hospital. Eventually with time and a tight nip with large quantities of toilet tissue he had managed to inhibit the bleeding.

Julia, oblivious to the fracas in reception, shakily tried to assimilate her bail conditions that the charge office sergeant was trying to explain.

"I'm sure, as this is your first offence," he told her, "that the courts will be lenient." He patted her reassuringly on the arm. "Shoplifting is hardly the crime of the century," he smiled.

He led her out of the interview room and into Reception. Her eyes widened with a mixture of shock and disbelief to see Luca, cradling a swollen eye sitting before her.

"Luca!" she gasped, smiling for the first time in days, "What are you doing here?" Her face fell, "Are they interviewing you?" Her voice began to tremble. "You must be so embarrassed, I'm so sorry." Pent up tears that had waited weeks to fall began to drown her eyes. With concern out-shadowing her shame, she walked slowly towards him.

"What have you done to your eye?"

Luca looked across at the officers and gave her a weak smile.

"It's a long story," he answered, holding out his arm sympathetically. "Hey, come here," he whispered. He felt her body tremble nervously in his embrace but the flurry of further flashes and clicks broke Julia's comfort. She couldn't deceive him any longer.

"Luca, I have so much to tell you." She looked into his eyes. "You were right, I am not the person you thought I was."

"Julia," he sighed, "let's go somewhere else to talk." Luca glanced around the foyer at the officers and sergeants straining to hear their conversation.

"Come on," he beckoned towards the door.

"No, I can't walk another step with you until you know the truth." She hung her head. "I did steal the outfit, Luca. I stole it to come to the races the day we met." She shrugged her shoulders and allowed her shame to tarnish her eyes. "You see, I had nothing to wear, but desperately wanted to be a part of the day."

He watched as humiliation smothered her face and heard her voice fall into a struggling whisper as she forced her words passed the crammed emotion lodged in her throat.

"I am a gypsy girl, Luca, I have nothing and I am no-one."

"Don't, Julia, don't say another word." Unable to bear witness to her painful confession any longer he pulled her close and encouraged her face to nestle into his shoulder. "Don't you see? I don't care who you are or where you have come from." His urge to say more was carelessly postponed by the blatant cough of the officer wanting to clear the reception area. "God, I've missed you so much," he whispered, drawing in the soft familiar smell of her hair. "Come on," Luca gestured to the door, "let's talk in the car."

Julia stared at him in surprise. "What, are you going to take me home?" she asked disbelievingly. "After all this?"

"Hey, I have to take my side of the responsibility in all this, those bastard reporters wouldn't be here if it wasn't for me, would they?" His eyes shone a smile onto her face. "Are you ready to make a run for it?" He smiled, pointing at the awaiting pack and the sheeting rain.

He pulled her by the hand, and the pair of them ran outside. With a stream of reporters chasing after them they eventually reached the privacy of the car. Unperturbed by the cameras and microphones bashing against the windows, Luca looked across at Julia. During their short sprint to the car the rain that had pounded against them had soaked her to the skin. Her wet hair, poker straight and as black as midnight dripped upon her clothes, and her skin, as smooth and as delicate as a butterfly's wing, looked pale and daunted by her morning's experience. He watched the raindrops running freely down her face and he worried she must be cold; he pulled at the travel rug that lay on the back seat of the car and slipped it across her shoulders. He looked back at her and thought how small and helpless she appeared beneath its woollen folds, but then she looked back at him and smiled. It was a smile that lit up her eyes with warmth and a love that he knew was only for him. He had missed her so much and just couldn't stand the thought of taking her home. Luca started the engine,

"Have you got any plans?" he asked.

"No why?"

"If I said I wanted to take you somewhere, would you come with me?"

Her smile grew. "Of course, anywhere."

"Right, buckle up. I'm taking you on an adventure, but, on the way you must tell me everything you know about Charles Lancaster-Baron."

"Yes, I will, but I will have finished by the time we get to the end of this drive," She buckled her belt, "so, that should give you plenty of time to tell me about your eye."

"Okay," Luca nodded with a playful smile, "You're father seems like a straight talking kind of guy, why shouldn't I be?"

Julia stared at him. "NO?" she gasped disbelievingly. "My Dad did…" she threw her hands to her mouth and giggled.

Luca laughed and turned on the wipers, it was then he noticed a piece of paper trapped within the blades. With the reporters now running to their own cars to get back to the warmth of their offices it freed him to open the door. He pulled the paper free.

"I don't believe it!" he groaned with a grin. "A bloody parking ticket!" Looking back at her his grin broadened. "For a lady of meagre means you don't half cost me a fortune!"

They both laughed as he drove away. Julia began to inform Luca of her short conversation with Charles on the evening of the ball. She had to concentrate on her every word, not because her words were untrue, but because privately she was battling with an exciting ecstasy. She was embarking on a mystery adventure with none other than the love of her life.

Chapter Thirty Three

LUCA had made their reservation whilst in the car; they were on their way to one of the finest hotels in North Yorkshire, Pendlestone Manor, which lay fifteen miles from the outskirts of York.

Whilst they had travelled Julia had become mystified at how much the weather had changed since leaving the police station. The black cumbersome clouds were beginning to fade into the distance, the storming rain had submitted to fine drizzle and everywhere a new day was dawning. A bright blue sky welcomed them with the distant poke of sun and a vibrant multi-coloured rainbow beckoned them through its large sweeping arms. She took the turnaround in the weather as a sign, a sign that even the unpredictable forces of nature aligned in agreement with their reunion.

They approached a tree lined drive with a generous brass shining plaque that read 'Pendlestone Manor, a gift for the discerning visitor.'

Julia nervously placed her hand on Luca's leg as they drove down the swirling drive. At either side of the giant oak trees that lined its path were acres of magnificent parkland. Among the traditional formality of the grounds long horned sheep and Charolais cattle roamed freely, untroubled by the sporadic passing of visitors' cars and all of them refusing to be distracted from their rightful opportunity to graze.

As the hotel began to appear into her view, Julia took a breath. Pendlestone Manor, once a private estate for four generations of the Sinclair family, stood peacefully, privately tucked away within the dip of rolling hills and woodland, offering a splendour that only the aristocratic heritage of the English countryside could bequeath. It was a sandstone stately home, its enormity moderately tempered by the gentle creep of rose bushes against its façade. It was the most romantic place Julia had ever seen.

"Oh, Luca!" Julia gasped, "It's the most magnificent place I have ever seen."

"Really?" Luca asked proudly. "Well, it's about to get a damn sight better, I've booked us a fantastic suite." He gently squeezed her hand; aware she might feel apprehensive. "I wonder what they will think of my shiner," he said, pointing to his eye.

Julia threw her hand to her mouth in embarrassment. "I bet they've never had a thief *and* a brawler staying in the hotel before," she said warily. Luca shrugged.

"Who cares?" he stated boldly, "It won't stop us paying, but," he added, "I wonder if they'll hide the silver when they see *you* walk in?" He burst out laughing and tried to protect himself with his arm from her playful tussle.

Julia laughed too, relieved and grateful that at last she had been released from her deceit. It was as though she had walked a thousand miles in sweltering heat, constrained by heavy steel armour, only to land in the safety of a cooling pool and been given permission to swim naked.

Luca watched her happy eyes dance as she took in the scenery and felt in awe of her confession in the station. To him, her honesty had merely demonstrated the guts and integrity she possessed. He really couldn't care less about her roots, he loved her no matter what.

Suddenly Julia sat upright in her seat, "Oh, no!" she gasped, "I don't have anything with me, no clothes, no underwear no make up, not even a hairbrush."

"Don't worry about that," he smiled, gently dismissing her concern "We'll buy some more, for once our problems are simple."

He reached for his phone and changed the message on his voicemail, redirecting all his calls to Thomas Markington. While he organised his work schedule Julia looked up at the building.

Numerous lead pained windows sat in haphazard rows across the breadth of the building, each window large enough to see the grand swags and tails hanging gregariously inside every room. A thick covering of ivy crept up the wall and caressed every window, the old sandstone brick appearing to warm the whole hotel in a duvet of affection. Luca turned off his phone and snapped it shut.

"That should piss them all off," he laughed. "Nobody knows where I am, who I'm with or what I'm doing!" Just like the ivy, he wrapped his arm affectionately around her waist and led her into the hotel.

Reception welcomed them with the glow of French standard lamps and the exuberant décor of mulberry and gold. Seeing them arrive, a tall impeccably dressed gentleman immediately made his way from behind the oak reception desk to greet them.

"Mr DeMario, how are you?"

"Hello Antonio, we're very well, thank you, how are you?" The pair exchanged a firm and friendly handshake before Luca turned to Julia. "This is Julia."

"Oh!" Antonio roared, causing Julia to blush as he eyed her approvingly from head to toe. "Pleased to meet you, Julia," he gushed, kissing both her blushing cheeks. He turned back to Luca "Are you staying with us or just dining?"

"We're staying. I booked a room on the way here."

Antonio surged back to the reception desk and checked on his list of new arrivals. "Pah! This room is not good enough for you," he looked over to reception "Harry!" Antonio impatiently clicked his fingers to the second man standing behind the reception desk. "Upgrade Mr DeMario's room to the honeymoon suite and send up one bottle of vintage Cristal. My friends' attendance calls for celebration." He turned to the couple "Take it with our compliments, it is an honour you are staying with us," he beamed.

"Thank you," Julia said gratefully, desperately fighting the urge to ask what Cristal was. "I hope you don't mind my asking, but is the room ready?" At this stage all she wanted was a shower.

"Yes, yes it is," Antonio replied, he clicked his finger again. "Paulo," he ordered to the man standing at the concierge desk, "take the bags from the car."

Luca laughed, "Err, that won't be necessary, we haven't got any."

Antonio shrugged, his professionalism instantly making them feel at ease. He threw his arms up in the air in careless wonder, "Of course you won't have any bags, what was I thinking? Who needs bags when you have love?"

They were shown to their room and again Julia was spellbound. Although she recognised she didn't have a lot to compare it with, the contrast between this and the accommodation she had been forced to endure only hours ago would have been laughable were it not for the fact that shame still burdened her mind. She sat down in one of the large high backed-chairs in the sitting area and watched Luca pour the Cristal which she now recognised as champagne. The gentle silence of the room lavishly tainted by the chink of glass and the fizz of bubbles allowed her to relish the moment.

"I can't believe I am with you. I've really missed you, Luca," she told him bravely.

He looked across and smiled at her. "I know what you mean; I never believed I would get the chance to be with you again, thank God for the police station, eh?"

Julia blushed again. He walked over to her and held out her glass of champagne. Reluctantly she took it.

"What will everyone say, when they find out one of the most eligible bachelors in the world is back together with the thieving gypsy girl?"

"Is that what we are? Back together?"

Shyly she looked down to the floor. "I hope so."

He chinked his glass gently against hers, "Cheers!" He paused, "Here's to honesty." He bent down and kissed her fleetingly on the cheek, "Because that, my darling, is exactly what you are." He lifted her chin with his fingers, beckoning her to look at him. "Stop talking about the past, Julia, we are living in the now and I never want to lose you again." He perched himself on the edge of the armchair.

Julia smiled back at him, but couldn't help another worry rising to the surface. "What will your parents say?" she asked. "You know your father hates me, don't you?"

"What makes you say that?" Luca asked, nervously shuffling against the chair.

"The day at the races at Ascot, he glared at me with such ferocity in the winners' enclosure I think he would have killed me if he had the chance."

"Don't be daft, that's just his way sometimes." Luca hastily changed the subject. "That reminds me, we are organising a surprise sixtieth party for my father the day after tomorrow, it's in the evening, will you come with me? You will feel differently when you meet him properly in person."

Julia nodded nervously.

"Anyway, more to the point of murderous father in laws, what will *your* father say?" Luca asked, cautiously tapping his eye wound.

She rested her head on the chair back and remained quiet for a second whilst she contemplated the question. "Probably, 'hey sorry about the pasting I gave you in the station but, Luca, now you are family will you lend us some money!'"

They both laughed. Contended and happy they huddled together in the chair drinking their champagne feeling truly ecstatic to be in each others' company again. As Julia drained the last mouthful from her glass she stood up.

"I really need a shower." She scratched against her clothes. "I feel grimy."

"Ok, you go, I'll put the racing on, I'll see how much shit I've caused." He reached for the remote.

Julia grabbed his hand, "No Luca," she said firmly, "I don't want anything to ruin our time here. You might hear or see something that annoys you." Her voice softened, "Please don't."

"No, you're right," he nodded, "I'll have a lie down." He winked. "I might bring you a glass of champagne in if you're too long."

"You do that." She kissed him on the nose and walked into the bathroom.

The shower that stood before her was the size of her sleeping quarters in the caravan. She opened the cubicle door and found it had buttons and switches all over the place. She read a sign that informed the user how to activate the 'tropical rain-showers', 'state of the art music system' and noticed knobs and brushes that could massage and exfoliate the body, there was even a broad padded seat inside that would easily seat four people. She looked back at the enormous oval Jacuzzi by its side and, after some deliberation, tempted by its unfamiliar gadgets, decided to take a shower.

She undressed and turned on the water. Stepping inside, she allowed the water to caress her before making use of the rich lotions and washes that foamed against her skin. She closed her eyes and allowed her senses and mind to escape into the unknown world of extravagance.

Luca had long since got changed into the towelling dressing gown that lay on the four poster bed. With the glass of champagne he had recently poured threatening to lose its fizz, he decided to act on his promise and take the glass to her.

He knocked on the bathroom door and waited for a response; he heard nothing so apprehensively, he opened it and walked in.

A waft of feminine scents, a heavenly concoction of Ylang Ylang and Lavender sensually enveloped the air. Luca stared through the frosted piece of glass and felt his legs and body become heavy with desire. Between him and the glass stood the alluring silhouette of a naked goddess.

Her head was thrown back as she allowed the spurting jets of water to immerse her face and hair. She ran her fingers across her long black hair that stretched the length of her tanned curving back. Her firm breasts were small and pert, her nipples erect from the forceful sensation of the pounding water against them. Oblivious to his presence she began to lather her long toned legs, leaving a trail of foaming bubbles against them. It was the first time he had seen her naked and revelled proudly that this moulding of feminine perfection was the woman he had fallen in love with. A new current of lust streamed through him.

Sensing a presence, Julia stepped away from the jetting water and opened her eyes, Luca immediately fought to explain.

"I brought you some champagne; I thought you would have been in a bubble bath and that…"

Shamelessly naked, she walked out of the shower and stood before him, allowing him the pleasure to freely roam her body with his eyes. Her wet skin glowed like an oil lamp in a window and secreted the sensual scents he had already smelt with further pungency. Tenderly, she placed her finger over his mouth.

"Ssshhhhh. I want the champagne." She hesitated, "I also want you," she whispered.

Slowly, still staring into his eyes, she slipped the belt of the dressing gown away from his body and, taking their champagne, she led him gently by the hand into the enormous cubicle. Taking hold of his face she kissed him and guided him backwards to the seat. She straddled her legs across his lap, never allowing her eyes to wander from his stare. Their gaze was fixed and Luca vowed with passion he would never forget this moment.

Reassured by the breathtaking intensity between them, Julia knew she wanted him more than she had ever wanted anything in her life and was well aware they were about to embark on a miraculous journey. Wildly, she threw her head back and let out a pleasurable gasp of anticipation whilst teasingly rubbing herself against his lap. Relishing every second, she drew away slightly, determined their time would be savoured. Gracefully she stood before him.

Luca stared at her awesome figure; her long legs were splayed astride and carelessly continued to stretch before melting effortlessly against the feminine slender curve of her hips. He reached for her breasts and gently caressed each one with his hands, softly teasing each nipple with his fingers, relishing the feel of them hardening in response to his touch. Her breaths began to increase in response to the touch of his hands against her flesh. With an aching need to pleasure him, she gradually lowered herself and crouched at his knees. In silence he tilted back his head and closed his eyes, aware she was about to send him into pure ecstasy. His gentle groans continued, each one urging her to continue and his every moan encouraging her to lose control. Her need was too much to resist, rising to her feet, once more she straddled her legs around his waist and with tender passion lowered herself onto his hardness. They both gasped in satisfaction as the release of the fulfilling pleasure engulfed their bodies. She raised herself up and down again and again with athletic ease, savouring each mighty thrust that entered her.

"I love you, Luca," she whispered in his ear, maintaining her tightened grip around him.

"I love you too. God, with all my heart I love you," he responded. "Julia," he gasped, "Julia," he asked again with urgency. With a firm hold his hands gripped her hips. His grip asked her to stop.

"What is it, Luca, what's the matter?" she whispered in panting breaths.

"Look at me," he asked. She looked down into his face. "Julia," he asked again, "will you marry me?"

Torrents of water fell onto her disbelieving face; she smiled back at him. "Oh Luca, yes, yes, yes, I'll marry you every day for the rest of my life," she answered honestly.

His grip tightened around her body as he allowed her movement to continue. They kissed passionately, neither one of them trying to break it. She writhed hard against him and then, almost reaching climax, she increased her rhythm. Luca sensed her urgency and responded; powerfully he began to push himself inside her deeper and harder. She screamed in delight as a forceful orgasm pulsed through her pleasured body. His strong arms held her quivering body tight whilst he continued to thrust. Moments later, she let out a satisfied groan as she felt him explode inside her.

They sat limp and weak in each other's arms, the water continuing to pound against their skin, running freely, like a myriad of country streams across their love- fuelled nakedness.

Chapter Thirty Four

DELAYED by Mary's heroic efforts to revive the rhubarb crumble to edible proportions and Kitty's indignation at the suggestion she should not drive, Charles watched as the pair clumsily jolted their way down the drive in the Land Rover on their way to the widower in Chelmsley.

"I won't be back until later," Kitty shouted through the passenger window, holding onto her headscarf as if travelling at speed. "After visiting this poor man I'm going on to have supper at the Santé's."

His conscience lurched, he hoped nothing would be mentioned about Paris, but Charles waved her off with a smile. Today was not a day to be clouded by the mere *possibility* of concerns.

He could hear his mother's declaration of love still ringing in his ears, and now she was surprising him a second time. Aided by a pleasant breeze, her hoots of gut-wrenching laughter, brought about by Mary's failing attempts to master the cumbersome vehicle, drifted merrily up the driveway. It made Charles realise just how long it had been since he had truly heard her happiness and that sound, he decided, for both of them, had been long overdue.

Appreciating Cedar's silence he headed straight for the library, one of his favourite rooms. His preference was led by the fact that it was filled with his father's polo memorabilia, mounted photographs of him with members of the Royal Family, winning polo sticks hanging upon the walls, along with trophies and water coloured portraits of his favourite horses, all of which blended perfectly with the room's hoard of expensive antiquities. He flopped upon the chesterfield sofa which was bathed in the welcome informality of worn conker leather and sprawled out his legs. Easily ignoring the buckling shelves of leather bound books, he sent Paris a text, giving her the 'all clear' and suggesting she picked up some snacks on the way to quell his hunger. He then sank back on the sofa to enjoy the tranquillity.

Charles stared at the fine stone fireplace at the far end of the room and remembered his own laughter. Back in January, he had organised a shooting party, and old school friends, some having travelled from as far as South Africa, had sat around its licking flames. After eating Mary's speciality, a succulent game pie which was rich with the decadent seal of chateau Margaux, he and his twelve friends had sprawled out, drinking vintage port and reminiscing on old Etonian times. They had all truly laughed, great giant guffaws that ricocheted off the wainscoted ceilings and echoed across the oak panelled hallways. They had teased one another avidly about past indiscretions and disastrous sporting events before their conversation had settled upon more customary grounding, with talk of privilege, fine wines, breeding, and connections all taking centre stage. It was the latter subject of discussion that caused Charles' mind to falter into pessimism, how many of those friends, if any at all, would be around him if they became aware of his reality?

He sat up, immediately feeling the anxious tug of his thoughts and, trying hard to focus his attention to more positive tones, he thought about how far he had come in such a short space of time.

Luca DeMario's winning streak was coming to an abrupt halt and that thought certainly made him smile. What a fucking mess he was in, after being penalised for the detection of drugs, many trainers he rode for would be wary of booking him. Nobody wanted to get involved with that kind of scandal at the moment. The racing federations were clamping down big time on race fixing with the looming threat of jail facing many who had tried. Even better was Luca's new dilemma, the thought of him cowering in embarrassment from reporters in his massive mansion was another call for celebration. A thieving gypsy girl! Charles laughed aloud.

Certain that Luca was taken care of for the time being, he moved on to his favourite subject, Rebecca Santé. Just the mention of her name, and the promise of a better future that her name held, made Charles want to groan in ecstasy. *My lovely Rebecca,* he mused sinking back onto the sofa. *Once I get her this baby she will need me desperately, she will fall in love with me all over again, and then, once we're married, this financial crisis and the potential shake I caused to the Lancaster-Baron name will all be ancient history.*

A cunning smile adorned his face as he heard the door chime, the crucial piece to the jigsaw had just arrived – Paris was here.

Paris bustled in, straining to carry an overflowing carrier bag.

"I got a taxi, dad wouldn't bring me," she blushed as she recounted the argument she had had with her father about her coming to Cedars Hall. "Anyway," she said brushing away her thoughts, "I stopped at the supermarket on the way, you said you were starving, I thought I'd cook for you." She looked at him and smiled enthusiastically before catching his eye and looking away. She followed Charles through to the kitchen and shrieked. "Wow!"

Charles turned to look at Paris with a knowing look, expecting that her exclamation was concerning the size of the enormous kitchen, just like all unacquainted guests arriving at Cedars, but it wasn't. Instead, Paris surged straight across the room and stopped before the aged and frequently faltering double Aga oven, appreciatively running her fingers across it as though she had found lost treasure.

"I love Aga's," she told him. "Mother refuses to get one, she says they are dull, old fashioned and," she made quote marks with her fingers, "the ugly things just don't retain their sheen." The pair of them laughed.

"It's the first time I have had the inclination to agree with your mother!" Charles answered.

"Well," Paris stated confidently, "I did a cookery course once and all they had was an Aga, I learnt so much, I'm telling you now your dinner tonight will be delicious."

She began to unpack the contents of her bag, pulling out sausages and eggs and other ingredients, and then she pulled out a bottle of ale.

Charles walked over to her in curiosity. "Real Ale?" He said picking up the bottle. He was completely oblivious to the horror that had solidified in his noble voice, and with a frown he read the label. "I haven't seen anything like this for bloody years"

"Oh, really?" Paris sarcastically threw her hands to her face, feigning horror "That's because you don't live in the real world, me Lord, come and live with the working classes. You could put a handkerchief on your head, park your arse on a deckchair and drink it in the garden whilst your misses washes your dirty kegs!"

Charles laughed until his sides ached, revelling in the candid humour that only his mother and Paris would dare to speak. He grabbed her hand, and Paris also giggling, willingly allowed him to hold it.

"I'm sorry," he said in between breaks of laughter, "I didn't mean it like that." He ruffled her hair, noticing it was newly washed and its usual dull appearance had been replaced with a soft shine.

"I should hope not too," she chastised, playfully shoving him away. "Anyway, pour yourself a glass of wine and go and watch some television or something while I cook. Or, better still," she walked over to her handbag, "read this book." She pulled out a slim book and handed it to him.

Charles examined the front cover, but having never heard of the author, Paulo Coelho, or of the title, *The Alchemist.* He stared back at her blankly.

"Have you read it already?" she asked

"No."

"I didn't think so," Paris answered bluntly. "You should; I think the author wrote it especially for the likes of you."

Charles raised his eyebrows. "I'm intrigued already," he lied. Charles felt too ashamed to tell her it had been probably three years since he had read a book and that even then it was finished under duress when he had felt bored and irritable on a holiday to the Maldives; the rain had pissed down for the whole fortnight, he remembered sourly. He poured two glasses of wine from a bottle he had allowed to breathe for the past four hours and handed Paris her glass.

"I never drink alone," he said watching her rummage through the unfamiliar cupboards for a suitable pan.

"I usually never drink at all, especially now," she answered, protectively touching her stomach.

"Red wine's not counted as alcohol. Have you not been listening to the recent research? It is packed with medicinal benefits, taste it, you'll feel like a different woman."

"Yes! That's what I'm worried about, Charles!" she laughed. "I bet you say that to all the girls!"

Paris took a sip and had to admit it was absolutely delicious. She smiled and felt unable to resist taking another mouthful. "Now go and sit down with that book, I want to get on with this meal. When I've finished it I'll give you a shout, if you can't hear me I'm sure I'll find you in this maze somewhere!"

She had been in the house for twenty minutes, but it was the first time she had mentioned the size of the Hall, Charles felt pleasantly bewildered by the fact that she was truly unimpressed. He patted her bottom cheekily, feeling the unattractive wobble of surplus flesh beneath his hand.

Paris shyly darted out of the way, picking up the book and handing it to him. "Go and read!" she persisted with a smile.

Once again, with the book in his hand, Charles sat in the library feeling strangely bemused by the effect Paris had on him. In a strange sort of way he found himself actually enjoying her company, she was funny, bright and so quintessentially straightforward. She would never be girlfriend material or anything preposterous like that, but, nevertheless, she was the kind of girl that would be a true honest friend. With a gigantic sigh he nonchalantly flopped back onto the leather sofa and opened the book. He read the first page, then the second and the third, he was gripped...

Charles put down his knife and fork. "You were right, that was absolutely fantastic!" Charles praised, rubbing his bursting stomach. "I haven't had toad in the hole for years, and that gravy was just perfect."

"Do you mean the ale gravy, me Lord?" Paris joked.

Paris had consumed two large glasses of wine and felt really quite drunk. However when she saw Charles pouring the second bottle, it was so delectable that she just couldn't resist pushing her glass toward him for a refill.

It was ten o' clock and the night was beginning to draw in, causing the dining room, where Charles had insisted they eat, to suddenly darken. Charles pulled his lighter from his pocket and lit the six crooked candles of the silver candelabra that centred the table. They lit the room with bright flickering flames, inviting a sense of romantic, yet rueful excitement within Paris all over again. He looked at her and noticed again how her eyes, captured by the glow, looked so amazingly pretty.

"Come on, let's go into the library," Charles said picking up the candelabra to lead the way.

"I can't, not tonight anyway," Paris said.

Surprised, Charles turned to face her; her face looked flushed from the excess wine and the candles' heat.

"I haven't brought my library card and I have three books that are overdue. Will you pay my fine for me?" She giggled and picked up her wine glass to follow him.

Charles laughed, "Come on you bloody daft thing." Sensing the alcohol was taking effect, he offered his hand and tenderly led her through the winding corridors.

Once in the library they both sat on the sofa, the candelabra flames gently wafting against the mansion's sporadic draughts. Paris stared up at the polo memorabilia hanging upon the walls.

"I am enjoying the book, by the way," Charles said, picking it up from the arm of the sofa. "It appears it will offer a philosophical slant to life, do you give a lot of credence to that sort of thing?"

Paris shuffled into the sofa and relaxed, "Definitely," she answered thoughtfully. "I believe that life is one magical journey, it delivers us safely to all kind of diverse destinations and scenarios, some of them are heartbreaking, some of them are scary, but all of these experiences, whatever they are, enable us to grow." She looked at him amid the glow of the candlelight. "It is a question of how we deal with these situations and how much trust we have in nature that determines whether or not we abuse life's protective safety net around us."

Charles raised his eyebrows, "Wow," he said quietly, "that's heavy stuff. I guess I'd better continue reading in order to gain some ground." Charles stretched out his legs along the sofa and wrapped his leg over hers. "And speaking philosophically now, how are you feeling today about the situation, Paris?"

"I don't know," she answered calmly. "I have thought a lot about the Santé's proposition but I am sure that, ultimately, when the time came, I would regret giving the baby away. I'm lonely enough already," she admitted earnestly.

"I didn't mean the baby, Paris, I was talking about us," he told her softly.

Her voice stumbled in surprise. "Wh…What?….US? What do you mean?"

"Are you telling me that our time together has meant nothing to you?" Charles asked bluntly.

"No, not at all, Charles, I just didn't think it would have meant much to you really." Paris blushed and took a massive gulp of her wine.

He ran his fingers through her hair causing her scalp to tingle beneath.

"People won't believe this, but I want children too, I can't think of anything more satisfying than bringing up a family."

"Really?" Paris said eagerly.

"Yes, definitely," he replied, "but, I know I couldn't feel that way if it were someone else's baby, even if it were Gerard's, as much as I loved him as you did." He searched Paris's face for her reaction and realised from her bemused look she needed clarification. "Paris? Do you understand what I am saying to you?" Another blank stare. "Paris, you would make exactly the kind of mother I would want for my children. I am sick of the false flashy bitches that I have around me all the time, they are not for me. " He shrugged. "Well, not for settling down with anyway." He sat upright and settled both his hands upon her shoulders, then, with utter conviction he looked straight into her eyes. "When I settle down, I want to be married and have a family with someone genuine," he gently rocked her shoulders, "someone like you Paris, do you here me? Like you." His smile almost turned into a laugh as he appeared to become excited by his admission. "You are the most amazing woman I have ever met, I am not surprised that Gerard fell in love with you," he paused, "but, I just couldn't take on someone else's child. I just couldn't do it."

Paris couldn't believe his words were real, she still felt confused. "What are you telling me? That no man in the world would take on somebody else's child and that in order to be with you I would need to get an abortion?" She asked.

"Hell, no!" he replied forcefully. "This is a human life we are talking about here." He smoothed his hand gently against her stomach, "I love the baby as much as you do, I don't want it to die."

"Then what?" she asked still unable to decipher his message.

"Well, maybe if the baby was going to Rebecca it would serve many purposes, we would know it was in safe hands, *and*, with Gerard's own family and secondly," he held her face in his warm hands "more importantly, it would enable *us* to share our life together and begin from a clean slate."

"Us?" she asked disbelievingly. She took another large mouthful of wine.

"Yes, Paris, us," he confirmed. "Have you not listened to a word I have said? I am sick of this life, I want you, and you are the only person I have ever met that is real."

Like a shoal of fish, Paris' emotions swam haphazardly from one side of her ocean of thoughts to the other. She felt her skin prickle, dance and flush as Charles slowly began to kiss the side of her cheek and gently inched his way towards her quivering lips. Her life suddenly began to look a lot clearer. Tenderly he kissed her mouth. She closed her eyes, allowing his affections to seep through her skin. *Yes, it all made sense,* she thought. She responded warmly to his tongue that tentatively prodded inside her mouth. *Yes,* she felt certain this was the right thing to do. He began to unbutton the collar of her sweatshirt, allowing the manliness of his experienced hands to warm against her skin. *Yes,* she could feel the love permeate through his touch, and *yes, yes, yes,* she felt her body float longingly to the world of affection, a planet that she never imagined travelling to again.

Moments later she was lying naked on the floor with her white plump body in full view. She grabbed a cushion and tried to hide herself; sensitively he pulled it away and stared into her eyes.

"Paris, stop that. Don't you understand?" he asked tenderly. "I want to be with you for the person you are, to me you are stunning."

His words melted across her mind drowning the years of pent up insecurities and vulnerability in an instant. Then she panicked as he began to kiss her again, she raised herself up onto her elbows, the concern in her eyes undisguised.

"But, what about Gerard?" she asked, responding only in brief dashes to his continued kisses "What will people say? Won't they think I am dreadful if I turn my attentions on someone else so soon?" Already she felt herself recoiling.

Already stripped to his underwear, Charles leant on his elbow by her side; he stroked her hair and her face whilst he answered, "Mmmm, I can understand your point. And yes, you are probably right, it is perhaps best to keep our relationship private for the time being." He kissed her cheek then whispered in her ear, "Everyone knows the special relationship you and Gerard had. I don't want people to think we are disrespecting him in any way, and neither do I want people to think we are doing this on a whim. But, I love you, Paris and always have done. We will take this a stage at a time."

Paris allowed his persuasive kisses that swept against her lips to charm her all over again. She closed her eyes and soon began to wallow in his slow, loving tenderness. *Yes*, she thought, *one stage at a time*. Softly, with remarkable expertise, his hands began to explore her naked body, her breaths became stronger and her desire for him grew. *Yes, he loves me, yes, he does, he really loves me.* She wrapped herself around his body and kissed him with an all consuming, hot, burning passion.

Coldly switching off from the fact that Paris was carrying another man's child, Charles realised it had been a long time since he had made the pretence of making love to a woman, but, this situation called for such action.

With the dim light from the candle flame veiling Paris's plump, fleshy body, he too was swept away. Her heartfelt emotion filtered through his skin as he became locked within the tangle of her passionate and adoring embrace.

Chapter Thirty Five

JULIA eased her way into consciousness from a deep sleep and instantly became aware of the warm loving tangle of Luca's arms around her. The room was still dark; the exuberant trail of the heavily lined curtains guarded the room of daylight and only a faint crack, a reminder of their haste to fall into bed the previous night, allowed a chink of determined daylight to peer through. She took solace in the sound of Luca's long restful breaths, feeling relieved that at last, they could both relax. She closed her eyes and took a deep breath, lazily languishing on the smell of his warm masculine skin.

Slowly her body began to spark back to life, and as it did so their previous night's passionate love making in the shower absorbed her mind. Every detail funnelled into each cell of her body causing them to quiver and prickle with the reawakening of desire. Then, "*Marry me, Julia.*" Her mind replayed his proposal and she gasped with elation. So, conscious of Luca needing rest, she pulled the bed sheet up to her smiling face and bit it like a playful child, trying to mask the elated shriek she thought might escape. Her laughing eyes searched the darkness for confirmation, was this miraculous life of hers really true?

She snuggled closer into Luca's arms and tried to calm her high spirits, fighting away the temptation to jiggle her restless legs against the mattress. She clamped her eyes shut and suppressed the innocent giggle that bubbled beneath her love-soaked heart, *Mrs DeMario,* Julia deliberated, *Mrs Julia DeMario.* She scrunched her toes into a jubilant curl, and then her restless legs told her, they couldn't stand the torture of lying still for a second longer.

She jumped out of bed and sneakily hoped that the sudden irritation of movement would cause Luca to stir, but it didn't. Biting her bottom lip she scampered to Luca's side of the bed and stared down at his sleeping silhouette, wondering again how she was going to keep quiet and allow him the rest he deserved. She tapped her hands incessantly against her joyful face in a bid to busy them from touching him, she flash-danced on tiptoes feeling the plush pile of the carpet sink between her toes, but within nanoseconds, her excitement overflowed, she jumped up and down on the spot before accepting; she couldn't contain her delight any longer and it was then that she let out an exhilarated squeal.

Luca stretched dreamily under the warm comforts of the duvet and the encouragement of movement forced her to fling herself upon him.

"Luca! Luca!" She shrieked, "We are going to be married, I can't believe it!" She began to smother the entirety of his face and hair with fast ravenous kisses. "Oh! I love you so much," she gushed.

Luca groaned sleepily and lifted the duvet for her to enter. She rolled inside and felt the snug security of his arm encase her with his love.

For Luca, waking to feel Julia's soft naked skin against him instantly encouraged his temptation to rise. Softly he kissed her face and drove his hands to trace the softness of her skin beneath the sanctuary of their secret domain. Julia responded lovingly, finding his mouth in the darkness and kissing him softly before winding the length of her leg around his body.

"Mia Bellissima," Luca moaned sexily.

Luca's words and the sensation of Luca's lips kissing her body as he inched his way under the duvet ignited a current of sexual electricity that softly crackled through her body. Julia closed her eyes, and arched her back in pleasure as Luca's mouth nestled between her legs.

Later that morning, Julia stepped out of the shower and walked back into the bedroom with a bath sheet wrapped around her. Luca watched as she slid on her only belongings since arriving at the hotel, black denim jeans and her white vest. Having just made some phone calls he pushed his mobile back into his pocket and revelled at the sight of her.

"You are so beautiful, Julia," he told her from across the room. Overwhelmed by the feeling of never wanting to leave her side, he walked towards her and pulled her towards him, inhaling the fresh, natural scent of her damp skin. "God, I love you so much!" he told her sincerely; he took a deep reluctant breath and drew away slightly from their embrace. "I have to work today," he informed her grudgingly, running his fingers through her wet curls. "There are two races I cannot fail to ride in. I've just come off the phone to Thomas and already it seems I am in the shit."

"Oh, no, I'm really sorry, are you in big trouble?" Julia asked hiding her disappointment that he was leaving her.

Luca smiled at her genuine concern. "No, don't be daft, I was only joking, I'm not really in the shit, I just really need to get back to work. But," he continued, "to keep you out of mischief while I am away I have arranged for you to go to Lancaster's, a boutique not far from here. A driver will pick you up in about half an hour and the owner is under no illusion, you can choose whatever you want." He took a step back and held her at arms length, eager to witness her pleasure.

She caught her breath. "Really? Are you sure?" she trilled with a twinkle in her wide eyes.

"Of course I'm sure, get whatever you want, the whole shop if you want." He hesitated, "But don't forget to choose something for tomorrow night." His mobile rang again, he ignored it but looked at his watch. "I'm sorry, I'm going to have to go, I am so late."

"Tomorrow night?" Julia asked with a frown and overlooking his urgency.

"Yes," he rolled his eyes, kissed her quickly on the lips then turned for the door. "Have you forgotten already?" He shouted over his shoulder, "It's my father's surprise sixtieth party."

"Oh yes, of course," Julia answered quietly. Luca had already left the room when Julia flumped onto the bed and heard her voice float into apprehension, "How the hell could I have forgotten that?"

She loved him so much and wanted desperately to impress his parents. She thought about his father and felt her nerves slowly begin to simmer into anxious foam.

It was late afternoon and Charles, driving his car along a country road, decided to pull over into a lay-by to take Rebecca's call. The swiftness of his decision forced the disguised works van following three cars behind to sail past.

"Shit!" The driver thundered, thumping his steering wheel several times in frustration.

"You're not going to believe this," Rebecca stormed to Charles, herself having to hear it a second time before even she could distil the information. Charles held his mobile from his ear, his crowded head already ached and Rebecca's shouting did not help.

"What the matter?" He asked her.

"A friend has just called me to say that she had seen Piers with Sofia DeMario having a great time in Harrogate last night."

Charles felt elated. "Really?" He said in joyful surprise before knocking down his elated tone a few octaves with a fake cough. "Really?" he repeated solemnly.

"Yes!" she snapped. "What a bloody pig. He was the one that supposedly hated it around here, so why hasn't he just buggered off back to Kentucky?"

"Yes, why hasn't he?" Charles asked, genuinely pondering the reasons. "Maybe he just wanted to make you jealous?" he suggested, thinking aloud.

"Oh!" she spat, "so he's not content with already making an idiot of me by sleeping with *her*, he now wants to rub salt into the wounds by flaunting his indiscretions in public. It is all so false, and he can go to hell!"

Rebecca's obvious jealously was contagious; he wished she didn't care what he was doing. He tried to ease her back into his world.

"Well, anyway, who cares what he is doing? In a few months you are going to have something very real that you never would have had if he had remained around. You mustn't lose sight of how you will feel when you are holding your baby, Rebecca. You are going to be such a fantastic mother." His conscience interrupted his flow and crunched like a foot upon frosted autumn leaves as Paris came to mind.

Rebecca let out an accepting sigh. "Yes, you're right." She said curtly, "Do you think this will *really* come off?"

"Yes, I'm sure of it Rebecca," Charles answered, casting away his guilt. "I spoke to Paris briefly about it this morning," he lied. "Although she is worried about the negative connotations people may construe of her giving the baby up to you, overall, she sees it as the best option for her *and* the baby."

"I wonder if I should call her to talk to her about the detail," Rebecca said.

"You mustn't do that Rebecca," Charles quickly interjected "It could ruin everything, I've told you. She wants me to be the go-between for the time being."

"But tell her though; we will always relay the story in a sympathetic way towards her."

"I'll tell her," Charles promised.

"What are you doing this evening?" she asked

Charles, embarrassed by the soothing secret of challenging Paris to their third game of Scrabble, immediately rustled for untruths. "Oh, I've got a boring meeting with the accountant which will consist of him trying to motivate me to catch up on all my paperwork and stuff, we can't all be as organised as you," he laughed. "What about you?"

"There's a polo match over in Beverley, I quite fancied going and wondered if you wanted to join me, anyway, perhaps another night then?"

For a fleeting moment the thought appealed, there would be several of his friends playing in the match and nothing would please him more than turning up with Rebecca, but the plan of getting back Rebecca had to be viewed in terms of 'the long haul', presently the need to appease Paris had to be a priority.

"That's a shame, I would have loved to have come, but, like you say, definitely another night."

"Okay."

"Well, I'm sorry to hear about Piers, Rebecca, I can't understand him at all, but remember you are too bloody good for him."

"Mmmm," she answered unsurely.

"Anyway, call me later if you need to. Bye Rebecca."

"Bye."

Charles was genuinely surprised that Piers could truly have chosen Sofia over Rebecca, their breeding was just incomparable. A list of probable scenarios and possible misdemeanours that Piers could be plotting began to form in Charles' mind, none of which made sense. Taking advantage of both privacy and opportunity, Charles called Hugo, the first on his list of people to call.

"Uuuuurggghhh!" Hugo croaked on answering.

"My God, man! You sound like shit. What's the matter with you?" Charles asked.

"I'm still pissed I think, I was partying last night in Belgravia, just for the record, 5 bottles of Cristal and 12 lines of coke between four of us, then getting in at 7 a.m. doesn't do much for the old telephone manner," he groaned.

For Hugo, in comparison to the last three months, last night had been a mild affair. He and the other traders in the city had been celebrating their anticipated share of a £25 billion payout in bonuses, set to be paid in a matter of months. For a lucky few, Hugo included, money was no object and as a result their nights out were becoming more and more competitive. Last night he had spent around £8000, a mere snip in comparison to his colleague the week before. His bill for champagne, alone, in a club had amounted to £33,000. Most of it had been given away to strangers, or shaken and then spurted against the pack of sexy women on the dance-floor.

For Hugo the money didn't impress him as much as the others, he never discussed his earnings, and why would he? He was used to having money. Both brothers had matured safe in the knowledge that they were wealthy young bachelors, known from one end of the country to the other for their inherited fortune.

"Listen, you waster," Charles said jokingly, "Get your arse out of bed and get into work. You remember that £450,000 investment I gave to you three years ago in shares?"

"Vaguely," responded Hugo, casually yawning and rubbing his bloodshot swollen eyes

"Let me know how the money's doing will you? I know it was on a long-term investment basis, but I need to sell the shares and have the money. I know I might have lost a few grand doing it this way but, hey, who's counting?" Charles tried to sound casual, secretly aware that he was counting every single penny.

Hugo staggered into his kitchen and shakily began to brew some coffee. He felt seriously baffled by Charles' request. "What the hell do you want that for?" Hugo asked, "It's two day's pay," he mumbled.

"What?" Charles asked

"Oh nothing," Hugo grunted, his head was feeling so bad he was fast losing the will to live. "I'll have a look and get back to you soon, now do me a favour, get off this fucking phone and let me get some coffee into my system."

Charles laughed and hung up, sitting in the lay-by, he thought of his brother and felt like a fraudster, utterly ashamed to be withholding information from him. He sighed, what option did he have? It was not an option to transfer his guilt and shame onto others within the family. It was his mess and he had to sort it out. He felt a little less tense having remembered about this investment, it would help things along in the short term.

Hugo, still feeling bemused by the conversation with his brother, drank some coffee before firing up his laptop to check out the details.

It was not good news. The shares, having been a dead cert three years ago, had plummeted drastically and were now practically worthless. "Oh well," Hugo shrugged, snapping shut his laptop. "That's the price you pay for investing in high risk portfolios," he croaked to himself. Potentially there was every chance they would rise again in the next few years, Charles would just have to wait. Why the hell was Charles interested in them anyway? He considered his reasons briefly before switching off his aching brain. It wasn't important he concluded, he would call Charles later and inform him he needed to keep the money where it was for now. Dismissing the subject in its entirety, he headed for the gym.

Charles continued with his calls. Doctor White was next on his list, he had tried many times to contact him and was surprised and relieved when the Doctor answered.

"Hello Doctor White, its Charles here," he announced

"Ah, yes, Charles," the doctor fumbled, "sorry I didn't manage to get back to you earlier, I've been terribly busy."

Charles wondered what the creaking elderly could possibly get up to that would result in *them* being busy.

"Right, no problem," Charles said, sensing an edginess to Doctor White's usually welcoming voice. "I was calling about Mother," he continued, "she appears to be somewhat ailing with something, she denies it of course, but I can tell she is seriously off colour. I have noticed, through telephone records, that recently you two have been in communication regularly. Could you help to throw any light on the situation?"

Charles listened to the silent emptiness that filled the phone; it lasted for a number of seconds before the doctor spoke.

"Charles," his voice wavered, "you know very well, it would be terrible practice for a doctor to discuss private medical records about another patient."

"Yes, I can understand that, but, she is *my* mother, she is also getting old. If she is ill, I should be informed."

Again, his comments were met with silence. Doctor White closed his eyes, tapped his aged finger against the telephone table and tried desperately hard to think of something that would get Charles off the phone. Picking up a squashy ball from the floor he threw it to the other side of the room causing his two Jack Russells to yelp and bark as they scampered after it.

"Oh blast, someone's at the door," he crackled, "I'll have to go Charles, all the best my boy."

The line went dead. A thick, heavy, menacing feeling lay in the pit of Charles' stomach, he knew with certainty a conspiracy was in operation between the doctor and his mother and his hypothesis regarding his mother's ailing health had been confirmed. But it was the hesitancy in the doctor's voice that now accelerated his concern. He knew that the situation was worse than he had thought, his mother must be gravely ill.

Chapter Thirty Six

IN DEEP THOUGHT, Charles made his way home. When he arrived, he found his mother in the kitchen reading the paper, readily awaiting her guests to arrive for a bridge party she had organised. To the untrained eye she looked every inch the perfect hostess, wearing a silk blouse which was heavily adorned in a multitude of brightly coloured flowers and neatly tucked into a pair of red trousers, her make-up was, as usual, meticulously glamorous, her hair was perfectly set, and her nails elegantly manicured with a fresh, bright pink polish. However, with this brief inspection, two things were immediately brought to his attention. The first was the decline in her weight and the second was the overbearing edge to her attire.

Her outfit, he decided, was over the top. There was too much colour and too many distractions, the numerous flowers creeping against her blouse appeared starker than ever when teamed with her red trousers, it was as though she was trying too hard to camouflage transpirations occurring behind this vibrant façade.

His mother looked up at him, "Hello," she offered simply, returning her attention to the paper.

"Hello," Charles replied, moving in closer and suspiciously scrutinising the remainder of her appearance.

He noticed that her face, beneath the concealment of her make-up, looked drained and tired. She glanced up at him for a second time, his motionless stance distracting her from the *Times*. He managed to catch her eye and, in the second their eyes met, he became aware she had a major problem. Their sparkle had gone, they looked lifeless, dull even, and just like bruised carelessly treated fruits, he witnessed darkened pain on their surface.

With a feeling of dread, he threw down his car keys against the oak table where his mother sat. The harsh sound made Kitty jump. Unable to conceal his concern any longer, Charles began to talk.

"I have just spoken to Doctor White," he informed her, allowing a silence to prevail.

Kitty eased herself off the chair, suppressing her pain as she moved. "Oh, yes?" She answered casually. "Would you like a coffee?" She turned her back to him; her hands scurried nervously against the buttons of the coffee percolator machine.

"No, I wouldn't," he seethed, "I would like you to sit down and tell me what the hell is wrong with you," he demanded.

"With me?" she laughed. "Why, Charles, I don't know what an earth you are talking about." Her eyes darted nervously across the room, happy to settle anywhere but upon his face. "Whatever gives you the idea there is something wrong?" she asked, turning once again to the distraction of coffee.

"Mother, look at me!" he challenged storming over to her. "Nobody wants a bloody coffee!" he shouted, grabbing the tin of ground coffee from her hand and swinging her forcefully around to face him. "Mother, tell me what the problem is!" he shouted. He glared furiously into her eyes.

Kitty squared her shoulders as she faced him and reciprocated his forceful glower. "Don't you dare shout at me like that, young man," she retorted, "you remember who you are speaking to, I am your mother." She pointed up to him aggressively and he saw the tremble to her finger. "I am not one of your cronies that you can order about and intimidate. Who the hell do you think you are?" She rubbed the wrist he had gripped. "Your father would be disgusted with you," she added.

Charles frowned in puzzlement. "What are you talking about? *My cronies?*"

Kitty threw her arms up in the air dismissively, "I don't know," she stammered, "you're like a bull in a bloody china shop going around, trying to force information out of me and Doctor White. Have you no respect?"

"How the hell can I force information from either of you if you have nothing to hide?" he shouted. "Don't you see, I've told you before," he slammed his hand against the table, causing Kitty to jump again and the dogs to scurry into the boot room. "I am worried about you?"

Kitty stood up to her son once again. "Yes." she answered in a booming voice, "and I have told *you* before, you get your own house in order before you begin to worry about mine, or anyone else's for that matter." Her eyes were screwed up in fury and her voice was now cold with the chill of resentment. "It strikes me you have a lot of work to do."

The doorbell rang but she held her icy stare for a moment longer. "Now, my guests have arrived for a relaxing game of bridge," she informed him, straightening her blouse with trembling hands, "so, if you will excuse me." Kitty walked from the kitchen with her head held high, leaving a seething Charles standing alone.

He could hear the distant rumble of laughter and conversation as Kitty led her guests through to the drawing room. He grabbed the bottle of cooking sherry that stood by the side of the Aga and angrily poured some into a glass. He took a large slug, replaying her words over and over. With a desperate need to get away from the sound of the vague jovial voices that echoed into the kitchen and be alone with his thoughts, he walked outside and into the garden.

The summer evening's close of day brought with it a warm yellow sky. The rich golden blanket lay in silence under streams of ivory cloud which wandered dreamily, like warm, freshly baked lemon meringue pie. A scattering of birds, the swift silhouettes of a daring few, made last ditch attempts like children five minutes before the close of mischief night, to twist through the sky before retiring to the confinements of their nests.

Charles sat down upon a wrought-iron chair and viewed the scenery before him. The fading power of natural light transformed a distant cluster of trees that had, by day, been rich with the luxury of green succulent leaves into black shadows of dark, angry faces. He focused on the gnarled menacing beckon of their branches, knotted and twisted like an evil hunchback waiting for the realms of night to fall before it could make its terrifying grasp upon an innocent passer-by. His eyes scanned the prevailing swell of the countryside, to most, it captured the core of nature's beauty, but for Charles it captured a different image. He smiled tartly at the ironic scene before him, feeling an immediate sympathy and commonality with the rolling land.

The fields, a collective masterpiece of mans' labour, and each separate field, like the personalities of individuals, had their own unique shape and size, with the soil in which they grew, the vegetation's soul. However, despite their differences, Charles noticed they all shared the same thing in common. They were imprisoned with the non-negotiable restrictions of fences and hedges, unable to grow freely, and forever beholden to a strange man's judgement and decision. Their freedom, just like his own, had been immobilised. He watched the birds in the sky, the last few that remained, and noticed their habitual temptation to follow in another's path. In the distance he noticed a line of juvenile oak trees. For whatever reason, their youthful exuberance had also been disciplined with the cold steely formalities of a wire mesh surround. Even the awesome power of the formidable oak tree had been unable to escape the lifetime sentence of captivation.

His hands began to tighten around the cold realities of his glass. His jaw tensed, his body stiffened. He felt an unquenchable urgency to scream across the sky as he realised, he was the biggest prisoner of all, and his jailor? Wealth.

The pressure building in his mind triggered his aching temples to pulsate, of all the sentences life could bestow; this was by far the cruellest. Yet the worst feeling of all was that he had no way of knowing how he was going to escape.

Charles was aware that the comforting retreat he had once found in his mind had been replaced. What had once been an egotistical haven, a personal dictionary for flattering words of encouragement and self-praise and a mechanism he had often called upon for cross-reference purposes to confirm that indeed, he was the greatest, had been replaced by a prison of verbal poison, a place that he now expended huge amounts of effort and time trying to avoid.

If he allowed his innermost thoughts and desires to enter this dark creepy vault, he would immediately feel a sense of claustrophobia caused by the slow, torturous strangulation and suffocation of his inner being. He would try internally to back away, forcing his thoughts to withdraw back to consciousness, but, its evil magnetism was such, it drew him nearer, like a weak, vulnerable hostage. His back was pinned against the wall of his mind, immobile; he was forced to listen to the fire of insults relentlessly unleashed from the diseased catapult of hatred and self-loathing.

Hearing another wave of laughter goad its way through the air towards him, Charles turned his attention to the house. Glancing through the library window he saw one of his father's winning polo sticks hanging against the wall. He let out a muffled groan as the solemn voices in his head once again came to life. "*You cannot be trusted with anything, even on my death bed. I asked you to take care of everything, you were the elder son, and look at the mess you have left behind you,*" his father's voice chastised. "*Oh, good heavens! My own grandson, a measly crook!*" His treasured grandfather disappointingly droned. "*What are you going to do now, you half wit*" an anonymous voice boomed. "*You have let everybody down, haven't you? All the work and effort that went into building up the respected Lancaster-Baron name, and then you come along.*" A haunting laugh echoed in fathoms. "*What will everyone say when they find out?*" a second voice screeched before pausing to let out a menacing laugh. "*Shall I pass you the gun now?*"

Emotion engulfed him. The venomous voices were right; he had squandered torrents of their hard-earned money and had let his father and his grandfather down. It would kill his mother to learn he had disrespected the two men she treasured most.

"Why did they show me this life?" he spat through gritted teeth. "Now I'm here, I can't escape it." The desperation in his voice did not deter the force of another voice. "*You have even failed in looking after your own mother.*"

Charles felt his body grow cold as he thought about his ailing mother and her stubborn insistence on freezing him out of her life.

His face began to crack as a tidal wave of shame and regret riddled his body. A solitary tear drizzled down his face; he looked up to the sky and secretly whispered a question.

"Does anyone in this world know what it feels like to be aware that neither your mother, nor your father will ever forgive you?"

He viewed the ensuing silence as confirmation; even the divine powers of nature had no wish to communicate with a waster.

Chapter Thirty Seven

IT HAD BEEN eighteen months since Bill Montford had acquired his Range Rover Vogue, yet today, he realised it was the first journey he had taken whereby he had actually appreciated its capabilities and refinements.

He cast his mind back to the feeling of trepidation that had flooded his body the day he had signed the finance agreement. His hand had visibly shaken as he gripped the pen before his signature was etched upon the dotted line, aided and cajoled by Francesca's insistent, stony, stare across the salesman's table. Bill shuddered as he recalled the detail of that day. There had been a time he would have done anything to keep Francesca happy, but now, like bath water frantically spinning to escape down the plughole, he saw freedom in sight. Freedom from the debt-ridden life she had caused.

In all the years they had been married, this was the first time he had harboured a secret from his wife. However, given that she had an almost addictive propensity to spend beyond her means, he had no option but to withhold this information from her, allowing the occasional feeling of guilt to rapidly wash over him. He straightened his back against the comfort of the leather seat. Yes, he thought, today's appreciation for the vehicle had been born out of sheer relief; there was now a chance it could soon be paid for. For that, he had only Frankie DeMario to thank.

Since Bill had informed Frankie of his financial crisis on the evening of the Ascot races, Frankie had given him a taste of *his* business world, and although it was only a taste, it was enough to enable Bill to reap business and monetary benefits that months ago would have been a distant dream. For once, things were looking up.

Bill had been brought up, like many from his era, to believe that only hard work would reward with monetary gain. Working with Frankie had been a true eye opener for him. With little, or in some instances, no effort, Frankie had introduced him to a shrewd concoction of business strategies. High-risk stocks and share strategies, spread betting and property investments had all been a part of Frankie's weave to get Bill back on track. Frankie had even been kind enough to loan him some funds to pay off the serious debts that were threatening court action. Bill would never forget Frankie's kindness toward him and hoped that one day he could repay him in some way.

He was travelling back from dropping Francesca off at the beauticians and since she had gotten out of the car he had remained in deep thought. It wasn't her voice, the voice that for so long now had grated in his ears, but quite unusually it was the words she had spoken which he felt compelled to evoke in his mind.

"Perhaps Paris and Charles will get together after all," she had stated while spraying herself and the entire car with a third cast of Chanel No 5.

Bill shot her a sideways glance. "What are you talking about?" he snapped, swerving the car away from the verge he had almost hit.

"Trust you!" she retorted, sharply pulling down the vanity mirror of the car to check her hair, "Have you not noticed how much they are seeing of each other? At present they are practically inseparable." She laughed disbelievingly, "I don't know how that girl does it, I really don't. The rest of us work like slaves to look good, and she, well she sits stuffing her face with all kinds of rubbish, barely summoning the energy to transport herself to the bathroom, has no regard for fashion or cosmetics, yet still manages to attract the most eligible men in the county." She tutted in wonderment, "Another one of life's bloody mysteries."

Bill rested his elbow on the armrest of the car and rubbed his thumb aggressively against his pursed lips. With his eyes glancing sporadically to the traffic around him, he consciously tore into his wife's statement. She treated him like a fool, and on reflection she always had. How could she twitter so nonchalantly about 'one of life's mysteries' when she was acutely aware of the reasons behind Charles' gut-wrenching actions? He had borne witness to Francesca encouraging Paris to go ahead with the adoption the day he had overheard their conversation. *How could she do it? Her own grandchild to be given away, and for what? All for the sake of money?* He shook his head, disgraced by his wife's utter vulgarity.

His vehicle swept into Goldsborough Crescent and, as though a goading partisan to Francesca's words, Charles' Bentley was perched arrogantly against the pavement outside his home. Just the sight of Charles' possessions caused the hairs on Bill's neck to stand, one by on, like the protective bristles of a porcupine. His words fought for freedom behind gritted teeth and fierce, tightened lips.

"Keep away from my daughter," he raged. He sat in his car on the driveway, willing himself to calm down before he entered the house.

Charles and Paris sat close upon the settee, neither one of them had heard Bill's car settle upon the drive, their conversation remained too deep.

"Truly, Charles. What do you think your life is about?" Paris continued, feeling strained by irrational emotion; her unrelenting eyes baited him for an answer. Charles immediately felt a sense of unease and shuffled awkwardly next to her.

"What kind of a question is that?" Charles asked, aggressively running his hands through his hair. "I mean, how many people could even begin to answer such a question?" He gave her a smudged smile, trying to conceal his annoyance as she continued to dig into his private domain.

"Many people could answer that question. I, for one, and certainly Gerard." Paris was oblivious to the look of agitation that coursed Charles' face, born as a result of another tedious comment about 'the perfect Gerard'. Like an elastic band stretched to the whites of its innards he felt his patience ready to snap. *She seems to forget* he thought savagely, *I knew him for a lifetime; he was far from perfect;*

"Oh yes?" he answered dryly, "And what did you two love birds conclude then?"

Paris laughed lightly. "There's no need to snap," she said reaching for his hand. "It's only a question, not an interview, I am just interested, that's all." She rubbed her warm hand against his. "You see, it's like Deepak Chopra says in his book *Syncrodestiny*," she paused, watching his curt nod of impatience, "he says that every person in the world has a destiny. When you are on the right path to fulfil your destiny, small or enormous coincidences will transpire, informing the person they are on the right track towards that destiny."

"Yes, I know what you mean, like all those touchy feely hippies who wear beads, smell burning sticks to alleviate their nostrils of their formidable B.O and believe in *fate* in other words?" Charles rolled his eyes, "No thank you. That kind of conclusion to life does not sit well with me." He sat upright feeling more confident to enter discussion. "Sitting on your arse and hoping that fate will guide you in the right direction is a pile of utter horse shit, in fact, that's where those tree huggers end up, knee deep in shit at that God awful place Glastonbury. God!" he said throwing his head up to the sky, "The bastard that dreamt that up must be worth a fucking fortune now." He turned to face her. "The fact is, Paris, if you want something, truly truly want something out of your life, whatever it is, you have to forge ahead by whatever means possible and make sure it happens." He raised his eyebrows and shook his head, sheer determination had burrowed in his eyes "If you don't force it to happen yourself, your dreams will never materialise."

"Yes, but Charles," Paris persisted, "Don't you see? Too many people continue with their dreams even though they are destroying their own soul in the process. Because ultimately if they were to listen to their inner compass they would have a sense of worry and disquiet when they were doing something that was not a part of their life plan."

Charles watched her emotion soar and sensed a troubled mind hid behind the pleas of her passionate lecture. He moved closer toward her, taking both of her hands into his.

"Paris? Now I have a question for you," he said sympathetically. "What's the matter with *you*? I get the impression it is you that feels disquiet?"

His words stung. They stung her mind, her heart and her throat that was now cinder hot from the snare of pent up emotion. She hung her head.

"I guess I am just worried," she admitted quietly. "You see my life is about love, if I don't have it in my life I feel useless. Gerard has gone now, as a result the coincidence that has settled in his place has been you." she looked up at him, her voice turned to a whisper. "I am scared that if I give my baby up and then you leave me, I will be alone again with nothing." Like rain against a window pane, one wide silent tear followed the track of the one before. "I'm confused," she admitted, her face beginning to scrunch.

Oh shit!, he thought, *please don't cry, please. You look so ugly when you cry.* With reluctance he reached out and held her in his arms. As her head sank into his chest he likened her, as he had so many times before, to a big, floppy, faithful Saint Bernard, she would always be there in times of need. He held her and waited for her to calm down.

Quietly, Bill walked through the front door and, as his foot rested upon the ivory carpet of the hall-way, he was met with Charles' cold calculating voice drifting from the sitting room.

"You have to think of our future together, Paris, nothing more," Bill heard Charles tell his daughter.

"*Are you sure* it is the right thing to give up the baby to the Santé's, Charles?" Paris asked, completely oblivious to her father's presence.

Charles looked down at her face. Her puppy dog eyes, crowded by dark circles, looked back at him for reassurance. Guiltily Charles battled with the cold selfishness of his resolve, deliberating ashamedly on how his own needs and wishes were causing detriment to human life. Only when his mind cast Rebecca's face into view and reminded him of the love he held for her did his shame subside.

"Of course it is the right thing, Paris, for all the reasons we have already discussed." He comforted her with a kiss on her damp cheek. "I love you, Paris."

The words threw her like a rugby ball over the posts into a brand new life. A life she had for so long wanted to reside in. Just like the Caribbean Sea, his blue eyes shone with promise and sincerity and made Paris feel alive all over again.

"I love you too," she whispered.

Bill was sickened. He wrestled with an almighty force that urged him to surge into the room and grab Charles by the throat. He would shake him, shake him so hard, he would twist and grip his throat until his innards were forced from his cruel selfish body. Bill's eyes narrowed in hatred, his fingers twisted and turned in his palms as he stood outside the room where his enemy sat sadistically infiltrating his precious daughter's mind. He thought of Frankie's words,

"Revenge must always be calculated and methodical. If there is one thing this life has taught me about retribution, it must never be exacted when emotion is soaring."

Bill inhaled a tight breath and, with the door still open behind him, he closed it with an intrusive click.

"Hi, Paris!" he shouted, "I need to use the bathroom. I'll be down in a minute."

He ran upstairs fearing the unfamiliar tremor of loathing and hatred that barged through his body. He locked the bathroom door and turned on the cold-water tap at the basin, the water pelted out fiercely, just like his hate for the man downstairs. He cupped his hands, throwing the water against his face, ignorant of the tidal wave of splashes that splattered against the carpet and walls.

It was several minutes before he was composed sufficiently to make his way back downstairs. He walked into the sitting room where his daughter sat with Charles close by her side. A bold slash of sunlight poured from the patio doors, innocently illuminating the bulge of Paris ' pregnant stomach and instantly Bill was reminded of the new innocent life beneath. This was a life that was a part of him, his future and his past. His thoughts turned to his own mother and how she, too, had protected him with her own womb in order to give him life. He had repaid her poorly; she had died alone, sacrificially singled out by the new life he had selfishly begun with his wife.

"Are you alright Dad?" Paris asked noticing the tight look of angst upon his face.

"Me? Oh yes, I'm fine," Bill smiled.

"You look like a man with a lot on his mind," Charles sneered.

"Yes, well you have probably hit the nail on the head with that one," Bill answered calmly. "Would anyone care to join me in a drink?" he asked, walking across to the decanter. "I feel I need a gin and tonic, it may help to drown my troubles and loosen my tongue. After all," he looked across at Charles and smiled again, "you know what they say, a problem shared is a problem halved."

"Yes, I'll have a drink, I think I have come out in sympathy for your lovely daughter here," Charles said, ruffling Paris' hair, who was now looking up at him adoringly. "I haven't touched a drop all day."

"How nice of you to be so considerate to her." Staring at the wall before him Bill managed to conceal his infuriated grimace whilst he poured the drinks.

Charles felt his emotion gurgle with a mixture of amusement and anger towards Bill's supposed stress. *What the hell has he got to worry about? He lives in the equivalent of a two up two down, he breaths free from the constricting mould of expectation, yes he has a bitch of a wife, but nobody forces him to stay.* As ever, Charles brought his attention to his own suffering and the conversation with Hugo only hours before. The money was unobtainable.

"Oh, it will probably be fifteen or twenty years before you see any major return on that investment," Hugo had informed him. "Who cares anyway?" Hugo had laughed. "It will be a little nest egg when you have retired that will see your nails are trimmed by some playgirls, Hugh Heffner doesn't look too bad on that plan!"

For Hugo the matter had been casually dismissed, for Charles another obstacle had been met. He took the drink that Bill was now offering.

"Thanks, Bill. So, come on, what is on your mind?" Charles asked.

Bill sat alone in a nearby armchair and shook his head. "Well, you see, Charles, it's really quite simple and when you are lucky enough to have children of your own you will understand my train of thought." His eyes narrowed as he looked back at the ghastly shallow man before him. "I am wondering what the hell you are doing here, in my home?"

The room was shocked into silence. Only Paris, disbelieving of her father's words, let out an uncomfortable laugh that fleetingly cracked the frozen atmosphere. Charles followed her lead and he too let out a reticent laugh.

"I am not joking, Charles," Bill went on, his anger assaulted further by Charles' apparent amusement. "I want to know. What do you want with *my* daughter and *my* unborn grandchild?"

The smile on Charles' face disappeared; he swallowed hard, ever thankful for Paris' swift intervention.

"Dad?" she questioned, confusion smothering her face, "What are you doing?"

"I am doing what every parent in the land would do. I am saving my daughter from heartbreak by a snivelling, no hoping bastard like this shit sitting here."

Paris was frightened by the menacing look that sat in her father's eye. Never had she seen it. Not even towards her mother, his wife, the wife that for years had tormented and bullied him into submission. "What are you talking about?" Paris asked, feeling another outbreak of emotion about to erupt.

Her father looked at her, his expression filled with disdain. "Are you telling me you are so stupid you can't see what he is doing? This conniving rat doesn't love you. He doesn't know what love means, he…"

Charles interrupted him. "Bill …" he stated forcefully.

Paris stopped him with an upright hand and stood to her feet. "How dare you?" Paris shouted. "How dare you talk to me about being stupid? There is only one person stupid in this house and that is you."

Bill stared back at the unrecognisable guise of his daughter.

"Just because I am your daughter I am not *your* property and this," she shouted, stabbing at her stomach, "is not *your* property either. I am sick and tired of being treated like the personal property of you and Mother. If you were so intent on standing by your daughter then, with all the opportunities you have had, why choose now? All my life she has bullied me and bullied you, and every time you have given in to her!" Paris screeched hysterically. "Even though you knew, that your pathetic, spineless submissions resulted in me," she prodded her chest angrily, "me, your daughter, paying the price." Her pregnant body heaved for breath; Bill sat looking up at her, stunned at the unexpected twist in his daughter's behaviour.

"So now," Paris continued, "you think is the time to protect me and save me from heartbreak?" She moved herself inches from his face, Charles stood and tried to draw her away but she pushed him back. "Don't make me laugh. That is the trouble with you two; you just can't bear to see me happy can you? Because you have fucked your own life up so badly, you want me to do the same." Tears were flowing down her face, but her words still managed to bubble through her broken sobs. "Well, I have news for you," she shouted, brushing her tears with determined strokes of her hand. "You can both go to hell. I do not want to be a part of this any longer." She turned and grabbed Charles' hand. "Charles and I are going to start a new life, aren't we Charles?" she asked, turning toward him.

Charles nodded awkwardly.

"You see, Dad. Whether you like it or not, for once I am going to start making my own decisions. And that will begin tonight." She looked back at Charles. "I am going to let you think this over, alone. Tonight I am sleeping at Charles' house."

The unexpected bolt of her words caused Charles to gulp in panic. *Shit, she can't possibly be serious?*

"Paris," Charles suggested, "Maybe you should talk about this with your father in a calmer manner; he is after all only trying to protect you."

Bill seized the opportunity. "Ah, you see – your first suggestion of commitment and he's backing away like a snarling dog. Go on," he goaded, staring with loathing at Charles, "tell her; tell her she can't come."

Paris turned to face Charles and waited for an answer, her mind was ready to face whatever anyone could throw at it.

"Well?" she asked vehemently.

Charles admired the unexpected yet indestructible strength that spilled from her being. He looked from Paris to Bill and retraced his glance again,

"Yes," he answered loosely, "of course you can come."

Chapter Thirty Eight

CHARLES started the car and wondered where the hell he would take her – Cedars Hall? Not a chance. Pendlestone Manor? Too expensive. The small budget hotel on the outskirts of Chelmsley? He hesitated, it had its benefits, impossible to bump into anyone he knew, but the thought of even walking through the doors of such an establishment filled him with instant dread. He heard Paris' timid sniffles by his side and at once the answer came.

"Don't worry, Paris," he reassured, "I'm going to take you to a place that will wash all of your troubles away."

"Where's that?" she asked hopefully.

"A place that even I haven't been to for years, but as children Hugo and I always visited it when we needed to escape. It's our family cottage at Wickruns Bay, a quiet little seaside village close to Whitby. Have you ever been?"

"No," Paris replied, staring pensively out of the car window.

"I think you need some time away, a change of scenery perhaps?" Charles suggested.

"Mmmm. Maybe you're right," she answered sadly. Suddenly panic prevailed. "Oh, no!" She turned to Charles.

He knew what she was going to say, *I haven't brought any clothes with me, I'll have nothing to wear,* he mocked privately.

"What about the dogs that I walk? How will they cope tomorrow if I let them down?"

Charles laughed; how unique she was. "Oh, Paris," Charles soothed, rubbing her overweight leg with silent criticism. "For once can you just think of yourself? The bloody dogs will be fine, and anyway they're not your sodding responsibility." He took a hold of her hand and kissed it. "You need a break," he insisted. "We will phone the owners and explain."

Paris felt too tired and too grateful to speak. It was the first time in ages she felt as though someone genuinely cared about *her* needs. She let her body sink into the bucket seat of the car and protectively rested her hands against her pregnant stomach. There was only weeks to go before the baby growing beneath her hands would introduce itself to her. Already it had experienced far more troubles than its innocence deserved. *Poor thing*, she thought. She closed her eyes and tried to push her upset to one side; it wasn't long before she began to doze.

"Only half a mile to go," she woke to hear Charles informing her. Paris opened her eyes to see they were slowly travelling down a very steep hill and beneath it was a breathtaking seaside cove. Old traditional street lamps lit the whole bay and illuminated a darkening marble sea. With sleepy blinks its calm waves stroked the sand clean before retreating again. Paris felt herself immediately relax; she sunk the window down, eager to smell and to hear the gush of the sea. As the fresh sea air hit her face she breathed in deeply, and realised that without doubt, this was her kind of place.

"I wish we had come earlier," she commented, "I would have loved to walk along the beach before the tide came in."

"The beach will still be here in the morning," Charles answered, he too also appreciating the view.

As Charles parked the car near the bay, Paris continued to scrutinise her surroundings. A cluster of cottages, maybe only a hundred, all perched on the cliff side and mingled together in a crooked hotchpotch patch. Paris smiled as she imagined them hunching up their shoulders to give their neighbours the opportunity to glimpse at the awesome bay before them. Some of the cottages and their small leaded windows hallowed the early evening with the welcoming glow of lamps; they looked cosy and inviting, a safe haven from the cool rush of the salty air. Between them she noticed hundreds of inching steps that meandered obliquely uphill, with sporadic streetlights at their sides, guiding visitors through the pathways that led to the various fishing cottages. Their beauty was incomparable and even though they were small dwellings, their strength shone in the midst of individual character. She wondered silently what they would have seen and survived, she imagined the sea storms bashing at their doors and windows, trying to force a way inside and cause destruction. These clusters of cottages, like hardy moorland ponies, would have stood firmly in unity. She imagined them with arms linked, their strength on occasion diminishing to a tremble, yet, against all the odds, their bravery had always prevailed. Already, she decided, she *really* loved this place.

Paris turned to Charles, who was waving his mobile through the air trying to gain a signal, "Do you actually own a cottage here?" she asked in amazement.

"Yes, it was handed down to my mother from my grandfather," he answered, briefly looking around the resident's only car park for vehicles he recognised.

Paris sniggered.

"Why are you laughing?" Charles asked.

"I'm just wondering if all the assets you term as *yours* have been handed down, is there anything you have that *you* have actually worked and paid for yourself?"

Charles felt truly angered and, although he didn't respond verbally, he snatched a carrier bag from the back seat and flung it past her face.

"I stopped by a shop while you were sleeping and bought some essentials for the cottage. For your information, *I paid for them.*"

Paris raised her eyebrows, a vulnerable spot, she realised. She opened the car door and the exhilarating smell of salty, oceanic freedom increased. Charles, still irritated and clearly oblivious to the raw power of the smell, lit a cigarette. Though he waited briefly for her to catch up, Paris was left to follow the trailing scent of cigarette smoke.

The Lancaster-Baron cottage was very quaint, it was as if its habitation over the past two centuries had left it feeling so relaxed that its only inclination was to lean on its elbow and languish in the spectacular surroundings. *And who could blame it?* Paris thought. A wooden name plaque was nailed by the side of the door that read *Keepers Cottage.* Charles fumbled beneath a stone by the door steps until he found the key.

"Keepers Cottage, what a lovely name, it gives me the feeling it will look after me." Paris saw the key. "Did someone know you were coming?" she asked.

"No. We always leave the key here; it's an open house whenever we feel the need to come."

Paris laughed. "God, this is like a different world," she gasped.

Charles ignited his lighter and fought with the key in the damp key hole. After some tugging, shoving and rattling of the door with the key, eventually he managed to shove his way in and reach for the light.

They stood in the sitting room, ornamental boats and old fishing nets hung upon the wall beside authentic photographs, all reminding a now lucky generation of the tough, gruelling fishing occupation of yesteryear. The décor, though dated, spoke of high quality and good taste. Old worn rugs lay upon a terracotta carpet, and a settee and two armchairs, obviously cherished with sentiment Paris presumed on seeing the numerous layers of re-coverings that peeped from beneath.

"God, it's bloody freezing in here!" Charles said, rubbing his hands together. "It stinks as well."

"I would be freezing too if I had been left alone for so long," Paris answered whilst continuing to admire the idiosyncrasy of the sloping walls and ceiling.

"First things first," Charles said, taking three bottles of Rioja from the carrier and placing them on the mantel above the fire before he bent down to light it. The fire was already laid and the log basket by its side was full with dry chunky logs.

"Who laid the fire?" Paris asked.

"We have a woman that comes in once a week even when we are not here; she airs the place and keeps it habitable on the off chance."

He struck his lighter and lit the papers beneath the kindling and, as he did, a huge puff ball of smoke crowded the room. Rubbing her hands together, Paris watched as the chimney initially refused to awaken from its dreams, continuing to cough out big balloons of smoke before slowly, the fire spluttered its way into life and once breathing freely, the chimney began to draw.

It wasn't long before the orange and sun-yellow flames began to belly-dance their way up the chimney and Paris, always appreciative of a real fire, turned off the main light and, instead, turned on the lamp by the fireside.

"Oh, how romantic and cosy," Paris gushed, drawing the curtains and standing back to admire the golden flicker of the flames. She sat down in one of the armchairs, feeling the heat of the fire already eating away at the chill of the room and immediately understood why this wonderful place had been cosseted for so many years. She submerged into the soft cushions of the armchair and watched Charles, still kneeling at the fire, in deep thought.

"What are you thinking about?" She asked

"Just old times," he said, reminiscing on all the laughter that had taken place in this very room over the years. "I have a lifetime of special memories here." He paused for a second, "I wish I had come back sooner. It could just do with a bit of money spending on it now though," he said looking around the room.

"What are you talking about? It's wonderful," Paris said, already feeling protective of the secret hideaway. "Anyway, where's the bathroom, I'm bursting for a pee?"

"Not again?" he laughed. "You only went an hour ago."

"Err, Charles, in case you haven't noticed I'm pregnant," Paris pointed sarcastically to her pregnancy bulge with a smile. "Pregnant women have to pee every ten minutes." She stood up and took some deep breaths, having sunk so low in the chair the baby had pushed against her chest making it difficult to breathe.

"It's upstairs, first on the left. What are you breathing like that for?" he asked screwing up his face.

Paris laughed and shook her head. "Oh, forget it," she answered.

It was freezing upstairs and Paris noticed the only form of heating was free standing plug in radiators. She blew into her hands and tried to stamp away the cold upon the creaking floorboards.

"Shall I plug in the radiators, Charles?" she shouted down the stairs.

"Oh, hell!" he groaned, "I bet it's sub-zero up there, I'll have to get pissed so that I can face going up."

"Stop moaning!" she shouted back.

Charles smiled and reached for the rest of the shopping. He unpacked the bread, cheese, ham, eggs and milk and placed them in the kitchen that led off the sitting room. He opened the kitchen cupboards. The same pans and crockery he had remembered throughout childhood still lay patiently inside and now, feeling hungry, he reached for the frying pan.

Paris explored the bedrooms; the first was a double room with a small wardrobe, a sink, and a dressing table with two drawers squashed into a corner. She plugged in the radiator and turned on the bedside lamp. She liked the room, it was cosy, with simple blue lined wallpaper and a blue bedspread to match. She walked over to the far wall where some old photographs hung.

A girl of about sixteen, Paris guessed, sat upon a wall. Paris looked closer and recognised it as the one outside this cottage. Sitting next to the girl was a man, he was broad and handsome, and although the photograph was depicted in black and white, Paris instantly saw the resemblance to Charles within him. He had the same blonde wavy hair and an energy to his eyes that charmed the camera lens, the same mysterious energy she had always seen in Charles' eye, but this man, quite unlike Charles, portrayed an inner contentment as though thoroughly at ease with life. The girl by his side had a wide ecstatic grin, her arm was resting upon the man's knee and her head was lovingly nestled into his chest. The love she held for this man was as clear as the day the picture had been taken. There were others, some of Charles and Hugo dressed up in cowboy outfits on the beach, but none of them captured her interest as this one did. Eager to learn more about the pair, she shouted down the stairs.

"Charles. Who is this in this photograph on the bedroom wall, the one with the young girl and the older man?"

Charles walked to the foot of the stairs. "It's my mother with her father, my grandfather," he answered looking up at her. "That photograph was taken the first day he had bought this house. The story is quite charming really."

Paris sat on the top stair, eagerly awaiting the story.

"My grandfather used to visit Wickruns Bay frequently with my mother. When she was about five, an old lady whom my father knew, invited her in for sandwiches and cake after she had played on the beach. She enjoyed her time in the cottage so much that she told her father, if ever they were lucky enough to own a cottage in Wickruns she wanted it to be this very cottage." Charles laughed. "As Grandfather became more successful, every year he upped his offer to the old lady, Mrs Cooper was her name, but she paid no interest to the money, telling him each time that she was leaving the cottage to her children." Charles shrugged and laughed. "When she died her children didn't hold out for sentiment, they bit his hand off with his first offer."

Paris took a deep breath then slumped her shoulders, "Oh how sad for Mrs Cooper, what shallow swine's her children were." Charles grinned.

"Still," Paris said, lightening the mood, "great for your mother and her father. I'm sorry for my comments earlier, I had no idea this place held such personal history."

Charles didn't comment.

Paris continued' "You mother looks to have absolutely adored her father, how wonderful that your child should adore you like that," she said dreamily.

"Mmmm, possibly, but sometimes I think too much adoration can be unhealthy," he answered, feeling an inner edginess build.

"Oh Charles, you humbug! Can you not imagine having a daughter and her loving you in that way? You look just like your grandfather, I bet your daughter would love you in the exactly the same way. Wouldn't it just be magical?"

Charles' voice fell low. "I can't imagine anyone loving me the way my mother loved my grandfather," he answered truthfully.

Paris fell silent as she traced his empty stare. "I can," she answered softly.

He looked back up at her and saw the sincerity in her blue eyes, romantically softened by the undertones of the lamps in the rooms upstairs.

"Really?" he asked in soft appreciation.

"Watch this space," she whispered, slowly walking down the stairs toward him. She didn't speak again; she just held him and felt the negative vibrations of insecurity temporarily shake his cool exterior. He pulled away.

"Are you cooking something?" Paris asked as wafts of melting butter poured from the kitchen.

"Yup! Croque Monsieur," he answered confidently, walking back to the oven.

Paris screwed up her face and followed him. "Croque Monsieur?" She chided "Do you not mean a cheese and ham toastie?"

Charles laughed. "No, I do not, I mean Croque..." He paused, "Well yes, okay then, yes it's a cheese and ham toastie."

Paris picked up a tea towel nearby and threw it at him "You pretentious prick!" she joked. "You're not with your cronies now you know!"

Charles winced as he recalled his mother's use of the word only days before. "Have you been talking to my mother?" he laughed.

"Why? Does she think your set are cronies too?"

"I don't know. Anyway," he said leading her by the shoulders out of the kitchen, "while I am cooking I want you out of here, go and sit by the fire and read a book or something. Or, there are some games in that top cupboard if you want to have a look. There used to be Scrabble, I could thrash you again if you are feeling brave."

Paris, already enjoying her time here so much, rushed to open the cupboard door. "Wow! There's Monopoly!" she screeched. "I haven't played that for years. Shall we play it, what do you think?"

"I think little things please little minds!" he shouted from the kitchen.

"Okay then, after supper we will go for a walk instead, shall we?"

"No, not unless you want to get washed away. The tide's in and, anyway, Monopoly used to be my favourite game, I'll play, but only if I can be the racing car *and* the banker!"

Paris giggled as she opened the box "Little things!" she teased.

Paris popped the last piece of the delicious Croque Monsieur into her mouth and savoured its presence. In one way she wished she had been at home, most certainly she would have gone for third helpings, but with Charles by her side, inching his racing car toward her hotel dwelling on Mayfair, the gluttony and comfort of a bursting stomach could never match the feeling of pure bliss that engulfed her now. Earlier he had turned off all the lights and insisted that their evening would be illuminated only by candlelight and the flames of the fire. Since then, every time she had looked at his handsome shadowy face and smelt the fading masculinity of his aftershave, a tide of excitement flipped her innards. For the first time he seemed real, authentic, as if the sea of this special place had already drowned his false inhibitions.

"Oh, no!" Charles cringed as he landed on Mayfair.

"That's two thousand pounds to me, please," Paris ordered, holding out her hand.

Charles looked down at his dwindling supplies in his bank and realised how close this game sailed towards his own life. "I'm bankrupt you bugger!" he laughed.

"Never mind, pooch, there's plenty of worse things that can happen in life."

"Pooch? Pooch?" he said with a smile "Where the hell did that word come from?"

"Sorry, it's just by this candlelight with your hair all ruffled and falling over your face, you reminded me of a Shit-zu I look after, it's called Pooch!"

"It's the first time I've ever been likened to one of those ugly little bastards."

Paris laughed. "Don't be so cruel."

She reached across the board, where they lay on the floor, to playfully swipe him, but Charles, also laughing, got hold of her arm and pulled her nearer. For a second he just stared and examined her smile. For the first time he noticed her small even teeth, and her lips, tinged with a red glow from the occasional sip of Rioja she had taken, and her eyes, playfully placid with a warming honesty that burst from their tide of blue.

"I've loved tonight," he said softly. "I wish my life could always be like this."

"When we are together," Paris suddenly felt shy, "you know, together as in, married and all that, it will be."

He inched his face closer toward her and closed his eyes, she kissed him softly. Her kiss, slow and tender, was the only kiss he had ever received that promised true loyalty. The feeling stirred a medley of new emotions. He broke away.

"Paris, would you mind if we stayed down here tonight, just you and I, in front of the fire?" He stroked her hair. "I could bring a duvet down." He hesitated, feeling intimidated by the truth, "I just want to hold you all night in my arms." He told her truthfully.

Tears welled up in her eyes; emotion bound her, making it impossible to speak. She just nodded.

Charles closed his eyes and took comfort from hearing her breaths by his side. He felt confused. Had a brand new world suddenly introduced itself?

Paris' head was free from thought, faster than ice cream, she had already melted.

Chapter Thirty Nine

JULIA skipped out of the boutique with the large carrier filled with her newly altered dress. Making her way toward the car, her emotions were on such a high that she barely felt her feet touch the ground. Luca's chauffeur opened the back door, a gesture she still couldn't bring herself to feel comfortable with, although she thanked him before slipping gracefully inside.

The carrier bag was large with gold embossed lettering running across the centre. Not wanting to part with it, she rested it upon her knee and took enjoyment from the crackle of the thick plastic, the soft rustle of the packing tissue inside and the faint exuberant waft of the boutique's luxury against her face. She couldn't resist another peek of the treasured outfit that lay inside.

Simon, the driver, looked at Julia through the rear view mirror. He had enjoyed chauffeuring her around. He had done this job for twenty-three years with the last four working solely for the DeMario's. He had seen some pretentious tossers in his time, but Julia was a good kid, she had a big smile, one so big that it showed a big heart beneath. She was a true beauty, Luca was a lucky man.

Replacing the tissue and still smiling, Julia rested her head on the headrest and looked out of the window. She had never owned anything as spectacular in her life; the dress was just perfect, well at least she thought it was. Luca had not seen it yet and she hoped he would think it suitable for her first formal meeting with his parents.

Her stomach lurched again; the surprise party tomorrow evening was creeping ever closer. She took a sharp intake of breath and began to slowly appease her agitated thoughts.

Together, she and Luca had faced many obstacles and, so far, they had conquered them all. Taking Luca to the camp last night to meet her father was certainly one of them. She let out a giggle that caused Simon to look back at her through the mirror again.

"Come on Luca," she had suggested, feeling confident that now nothing could come between them, "we have to get it over with at some stage; if we are to be married you have to make amends with him sometime."

"What do you mean, me make amends with him?" Luca had laughed. "He smacked me straight in the eye." He began to examine his fading wound in the mirror. "I know," she said calmly, walking over to him, "but in a way he did you a favour, you were a bit sweet looking before." She grinned, staring back at his handsome reflection. "That black eye made you look like a handsome rogue." She slid her hands against his thighs, "It made me fancy you even more, at least thank him for that," she joked.

Luca responded to her touch and turned to kiss her. "Mmmmm," he said adoringly, "I suppose I could be persuaded."

So they had set off and, with each mile that flashed by, Julia remained unperturbed by the outcome. Whatever the conclusion to the reunion, she would be marrying Luca, the absolute love of her life.

In nervous silence, the two of them walked hand in hand through the heart of the site, past the pile of black embers from last night's camp fire and through the gaps between the other caravans, until eventually they neared the door of Julia's 'home.' As they approached it, the tree to the side of the caravan caused her to cringe, and a slow blend of both embarrassment and amusement to gently rise. She bit her lip to conceal both emotions and, internally, she groaned.

It had slipped her mind when she had suggested they visit that today was Friday, her father's habitual 'wash day'. The tree was festooned with the entirety of his wardrobe, two pairs of trousers; three shirts, four pairs of underpants and one jumper, and all now swished happily along the tree's branches.

With Julia still internally groaning and Luca nervously stepping from one foot to the other as he remembered, and waited, to be reintroduced to the man that resembled an American barn, Julia knocked on the door.

There was no answer, so she knocked again.

"Can you not just go in?" Luca asked looking puzzled.

"Not today," Julia answered, still biting her lip and feeling unable to look at Luca in case she became hysterical with nervous laughter.

"Who is it?" His gigantic voice ricocheted from the caravan.

"It's me," Julia answered, noticing Luca shrink beneath his shirt.

"Well, why the bloody 'ell do ya' not come in then?" The door swung open and there he stood, filling the doorway with his enormity.

With eyes as wide as a lagoon Luca fleetingly traced the vision before him, and on seeing Luca's face, Julia shrieked with laughter.

There her father stood, in his customary glory of 'Friday scarcity', wearing his remaining pair of underpants and holding a can of cider in his spade-like hand.

"Oh!" he said in a deep rumble, making no attempt to apologise for his lack of attire, "I wondered when I would see you two buggers 'gain." He stood to one side of the door and beckoned them inside with a nod of his head. "Come in."

Julia walked in first followed by Luca who was immediately dwarfed by the gigantic stature of her father standing before him. Julia felt protective of Luca and tenderly linked her fingers into his, leading him to the worn settee which faced the small portable television.

A can of Woodpecker Cider was thrust in front of Luca's face which he accepted with a nervous smile. With interest he scrutinised the description on the can.

"What's up with you?" Julia's father boomed, "'ave ya never drunk that before?"

Julia sniggered as Luca jumped to his own defence.

"Er, yes, yes I have," he stammered taking a slug from the can. "It's delicious," he concluded, his taste buds smarting from its overbearing sweetness.

"Delicious, my arse!" Mr Smith laughed. "It does the trick, that's all we need to know, it gets ya pissed!" He let out a huge laugh.

"Don't be horrible to Luca, Dad. I've brought him back to meet you again. There is no need to be nasty to him," Julia scolded lightly.

"'Orrible to 'im? What are you on 'bout? 'Ow often do I share me cider?" Julia's father laughed again and got up from his armchair, which was exposing a mass of foam from both armrests, and banged his can against Luca's. "Cheers lad!" he gestured. "Let's make a fresh start, shall we?"

Luca nodded with relief. "Yes, that sounds good to me, Mr Smith," Luca smiled.

"Ey, while your 'ere," Julia's father sat back in his chair and looked across at Luca, "I've seen on the news that one a your lot 'as been up in court for fixing races."

"Mmmmm," Luca answered, not daring to pluck up the courage to protest his colleague's innocence.

"What's the betting you and I can't 'atch a plan like that?"

"He's only joking!" Julia shrieked, seeing Luca's horrified face and trying to reassure him.

"Wor?" her father exclaimed, "Doesn't everyone want to make a few quid in this world?"

Julia turned back to her father. "Stop it, Dad. You have had your fun, now stop it!" She stood up. "Anyway," she said, straightening her jacket from creases, "We are going now, I only wanted you and Luca to patch things up."

"Give over," her dad interjected, "that lad's not goin' anywhere until 'es 'ad another few drinks wi' me."

So, Luca's fate was sealed. Five cans of Woodpecker Cider later he staggered out of the caravan with his gigantic new friend, still in only his underpants, slapping him hard on his back as he left. As Luca wobbled down the steps, her father took Julia by the arm and turned her to face him.

"Ey, now you be careful do ya 'ear me?" he said in a protective whisper. "I'm pleased you've found someone that 'as a bit a brass in their pocket," he rubbed his fingers together "but, there's not a better feelin' than freedom, remember ya' roots and don't ever feel trapped." He rubbed her shoulder lightly. "You'd better get off," he said nodding over to Luca, who was visibly swaying in the darkness. "'E looks as green as a cucumber."

She nodded. "Good night, Dad," Julia said softly.

In unison, they zigzagged back to the car and Luca only managed to contain himself until he reached outside the camp before he vomited violently upon the grass verge.

Returning from her thoughts, Julia realised they were now only minutes away from the hotel and she smiled to herself in the back of the car. Could meeting his parents really get any worse than that? *No*, she concluded trying to settle her jittering nerves, *it wouldn't be anything like that. Luca's parents will be much more dignified.*

On ringing only twice, the telephone was answered. Both the caller and the receiver of the call were now well acquainted.

"Charles spent the evening in Wickruns Bay with a lady by the name of Paris Montford." The voice was remote and to the point.

"Wickruns Bay? Paris Montford?" The receiver of the call fell silent for a second whilst the information was distilled. "What the hell for?"

It took the caller ten formal and difficult minutes to explain. The conclusion was met with a second, much longer spurt of stony silence before the whole operation was brought to an abrupt end.

"I have heard enough. There is no further work I want you to complete; I have all the facts I need. Please send me your invoice along with the evidence and you will be paid without delay."

The line went dead. The chair creaked solemnly as the recipient of the call sat upon it. A determined voice swept icily across the room.

"Oh, you have done it this time Charles Lancaster-Baron. You have really done it this time."

Chapter Fourty

HOLDING UP her floor length dress with one hand and allowing the smooth mahogany balustrade to steady her with the other, Julia took a deep intake of breath; then gracefully made her descent along the long winding staircase of the hotel.

Below in Reception, her spellbinding appearance caused a rare scene within the hotel. The concierge, positioned at the foot of the stairway, had never been so busy, with a burst of customers gawping wantonly up the staircase asking nonsensical questions that even they, let alone the bell boys, recognised as irrelevant. Receptionists, perturbed by their obscured view, huddled discreetly together, some smiling up in admiration whilst others had soured faces that indicated nothing more than an all-consuming jealously. It was indisputable; the vision before them was awesome.

Wearing a full length powder pink gown, her dark treacle skin glowed like a melting candle. Tastefully sprinkled sequins and crystals upon her dress flickered and danced alluringly whilst delicate pink straps, drizzles of modesty, were almost hidden beneath large waving tresses of her long dark hair and then disappeared beneath a figure-hugging bodice. So proud to hold her close, the bodice refused to relinquish responsibility and cosseted every inch of her ribs, her waist, her stomach and her thighs until a dramatically jewelled mermaid fishtail that splayed from her knees forced it to let go of her.

With each demure step she made, her curvaceous hips sensually rocked with the soothing momentum of a baby's cradle, hypnotising her audience and forced most of her male admirers to ask a wishful question. Was there any chance they could be the lucky beneficiary of this gift and unwrap the fascinating promise that lay hidden beneath?

Julia, oblivious to her spellbound audience, had appreciated preparing herself for the evening in privacy, taking time and great effort to perfect her appearance, but, in this instant, with her body filled with angst and nausea, she wished Luca was by her side.

As she made her way to the hotel's cocktail bar to meet Luca, she had never recalled her senses feeling so alert, every detail of her magnificent surroundings appeared to magnify in her path. She felt her diamante shoes, so delicately feminine, sink into the opulent royal blue carpet that trailed regally beneath her feet. Her nervous eyes, swamped with vulnerability, studied the enormous rotund chandelier that hung from the high domed ceiling above. It reminded her of the story 'James and the Giant Peach', the last story her and her wonderful mother had read together before her tragic murder. Her emotions slumped; she wished she was with her now, to reassure her and guide her down this daunting staircase. Her gorgeous eyes then swooped upon the vast authentic portraits that hung upon the wall, their lifelike presence, were portrayed in colours so vivid and striking that the masterful strokes of oil still appeared damp. These were the 'blue blooded' ancestors who had once called Pendlestone Manor their home, she realised. They stared back at her with austere questioning poses, seeming to challenge her to state a legitimate reason for her attendance amongst the grandeur that surrounded her. She rapidly looked away, though still feeling their stare. She glanced back at the chandelier to rekindle more positive images. Hundreds of crystal pendants, like giants' teardrops, captured her with a magical twinkling dance. Julia imagined they looked like fairies living in a secret land, and wondered hopefully if they would be kind enough to cast some lucky fairy dust upon her to alleviate the hammering of her stamping nerves. Then, on closer scrutiny, she saw the truth.

This time each crystal was a unified group of malicious imps and each twinkle was a cruel nudge of amusement brought about with the knowledge that, amongst this genuine finery, she was indeed a genuine fake.

She searched for a reason that would explain her sudden twist in emotion. It was her dress she thought; it was so comfortable, almost too comfortable. It made her feel as though she was naked, bearing herself to the world, and she hated the thought of that. As much as Luca knew everything about her, she despised the thought of anybody seeing the truth and deeming her unsuitable for him, especially his parents. She felt her stomach loop in trepidation; it reminded her again that she was now only hours away from meeting them formally.

As she approached the final step, she lifted her dress a fraction before releasing it to walk through Reception, and the splaying fishtail, adorned in sequins, followed on behind, romantically trailing across the floor. Unbeknown to Julia, as she walked through the hotel with a smile on her face, and the occasional, "Good evening," she had fooled every member of her audience into thinking *she* was as authentic as the very portraits that had just intimidated her.

Julia had not yet frequented the cocktail bar in the evening, but as she neared she felt comforted by the sound of a piano and the cool mellow voice of an accompanying jazz singer. She paused by the door and was surprised to experience reprieve from the formal décor of the hotel. Within the bar the lights were subtly dimmed and small ceiling lights cast targeted rays towards a long chrome bar and slim, glass bar stools.

Julia stepped inside and felt eternally grateful to see Luca sitting straight ahead of her on one of the bar stools; her heart sprang in excitement, he looked so handsome in his tuxedo. His shoes, that she had watched him polish only an hour before, tapped playfully to the music against the glass stool, and he casually slid an olive off a cocktail stick into his mouth. *How the hell can he eat?* she wondered.

Casually he looked up toward the door. Seeing Julia walking

towards him brought a beam of pleasure to his face. He stood and watched her approach, aware that every other eye in the bar was also tracing her steps across the room. He smiled proudly as she reached him. Gently he kissed her on both cheeks.

"You are the most striking looking woman that I have ever seen in my entire life," he told her genuinely. "I am so proud to be with you." He paused. "And especially proud to be taking you to meet my family. They are going to love you, just like I do," he told her with certainty.

She gave him a huge smile, hoping that its enormity would hide her sickening nerves. Having never taken a girl home to meet his parents formally, she knew that tonight meant everything to Luca.

"I'm having a champagne cocktail," he told her, "it's fabulous, would you like one?" he asked whilst he drew out a stool for her to sit down.

"Yes," she nodded, "that would be lovely, thank you."

Luca beckoned the barman and whilst he waited for him, he took in her appearance once more.

"You look absolutely fantastic," he told her again. He nestled his head adoringly to the side of her face and lowered his tone, "Do you know what I am going to do to you tonight when we get back to our room?"

The breath of his warm sexy voice tickled her face, causing the skin on her body to respond with a sensual crackle that travelled rapidly down her spine.

"What?" she whispered with a coy smile.

"I am going to make you...."

"What can I get you to drink, madam?" the waiter asked.

Julia giggled whilst Luca ordered her cocktail and slowly felt her nerves begin to thaw.

They sat at the bar, talking, listening to the music and enjoying the decadence of their cocktails. Julia felt so relaxed and privately wished they didn't have to leave but Luca's words jolted her into reality.

"We had better leave," Luca said, looking at his watch and pushing the remainder of his cocktail towards the waiter.

"Are you going to waste that?" she asked.

Luca laughed. "No, I'm going to share it with him," he nodded toward the waiter polishing the bar.

Again Julia wished she could postpone their departure. "Are we late?" she asked, shuffling nervously on her stool. "Surely we have time to finish our drinks?"

"You have, but may I remind you I am driving." He kissed her on the nose. "That was my second; I better not drink it all. And anyway, I don't know what the traffic will be like, it's about an hour and a half's drive from here and we have to arrive before he does," he reminded her.

Oh God! Julia thought, reality sinking in, *the 'he' Luca is talking about is his father, and he hates me, I know he does*, she began to panic. Standing from the stool with Luca's assistance, she asked him a question.

"Luca, if we get there and your father is nasty to me, can we leave with a promise that you will remain by my side?"

"There are two things you can be sure of," Luca answered, reaching for her hand. "I will always be by your side whatever he thinks of you, but secondly, *he will* love you." He took a step back from her. "I mean, come on, Julia, look at you, show me a man in the world that wouldn't." He took her arm. "Now come on, let's go."

Luca's words had done little to alleviate Julia's nerves, but moreover, his words had done little to alleviate his own.

Chapter Fourty One

THE ROBOTIC FLINCH of the electric gates and the neutral stir of the car's engine forced Julia shoulders to tense. Unlike the rest of the seventy-minute journey when she had chattered indiscriminately, now, her nerves deemed it impossible to speak a word. Luca sensed her unease and sympathetically placed his hand on her knee then, when the thick wooden gates allowed, he drove on.

The day was beginning to disappear, inviting the grounds of the DeMario mansion into the realms of a shadowy dusk. As they travelled down the drive Julia could see an enormity of land, fenced by post and rails and offering home to a small collection of retired horses. Luca slowed the car. "They are some of our horses that have had serious injuries or seen the end of their racing days," he told her forcing conversation. "There are five of them that love to stay out as long as they can, we let them until the weather really turns then we bring them in for the winter."

Julia nodded, though still remaining silent, all the while keeping her eyes on the driveway ahead. They passed lines of trees and clumps of woodland. The sound of the car intruding on the privacy of the wild inhabitants sent pheasants and rabbits scurrying back to safety. She rubbed the palms of her warm clammy hands and wished she could follow them. At this moment the thought of a rabbit's burrow, dark, small, and cooling offered the perfect hideaway and a strong appeal. The car continued.

As the mansion came into view Julia felt her jaw physically drop. She stared at the vast residence; halogen lights radiated a dazzling luminescent glare onto the façade of a huge white building.

"Here we are," Luca said glancing at her. "Home sweet home!"

Julia didn't think it looked anything like a home, more like the formalities of a British Embassy, a building that would only be visited in times of trouble when travelling abroad. Her stomach clenched harder. Her eyes searched for welcome and managed to find brief solace from the broad oblong stance of the windows.

So many of them lined the building, like obedient toy soldiers, and cast a carroty orange glow from within and winked in greeting to external life. It looked as though America's White House had been transformed into Santa's grotto.

Luca parked the car between the enormous front entrance and an elaborate water fountain which now, aided by the halogen lights, spurted water that looked like molten gold twenty or thirty feet into the air. Then, the sound she had been *really* dreading. The harsh cease of the engine followed by the irrevocable sound of the keys sliding from the ignition, it was all so final. They had arrived.

Luca saw the look of trepidation in her face. "Look," he said, trying to lighten her mood, "it's half-past eight now, my father is expected with my uncle at nine, it will give me a chance to introduce you to Mamma and some family friends before he arrives." He rubbed her leg affectionately. "There aren't going to be many people here tonight, just a selection of close friends and family. My father thinks his surprise has already been dealt with when my uncle arrived from Italy this morning to take him to play golf. He has no idea that more celebrations are planned, he will be tired, we won't be here long, I promise."

The illuminated driveway lit up Luca's pleading face and Julia could see his greatest wish was that tonight would pass smoothly. *His* nerves, she reminded herself, just like her own when she had taken him to meet her father, would also be on a knife's edge. She chastised her selfishness and forcefully unbuckled her seatbelt.

"Anyway," Luca continued, "did you remember to bring your wellingtons?" he asked also unbuckling "Whatever you do, don't be impressed by the façade, the place is full of cockroaches inside."

"Who said I was impressed?" she retorted with a smile.

He burst out laughing. "That's my girl!" He leaned over and planted a grateful kiss on her cheek before the scrape of bolted doors opening caught their attention.

"Oh mia Bellissima!" Luca's mother sang from the immense doorway.

With her short chubby arms lovingly outstretched she walked toward the car. She was wearing a turquoise gown with reams of flowing fabric that swished one way and then the other as it followed the sway of her ample hips. The lights on the driveway shone against her face and Julia's disposition began to lift as she saw the warmth in his mother's eyes. Her face carried a smile that was as large and as warm as pure sunshine, and as his mother tried to peer through the windows of the car, Julia could see that her welcoming smile was also for her.

"Chow, Mama!" Luca called as he walked around the car to open the passenger door to help Julia out.

"Oh my Lord! Bellissima! Bellissima! " Maria threw her hands to her face as Julia walked toward her.

"She is telling you that you look beautiful," Luca whispered.

Maria's cautious pigeon steps were discarded and replaced with enthusiastic leaps as she neared her son and his guest, once she got hold of them both they were covered in Italian kisses and swamped with gripping hugs.

"Come in, come in!" she beckoned eagerly, grasping Julia's hand and pulling her towards the house. "Let me get you a drink before Pappa DeMario gets home, I want to know all about you."

"Mama!" Luca chastised lightly.

With a beaming smile Julia turned and shook her head at Luca indicating him to hush; his mother's affectionate sincerity was more than she could ever have hoped for.

As Julia was whisked into the kitchen, it was impossible for her to tell Luca's mother *anything* about herself. Not only was she spellbound by the mansion's décor and lavish pieces of furniture, but in addition, every time she looked at Mrs DeMario she realised her nerves had been exchanged for excitement; this gregarious lady before her was to be her future mother-in-law. Her face began to glow and her nerves, that up until minutes ago had threatened to remain a lifetime, were being forced to surrender to the unstoppable charm of sheer elation.

Luca watched proudly from the sidelines as he witnessed Julia's spirits revive under his mother's caring wing. He grinned as he saw his mother enthusiastically waving over relatives and friends, introducing them with a crafty knowing nudge to meet Julia, her son's 'new friend'. He lingered cautiously, for a hint or a gesture that indicated Julia's wish to be rescued, but, contrary to his concern, he saw only her dark eager eyes flashing him a sexy look across the room, each one lasted just a second, though long enough to make him feel like the luckiest man in the world.

Emma and Sofia stiffened with rage that Julia should even be invited *and* that all their family were now crowding round to meet her. When they thought Luca was suitably distracted, they circled the outskirts of the group, like a duo of preying hyenas, eyeballing her menacingly in the hope that the opportunity to pounce might come. Sofia was the first to recognise that their efforts were fruitless. Julia was so busy impressing *her* relatives that she was not even aware of Sofia's presence *and*, to cap it all, she saw Piers, also standing on the sidelines, laughing openly on seeing that her intimidating ploy had clearly failed. Sofia stamped over to him.

"Pick up your pet lip, little princess, we wouldn't want you to trip over it and scuff your Jimmy Choos now would we?" Piers teased.

Sofia shoved him playfully but, with a sour face, continued to glare across at Julia. "She's just too good to be true that one, she doesn't fool me," she told Piers.

With a continual trail of adoring company by her side, Julia was ushered toward the drawing room, the room where apparently the bulk of the surprise party was to be held. Luca marched ahead of the other guests and for the first time since they arrived actually managed to walk by Julia's side.

"I feel like I need to ask for your autograph, Maam," The pride in his voice mirrored the pride in his heart. He smiled and placed his arm tenderly around her waist as he walked her into the room.

The room was so magnificent it took her breath away. "Wow!" she exclaimed. "This is, this is just, just amazing!" Her eyes raced disbelievingly across the room.

Pasted in ivory and gold the room swept on forever. An endless oak floor, polished to a glass like sheen, was comforted with huge ivory rugs that moulded effortlessly against dozens of ivory backed chairs and golden sofas. Numerous coffee tables with family memorabilia aboard also played host to golden coasters and newly- lit candles that flickered gently around the room. A medley of vast oil paintings and water colours graced the walls, but her eager eyes, sweeping so willingly from one facet of the room to the other, failed to take in their detail. Natural curiosity beckoned her to casually wander towards the family's more personal collections. She perused several years' worth of family portraits, all of them depicting a solid, loving family unity that silently reminded her of childhood yearnings; she examined trophies within an enormous glass cabinet that Luca had won over the years; scattered thoughtfully upon the coffee tables were bronze ornaments of thoroughbred racehorses with whip-cracking jockeys aboard, surging the horse across the winning line. At the far end of the room was an enormous ivory and marble fireplace. At either side of its mantel were fiery carvings of horses' heads that majestically sprung toward the room as if they, also, wanted to be a part of the cosy retreat that the now crackling log fire and the surrounding sofas offered. A gilt mirror above the fireplace filled the entire wall; its position was so high it would be impossible for a person to peruse their reflection, though on closer inspection its purpose became clear to Julia. Its purpose was to echo the grandeur of this time, three 'Giant Peach' chandeliers that hung in symmetry from the ceiling above, flooding Julia once again with special memories. With that thought Julia stared across at the enormous window that looked outside, although the black cast of the night inhibited any external view. She gave a private thank you to her mother, without whose spiritual intervention, the previous tide of apprehension that had swamped her could not have been transformed into such excitement. She turned to Luca and gave him a gentle peck on the cheek.

"It's wonderful to be here, thank you for including me," she told him.

Mrs DeMario looked across her and her husband's favourite room in quiet contemplation. With great comfort she watched her son and his new love. She had immediately warmed to Julia, yet, unlike some of the others within the room, it was not her beauty that had swayed her decision.

Beauty was like money to Mrs DeMario, easy come easy go, but she had sensed, Julia was a natural, genuine woman and she could understand exactly why her son had fallen in love with her. And fallen in love he certainly had. She had watched him looking at Julia, his eyes had shone as they followed her every move and she had noticed how their little touches, that neither of them could resist bestowing to the other, electrified each others' skin. She remembered that feeling of new love and was ecstatic for them both. To love and to be loved was the greatest gift of all.

Outside, a car had parked to the side of the mansions entrance. Two men got out and stood together and, as they did, even the cool night air received a chill. Like threatening jackdaws, their dark glossy hair submerged into the black of night. Their jet eyes, eerily distinct and mounted against muddy grey skin, pricked their surroundings. Slowly, enormous footsteps crunched menacingly against the gravel as they made their way towards the front entrance of the DeMario home.

Tonight there was definitely to be a surprise party only this one would surmount every other.

Chapter Fourty Two

MARIA'S EYES shone like warm polished conkers and the elaborate trails of sheer turquoise fabric that fell from her sleeves span, like celebratory Catherine wheels, as she waived her arms through the air.

"They're here, they're here!" she informed her guests with a squeal. "Everyone, try to be quiet." Then, with a bursting smile of pride she turned on her feet and hurriedly tip-tapped away.

In the drawing room the request for silence was sympathetically broken by the tickle of hurried whispers, tiptoeing feet that rushed across the floor in pursuit of a better position, the gentle clink of glasses being placed upon golden coasters and, for Julia, the thunderous vibration of re-emerging nerves that clamped her body.

She felt annoyed by their presence. Just as she was beginning to relax, yet another situation transpired to jolt her into inexplicable turmoil. Nervously, she took a sip of her champagne, feeling confident that everyone would be oblivious of the tight grip that encased the crystal champagne flute within her hand. She glanced toward Luca and tried to find comfort from his smile before the creak of the opening door anchored her attention.

Frankie DeMario, looking powerfully handsome, walked into the room, dressed in the smooth informality of a gold coloured suit. A broad grin covered his face as his guests and the surprise party registered in his mind. Whilst his guests greeted him with a rapturous applause followed by singing the Italian rendition of 'Happy Birthday', for the first time Julia saw the resemblance between Luca and his father as the genuine warmth of Frankie's smile thawed the dark moody face she had witnessed in the past.

His guests continued to enthusiastically sing, and his eyes, drowned by the recognition of friendships, danced cheerily across the room and gestured a grateful 'hello' as they fell on each familiar face. Maria handed him a glass of champagne and stood by his side, looking up at him, like a faithful puppy searching for her master's approval. In true Italian style, he threw his arms exuberantly in the air, then gratefully rested his arm around his wife's shoulder, the two of them, portraying a symbol of unity, swayed together to the room's song.

Frankie's eyes rested proudly upon his son standing at the back of the room and his head nodded with subconscious approval, then, suddenly, the face that had appeared to be melting, darkened with the unstoppable ferocity of a thunderous sky.

The change in his demure was apparent to all that stood before him. Only Maria, her hips still swaying by his side to the birthday rendition, failed to notice the nervous hush that had permeated the room. One by one the guests turned their heads to witness for themselves the source of Frankie's obvious alarm.

Julia felt his stare burn into the depths of her soul. Two hell bent rays of fire bolted from his eyes and bore into her, leaving the unmistakable scorch of public humiliation smouldering across her skin. Her eyes flickered with confusion across the grandeur of twinkling dresses and the sea of now blurred questioning faces. The silence boomed in her ears and for a second she heard the crashing thud of her solitary heartbeat clambering for life. Her eyes rested on Luca standing by her side. They pleaded with him to save her from the oblivion of her crime. He moved closer to her, his eyes also drowning in confusion, he reached for her arm then the drawing room door opened once again. It was as the next person walked into the room that Julia's torture exploded.

Her champagne flute that had only moments ago been held by her tightened grip smashed violently upon the wooden floor. Then she screamed.

It was a scream so terrifyingly piercing that it whirled hysterically around the room like an icy bitter wind. A petrified Julia felt her heavy shaking legs step backwards, fearful that at any moment he would approach her. She held up a trembling finger and pointed toward the face she had seen for an eternity in her nightmares.

"No! No! It's you." She pointed disbelievingly towards Luca's uncle. "You…you killed my mother!" She felt her heavy arm crash to her side, then let out another frenzied scream, she pulled at her hair, gasped for breaths and continued to inch backwards, "You are a murderer!" she shrieked.

It was the cold, hard wall that pressed insistently against her back that prevented her from moving further. Her instinct was to run, but she was trapped; trapped in a room that only moments ago had seemed enormous, but now had the claustrophobic confinements of a toilet cubicle.

Luca reached out to the woman he no longer recognised. "Julia, stop, talk to me."

With force Julia pulled her arm away from his touch.

"What the hell is going on?" Luca shouted.

Julia was oblivious as to who had asked the question, but she answered, as if trying to confirm for herself the sordid facts that now framed the bloody image in her mind.

"He," she trembled, "he shot my mother." She rubbed her forehead savagely, hoping that her vision was a sadistic hallucination. "Yes, he shot my mother," she confirmed. "I was with her, I saw his face, I could never forget it." Silent tears rolled down her cheeks as the intensity of her childhood pain was rekindled. "He did, he murdered my mother," she whimpered in terror. "He is a cold-blooded murderer." She fought for breath as her sobs burst form her throat.

"She is a maniac! Stop her, tell her to shut up!" Sofia screamed across the room at Luca.

The uncle's black brows angrily lowered creating a blanket of fearsome evil across searing black eyes. He had listened to enough. Julia heard the murderer's footsteps pound eerily towards her and saw his black wicked eyes fixed upon her. She screamed again and without hesitation Luca moved in front of Julia to protect her.

"What the fuck is going on?" Luca bellowed towards his uncle.

Frankie DeMario threw out his arm and flattened it forcefully against his brother's chest, preventing him from taking another step. "Stop!" he ordered his brother; Frankie's eyes swept the room with a torturous glare. "Everyone leave."

A sea of stunned faces stared back at him.

"Did you hear me? Everyone who is not my family get out of this room now." he scanned the room, looking for someone who had the guts to disobey. "In fact, get out of my house!" he shouted.

Like the bubbling inferno of champagne that had only an hour ago glugged happily out of luxurious bottles, the guests spilled from the room.

Chapter Fourty Three

FRANKIE DEMARIO stood in silence, only the thick haunt of the atmosphere held court. Five faces, his wife, his children and his brother stared back at him and he remembered, as if his life was now over, what each one had all meant. His thoughts, as rapid as wild fire, drove him through fields of memories. He recalled his words as he had proposed marriage to Maria; he relived the burst of pride as his first child, his only son, Luca was born; he felt the warmth of his baby daughters' skin against his arms as he had held them tightly, and he felt the bonding thud of his brother's hand against his back as they had celebrated previous victories. Now, he felt their stare upon him, stares that demanded explanation and reprieve from the torment that now agonised them.

Guilt gripped the innards of his stomach and wrenched searchingly for long- buried truths causing the greatest pain of all; after this evening he knew, he would never be able to look his beloved family in the eye ever again.

Anger fuelled his will for endurance as he glared at the sixth face in the room. Just looking at Julia made him feel physically ill and her presence, a torturous reminder of past indiscretions and sheer wrongdoing, permeated his body with pure boiling hatred.

He examined her face, it was an exact replica of the perfected mould he had once held in his hands and the mere thought of that exaggerated his every sense; he could smell the woman, he could hear her smoky voice, taste her sensuality and feel her warm lips against his own. He bit ferociously into his lip trying to dispel the lost comfort that had once rested upon them.

He clamped his eyes tightly shut, trying to scold her from his memory. Briefly he wondered, was it hatred or was it love that he had buried? Afraid of his emotions and the words he was about to speak, he felt his legs begin to buckle. Then, as if bone by bone, his body was surrendering, he slumped into a chair.

Luca became engulfed by terror. Although he could hear the soft pleading whimpers of his trembling fiancé beside him, the sight of his father distracted him from comforting her. Everything his father had stood for was crumbling before his eyes. His handsome swarthy face was now ashen, his black eyes, only minutes ago alive with zest for life, had now sunk into a grey hide of skin, and his powerful shoulders, dependable and always ready to protect, had now wilted into his chest. Luca's heart pleaded with banging beats to forbid the signs of fragility and weakness from being displayed upon his hero and he wished with all his heart he had taken heed of his father's words to "Get rid of her," spoken so long ago. He hated this apparition before him. His powerful father was sinking before his eyes and, if Julia had stayed away, it wouldn't be happening. Luca was filled with dread and panic as he recognised it was all too late. With the aid of the stony silence, his instincts were able to warn him that, whatever his father had to say now, he would never view him in the same light again. For that, momentarily, he would hate Julia too.

"Listen," Frankie's voice hissed through gritted teeth, chilling the air and transporting fear into the family members that remained. His eyes narrowed cruelly as he looked at Julia. "Since seeing you for the first time with my son I knew this night would come. Now the Lord has sent this situation because it is my penance to be paid, AND," his voice rose, "I WILL PAY IT!"

His brother stepped forward. "What are you talking about? Don't say anything you are going to regret." He grabbed Frankie's shoulder. "Frankie!" he pleaded, "Stop!"

"Be quiet!" his brother ordered. Frankie DeMario continued to glare hatefully into Julia's eyes. "Many years ago I had an affair with your mother. You are the image of her. Just like you, she was a beautiful woman." He shrugged dismissively, "Foolishly, I could not resist her."

Luca tried to walk from the room feeling that, if he didn't, his anger was so great he could kill his father.

"Stay here!" his father ordered with a fierce bark.

Sofia grabbed her brother's arm in search of reassurance and pulled him back and, as they stood dealing with the life changing shock, both of them looked across at their mother.

Maria was suffocated by his words but she had no wish to run from them. Her children were here, she would never leave them because, just like them, she too was a prisoner inside her once favourite room. She listened as her husband continued, aware that each word he spoke cracked her heart like a blow to a fine porcelain jug.

"Your mother may have been beautiful," he paused, "but she was stupid!" he spat venomously. "After a while she began to try and put pressure on me to leave my family, when I refused she tried blackmail tactics, telling me I was the father to her child." He turned to look at his wife and watched her head hang in shame. "She started to tell me that if I didn't tell my wonderful wife about us, then *she* would." His voice lowered and his eyes wandered. He stared at the wall as he recited his experience. "One evening," he continued, "around midnight, I let out the dogs, and I found her." His eyes were distorted with hatred. "There she was standing on *my family's* doorstep, thinking she had some kind of right to knock on *my family's* door. Oh, no." He shook his head with slow determined sweeps, "It was not going to happen, I had built up an enormous empire, I had worked day and night for what we had, for me and my family, they were dependant upon me and I loved them all very much." He pointed at Julia and yelled, "And your mother, your fucking bitch of a mother, thought that she had earned her slice of the cake simply by lying on her back and opening her legs!" He spat upon the floor. "No fucking way! I had to do something about her and fast." As his cold words menacingly rolled, each one sliced through Julia with the same ferocity as an executioner's axe. "I knew she was as determined as a child was to walk to get what she wanted." His voice began to waiver and his final words almost lodged repugnantly in his throat. "I decided the only way to sort the problem, was to get rid of her. For good. And yes," he thundered, "for the sakes of all of you." He pointed to his three children and his wife with determined stabs to the air. "I had her murdered!"

His final admission of guilt sapped his body of power and with a heave of his chest, he began to sob.

For the first time Maria DeMario's silence was broken. She stared at her husband and her words, stumbling with a hesitant uncertainty began to spill. "No, No?" Her voice was weak "You had her killed?"

She looked back at his brother, allowing Julia's accusations to ring loudly in her ears. Her brother-in-law did not look at her, nor anyone else within the room. He couldn't listen. He turned for the door.

"You stay here!" Frankie ordered.

Luca made a lurch toward him to grab his arm and force him to stay, but he swiped his nephew out of the way and turned to his brother.

"The admission is yours!" he roared with a heaving chest. He stamped from the room, slamming the doors behind him.

Frankie looked back at the remaining people in the room. "Yes," he said quietly, "this is my admission, and now I know I must pay."

Luca's rage flared. He picked up a glass and flung it toward his father, it splintered by his fathers' feet. "You fucking bastard, you talk of love, what do you know of love?" He bawled. "You cheated on my mother and on us. You have an affair and then, because it isn't working out the way YOU want, you take her life and leave a defenceless child without a mother?" Raw hatred was exposed in Luca's voice. He grabbed for Julia and took her into his arms. "I despise you, you gutless bastard."

"Daddy, no, no! Say it isn't true, please." Emma's voice held a vulnerable whisper; it was a sound that crucified her mother.

Maria DeMario stared up to the ceiling and ignored the breathtaking pain she felt, allowing her thoughts to transmit through her mind in consistent, logical steps. She was not naïve, affairs happened, it was the Italian way, this affair had not been mentioned for over ten years. When he had told her it was over she had trusted his word, the detail of the split she had not wanted to know, but this? *Murder?*

"Get out of this house, you monster!" Her voice was distant and emotionally barren. Unable to look at him she continued to stare up to the ceiling. She heard no movement and the only sound was the desolate weep of an innocent girl grieving for the loss of her mother. Slowly she lowered her head and turned to look at her husband still sitting in the chair.

"I SAID GET OUT!" she yelled.

In all the years the two of them had been married, this was the first order she had ever given to her husband.

Silently, he obeyed and left the house.

Julia watched him leave and felt paralysed by emotion as a cold sweat covered her forehead. She felt Luca hold her beneath her arms and edge her towards the door. "She needs air," she heard him say.

The fresh cold night air whipped against her face and alerted her to a second trauma.

"Luca, you know what this could mean, don't you?" she whispered almost too frightened to say the words.

She felt his shaking hands trying hard to give her comfort as he stroked the length of her hair.

"What?" he answered distantly.

"If your father was speaking the truth, about the child, I mean." She fell silent before forcing herself to speak again. "You know what that would mean for us, don't you?"

His soft caring strokes ceased and he pulled her around to look at him. "You mean…" his voice trailed off.

He looked deep into her brown eyes and noticed that just like his fathers, they too were almost black. For both of them their nightmare slowly began. The apparent, many coincidences and similarities that had initially amused them now paralysed them with sickness. The possibility of being half brother and sister slowly began to sink into their every being.

Four hours later at 3.30 a.m, Frankie DeMario was found hanging by his neck within the woodland of his hard-earned estate.

Chapter Fourty Four

An old weak hand, a haunting place
Can nobody see this pained hard face?
A broken heart, scorched with regret
To whom do I owe this incalculable debt?
My body is heavy, though my spirit light
Please let it guide me to the land of right
My time has come, I will soon be gone
Who will continue to sing my song?
The lyrics are here, embossed on my quilt
But I have failed to mention the tide of guilt
Goodbye my loves, please heed me well
I loved you whilst enduring, this burning hell.

The author looked back at the words only for the torture to worsen. The handwriting that for a lifetime had illustrated exemplary standards could now barely be deciphered. The pen was dropped, the author watched as it rolled to the floor.

Paris stood in front of the full-length mirror in her bedroom. She pulled up her top against her breasts to bare her midriff and slowly, with great tenderness, she slid her hand against the swollen bulge of her stomach. It felt hard, much harder than she had expected it to; she smiled as she felt an intrusive kick beneath her hand, the foetus, her baby, responding to her touch. She had grown a new life within her, a life that now, her midwife had informed her, had almost one hundred percent chance of survival. There were only two weeks to go before the due date and Paris couldn't wait to meet the new arrival.

Her thoughts turned to all the women out there in the world that felt desolate at being unable to conceive a child, prohibited from motherhood by the ultimate hand of nature, a decision that to those desperate women would be impossible to understand. It was to Paris, life was so cruel. *Why have I been given this chance when I didn't have that yearning?* She asked herself for the thousandth time. Her mind fired the answer. *You have to go through this to find true love, and what better way for sufferance than to help someone that is less fortunate?* Poor Rebecca she concluded, she must have gone through hell.

She cast her mind back to the day before, when Rebecca, out of sheer thoughtfulness, had invited her to see the nursery. It was beautiful. A hand-crafted oak crib had stood majestically in the centre of the room. Paris had walked to it, tenderly stroking her fingers across the smooth wood, and rocked it gently with her hand, imagining how her baby would respond whilst she did so. Rebecca had proudly opened the matching wardrobe to show piles of neatly folded clothes, nappies and muslins all in colour co-ordinated sections. Paris took some comfort from knowing that her baby would be loved and well cared for with Rebecca. She was all too aware that this kind of organisation would never be part of the baby's life should she be in charge.

Today she stared at the floor of her bedroom, at the hoards of clothes that now carpeted the floor and consoled herself with some home truths. She wasn't fit to be a mother, and there were many people worse off than her, some girls had to give up their babies for adoption and never know who had them. Every night must be a constant struggle to those mothers, the torturous wonderings through ailing sleep of who they were with and what they were doing; it must be nothing but a living hell. Thanks to Rebecca she would never have to endure that suffering.

The sound of the front door slamming closed made Paris jump. Quickly, she pulled down her jumper and promptly fell onto her bed.

Breathless from the brief exertion, she pretended to casually flick through some magazines. She had been back just one day from Wickruns Bay since the fall out with her father – still not enough time to allow the dust to settle between them. She felt her apprehension rise as she heard his footsteps nearing her room. He knocked timidly.

"Come in," Paris answered. Her father looked drawn and fragile. "What's the matter?" she asked.

Bill walked over to her bed and just like the old days perched on its edge.

He bowed his head. "It's Frankie DeMario. I just can't believe it." His voice wavered. "He's dead."

The news had not yet filtered its way to Cedars Hall. Charles was seated at the dining table beginning his breakfast and was taking his time to stir his cup of tea. Unusually, Kitty had reneged on her duty of dressing for breakfast, so wearing her dressing gown she sat in her usual chair opposite to Charles. She watched the thoughtful glower upon his face as he blankly stared out of the window.

"A penny for them," she snapped, irritated that her entrance had gone unnoticed.

"Mmm?" Charles blinked his way from his trance. "Sorry mother, good morning. I didn't see you come in." He passed the toast rack along the table. "Would you like toast?"

"No. No thank you." she grimaced. She managed a weak smile as Mary walked into the room.

"Oh, Mrs LB, you are not dressed, your dressing gown won't keep you warm. Shall I bring you a blanket for your knees?"

Kitty shook her head with brisk indignation.

"What would you like for breakfast?" Mary continued timidly.

"Nothing, thank you, just a pot of tea." Habitually she placed her linen serviette on her knee and awaited Mary's return.

"Why are you not eating, Mother?" Charles asked.

"Quite simply because I am not hungry," Kitty snapped again.

Charles had spoken to Mary yesterday; she had told him that his mother had barely eaten enough to keep a bird alive in the last week. Her weight loss was dramatically evident, when would she allow him in?

Mary walked back in with the pot of tea. "Shall I pour it for you, Mrs LB?"

Kitty nodded and looked back at Charles. "Mary drove me into Chelmsley yesterday," she said casually. "I was very surprised to see the Montford girl, is it Paris, so heavily pregnant. Victoria told me of the news some months ago; I naturally assumed with the events of Gerard's death she must have done something about it."

Charles shrugged.

Kitty persisted. "What is she doing? With the baby, I mean?"

Again, Charles shrugged. "I don't know. I barely know the girl."

Kitty felt her hackles rise, but his mobile rang, deterring her from prying further.

Charles listened to Paris. "Have you heard?" she asked solemnly, "Frankie DeMario has committed suicide. Dad is devastated."

Moments later Charles cut off the call and was pleased to have a fresh topic to discuss with his mother.

"Frankie DeMario has died. He killed himself last night, apparently," he informed her in a matter of fact way.

Kitty drew her hands to her face. "Oh God, that is dreadful. I didn't particularly warm to the man, but nobody deserves to feel that kind of misery."

"Huh!" Charles puffed without thought. "Well I'm glad he's dead, it may well bring that family down a peg or two."

Kitty screwed up her face in disgust and struggled with discomfort to free herself from the carver chair.

"How could you say such a thing?" she said, pushing herself from the table. "How low have you sunk to be wishing someone dead?"

She had no wish to await her son's response. With purposeful though timid strides she left the dining room.

She had barely left the room before Charles' phone rang again. Paris' name flashed up for the second time. "What is it this time?" he snapped at her.

"Charles, I'm sorry," he heard her whimper, "I need to be taken to the hospital, my waters have just broken."

"Shit!" With irritation he ran his fingers through his hair. "You will have to get your father to take you there. I will arrive as soon as I can."

"Why?" Paris shrieked. "You promised you would be with me."

"And I will be, Paris," he quickly soothed, sensing her panic. "I will only be minutes behind you."

He snapped his phone shut and cursed his disorganisation. He still hadn't sorted out the paperwork for the adoption. He had to make his way over to the Santé's for their signatures before Paris had the chance to change her mind.

Chapter Fourty Five

"I CAN'T BELIEVE that the time is here already," Rebecca gasped, putting the lid back on her Cartier pen. "The time has really flown hasn't it, Charles?"

"Mmmm," Charles nodded, secretly wondering why this year did not depict a century on the calendar of time.

"When do you think we can collect the baby?" Victoria asked, following her daughters enthusiasm. "Gosh!" she said covering her mouth with her hand. "That sounded terribly cold, didn't it?" She let out a demure cough. "Has Paris discussed anything with you about when she will feel ready to hand the baby over?"

"Tomorrow morning, assuming all goes well tonight, that is. Her feeling was that the sooner the baby got acquainted with its new home and routine the better for everyone," he lied

"You had better get to the hospital, Charles," Rebecca encouraged. "Let us know, won't you? And do give Paris our love, if there is anything we can do don't hesitate to let us know."

"I will. I will call you as soon as there is any news," he promised.

"Oh goodness!" Rebecca shrieked excitedly, "The thirtieth of November, I will never forget this date."

"Hang on a minute, Rebecca," her father interjected. "It may not be born today."

"Well, it's only ten o clock in the morning," Victoria said. "I hope for her sake it is, let me assure you!"

Charles smiled and turned for the door. Rebecca rushed over to him.

"Charles," she beckoned. He turned to her. "Thank you. Thank you so much for everything you have done for me." The look in her eye and the unusual sound of love in her voice made him realise that the reasons for his plans were worthwhile. There was a flicker from her, in fact, more than a flicker. Just as he had suspected, her days for needing him were inching ever closer.

"No problem," he answered with a smile. "You are special; you deserve to be a mother." He kissed her on the cheek. "I'll call you," he whispered tenderly.

He closed the door behind him and heard James Santé's words praise him to his daughter.

"That man is a true gentleman," he assured Rebecca.

"Yes, I know," he heard her reply. Charles smiled, then got into his car.

Seven hours later, to the relief of Paris and Charles, the midwife greeted them with liberating words.

"Congratulations, Paris, you have a beautiful baby boy!" A gurgled wail ensued. "Do you want to hold him now?" she asked, holding up a, to Charles, shockingly ugly blue and grey alien.

"No," Charles answered quickly, not wanting the baby to gain even an inch closer. "She would prefer him to be gift wrapped, wouldn't you Paris?" he asked, stroking her forehead.

Paris nodded reluctantly. A brief silence followed whilst the sound of scissors cutting through the gristly umbilical cord punished Charles' decision before the baby began to scream deafeningly again.

"Steady, little man, I just want to weigh you."

As if oblivious to his screaming, the midwife wiped the baby's face and body and looked over at Paris.

"You've done well my love to say he is two weeks early, he's seven pounds ten," she told her.

"Is he alright then?" Paris asked the midwife. "Truly, is he alright?"

"He's absolutely fine, a fighting weight with a fighting personality," the midwife assured.

As if on cue, the positive confirmation allowed Paris to relax causing her teeth to clatter against each other and her body began to violently shake.

"I think I am going to be sick," she shouted, trying to shove herself up the bed.

"Oh shit!" Charles choked as he watched her wretch. "Do something, quick!" he shouted at the midwife.

"It's okay," she said gently, "Quite normal. You be sick in there, Paris," she said, handing her a cardboard bowl.

Charles, with a contorted face, stroked her head whilst Paris excreted spasms of bile from her mouth. "You poor thing," he soothed, "you poor, poor thing, it's okay, Paris, it's all going to be okay, I promise," he assured her.

"Now, are you ready to hold him?" She asked, clutching the baby that had now turned a healthy pink and was wrapped in a blue blanket.

"Hold it?" Charles exclaimed. "How can she do that? She's half dead," he said looking back at Paris, deathly pale with chattering teeth.

"Nature has a funny way of bringing the dead back to life," she laughed, passing the baby to Paris.

"Are you sure I won't drop him?" Paris asked, looking at the bundle of joy before her.

"You'll be fine, trust me," the midwife answered.

Moments later, the moan of Paris' chattering teeth had been replaced with intermittent giggles as she stared down, disbelieving that she had produced such a beautiful being. She stared at the miracle of his finger nails, examined the creases of his waxen fingers, gently touched his button nose and tried to count every one of the delicate sweeping eyelashes that graced his sleeping eyes.

"I told you you would be fine, didn't I?" the midwife stated. "I need to go and fill out some forms; I will be back in a minute." The door swung shut leaving the three of them in the room alone.

"He's a miracle," Paris whispered, looking down at her baby.

Charles witnessed the purity of her love as she stared at her son and for a second was almost washed away by the sight. He reached out and touched the boy's face and marvelled at the size of his fingers against his small innocent features.

"Yes, he is," he answered, "and so are you."

Paris' flushed face, glowing with the perspiration of labour and pride, looked back at him and smiled hopefully.

"That is why I want to be with you forever," Charles continued, "and one day, I promise we will have a baby of our very own," he told her tenderly.

He saw her face plunge and additional words failed him. "I need to make a call," he told her. "Have some time, to...to....." he shrugged, "Well, you know."

"Are you calling Rebecca?" Her voice was weak. Charles nodded. Paris looked away.

After Charles had left the room it wasn't long before the midwife returned. She peered across the bed at Paris' baby with a broad smile.

"He's absolutely beautiful," she cooed. "What are you going to call him?" she asked.

The question stabbed Paris. She didn't answer; instead she closed her eyes and concentrated on the comfort of her son's bodily warmth against her chest.

"Your mother and father are outside, they would love to come in and see you," the midwife told her.

Paris shook her head, her eyes remained closed. "Not yet," she answered. The baby began to let out small yelping cries.

"He'll want to be fed," the midwife said. "Will you be breast feeding Paris, or shall we give him a feed from the bottle?" she asked cheerfully.

"The bottle option will be better," Paris answered miserably.

"Do you not want to try breastfeeding? You know it is better to just try, it is better for the baby, he will get the best nutrients from you."

Again, Paris didn't answer. Sensing Paris' sudden dip in spirits the midwife sat down on the edge of the bed.

"Are you okay, Pet?" she asked, rubbing Paris' hand.

Paris immediately felt the flood gates open. "I want to breastfeed, but you see..." she stopped talking and buried her face into her baby's blanket. "It hurts so much to say it, but, my baby is getting adopted." She looked down at his fidgeting chubby arms. "So I will have to bottle feed him."

"Oh. I see," the midwife answered quietly. She squeezed Paris' hand. "You know, Paris, I have been doing this job for many years and you wouldn't believe the amount of mothers who have planned to give their baby up for adoption. Only, when it is born, they feel differently, Mother Nature kicks in and they feel they just can't go ahead with it. You must not feel pressured and go ahead with this if you don't want to. It's a massive decision that will affect the rest of your life."

"Please don't think I am a horrible person," cried Paris. "I will be a good mother one day; I know I will, it's just that I have to do this now, it's my only option," she sobbed.

"Hey, it doesn't matter what I think, my darling," the nurse reassured.

Paris hoisted herself further up the bed. "Oh, but you see, it does. It does matter. The thought of anyone thinking I don't love my baby would kill me. Especially if, especially if it was him." Paris looked down at her baby and began to sob.

The midwife remained silent; it wasn't her job to influence life-changing decisions like this one. Only when the baby began to scream with hunger did she get off the bed to bring a bottle of formula milk.

Paris touched his tiny hand and felt his instinctive grip against her finger. "I can't do it," Paris whimpered. "He needs me."

She stared at the small upturned nose that was so definitely a trait passed on from Gerard, instantly recalling a loving memory that was almost lost. Tears rolled down her face as she repeated again.

"I just can't give my baby away."

Chapter Fourty Six

THE FOLLOWING MORNING, Paris heard the door of her room swing open and looked up to see Charles peer around the door. Paris closed her eyes again; she didn't want to talk to him or anyone else for that matter.

Slowly he walked into the room; a loud rustling noise made her curious enough to open her eyes. From behind his back he produced an enormous bouquet of flowers.

"How are you?" he asked softly.

She shrugged in response.

"These are for you," he added passing her the bouquet.

"Thanks, they're beautiful," she said flatly.

"So, how are you?" he asked again, sitting on the edge of her bed.

Paris moved her legs to allow him more room and looked at her baby sleeping soundly in the glass cot beside her. "I might have been better if it weren't for the fact that this little chap kept me awake all night wanting to be fed every hour." She began to smile "In between that, he just wanted to be cuddled." She couldn't disguise the happiness that welled in her voice.

Charles sat very quiet and still; he couldn't bear to even glance in the cot's direction.

Paris immediately drew on his solitude and examined his face. His eyes looked tired and swollen, as if he had been crying, and their dark cloudy circles against his unusually pale complexion indicated that he too had suffered from lack of sleep.

"What's the matter, Charles?" she asked reaching for his hand.

In that moment he felt intense emotion gush through his body, and, for the first time, he felt a burning desire to tell her everything. He was tired of the lies and deceit that surrounded his life, he needed to feel warmth and security, and her hand, reaching out to hold him, signified she was the only person that could give it.

As he stared into her face she witnessed the fear and terror that lay beneath his eyes. She inched her legs out of bed and grabbed his shoulders.

"Charles, tell me, what is the matter?" she pleaded, gently shaking him.

He pulled her arms towards him. "Paris." She could barely hear his faint words. "You know, I need to tell you the truth about something."

"Go on," Paris urged. "You can tell me, whatever it is."

Charles began "You see…"

The door was bulldozed open.

"Good morning!" The midwife sang, pounding over to the curtains, allowing the morning light to engulf the room. "What beautiful flowers!" she gushed. "Shall I put them in a vase for you?"

"Yes, yes," said Paris, she looked back at Charles. "Could you leave us for a moment please? she asked.

The midwife took the flowers and left the room.

Paris turned back to Charles. "Go on Charles. Tell me." Paris clasped his hand within hers.

For Charles, the moment of confession had disintegrated. "Paris," he said, "I can hear in your voice the love you have for your baby." He sighed. "It hurts me to think of you in pain." He squeezed her hand and looked deep into her eyes. "I love you."

Paris looked back at him, "really, do you really love me, Charles?" she asked with appealing hope.

His eyes flickered in response to her blunt question. "Yes." Momentarily he looked away then returned his powerful, persuasive stare. "That is why I want to spend the rest of my life with you. When we get married, Paris, we will have many children, an enormous family that fills our home. You will be a fantastic mother to each and every one of them, I know you will. But those children, they will be *our* children, Paris. Not anyone else's. Remember, we are lucky, we have each other, what about Rebecca? She has nobody." He stood and walked towards the cot and looked inside at the sleeping baby. "There is no question about it, Paris, he is perfect, I can understand your reluctance at handing him to Rebecca." He walked back over to the bed and gently held her face within his hands. "But, our time will come, my darling, our time will come. I promise you it will."

The tears burnt her eyes as she fought not to let them fall. She had to be strong. She had never seen him so upset; she had been foolishly oblivious of the emotion he had been harbouring for her. It was true, he really did love her.

"Look," he said, delving his hand into a pocket on the inside of his jacket. "I have the papers, they have all been legally drawn up." He passed them to her and handed her a pen. "Sign them now," he said sympathetically, "then you know you have got that part over with."

Apprehensively she took the papers and looked back into the cot.

"Paris," he said gently, "within this agreement you have access twenty-four seven to see this little baby, Rebecca insisted on it. He will be well looked after and loved."

Her body felt rigid, her mouth felt dry and as she lifted the pen her hand shook. She felt Charles staring at the papers over her shoulder; she loved him and the promise of a happy family that he offered. Edgily, she forced her hand to sign on the page and then handed them back to him.

He smiled delicately. "Well done."

"When are they coming for him, Charles?" she asked weakly.

"A little later, when you are ready to leave the hospital."

She nodded, not daring to talk.

Charles began to put the papers back inside his pocket as the door opened again, this time it was her father.

"Oh, Dad!" She was pleased to see his kind face. "I'm so pleased to see you!"

Ignoring Charles' presence he walked swiftly to his daughter's bedside and kissed her.

"We left you to rest, the midwife told us you needed it. Your mother will be here in a minute. She's gone to buy some clothes for the baby."

He walked over to the cot and stared lovingly, proud to be seeing his grandson for the first time.

"Dad," Paris said gravely, "please go and get Mother from the shop. There is no need for her to buy clothes. Where he is going he will have plenty."

"What do you mean?" Bill asked darkly.

"Rebecca Santé is adopting him. Charles and I are to be married," she added quickly trying desperately to appease her own words.

"What are you talking about? What about my grandson?" Bill demanded.

Paris took a deep breath. "Like I said, I am having him adopted, Rebecca Santé is adopting him. Charles and I are getting married, it is the best thing to do," she said shakily. "We want to start our married life with a clean sheet."

Bill exploded. "Having him adopted? Are you insane? You haven't let him convince you that getting rid of this baby is the best option, surely? You are no more getting married to him than I am, you stupid, stupid girl." He thundered over to her bed. "Don't you see? He doesn't love you, that man is a bastard!" he yelled.

"What the hell do you know about anything?" Charles retaliated, desperately trying to claw back Paris' thoughts. "I love Paris and we will be married." He was then faced with a silence to the room as two pairs of eyes, father and daughters', stared back at him. For a second time, his eyes flickered.

Bill shook his head, utter revulsion covered his face. "You are beyond words," he said angrily.

The commotion alerted a passing midwife who quickly rushed into the room. "Stop this shouting immediately," she ordered.

Bill swung round to face her. "Are you lot in here going to allow this to happen?" he shouted. "Do you advocate babies being given away freely in here?"

"Stop it!" Paris shrieked, glaring at her father. "Get out!" she ordered frostily, "Just get out!"

The midwife stared at him. "You heard the lady," she said clinically, "if you don't leave I will have to call security."

Without another word Bill followed his orders and stamped out of the door.

Tears rolled down Paris' face and sobs escaped freely from her mouth. Charles watched as she tenderly picked her baby son from the cot and cradled him lovingly in her arms.

Paris was oblivious to anything or anyone; she knew that every remaining second with her baby son was truly sacred.

Chapter Fourty Seven

LUCA'S FACE was stained by the shadow of stubble; his hair was unkempt with a fringe that flopped sloppily against his forehead. His blue denim shirt, one of the few items of clothing that he felt had no association with his father, had only three studs fastened, leaving the rest of the shirt to hang like a loose napkin against mud splattered jeans.

For an hour that morning he had trawled through the wet muddy grounds of the estate, he didn't know why; it had been years since he had walked upon the land his father had treasured. Whilst he had walked he had recalled seeing his father's proud purposeful strides, as he had watched from the house, and had witnessed his father's superior satisfaction in his walk alone, almost tasting the sweet pleasurable breaths of country air he had inhaled, and at the time, Luca had smiled. This morning, as he had followed his father's conceited footsteps with delirious stamps, he was angry – so very, very angry. For all these years he had lived, he had loved a fraudster. Everything that man had achieved had not been from his own merit, but from the dark, cruel world of deceit.

Now, he sat at the kitchen table. The stale smell of whisky lay heavy on his breath, but as he had he poured himself another, he was adamant those whisky fumes were about to be refreshed. He swirled the glass in never ending circles against the marble table top and, like a zombie, watched the dark golden liquor spin wildly around the tumbler. Initially he had tried to take control of the situation, just as a 'true Italian son' should, making calls, standing strong and giving comfort, but as the time had ticked away and the proud memories of his respected father died, his spirit for tradition and responsibility died with him.

Even though a thick duvet of grief and depression hung heavily within the house, he was able to switch himself off. He could hear the hysteria of the DeMario women, his mother and his sisters, and he could decipher their repetitive conversations that sourly raked up the story over and over again. He could see their tears, he had felt them yesterday drip onto his shirt as his sisters had clung on to his body for comfort, and still he felt able to coldly keep his distance.

Even his mother, currently preparing to go to Italy to seek comfort from her sisters and organise the finer details of the funeral, had also been defeated by emotion. For once, she too, had broken her tradition of protecting her children from her personal pain. Last night she had sat and sobbed before them at this very table, unafraid to show them that her own heartbreak was just as real and as painful as theirs.

As he recalled the painful image, Luca drained the whisky, slamming the glass back down against the table. The aggressive burn that roasted the back of his throat bore him mild satisfaction, *what a mess!* he thundered internally. His world had crashed and he had no idea how to deal with it. Unknown forces were telling him that his once treasured idol was not only dead, but in fact, had never even existed. That man, that stranger, had suddenly plummeted into being the archetypal enemy, an enemy that had scarred him for life and, worst of all, driven away his only true love. Since the deathly realisation of the possibility they could be related and the fact that she had come face to face with her mother's murderer, Julia, overcome by nausea, had fled. He needed her, he wanted her here. He reached again for his phone.

"When will you be coming back, Julia?" he asked quietly into her voicemail. "I need you, regardless of anything, I need you here."

He placed the phone upon the table and watched it respond with another blank stare. His anger raised another dangerous notch upon the Richter scale; forcefully he snatched the fast diminishing whisky bottle and refilled his glass. His mother walked into the kitchen, their eyes met.

"I'm sorry, Mama," he said staring back into his glass.

"For what?" she asked weakly standing by the table.

"For your life's commitment proving to be in vain."

"My son," she said, stroking his arm, "if there is one thing that my life is not, it is in vain. I have you three to show off for my success."

"How did you do it?" He looked up at her, "How could you stay with him knowing what he had done?"

She turned her back and began to reorganise the crockery in the dishwasher. "I didn't know what he had a done, well not all of it anyway. And Luca, there is not a man in the world that does not have a problem with the obsession of lust. That would never have stopped me from staying and loving you all."

"Did you never feel hurt and betrayed?" His voice displayed hesitant anger. She turned and looked at him, her waterlogged eyes illustrating the answer. "That, my boy, is a conversation never to be undertaken between a mother and her child."

"But I am not a child," he shouted suddenly. "Because of you I have been forced to believe that bastard was a good man."

"He was your father," she responded hotly.

"He was a bastard!" he shouted, and you have deceived us also." He stared at her menacingly and saw the pain of his words cruelly agonise her. He stood from his chair and grabbed her arm.

"Mamma, I am sorry, I am sorry!" he begged, "Forgive me."

Slowly she nodded her head and stroked his hair. Her touch tormented him, making him want to shun the comfort. He sat back at the table and grabbed his glass.

Maria looked out of the window. "My taxi is here," she informed him, guiltily relieved by the promise of escape.

He looked up and nodded. "When will you return?"

"Tomorrow evening. Your Aunts will be returning with me. " She hesitated. "They will be attending the funeral."

"What about Uncle?" he spat. "Will a murderer be attending too?"

She grabbed her handbag from the side, "Your uncle will never be welcome in my life again, and anyway, like most criminals," her voice wavered with emotion, "since his exposure, nobody has seen him."

She held up her hand in farewell, the knot in her throat inhibiting her from speaking.

Luca remained brave, especially as he heard Piers approaching.

"Goodbye, Maria," Piers said lightly, "have a safe trip."

"Goodbye, Piers," Maria answered solemnly.

Luca heard the front door close and grabbed the bottle to refill his glass.

"Believe me, Luca, that won't help," Piers advised, walking past him and placing the two mugs he had brought down from Sofia's room onto the side.

Luca allowed a hateful slice of anger to escape. "And what the fuck do you know?" Luca replied. "You're as bad as the dead stranger."

Piers had never left Sofia's side throughout this whole disaster and he, too, felt tired and physically drained. "What do you mean by that?" he asked aggressively.

Luca turned round in his chair to face him. "I mean, you are also a two- timing bastard just like he was. If it wasn't for the fact that you are also a liar and a cheat you wouldn't even be here, you would be with Rebecca. What *are you* doing here anyway?"

Hostility between the pair baked in the air before Piers backed down.

"Look, we don't want anymore problems than we already have," Piers insisted, making his way out of the kitchen. "I was only trying to help you. But," he couldn't resist, "just for the record, I have Charles Lancaster-Baron to thank for my being here with your sister."

"What has that bastard got to do with anything?" Just the mere mention of his name had caused Luca's hackles to rise.

"Oh, it's a long story, another time perhaps."

Arrogantly, Luca sat back on his chair. "I've got all day, I'm not going anywhere, tell me, a change of subject matter will do me the world of good, what has that piece of shit Lancaster-Baron got to do with *you being here*?"

Piers walked slowly back into the kitchen. "Well, if you must know, the first night Sofia and I spent together was a set up, a trap to get me away from Rebecca. He blackmailed your sister."

"Blackmailed her?" Luca began to sober. "You'd better sit down and tell me everything."

Piers sat down at the table, *I may as well tell him* he thought, *after all, nothing could be as bad as the events that had recently transpired round here.*

Rebecca and Victoria Santé made their last checks from the list before they left the house; Victoria scurried upstairs to the Nursery.

"I've forgotten the Cashmere blanket," she shouted behind her.

Charles noticed that excitement had caused Rebecca's face to look flushed against her brown rabbit fur hat. She spun round to face him as he stood in the hallway.

"Oh, Charles, are you sure you won't come with us to pick up the baby?"

"No, no," he answered quickly, "I will wait here with James, you know, he will need company whilst he drinks his celebratory port and waits for his grandson to arrive." He tensed his arm muscles in jest. "It's man thing!"

Unexpectedly she flung her arms around his shoulders. "Oh, thank you, thank you so much for everything," she squealed. She stood back and kissed him hard on the lips. "How can I ever repay you for what you have done for me?"

The unusual spill of her emotion made him smile, he shrugged, "I dunno, possibly marry me?" The words rolled effortlessly off his tongue and as they hung in the air, even Charles felt a sudden surprise by their arrival.

Rebecca fell silent and her smile began to dampen. "Are you serious?" she asked.

Charles grew certain. "Yes, why wouldn't I be?"

"But, we're such good friends," she answered hesitantly.

"This is a good sign, you haven't said no yet."

Rebecca smiled, "No, you're right." She paused. "I haven't."

Charles waited for further comment whilst Rebecca continued to stare at him; her eyes searched his face, eagerly trying to uncover the hoax.

His heart galloped in anticipation, her answer determined his future and could potentially change his life.

Suddenly her smile vanished. "Charles, how can I say yes?" she said soothingly. "We have only just rekindled our friendship. What we have now is more than I could ever have hoped for, you are like a brother to me, and I don't want to lose another one."

For a moment he had thought she was going to accept, how foolish of him. *Why the fuck would she want to marry you?* he asked himself. If she was aware of his reality, he doubted they would invite him in the house. The voices returned, bolting him into a rigid stance. Victoria rushed back down the stairs.

"I've got it," she announced cheerily.

"Go on. Go now," Charles told Rebecca.

Paris sat with her baby for what only felt like minutes before she heard the sickening creak of the door opening again. Rebecca and her mother nervously walked inside, then stood, rooted to the spot as their hands fidgeted uncomfortably with their sophisticated designer handbags.

Paris looked down at her son, and wondered how desperate a person would have to be to take a baby from its mother's arms. The baby murmured, and Rebecca inched her way closer toward him with a maternal grin on her face.

"Oh he's so beautiful," Rebecca cooed as she peered closer.

Instinctively Paris felt her arms tighten around his body.

"Oh, he looks just like Gerard did when he was a baby. It brings back so many memories." Mrs Santé's face began to crumble as she recalled her happy days.

"Are you coming out with us, Paris?" Rebecca asked.

"Erm, no. You go first, then I will be leaving." Paris couldn't bear to part with her baby in a car park. "I can't get home, I'm waiting for a lift," she added.

Neither of them gave a response, Paris didn't even know if they had heard. The pair just continued to coo and babble at her baby, pulling at the white blanket to get a clearer look at his face.

Rebecca held out her arms. "Can I hold him?" she asked.

Paris felt her heart begin to thump; a knot had anchored and was growing like a rock in her stomach and throat. She wanted to scream at them to get out, *what am I doing?* She asked herself. *Where are you, Charles? You promised you would be here,* she hollered internally.

Sensing her hesitation, Mrs Santé opened her Mullberry handbag and handed her a crisp clean envelope.

"There you are, my dear, there's a cheque inside," she smiled tentatively.

"No thank you, Mrs Santé, I don't want the money, I just want my baby to be looked after and loved. There are some things that money just cannot buy." She glared at the purchaser. "Please, keep your money. Just promise me and him you will love him with all your heart."

Paris looked down at the most precious commodity she had ever held in her life and rested her soft lips against his forehead. She closed her eyes and cherished the feeling of his skin against her lips.

"I will never forget you," she whispered. "Our time has come to say goodbye." She kissed him again and slowly handed the baby over.

Rebecca reached out for him.

Paris began to sob uncontrollably. "Now, please, just take him."

"Paris? Please don't cry" Rebecca handed the baby to her mother and moved towards her.

"Just go, please go!" she shouted.

They left the room, taking her treasured baby son with them.

Paris was alone; she fell upon the bed and screamed into one of the pillows. Reaching out a clenched fist, she beat the iron bed head. Its only response was to rattle coldly against the bare wall.

Bill Montford had been waiting outside and watched in disgust as the Santé's left the hospital with the grandson he had never held. He quietly walked into the room and placed his dependable arm on his daughter's shoulder. All he could do was listen to her heart rending sobs.

"Charles will be here soon," she cried. "He's going to take me away, I need to run!" she screamed.

Her father did not utter a sound, though he felt sure, Charles Lancaster-Baron would never be returning to his daughter's side.

Chapter Fourty Eight

BILL watched his daughter sleep, cocooned in her duvet, safe at last from the misery she had to endure. It had been twenty-four hours since he had walked a trembling Paris through the front door. Once inside, he had sat with her for eighteen hours, hardly daring to leave her for a minute whilst he witnessed her shrieks, her whimpers and her pain. His daughter was heartbroken, and as a result, so was he. He stood at her bedroom door, his eyes red and swollen from exhaustion, but felt temporarily appeased by her body's decision to shut down into the welcome land of sleep.

Francesca walked past the doorway into her bedroom awakening Bill from his paternal concerns. Disdain seeped from his sideways glance as he chose to disregard her presence. He glanced through Paris ' bedroom window and saw that today, the first of December, was being greeted by falling flakes of snow. He crept back into his daughter's room and slowly drew the curtains with a silent wish that he would protect her from further cold. *But how can I?* He mused. *Internally, even I feel colder than the snow that is falling.*

He walked into the bedroom, to find Francesca sitting at her dressing table. He sat on the edge of the bed and reached for his socks and began to wrestle them on to his feet whilst he contemplated the role Paris ' *supposed* mother had undertaken in this eighteen-hour plight. He didn't have to think long; she had made one solitary cup of tea; that was all she had managed to do, boil the bloody kettle. He reached for his shoes from the wardrobe and shoved his feet inside.

"What are you doing? I would like you to take me into Chelmsley today, are you going out?" Francesca challenged with a frown.

"Indeed I am," Bill answered without looking up. "I'm going to the DeMario's house. I am going to pass on my condolences and see if there is anything I can do for any of them while *my daughter* sleeps." He stood up from the bed. "After what Frankie has done for me, that is the least I can do."

"Why. What has he done for you?" she snapped

"A damned sight more than you have," he retorted. "He has been my friend." He stormed from the room and down the stairs.

Francesca caught her breath and pursed her lips whilst she thought of a suitable reply. "Bill!" she shouted after him.

His idle response floated back up the stairs. "You will have to make your own way to Chelmsley today, my dear; for once some people have needs much greater than yours." She heard the front door close behind him.

"Of all the bloody rotten tricks!" Francesca fumed throwing her hairbrush to the floor. "Just wait until he gets home."

Luca heard the tyres of a car crunch against the gravel outside, he ran over to the kitchen window to investigate and was so relieved to see Julia sitting in the back of the limousine. She had called him back an hour ago and had promised to come to see him. As he rushed to open the front door, he was eternally grateful she had arrived.

She stepped from the car, wearing a long black leather coat, black jeans and black leather boots, Luca wondered if her sombre attire was indicative of her mood. He searched her face as she walked tentatively toward the house and noticed her usual dark complexion looked as pale as the feathery snow falling around her.

"Are you alright?" he asked softly as she walked up the steps.

"No, not really," she answered truthfully. "I feel very ill. I have not stopped being sick since I left this place." She looked up at the vast residence and felt ashamed she had allowed it to impress her only days ago.

"You don't look very well," Luca said holding out his hand in concern. Julia ignored his hand and walked through the door.

"I'll be okay," she responded frostily.

"Julia," Luca hesitated, she turned. "Thank you for coming; I appreciate how hard this must be."

"You said you needed me, Luca." She couldn't look in his eyes. "So I am here."

She followed Luca toward the kitchen, all the while reviling every step she trod within the 'murderous mansion.'

"How is your mother?" she asked Luca whilst unbuttoning her coat and shaking off the snow.

Luca watched the snow melt against her hair; its damp forced her hair to look so dark that it bullied her pale, tired face into the largest snowflake of all. Luca thought she looked so fragile, almost as if she could faint; he pulled out a chair for her to sit down at the table.

"As well as can be expected." Luca shrugged and sat opposite her at the table. "She's gone to Italy to sort out the funeral details."

Julia observed his hurt and embarrassment as he hung his head. She knew all too well how it felt to lose a parent; she couldn't imagine how Luca would deal with that pain *and* have the revelation that his father was a murderer cemented with it.

"And, more importantly, how are you?" she asked tenderly.

His voice was quiet. "I feel as if I am in another world, if I'm honest." He reached for his empty glass of whisky and encased it in his hand. "One minute I was the happiest man alive, engaged to the woman I know I will love for eternity, surrounded by a family I adored and doing a job I love." His eyes scorned his words. "Now, that family I no longer recognise, I feel I will never be able to summon the drive to work again and ….." his voice trailed, he looked up at her, "and now, worst of all, I don't know if my fiancé is also my half sist…" He couldn't finish and Julia didn't want him to.

She scraped the chair from behind her and raced to the kitchen sink. She wretched hard, her hands shook against the marble top she was trying to cling to. Luca stood by her side, holding back her hair and rubbing her back in slow circles of concern.

"Sssshhhh," he soothed. "It's okay."

Eventually, after a few minutes, Julia felt able to sit back at the table. Luca poured her a glass of cold water from the fridge, she sipped it cautiously.

"Have you eaten anything?" he asked

"No. Stop asking about me," she snapped. "The purpose of this visit is not about me, it is about you."

"Don't you see, Julia? *You* are about *me.*" He reached for her hand and thought fleetingly how small and helpless it felt before she snatched it back. "I need you to talk to me." Luca persisted.

He reached out to touch her again, this time she physically flinched to avoid him.

"Luca, don't," she said with heartbreaking clarity.

Julia hadn't yet worked out what it was that caused her the greatest torment. Was it the fact that his relatives had murdered her mother? Or, was it the touch and sight of the man she loved with every cell of her heart, that was now poisoned by the threat they shared the same blood that beat it? In the silence of the room she looked at him, his eyes were filled with tears and the hurt that smothered him crowded every facet of his face.

She took a deep breath, goading herself to be strong before she felt unable to hold back any longer. She leapt up toward him and sank her face into his neck. It was a guilty request for comfort from the only man in her life that had ever been able to give it.

"Oh, Luca!" she cried "What are we going to do?"

It was then that Sofia entered the kitchen startling them into breaking free from their embrace.

"Well, if you have the nerve to ask Piers what he is doing in this house, I am damned sure I am going to ask you the same about *her.*" Like a baited dog she snarled at Julia, "Don't you think you have caused enough fucking trouble in this family?"

Luca couldn't take any more. He flew across the kitchen, "You fucking slut, how dare you?" he shouted. He pulled back his hand and slapped her hard across her face knocking her forcefully against the kitchen table.

"Luca!" Julia gasped, "What the hell are you doing?" She ran to Sofia and helped her to stand.

Sofia wrenched her arm away from Julia's grasp and stood before them with a red handprint emblazoned across her cheek.

"Well," she laughed sarcastically, "it didn't take long for you to step into Pappa's shoes, did it?"

Luca blazed and stepped toward her, Julia pulled him back.

"You what? You fucking what?" he shouted. "After speaking with Piers this morning, it made me realise you are every bit your devious father's daughter." He jutted forward, escaping from Julia's grip. "You are a filthy evil bitch. Just like him you will do anything for money, he murdered to save it." He turned to Julia and looked back at his sister. "She fucked a wanker like Charles Lancaster-Baron on video to gain more of it."

Julia shrunk at the crudity.

Sofia's eyes darted from Luca then back to Julia, ironically wishing that the woman she despised could now save her from her shame. "But, you don't understand," she whimpered, "he forced me."

The doorbell rang, and Julia took it upon herself, with sheer relief, to walk from the room to answer it.

Bill looked small and drained between the vast marble pillars of the doorway.

"I've come to offer my condolences to the family," he murmured. "I think it was Emma I spoke to on the intercom, she opened the gates," he said weakly, peering behind Julia.

"Er, I'm not sure this is a good time," she suggested, still hearing the heated argument ensuing from the kitchen.

"I won't stay long," Bill offered feebly.

Julia stood to the side of the door to let him through and followed him into the kitchen.

"Do you realise that the Charles Lancaster-Baron that you had so much fun with drugged my fucking horse?" Bill heard Luca shout.

"Oh, no!" he heard himself groan. "A time like this and that bastard is still the centrepiece of the conversation."

Luca and Sofia simultaneously turned to face the new arrival.

Julia slumped upon a chair, remembering the night that Charles had persuaded her to sleep with Luca whilst he drugged the horse.

She looked at Sofia's tormented face regarding a sexual indiscretion he had forced her to undertake, and then squirmed in her chair at the thought of sitting in the house of the man who had ordered the murder of her mother. *What kind of a world am I involved in?*

Charged by the emotion in the room, the conversation continued, and Bill listened as the story of blackmail slowly trickled into a semi coherent tale.

"I can't imagine what your father, my good friend Frankie, would do if he were here now listening to what Lancaster-Baron had done to his daughter," Bill said.

Julia felt her stomach churn.

Bill looked across at Sofia. "I don't know what hold that man has on you women, really I don't." He leant angrily against the table "But, I wouldn't blame yourself Sofia, he's evil. And at least you have had the good sense to walk away from him. Paris has not been fortunate enough to do that."

Luca saw the pained expression on his face as Bill's head collapsed into his hands.

"Why, what do you mean Bill?"

With his daughter's heartbreak preying so heavily on his mind, he couldn't keep his words from spilling. "He has also blackmailed my daughter; he forced her to give up her own baby." Bill's fists tightened.

"He's done what?" Julia gasped.

"He made her promises of marriage and children but only if she gave my grandson up to the Santé's. Paris handed over her son yesterday; she has never seen Charles since."

"Why the hell would he do that?" Luca asked in astonishment.

"Only the devil will know the answer to that," he said aggressively. "I shouldn't have told you, for my daughter's sake, please don't repeat it." He searched the room and saw the silent promise in their eyes. "And going back to your father, Luca, he hated Charles. He was already trying to plot revenge when you told him about the drugging of your horse. He told me that. But," he sighed, "he died before he could. I know he would *kill him* if he was here now," he spat. He thumped his hand onto the table. "Why the hell did he kill himself?" Bill asked in oblivious wonder.

Julia jumped to her feet and ran to the downstairs loo, Luca ran after her.

Julia had slumped to the bathroom floor and felt grateful for the cooling effects of the cold marble that surrounded her. Luca sat next to her and, having held her hair back again whilst she vomited a second time, he played nervously with three of its strands that had come away in his hands.

"What are you going to do about him, Charles, I mean?" Her voice was nervous and apprehensive.

"I'm not going to do anything," he told her pointedly.

Julia looked back at him in surprise. "Really? Nothing?" she clarified.

He shook his head. "Since all this with my father, I have made a vow; I will never live my life as he has. Honesty and the truth is the only way for me. Revenge is something for the likes of *him*. I will never do it, *never*," he added forcefully.

Weakly, Julia smiled back at him, and for her mother's sake felt comforted by his answer. She felt sorry for him; all he had ever done was live and speak the truth, and now, here he was picking up the love-wrecked pieces that had occurred through no fault of his own. She was going to miss him. She heaved her weak body up from the floor.

"Luca," she said faintly, "I have to go. I can't stay here any longer."

"When can I see you again?" he asked, nervously rethreading the strands of her hair through his fingers.

"I don't know that I can ever see you again," she answered frankly.

"Don't do this, Julia, please don't do this!" He grabbed her arms in desperation.

Julia wriggled and managed to free herself. "Luca, please," she begged. "Will your driver be kind enough to take me home?"

"I thought you loved me, Julia, I really thought you loved me."

"Of course I love you!" she shrieked, "Don't you see that? How else could I come here if I didn't?" She pointed to the cold hateful walls of the house. "This place makes my blood run cold, but I came for you, you said you needed me."

He reached out to touch her again and watched her grimace once again. He read her thoughts. "You are not my sister, Julia, I know it. Please don't believe it, I…"

Julia placed her shaking fingers against his mouth. "You don't know that, Luca." She trembled. "You don't know that."

She opened the bathroom door and the sound of her heels echoing coldly across the hallway almost deafened her.

Luca grabbed her arm and swung her round to face him. "Julia, wait." His eyes searched her face in desperation. "I can't live without you," he said anxiously. "Trust me, Julia, let's leave all this behind." His eyes searched around the house before he looked back at her. "This DeMario name means nothing to me, I can walk away from it all, here, now. I will never look back, I promise." His eyes filled with heartbroken tears. "I love you, Julia."

Julia stood still, longing for him to repeat his words, yet simultaneously wishing she had had the strength never to have arrived in the first place.

"I love you too, Luca," she managed to whisper, but *you* must trust *me*, I cannot take any more pain, I have faced enough heartbreak in my life." Her voice began to crack. "We have had our chance, and, for whatever reason it has been taken away." She reached for the door. "I have to leave."

Luca was depleted of energy. He stood in the doorway and watched her slide onto the back seat of the awaiting limousine.

Julia looked back at him and their eyes held contact for the last time. The car began to drive away and she craned her neck and watched his image fade from the rear window. Once Luca was out of sight, Julia realised she would never be fearful of anything again, because living without Luca would be the hardest thing she ever had to face. With that thought in mind she reached for her mobile and dialled directory services.

"Hello" she said, "I need a number, it is a private residence. The name is Lancaster-Baron. The town is Chelmsley."

Moments later she closed her phone and sat back against her seat. She had obtained the number. Others were either too busy or too frightened to take him on. *I however, am not.*

Chapter Fourty Nine

THE LINE began to ring. It was not nerves that she experienced as she waited for an answer, more surprise at the cold calculating resolve that directed her mind.

"Good morning, Cedars Hall," a cheery voice answered.

"Good morning," Julia replied, "May I speak to Charles Lancaster-Baron, please?"

"May I ask who's calling?" the lady asked.

"It's a personal matter," Julia replied confidently.

"A personal matter, you say?" the lady repeated.

Kitty overheard the telephone conversation and became concerned that the call Mary was taking was for her. She gradually inched herself up from the chair and heard the conversation continue,

"I'm not sure whether Mr Lancaster-Baron is around at present, are you able to be more precise?"

Kitty became plagued by a distrustful notion. Though hunched in pain, she slowly made her way to the library, a room she rarely frequented, but there was a telephone within. One hand clenched the pain that dug ferociously into her side, the other picked up the receiver and listened.

"A personal matter in regard to the DeMario estate?" Mary repeated. "Just one moment, please"

Kitty sat down upon a nearby chair, a deep frown of suspicion and confusion furrowed her forehead. Kitty heard Mary's footsteps tapping across the hallway to find Charles, leaving both Kitty and Julia to wait patiently upon the line.

"Can I help you?" he asked cautiously.

"Is that Charles Lancaster-Baron?" Julia asked.

"Who's calling?"

The suspicion in his voice told Julia it was most certainly Charles.

"I can understand you asking, Charles, after all, I am sure, with the deceitful life that you lead there must be all kinds of people wanting to speak to you."

"I beg your pardon, who the hell is this?" he demanded.

"Oh, yes, forgive me, I haven't introduced myself, you see I am one of the women that you will have forgotten all about, to you, a grubby little pawn in your game of *snakes and adders*," she hissed. "I am Julia, you know, Luca DeMario's friend? You encouraged me to sleep with Luca in the hotel in Ascot so that you could drug his horse, you have maybe forgotten that have you? After all since that time you have become a whole lot busier deceiving others.'"

Kitty sat back in the chair, wide-eyed in horror.

Charles, three rooms away, looked concerned. He answered in a guilt ridden whisper, "Who the hell do you think you are calling my home and casting all these false aspersions on my character?" He looked over his shoulder. "You…"

Julia refused to allow him to continue. "Well, you see, Charles, I happen to think that I am someone who is worth so much more than the likes of you. You see," her voice was determined and grave, "I know I will never have to associate myself with a person who blackmails the likes of Sofia DeMario into enticing someone else's partner away from them out of jealousy. I know that I will never have to look into the eyes of a bastard that has forced a kind girl like Paris Montford into giving up her child, and I know I will *never* have to keep quiet council about my opinions purely because I feel the need to keep social status in your false, grubby world."

Charles was stunned. How did this stupid whore know all this? He gave a false, condescending laugh.

"I have no wish to speak to the likes of you," he patronised, "You are talking absolute…."

"Oh I know you don't want to talk to me, Charles, after all, I am a gypsy girl who has nothing and lives in a caravan. What use am I in the falsities of your privileged world? Don't you see? You should be ashamed, and so should your parents."

With her final comment, the dagger had not only been drawn but it had stabbed him hard and he felt the sharp blade maliciously twisting inside his guts.

"Fuck you!" he shouted and cut off the call.

Kitty replaced the receiver and felt her tears of shame and misery trickle down her face. She heard the front door slam shut then gazed out of the window and watched as her son drove his pretentious car down the drive. Never in her life had she felt the heavy burden of disgrace.

Julia deciphered an inch of wounding in Charles' tone, yet, it did not fill her with the satisfaction she had hoped it would. As the car drove on, she watched the trees and the buildings scurry past her view. Occasionally it slowed for traffic lights, allowing her to notice a couple of shops, their windows dressed with Christmas decorations and she realised that today was the first of December.

It seemed amazing how the time had flown by, so much had happened since the day she had decided to go to York races back in May. Possibly, she pondered, that was where the problems had begun, right on her doorstep in York, but she didn't feel it was the actual events that had caused the problems, more the arrogant pull that had guided her into thinking she deserved more than the tedious gypsy life which she lived.

She rested her back against the backseat and once again felt the labels in the leather coat she was wearing prick her back. She loathed herself because, even today, knowing what she did, she had worn clothes she could not afford simply to impress the egotistic jurors of a false, condescending, and even murderous world. Whilst she wore these clothes, she was as bad as them, all of them, because each criminal and deceptive incident that she had witnessed since entering this world had been born out of the love and the self-imposed sentiment of status and money. These people, she knew, would preserve both – at any cost – her mother's grave bore huge testament to that.

She struggled to free herself from the arms of the coat then threw it with disdain to the carpeted floor of the limousine. This was a life she had always dreamed of, and now, for her mother's sake, she took pleasure from turning her back on it. But, that was a *way* of life, she recognised. It was the one person within it that pulled her to stay.

Regretful tears scorched her eyes and the thought of being without Luca unearthed a feeling of loss and longing that seemed so hard to bear. Confusion spun around her head. Only forty-eight hours ago they had made a pact that they would be together for life. Her heart overflowed with love and respect for a man whose only crime had been oblivious honesty. She felt her lips begin to tremble as the strength of her emotional flood-gates began to lift. Her waterlogged eyes glanced up at the driver through the privacy glass that had long since separated *staff* from *the privileged few,* and realised that, with her as his passenger, she eradicated that tradition. He was a person just as she and she felt comforted by the fact they shared the same commonalities as the everyday man. The chauffeur continued to drive, wrapped up in his own world, and whilst she sat on the back seat she knew she bore no part of it.

Presently, she told herself she lived in No Man's Land and only the calming essence of time would ease her back into her old way of living.

Charles ripped down the road towards Chelmsley Manor. The Santé's house held the only sanctuary; he knew that just seeing Rebecca would appease his angry mind. With every corner of the road he pressed his foot harder on the accelerator, testing his nerve to the limits in the vague hope the viscous voices that had returned in his mind could be drowned.

He parked in the drive and turned off the engine. With rough strokes he rubbed his face with his hands in an attempt to clear his head of the worries that for so long had lain deep beneath. He took a deep breath, realising that just the art of paying his problems attention would only make them swell. Then, like a man having been found guilty of murder, he held his face in his hands.

He tried to regain his composure, and watched as the many treasured faces glided through his mind – his father, his grandfather and, of course, his mother. What had his life come to whereby a fucking gypsy girl would read him what she would interpret as his last rights?

"Fucking peasant," he snarled through gritted teeth.

"Charles!" He heard Rebecca's voice shout across the gravelled driveway. He followed her voice and saw Rebecca peering out of the bedroom window above. Her hair was unkempt, her face as pale as morning frost and her expression one of anxious concern. He got out of the car and, immediately forgetting his woes, greeted her with a dashing smile.

"Hi!" he shouted up.

"Come up here quick!" she snapped.

Her head popped back through the window and, from it, Charles began to hear the ear-piercing screams of a baby. He grimaced, then, as he walked toward the entrance, he began to smirk. He had known all along that Rebecca was going to need him; it just came as a surprise how quickly his intuitions had materialised.

Kitty had sat for over an hour in a contemplative silence. Her tears had drained away, the shaking of her hands had ceased and her whirling thoughts had settled. She was left with the icy severity of hard, tough, facts.

"Mary!" she called from the library. "Mary!" Kitty heard Mary's trusted footsteps tap down the hall.

"Yes, Mrs L.B?" Mary said, standing at the door with her usual smile.

"You can take the rest of the afternoon off, Mary," Kitty said, unable to look her in the eye.

"Is there something wrong?" Mary asked moving closer toward Kitty.

"No, there is nothing wrong at all," Kitty answered, feeling nervous of her approach. She looked out of the window to avoid eye contact. "I would just like to spend the afternoon alone, if it is all the same to you."

Mary stood quietly wishing she had the guts to advise her mistress to rest. She had looked so unwell today and now there was something in Kitty's mood that spoke of a deep-rooted unrest.

"Shall I just finish the ironing and the laundry first?" she asked quietly.

"No, Mary, thank you." Kitty's voice wavered. "I appreciate everything you do for me and now I want to give you some time for yourself also."

Mary knew Kitty well enough to know when her word was final. She wanted to walk over and stroke her arm, to tell her that, whatever was on her mind, everything would be alright, but she couldn't, her kind, faithful mistress would recoil.

"I'll get my coat," Mary said sadly. "Goodbye, Mrs L.B."

Kitty, too pained to talk, held up her hand in gesture of farewell and seconds later heard Mary's footsteps return down the hallway.

Kitty waited until she heard Mary's car drive away and then made the call she had been dreading.

"Hugh?" Kitty confirmed.

"Yes, hello, Kitty," Hugh Stephenson replied.

"I want you to come to the house, I don't care what you have got going on, I need you here this afternoon. I will apologise now for any inconvenience I will be causing you, but this is urgent."

Hugh was alarmed by the urgency in Kitty's voice. "I'll be there," he answered without hesitation.

"Good, bring *all* my legal files. I will expect you at three o'clock."

Kitty replaced the receiver and looked up at her husband's memorabilia crowding the library walls. The sight of them offered her a fusion of pain, regret and strength. She drew on the latter, without strength it would not be possible to get through her meeting with Hugh.

Chapter Fifty

December 2nd, 12.30 p.m, Chelmsley Manor

THE PAPOOSE seemed to be the only thing that stopped his piercing screech, Rebecca realised as she stomped angrily around the yard outside. Up until now he had never stopped. She stood to fill a water bucket and rubbed the small of her back, *this bloody thing hurts* she thought in frustration. The ceasing of her movement caused the baby to murmur. Hiding her irritation, she carried the water bucket to the stable.

Having only had three hours sleep last night due to the baby's insistent screams, she felt so tired, and then fleetingly, she wondered how single mothers managed to cope. But, she was a single mother she told herself, after all Piers was no longer around, she had everything to do herself.

"Rebecca!" her mother shouted from the kitchen door, "Do you want me to have the baby so that you can get on?"

"No," Rebecca bit back "He needs to get familiar with my scent." She noticed her mother's baffled look and turned away.

She had read it somewhere a couple of weeks ago, just like she had read many books on parenting and babies prior to his arrival, not that they did any good. She scoffed at their tenuous words; 'most babies sleep a lot of the time when they are first born,' they had told her. That hypothesis stood to be corrected where Gerard's baby was concerned, she thought bitterly.

"She looks so tired," Victoria said to her husband in the kitchen, "but she's being as stubborn as ever in not letting me help her."

"Maybe she just needs some time on her own with him," James consoled. "You know, it's not easy when you feel as though everyone is watching and judging everything you are doing."

Victoria nodded reflectively, thinking of when she brought Gerard home for the first time and didn't have a clue what to do.

"I tell you what," James offered. "Why don't we go out for lunch and give her some space, she'll be different again when we get back, it will give them some peace to allow them to sleep."

Twenty minutes later the two of them waived goodbye to Rebecca and drove towards the village. Rebecca watched them leave. *Freedom*, she thought, watching the car disappear, after only forty-eight hours she was already missing its luxury.

She looked down at the sleeping baby, his tiny fingers clutched into a petite fist and his sleeping face snuggled into her chest, at last, a chance for reprieve. Her shoulders and her back were aching badly, she quietly opened the car door and tentatively unbuckled the straps that held the papoose against her and placed him into his car seat. She could now get on with the rest of her jobs before possibly being able to snatch some sleep herself.

She tiptoed away toward the stables. She managed five small steps before he fired up his frenzied screams.

"Oh pissing hell!" she shouted.

She scooped him roughly from his seat and took her mobile from her pocket to call Charles. He answered after only one ring.

"Charles, you're going to have to come and help me again," she shouted, turning her head away from the deafening screams. "Will you come now?" she pleaded.

Charles smiled. "I'm on my way."

Charles snapped his phone shut, this plan was unfolding much easier than even he had ever envisaged.

December 2nd, 1.15pm, Cedars Hall

"Right, I'll be off then, Mrs L.B," Mary told Kitty who was sitting yet again in the cold library. "Sam is here doing the gardening so, if you need anything, give him a shout." Kitty heard the concern in Mary's voice.

"Off you go, Mary. Don't you worry about me, I'll be fine."

"Don't forget that Doctor White is calling at 3 p.m."

"Yes, I'll remember," she answered brusquely.

Mary loitered for a second, feeling very uncomfortable at leaving Kitty. For the second day she looked so frail and needy, yet she knew, if she made an excuse to stay, Kitty would not be appreciative of her sympathies. Mary fidgeted at the door. "I'm going to stop in at The Durham Ox in Crayke tomorrow morning and pick up some of their marmalade that you enjoy; you know their jams and pickles won several awards this summer?" Kitty didn't answer. "Anyway," Mary said in a jovial tone, "you'll be able to have some for breakfast tomorrow, won't you?"

"Yes, that will be lovely, but don't make a special trip on my account," Kitty forced. "Goodbye, Mary, have a lovely afternoon."

Mary hung her head and turned from the room. "Goodbye, Mrs L.B."

"Oh, Mary," Kitty called weakly as she left the room. Mary popped her head back round the door and Kitty turned to face her, feeling frustrated at herself for being sharp with Mary the day before. "Thank you. Thank you for everything you have done."

Mary searched Kitty's face, her voice sounded sincere, yet as distant as bird song.

She frowned. "Mrs L.B?" She edged cautiously back into the room.

"Like I said, goodbye Mary, have a wonderful afternoon."

Kitty listened as she heard Mary's car travel down the driveway. She gripped onto the chair and braced herself as she heaved herself up, delivering excruciating pain to her body. She felt every grate and creak that gnawed at her joints, but slowly she hobbled her way into the kitchen.

Her dogs, lulled into sleep by the distant repertoire of Radio Four, slept by the Aga, but on hearing her approaching steps they sprang into action and danced to the rhythm of their wagging tails.

"Hello my beauties," she soothed. It had seemed like months since her deteriorating body had allowed her the joy of sitting among them on the floor. If ever there was a day she had to force luxury upon herself it was today. Slowly, she sank inch by inch, and as if they understood her plight and her pain, the dogs stood to one side and allowed her the space and time she needed to join them. As she sat on the floor, bending her legs in search of comfort, she noticed again how thin and scrawny they were, like skeletal forms beneath her royal blue trousers. She shuddered at their sight, then felt comforted by her dogs' affections. They didn't care how she looked.

She stroked their heads and watched their eyes melt with appreciation as they stared into her eyes. One after another she stared back into their eyes and felt the connection of their souls with her own. A connection of souls, she thought, only truly possible with animals. The floor was amassed with an assortment of wagging tails, some flitting, some pounding the Indian stone beneath. Their wet noses nuzzled her arm to continue her stroke and some rolled onto their backs, unafraid to show their appreciation for her attention she was bestowing. *What a happier life this would be if all humans were as honest as our faithful dogs.* She saw Sam, the gardener, walk past the window and inched her way up.

"Sam!" she shouted, knocking faintly against the window; he turned and smiled, respectfully taking off his flat cap to greet her.

"Will you do me a favour please, Sam? Will you yoke up Wessex for me, I want him to take me for a ride in the cart."

For a moment she thought he was going to refuse. "It's very cold, Madam." he warned.

"Nonsense!" Kitty retorted with a determined smile, "I'll be out in ten minutes."

She turned from the window and listened as the radio apparently repeated the weather warning: "Please, it is one of the coldest December days since 1956. Do not make a journey unless it is absolutely necessary."

Kitty turned off the cosseting drivel; *people were so mollycoddled these days.* She looked outside; the sun was out, causing last night's sheen of snow to twinkle like a million winter stars. Yes, it was crisp, she concluded, but that was just as she liked it, in fact it was her favourite weather. She started to quietly hum the tune of *Good King Wenceslas*. Yes, she thought, looking outside again, deep and crisp and even. She felt her spirits lift. For once, she had plans all of her very own and she was going to enjoy her day.

December 2nd, 2.00 p.m, Chelmsley Manor

Rebecca held the baby in her arms and continued, with greater ferocity each second, to jiggle the screaming baby in her arms.

"This is just a bloody nightmare!" she cried. "He's been like this now for two sodding days. I haven't slept, I haven't eaten and he screams his head off even more when I take him onto the yard. I don't know whether you should go and ask Paris to come, I need help."

"God, no!" Charles answered in panic. "We need to sort this out for ourselves." He looked back at Rebecca and realised he had never seen her look so traumatised. Clearly she was out of control, she was exhausted, her hair looked like rats' tails, squiggling out of a scruffy French knot, her blue Cashmere jumper that she had bought especially for collecting her new son, had still not been changed since his arrival and had just been christened with the fifth douche of baby vomit that morning.

"I can't believe that Mummy and Daddy have just pissed off," she tutted and rolled her eyes disbelievingly. "Mummy only stayed up until 3 a.m. you know, then she went to bed and left me with him."

Charles laughed, never had he witnessed her being so dependant on others. He looked around the normally immaculate bedroom and stared at the piles of clothes, nappies, wipes, empty feeding bottles, all carelessly discarded upon the floor in her attempts to pacify the needs of this tiny being.

"It's not funny, Charles," she reprimanded with a sour face. "No wonder I couldn't have them naturally, it was nature telling me I would be a pile of shit at this motherhood thing." Rebecca burst into tears, but failed to drown out the baby's screams.

"You're not shit at it, Rebecca. It would take anybody time to adjust. Here," Charles offered, walking toward her, "here, let me take him." He fumbled with his arms and hands as he tried to fathom out which end was which and the best way of tackling such as enormous project. "Where have your mother and father gone, anyway?" Charles asked, wishing Victoria was also here.

"Out for bloody lunch and then they're going to pick up some colic drops or something," Rebecca answered, picking up some of the untidy debris. "Mum thinks he might have colic." She tripped on a feeding bottle, stubbing her toe "Aarrgghhh!" she shrieked. She fell to the floor and wept. "This is just such a nightmare, I can't believe it!"

With the baby securely drooped over his shoulder, Charles continued to rub his back in relaxing circles and walked across to her. "Come on, Rebecca," he said, taking her hand. "Follow me."

Grateful that someone was taking charge, Rebecca didn't ask any questions. Instead she took his hand and allowed herself to be led toward the luxury of her unmade four poster bed.

"Rebecca, don't say a word, lie down there and get some rest. I am going to take him downstairs."

"But…"

"Rebecca," Charles continued more forcefully than before, "I said get some rest, we will be fine."

Rebecca looked at Charles smiling down at her, his navy blue jumper and the collars of his white shirt peeping out through the top of the crew neck suited him. His hands, so strong and masculine, looked even more so against the tiny body of the baby. Suddenly, as if a light switch had been turned on, she felt she needed him more than she had needed anyone in her life.

"It's just that I don't want you to leave me," she said with a quiet vulnerability to her voice. "I'll lie here and close my eyes, but I really want to know you are here, in this room."

He smiled down at her; this was all just too good to be true, and out of chaos comes… he couldn't remember the phrase or he was distracted from deliberation. Rebecca and Charles stared at each other, he managed to perch himself on the edge of her bed, for in this instance, out of chaos had come silence. A miraculously golden silence. Neither of them dared move, they remained still and Charles, secretly dazzled, listened to the amazing short snuffly breaths that this tiny baby was taking against his broad chest.

"I think he has fallen asleep," he whispered to Rebecca.

"You're a genius," she whispered back with a huge appreciative smile.

"I know," he mouthed back.

Inch by inch he lowered the baby boy down into its Moses basket at the side of the bed and, as he managed to lie him down, he stood still, wincing with expectant trepidation, only to be greeted with further silence. He looked back at Rebecca in amazement.

"Lie here and hold me," she whispered, feeling her own exhausted body desperate for comfort.

Charles slowly lay down and placed his arms around her. Having not had any sleep, Rebecca was beginning to feel cold, but feeling his body against her now comforted her with a familiar blanket of warmth. She cuddled up to him and looked up at his face only inches away from her own.

"God, you're a natural," she told him.

"At what?" he teased with a smile.

She thought for a second. "Everything probably." She smiled and drew her face even closer toward him, their lips were almost touching.

His heart pounded nervously as the moment he had dreamt of for so long had finally arrived, here, now, and without a second of warning or preparation. Suddenly, as clear as day, he could feel his life was going to turn out just as he had always planned; he had been made to suffer, but only so that he would be forced to relish and appreciate the good times ahead. He seized his moment and slowly bent his head to kiss her. As their lips touched he was magnetised into a new wave of dreams. *Oh and I will appreciate these times*, he promised himself, *with my every being I will.*

December 2nd, 2.30 p.m, Cedars Hall

The timeless sound of the faithful hooves plodding against the road soothed Kitty's soul just as it always had. She connected with the rhythm of their steps, *please just relax, please just relax, please, just relax.* Kitty took heed, immediately allowing her shoulders to loosen in retaliation to her tense upright posture.

The clear fresh air gently stroked her face and caressed the jovial tresses of blonde hair that had escaped her head scarf. With conscious effort she drew in fine though frequent breaths, feeling grateful she had the time to appreciate the cleansing clarity of just one of the gifts nature had to offer. Her weary blue eyes scrutinised the countryside in search of more.

Faintly she smiled in gratitude at the surrounding scenery and gently wafted the reins against Wessex's neck, encouraging him to continue their private tour. This very road she had travelled for years, by car, by foot, by carriage, but never had she seen it in the same light as today, it was a sight that would be etched in her mind forever. North Yorkshire, she sighed with satisfaction and pride, the only place in the world to offer such unrivalled beauty.

The cart wheels rolled against the road, creaking intermittently in thirst for oil and reminding her of added duties she had failed to complete. However, today she told herself, she refused to be distracted by negativity, and Wessex, with his head held high and his attentive ears pricked, gave a huge satisfactory snort as if in agreement to her decision.

"Good boy," Kitty encouraged. "Walk on my friend."

His ears twitched in response to his mistress' comforting voice and, happy to oblige her requests, he continued to pull Kitty and the cart along the winding roads.

His warm breaths cascaded out of his nostrils like the welcoming smoke from chimney pots and made Kitty realise the strength of the cold around her. A light sprinkling of snow had fallen, and already a determined frost was busy transforming it to ice. But, Kitty didn't feel cold today. She was surprised; the cold was something that had always managed to quickly permeate its way through several layers in the past. She concluded it must be her head, simmering her many troubles and sharing its heat to warm her fragile body. She forced herself to listen once again to the restful beats of her horse's hooves, she was determined that even thoughts of her son were not going to sabotage her time.

The roads were quiet. She supposed she had the preposterous weather warning to thank for that, yet thank it she did. Without this heavenly silence she would miss the echoing chorus of birdsong that rang in the distance. Kitty's smiling eyes greedily fed upon the rich detail of her surroundings. A robin, with a breast as large and as red as a summer tomato, perched on a nearby hedge and watched her pass. She witnessed its intrigue as it nipped its head in cautious sprightly jerks before flying away in search of more restful company. She watched it fly and wondered where its flight path would take it? Did that little creature really know? The mysterious wonders of life, what fools people were if they thought they were in control.

The fields that only weeks ago had allowed its crops and purpose to be recognised by a mélange of colour were now disguised by acres of virginal white. Like a waving white ribbon, the snow had settled contentedly across the hills. A winter wonderland, she concluded, one which only few would appreciate. She looked up at the enormous trees that lined either side of the road, their branches all delicately covered by inches of white snow. They held a crystallite magic, so still and yet alive, looking like graceful ex-debutants with hair that was silvered by a lifetime's experience and now, as ever, they patiently waited, like the true ladies they were. All they wanted today was to be asked to dance again, only this time they were cold, they wanted to dance with the sun.

Kitty shuddered. The freezing icy air began to sink disrespectfully into her frail, aged bones, the cold gnawed into her hands, she felt them ache, but in stubborn retaliation she forced them to waft the reins against her horse's neck. Kitty looked up at the snowy clouds and noticed there was hope, the sun was peeping behind them. She was certain its warm nobility would be victorious in its quest to shine; soon there would be the opportunity to be thawed. Would Charles ever be as lucky? she pondered. Again, she cast the subject matter from her mind; there was a clearing ahead large enough for farm vehicles to park, it beckoned her to pull in.

It was the perfect place; like the eyelashes of a sleeping giant, strobes of warm sunlight, broken by cloud, swooped down from the sky and stroked the wild grass upon the ground. As she slowed her horse, she felt the sun melt her face and the relaxing feeling encouraged her to rest a while and take in the views. Trustingly she released the reins and allowed Wessex to graze on the flickers of grass that peeped through the snow. Kitty closed her eyes and listened to the company of bird song.

December 2nd 2.30 p.m, Chelmsley Manor

As their kiss continued, Charles ached with longing, this was the moment he had yearned for since his teens. Oh the sweet utter joy of making love to Rebecca Santé! He dreaded the prospect of her pulling back, but as the seconds passed by and his lips continued to glide against hers she lay without even the slightest signal of a wish to escape. His confidence that this was really going to happen began to soar, and, like an eagle relishing the freedom of full flight, his manhood followed suit.

He kissed her with increasing passion, her momentum remaining unchanged. He remembered how tired she was, though his desire drove him on. With a cautious respect he would only bestow upon Rebecca, he gently stroked his hand across her jumper and rested it casually upon the curve of her breast. As he held his hand still, he simultaneously held his breath and wished upon his dream that she wouldn't break free. She didn't; she lay still, her breaths remained the same. He looked at her face in search of response but her eyes remained closed as they continued to kiss.

"Rebecca," he breathed, "you are so beautiful, the most beautiful woman I have ever met."

She touched his hair before dropping her hand back down to his waist. His hand crept beneath her jumper and rose with trepidation as he allowed his soft manly hands to explore. He gasped with pleasure as his fingertips touched her naked breast, her nipples hardened. Charles let out a second groan and kissed her harder, flicking his tongue passionately inside her mouth, unafraid to show how much he wanted her. Her hardened nipples were the only sign that her body had responded to his touch, for Rebecca remained motionless. He clamped his own eyes shut, unsettled and disturbed by her lack of response, but he couldn't stop now for the images in his mind and the ache in his groin urged his hands to persist.

"God, I want you," he assured her huskily.

His hands slid across her flat stomach and rested with wavering tenderness at the top of the waist band, then, free from rejection, his fingers slipped beneath. He thought he would burst as his fingers stroked the lace of her underwear, circling round and round in small ever decreasing circles until he met with the warmth of cotton in between her legs. He wanted her to thrust her hips to prove her longing for him to probe deeper, he wanted her to moan demurely at what was to come, but she didn't. Her only response was to inch her legs shyly apart. That movement was his only sign that she wanted him to continue, his fingers blindly searched their way beneath her panties, and it was there that he felt the soft, warm fertile land of home.

He gasped with pleasure at the thought of entering her, and now, throwing caution aside, that was exactly what he was going to do. With a passion too forceful to ignore he began to yank at his belt and tore at her joggers to come off. He looked down at her face, for the first time. Her eyes were open; she helped him by shuffling gracefully out of her pants. Then, she resumed position and lay back down. Charles wanted to please her and wondered what he would have to do. He felt uncomfortable, this was not as he had imagined their love making to be, but he sensed, if he were to ask the question, she would freeze with embarrassment.

Enormous throbs of desire tore through his body. In terms of Rebecca's needs, he would have to save his wonderings for another day, for now, he knew exactly how to please his own.

December 2nd, 2.40 p.m, Chelmsley Manor

Charles pulled on his trousers and watched Rebecca redress. She was detached, devoid of emotion, with only an occasional shy smile to inform him she knew he was still in the room. He zipped up the fly of his jeans and wished his dream of making love to Rebecca had never been realised. Never had he been unable to bring a woman to orgasm and never had he felt such a plummet in confidence. After all, having sex with hoards of women was usually a pastime that had ensured it escalated. It was definitely the first time he had ever walked away from having sex and been unsure as to whether the pleasure had been all his.

Maybe, he assumed, this was the feeling that women get when they find they have been used? Charles knew he hadn't been used for sex. Rebecca was too proper for that, but the feeling of emptiness and isolation that presently rolled around in his head consumed him.

The baby murmured and, with the transparent look of panic that crowned Rebecca's face, he thought of Paris and wondered guiltily how she felt. With that thought, as if a colossal cruise liner had bashed into a sky-scraping iceberg, he was jolted into comparison.

He remembered the hot passionate grip of Paris' buxom legs around his waist and her loving tender kisses that had trailed against his body, the way the soft fingers of her hands had traced every part of his physique and the adoring look of love for him in her eye. Now, he watched Rebecca washing her hands in the basin in the corner of her room, as if she was trying to dispel their 'act' from her mind and her skin.

A comparison? he argued internally. *There just wasn't one.*

December 2nd, 2.45 p.m, Chelmsley countryside

The unstoppable shivering that had controlled her body for the past ten minutes had ceased, leaving behind a numbing freeze that enveloped her with a sense of peace. It was a calming wave, as though a tide of Mediterranean sea had washed over her, dissolving the aches and pains that had held her body captive for so long. The sun gently unmasked itself from a floating cloud and shone sympathetically against her face; Kitty gave a faint smile and basked in its predicted victory. Its sympathetic essence basked her skin and like a long lost friend melted away every grain of anxiety her journey had begun with. It cosseted her, wrapped her troubled mind in a warm blanket of reassurance and told her that her fears and regrets were for yesteryear, before finally, it consoled her with the truth; she had quite simply done her best. She felt her mind sail away within the plasma of surrounding light and only the distant sound of Wessex's munching temporarily reminded her of her presence on earth.

Then with an empathy that could not be ignored, an unknown

force, a greater being that appeared to be encapsulated with some romantic mystical promise, slowly drew her away to another land. She felt there was a place it wanted to introduce her to, a land she had never seen and it was giving her its oath it was better than the one she had known. She felt her body, inch by inch, relax and her every conscious thought fly away to the comforting land of nothingness.

Kitty's soul left her body and sailed through the skies like a caged bird that had been authorised a natural freedom. Resembling the magic it had bestowed in life, it sprinkled its effervescent appreciation, like magical fairy dust, upon every fragment of the glorious earth below. In life on earth, Kitty's soul had shone behind the light of her bright blue eyes. From this day on it would shine for an eternity in the land of graceful infinity.

Chapter Fifty One

ABANDONED AND DISCARDED. The letters were etched aggressively on the page, piercing the paper as she scrawled the words. Paris had lost track of time, she had no idea how long she had sat at her dressing table writing these words over and over and, likewise, she had no idea how long it had been since she had last seen her baby. All she knew was that she didn't want to live; she wanted to be saved from this insufferable torture and for the finality of death to take her away from it. Suicide had entered her mind, there were many options available, but the cowardly tears that fell as she contemplated which method would suit her best reminded her she was not so brave.

Charles never answered any of her calls, nor answered the door when she tried to visit him. He had left her at the most desperate time of her life. What she had done, she had done for him and the promise and assurance he had given of the secure loving future she had always wished for. One day, if she ever regained her strength, she would maybe seek her revenge. For now, she would just concentrate on how she would inhale her next breath.

Bill peeped through the crack in the door and saw his daughter sitting at her dressing table. Her hair was matted into a large knot at the back of her head from tossing and turning deliriously on her pillow. Every evening he had rushed into her room when she screamed in terror and calmed her with his soothing voice. He had made her warm drinks that she couldn't face, sprayed lavender on her pillow and her dressing gown, the same one she wore now at four o'clock in the afternoon, all in the vague hope she would have a good night's sleep.

She hadn't eaten at all since her arrival from hospital, only sipped on water, and this morning even that had been vomited up when a trainee midwife had called mistakenly to see her and her baby. He had buried her head into his clinging arms and sobbed with her whilst she had hysterically clawed his body in search of comfort. Silently he watched her now and wished he could do something that would mend her heart. On many occasions he had thought of killing Charles Lancaster-Baron, the only time in his life such contemplation had ever arisen. That, maybe, was an option for the future. At this moment, how to mend Paris consumed his every thought.

He walked from her door and down the stairs and stood briefly in the hallway. He looked around at the glass chandeliers, the cheap reproduction oil paintings and the freshly arranged flowers in the cut glass vase and felt disgraced. His wife replenished those flowers every week and, even now, her responsibility to external image didn't fail. Her attentions would always be devoured by external image.

This place had never felt like home to him, it had been a house where false pretence, ridicule and worry filled every room. He walked into the sitting room and felt the cruel irony of what he was about to do. For the first time he knew he had everything that Francesca had been craving for, the only thing that could make her truly happy. Money. And now, thanks to Frankie DeMario, God rest his soul, he had plenty of it.

He shouted his wife's name upstairs and sensed each syllable lodge in his throat. He walked back into the sitting room, sat in his favourite armchair and waited.

Francesca appeared in her dressing gown with her face painted with the green armour of an algae mask. She stood impatiently before him, tapping at the drying mask with her fingers.

"What?" she snapped.

"You'd better sit down," he said quietly.

"Bill, I haven't got time to sit down, this face mask has to be off in five minutes," she barked, looking at her nails admiringly. "What's the problem?"

Bill didn't care whether she stood or sat, his words were ready to pour. "I am about to tell you something, Francesca, and for once," he gave her a foreboding stare, "I do not want any interruptions, do you understand?"

Francesca, surprised by his unusual bluntness, nodded.

"You know, when I married you I loved you, not because you were pregnant with our child, but I honestly thought we could build something that was real, something that would last forever. I made myself believe it because I wanted it to happen so much. When Paris was born I felt like a king, my heart overflowed with the love and pride I had for my family, the three of us together. But you see, now Francesca I am sick," he said solemnly, "I am sick and tired of you and your incessant moaning and complaining about what you haven't got as opposed to what you have got. I am sick of the years you have spent telling me how inadequate I am and how I would be nothing without you. I am sick of the years you have spent telling me who I should speak to and when. Oh, and let's not forget what I should be wearing when I'm doing it. You have wasted your life being nothing but a frantic social climber, eager to be around the people who appear to have it all. It has made no difference to you whether they are genuine people or not, just as long as you thought they were going places. Well, I refuse to waste my life in this trap of yours any longer and that is why I am leaving you." He watched her jaw fall and her eyes widen in disbelief.

"What?" she gasped, trying to hold her cracking face-mask together.

"Yes, Francesca, that is right, I am leaving you. That way you will have the chance to be with someone that matches up to your standards, furthermore, so will I."

He stood up from his chair and even though his voice remained composed Francesca realised his next line was his second vow to her.

"And mark my words, I will never ever return to you."

For a second she couldn't speak, her mind was caught up in

deciphering the words she thought she would never hear. The years they had shared flashed before her in alternating memories. One picture after another danced through her mind, his genuine manner, his gentlemanly habits, the kind, loving fatherly traits he still held to this day, but most of all, the patience and kindness he had shown in order to make their marriage work.

She shook her head disbelievingly. "Bill, please, please! No, you can't mean this, I have always loved you. I know I may not have shown it, but I have, it's true." The pain lingered in her throat with every plea she made. "I need you, Bill, I need you by my side. I will change. I promise you I will, you haven't given me a chance to prove that I can."

"Francesca, these words are spoken too late. No, you are quite right I haven't given you a chance to prove you can change, but anyone with a sense of loyalty or love towards their husband would be able to see how you have continually broken my heart and, at times, even my spirit. Well, I am here to tell you this will continue in my life no more. You can have the house and everything we own today and, you will be delighted to hear, it is all paid off, giving you a free rein to continue impressing your fancy friends at their fancy dinner parties." He inhaled deeply. "I am going to be doing something for me for a change. I will be taking what's left and starting a new life in Spain. I will give Paris the option of staying here, or she is welcome to come with me. You, however, are not. I will be giving you no more promises, Francesca, aside from this one – I will never be in contact with you again." He could talk no more. Sombrely he bowed his head and walked out of the room.

"Please come back, Bill," she begged. "Please, I am nothing without you," she pleaded. "What will I do?"

Bill continued to walk out of the house. As he did so, with the exception of Paris, he said his final farewell to everything that was in it.

Chapter Fifty Two

WITH THE AID of a powerful gusty wind, icy sheets of rain were clearly visible in the sky and they slashed through the air with an unrelenting wrath. Even Charles, with his grief-stricken head bowed at his mother's graveside, did not escape its unsympathetic determination. It was three o' clock in the afternoon and the dark wintry sky was forcing the day to close fractionally earlier than usual.

The day's general mourners had long since left the wake, and Charles, having returned to the scene of the burial, stood like a solitary shadow with his presence illuminated only by a dimly lit streetlamp standing only feet away. He stood staring at the mound of earth where she lay freshly buried beneath and watched the muddy rivers pouring down it to the grass at his feet. His long black Cashmere coat, completely sodden, blew up from his knees and only his tightened fists, anchored in his pocket, prevented the coat from rising further. The biting rain saturated his hair and face with ice-cold streams that trickled and dripped to the ground, but Charles, feeling emotion too great to express, allowed them to mingle with the invisible tears he wished he could shed.

He cast his mind with regretful sentiment over the past year and recalled with depressing clarity the now irrelevant and foolish woes and troubles he thought he had faced. Throughout it all, he had forced himself to be an outsider, ostracising himself from the love that had really mattered. Guilt then shamed his body. He began to think of all the times he had disrespected her, the times when he knew he had wounded her with his frustrated words, and worst of all, the times, he had been given the opportunity but had never told her, how much he loved her. He thought of the summer and the rhubarb, he had told her then, she had told him too, and that tender moment, for both of them was special.

He wondered if she had known then that she was dying. Had that been the reason for her tenderness? All the recollections of the secret meetings and phone calls that had come to an abrupt end when he walked into the vicinity came flooding back. *Oh yes, the stubborn selfish woman knew alright.* Angrily he wiped away the raindrops that had soaked his face with their fierce pelts. Simultaneously a gust of wind froze his body beneath his coat. *How could she do that to me? How could she know she was dying and not give me that chance to make amends and say goodbye?*

His head sank, he already knew the answer, she would have hated the thought of people pitying her and she would have despised every second of a tearful, sentimental goodbye even more. She had shown bravery and strength to the very end and Charles knew that, as with everything else in her life, Kitty Lancaster-Baron had done it her way. A lump engulfed his throat. *Her way*, he mused gloomily.

He thought about her funeral today, the only part of her will to have been so far divulged. She had requested that only close friends and family attend, for all donations to be shared equally between the church and cancer research, and for her coffin, the cheapest one possible, to be buried within nature's rich and fertile earth alongside her husband and her father. That was it, as simple as that. A woman of such nobility, seeped in dignity, yet buried with such simplicity. He looked down to the ground and watched a muddy puddle collect at his feet by her grave.

Charles didn't know why he was so surprised. Her old adage of 'money talks, wealth whispers' crept into his mind, as did her adoration for her father and her husband. Everything spoke of standards that *he* had just found impossible to live up to. He wished he could have lived up to them, he had occasionally prayed for the day to arrive. Maybe, he reflected, that was when his draw toward atheism had transpired; his prayers had never been answered.

Another icy gust of wind blew against his face, permitting his mind to revive itself with a fresh slant. He was different to her – there was no crime in that. They were mother and son, certainly that bond would never die, but that didn't mean to say his beliefs and his thoughts had to be cemented into her gravestone. That was a place for hers alone. Suddenly he felt a sense of freedom; it was a feeling, when standing by the side of her freshly dug grave, that made him feel guilty, but it was liberating nonetheless.

He was tired of her penny pinching habits and her unrelenting advice that forced him into a land of shame. He was sick of her moralistic codes that for so long had been forced down his throat. Now he had his own life to lead, she had made *her* choices, and from this day, *he* would make *his*.

He took a deep breath. However irritated she had sometimes made him feel and whatever his thoughts, it would never alleviate the love and pure respect he would always hold for her. He knelt upon the soaking ground and felt the mud and the rain seep coldly through his trousers to his skin. He reached out and touched the muddy mound of earth with his fingers, still feeling saddened by the simplicity of her grave.

"I'll miss you, Mother," his wet lips whispered. "I love you."

He felt proud; proud to have had the privilege to have known and loved her, but, moreover, he was proud that she, Kitty Lancaster-Baron, had been his mother.

With a look of superiority, his spellbindingly handsome face, soaked and swept by the ravages of the weather, glanced up at the church clock. Its blue and gold face indicated it was nearing three fifteen. There was so much time left before the day was over and, though his heart ached with grief, he had to look on the bright side. He was Charles Lancaster-Baron, elder son and heir to one of the largest fortunes in Britain. Just his name alone spoke volumes, it screamed fine breeding, privilege and wealth from the rooftops, he was 'the elite', and unlike the unique eccentricities of his wonderful mother, he would feel it an honour to let that elitism shine.

Hoisted by shoulders that looked broad and strong, he stood up and turned his back on his mother's grave. Then, standing the collars of his coat on end, he burrowed his head protectively between them and made his way towards the only thing he could presently think of that would illuminate that 'shine.' *The Ferrari garage*, he thought with glowing satisfaction, only two weeks ago he had seen the exact model he wanted in the showroom window. He made his way from the cemetery and was so thankful to have been blessed with a purpose to his strides.

Luca's hand shook and the photograph, worn at the edges by the frequency of contact, trembled within it. It had been three weeks since his father had died and, with the funeral over, he, being the only son, had been given the duty of sifting through the hoard of his father's paperwork. It was within his father's personal writing desk, a desk that for years had been under lock and key, that this picture, this depiction of ultimate beauty had been found. Luca had no intention of revealing it to any other member of his family, for he knew who it was, he could see it in her eyes and he could see it in her smile. The woman in this photograph was Julia's mother. He placed the picture in his wallet, determined to protect its anonymity from all it would hurt, and then rushed to his bedroom.

He took his mobile from his pocket and sat on the bed to make the call. He heard his sisters, Piers and his mother leave the house to go into Manchester for the day, they had already bid farewell five minutes ago but had been delayed in leaving. He waited until he heard their car drive away; then dialled her number. Her line rang and, as it did, he realised that his action may have been too impulsive. What would he say? How would he tell her? The line rang for a second time, the words didn't matter, he consoled himself. What mattered was doing the right thing, there had already been too many lies and too much deceit, she deserved to know because this photograph was Julia's property, this was her life. His heart missed a beat as she answered.

"Julia. It's me," he said nervously.

"Hello, Luca," she answered in a faint voice.

"Julia, I need to see you." He rushed on. "Before you say no, I have found something of my father's that you need to see." He hesitated. "It involves your mother."

Luca thought she had gone, "Hello, hello, Julia?" he urged.

"I'm here."

"It's so dreadfully important that you see this, Julia." He thought quickly about where they should meet, he wanted to show her where he had found it, tell her what time, every detail about his find. "Come round here, Julia. Please."

She heard the insistent urgency to his voice. "Okay," she agreed cautiously.

"I'll send my driver now," he told her.

Luca had sat in the empty house and waited for what seemed like an eternity, but now she was here and as ever, he rushed to open the front door.

She stood on the steps and looked back at him; he was shocked to see how much she had altered in only a matter of weeks.

Her face looked determined and an unusual resistance in her eyes created a sharp edge to the customary cheer in her face. She looked exhausted, and her clothes, jeans and a simple sweater, hung limply off her now skinny body, exaggerating her look of misery.

She noticed his reaction to her appearance and immediately felt both angered and vulnerable. "What's the matter, Luca, are you surprised to see the real me?" Her voice was smothered by sarcasm.

She had shocked him for a second time; he had never heard this tone in her voice before. "To my knowledge, I have *always* seen the real you," he reassured, refusing to retaliate and standing to the side of the door to allow her to pass.

She walked through the door, "Shall I take my trainers off, Luca? They are very dirty; I wouldn't want to *soil* this *immaculate* house."

This time, though sarcasm was still the intention, her voice was loaded with a hateful scorn.

His annoyance rose. "Have you ever had to take your shoes off before when you have walked into this house?" Luca asked pointedly, shoving the door closed.

She shook her head.

"Then don't bother now," he answered curtly. He instantly regretted his abrupt reply; he looked fleetingly into her eyes and saw their emptiness as a disguise for the raw hurt behind. "Can I get you a drink?" he asked her soothingly, trying to make amends.

"No," she answered abruptly, "I want you to show me whatever it is you want me to see."

For a split second he closed his eyes, not knowing whether he wanted to dig himself in, or dig himself out of this never ending nightmare, but then his sympathies led him to her mother and Julia's understandable pain. He walked over to her and rested his hand on her shoulder, hoping that the offer of affection might ease her hurt. Immediately he felt her physically recoil beneath his touch.

"Okay," he replied quietly, dropping his hand from her shoulder. "Follow me."

She followed him through a myriad of bright, airy corridors that led, eventually, to the rear of the house. They reached a large oak door. Luca unlocked it to reveal a short staircase harbouring only eight steps. At their foot was a second, much larger oak door.

"What's in there?" Julia asked, already feeling uneasy.

"My father's office," Luca answered.

She followed him down the stairs and watched as he unlocked the subsequent door. Walking behind Luca, she entered into his father's office and, with only one foot placed upon the dark plum carpet, she shuddered at the austerity of the surroundings. Far from the clear, fresh, ivory trail that ran through the rest of the mansion, this room was outspokenly dark, dark mahogany furniture, dark plum walls and dark shaded lamps, a place where she could understand the dark businessman, Frankie DeMario, feeling at ease. It was a room she could just imagine him thriving in, devoid of emotion, sentiment and light, a place where probably hundreds of deals had been agreed. She wondered angrily if her mother's murder had been one of them.

She hated being here, reviled everything about it, the whole room reeked of underground dealings where anonymity was paramount. There were no windows in the room, a large key in the lock and huge bolts scarred the inside of the door. She looked at the black leather sofa, it had a table by its side which hosted a crystal decanter with dark liquor inside, six crystal glasses surrounded it, and again, she wondered who had accompanied him whilst he toasted her mother's death. Suddenly, without warning, she began to hate Maria DeMario, how could his wife have allowed this repulsive underworld to exist within her home?

Luca had walked over to the vast mahogany writing desk that sat against the wall. He opened its lid to reveal a set of six slim drawers that made up the left hand side of its interior.

"I've had to go through his paperwork," he told her gravely, unable to refer to him as his father whilst she was in the room. "Rarely were we allowed inside this room." He looked around sourly; then returned his attention back upon the desk. "This desk was always held under lock and key, I often wondered what was in it when I saw him lock it up." He shrugged a solitary shoulder in regret. "Naively I respected his privacy, but I found something today that probably explains his actions. I opened this drawer." He pointed to the third drawer down. Julia inched closer toward the desk. "Do you see?" Luca continued, pulling at it to show it was fixed. "It's the only one with a lock?"

Julia nodded. He twisted the small key to unlock it then pulled the drawer open. "I found this inside." He had put the photograph back exactly where he had discovered it, as if trying to allow Julia the bitter-sweet consolation of being the first to find it, he stood to one side.

Ignoring the obvious unease that choked Luca's face as he looked on, Julia reached for the only thing in the drawer, a photograph that was laid face down within it. She picked it up.

Her hands trembled, her heart raced and she felt a flush of boiling blood expand throughout her body. She flopped down upon the leather sofa, forgetting that only minutes ago it was a part of the room's furnishings that she had berated for its look of brutality.

"It's my mum," she said in a hysterical whimper. "It's my mum," she repeated, staring down at the picture.

Luca moved to sit by her side and curled his arm securely around her shoulders "I know," he whispered.

"How did you know?"

"Because you are the image of her, she is beautiful," he whispered. He looked at her forlorn, fragile face and watched her chin tremble like a frightened child. He gently pushed her hair behind her ears. "You have her smile, you have her eyes," he paused, "and you have her strength," he told her gently.

Julia couldn't speak a word. She felt a sadness that delved too far to admit. Frankie DeMario had been speaking the truth about her mother, causing her a cruel awakening. She had spent hours over the past weeks, negating sleep and numerous meals, telling herself over and over that there had been a terrible mix up, that he had got the wrong woman and that somehow the real truth would be exposed, leaving Luca and herself free to be together. But now she held the evidence in her hands, she thought grimly. This photograph confirmed every fact that he had shouted and hissed from his mouth that night. How else could this photograph be here?

She ran her shaking fingers around its worn edges, instantly recognising he must have scrutinised this picture over and over again for it to be faded the way it was. Somehow, from somewhere within the realms of her young, good, loving heart she found a reason for solace. She remembered the look in Frankie's eye the night of the confession. At the time, she had witnessed his loathing for her mother, but now, unable to take her eyes off the photograph's cherished shabbiness she realised that his anger had possibly been a disguise for the one true love he had lost.

"Do you think he loved her, Luca?" Her voice trembled.

"He must have done," he said quietly, concealing his own pain. "Why else would he have kept her picture alone in that drawer?"

It was the answer she had hoped for. Julia closed her eyes and took a deep, shaky, breath. She wanted Frankie to have loved her mother and couldn't bear to think of her mother loving a monster. At last, within the dark bowels of this man's house and this sinister cave of iniquity, she had found a tiny symbol of tenderness, a true identification with love.

The thought confused her, but how was it that a person could be so multi-faceted? On one side of his heart, a cruel sadistic streak ran terror right the way through it, where murder, lies and deceit thrived within its undeserving beats. She ran her fingers again across the edges of the photograph, but how did the other side find the strength, against all the odds, to retain the natural compassion of love and sentiment? At once a vile thought blazed across her mind, if she *was* his daughter, could he have passed this schizophrenic heart onto her?

She felt her mind migrate from the agony of confusion and lead her instead to a tidal wave of hysteria. She bent over as if in pain, crossing her arms around her stomach and gripped her sides with an aggressive clench.

Luca didn't recognise the sound of her wails – they were so hoarse and deep that the sound scared him. They continued with long drawn out hollers and their gravity illustrated the magnitude of her pain. He threw his arms around her body, trying frantically to eradicate her torture, but the rolled up ball of her body continued to rock with a madding sway.

"It's okay, Julia, it's okay, Julia, it's okay," he repeated helplessly.

For minutes she listened to the repetitive momentum of his words and suddenly felt angered by his obvious oblivion. She lifted her head from the painful frenzy of her cocoon.

"But it's not okay!" she screamed. "It will never be *bloody* okay, Luca." Her face as she looked back at him was distorted with horror. "I'm pregnant!" she bawled. "I have an incestuous baby growing inside my womb and that will *never* be okay!"

Chapter Fifty Three

HER TREMBLING FINGERS looked as delicate and as frail as the pages she was turning, but Julia, led by confusion and a cauldron of fizzing hormones, continued to search for help. She was looking for 'a clinic.' A clinic that supposedly would take away her problem, she shuddered at the thought. No wonder they called them a clinic, she pondered anxiously. She could only imagine how clinically impersonal the procedure would be. To them, she would be nothing but a name and a number on a morning's appointment list, a list she had never ever foreseen herself being upon.

She could visualise the stark, austere appearance of these kinds of places, the staff's white uniforms, camouflaged by the harsh nudity of whitewashed walls. A steel bed frame as cold as the act that would occur upon it, and professionally tucked into the hard worn mattress, were frost white bed-sheets, stiffened by the freeze of heavy starch, reminding each patient their purpose was to offer meagre privacy as opposed to comfort. Her senses, swamped by belief she was already there, began to smell, almost taste, the smothering smell of antiseptic that burnt away the surface germs of the walls and floors. She could hear her feet tapping nervously down the barren corridor towards her allotted room and with anxious trepidation she began to grate her pen against her teeth.

This decision she had come to had not been instantaneous, nor had it been an easy, but it was one she could not renege on. Until this embryo was removed she would be trapped inside the DeMario Dynasty for the rest of her life – the thought of that filled her with dread. Then she thought of Luca, how could someone so kind, the man she adored, be a part of that DeMario family she so wanted to turn her back on? Once again, her question was met with heart-stinging emptiness.

Pressing hard against the page and almost tearing the thin pages of the directory, she circled the advert that appealed to her the most. It was the only one that included the word 'care' within its description. Only moments later she had made her initial appointment; she lay down on her bed and solemnly stared up at the ceiling. If only she felt able to accept the love and support that Luca offered. She felt so desolate without it. She wondered what he was doing now, was he thinking of her?

Professor Sanderson was a man of great integrity who had received hundreds of respectful acclaims from fellow scientists over the years. Since he was a faithful follower of the racetracks, Luca had met with him several times, but today, far from chatting casually about the form, their conversation had born a very different slant. Just as he had been instructed, Luca placed three strands of his own hair and the strands of Julia's into two separate plastic envelopes and sealed them at their edges. There was only one exception he made to Professor Sanderson's instructions. Instead of posting the packages by recorded delivery he would drive the three hundred miles and deliver them by hand. The results of this analysis would, either way, have an effect on every aspect of his future; travelling the three hundred miles was immaterial.

As Luca left the house he overheard an argument strike up between his sisters upstairs.

"Why do you want to see him?" Sofia hollered. "Just because his mother has died, it will not suddenly create any feelings within his body. The man is made of stone. He is a heartless bastard, why can't you see that?"

There was momentary silence.

"Because I love him, that's why!" Emma screamed in retaliation. "Now just piss off and get out of this room."

Luca heard the slam of a bedroom door. *What did anyone know of love?* he seethed.

"You are a bloody doormat!" Sofia screamed in response to the slamming door.

"Fuck, it feels weird here without her." Hugo's persona matched his disposition, moody and uncomfortable. "I can't stay here much longer, it's sending me insane; she's everywhere."

Charles, standing at the newly lit fire, swung round to face his brother. "Oh don't worry Hugo, you get yourself back off to London, after all, *you're* the *only one* that feels mother's presence and is reminded of her." Hugo was oblivious to Charles' sarcasm.

"Shall we go and get a Christmas tree?" Hugo asked, glancing at the television and noticing the backdrop of *Songs of Praise* was festooned with Christmas decorations.

"A fucking Christmas tree?" Charles snapped. "What the fuck do we want a Christmas tree for?"

Hugo didn't respond. Charles watched as his shaking brother began to arrange a line of cocaine upon his mother's favourite coffee table. The sight incensed him. He was about to speak but his phone vibrating in his pocket distracted his attention. It was Rebecca. Once again he chose to ignore her call.

"Mmmmmm," Charles heard Hugo murmur with a gigantic sniff, "the bullet of freedom."

He watched as his brother flopped back against the armchair, the effects of this 'bullet' already taking their hold. "God, you're low," Charles snapped, secretly feeling a creep of envy at Hugo's relaxed and seemingly gratified pose.

"Why?" Hugo answered with his eyes closed.

"Taking that shit on Mother's favourite coffee table. She would kill you if she was here now."

Hugo sniggered and opened one eye. "Cut the holier than thou act with me. You want to have a line yourself. It will ease you out of this uptight conundrum." He leant forward in his chair and began to straighten a line out for Charles.

Charles' phone beeped indicating a message had been left. He listened.

"Charles," Rebecca's voice sounded sophisticatedly soft. "Please come round, I haven't seen you since the funeral. Mummy and Daddy want to see you too." Her voice tapered off, "Please. If you're there, call me back."

"I can even smell her everywhere," Hugo mumbled, sitting back again and reclosing his eyes. "It's no good, you know, living here. We're going to have to sell this place," Hugo stated in a matter of fact way.

"Sell it?" Charles gasped. "Mother would be devastated."

Hugo sat up. "When will it sink in? She's not here anymore, Charles," he snapped. "Take a line of this." He kicked the coffee table shaking the virginal stripe of cocaine from its moulding. "It will help you to face up to reality."

Its beckoning was too great a temptation and Hugo was right, it had always worked in the past.

Moments later, Charles sat back in the chair and smiled, 'the bullet', with sophisticated precision had worked for him too, as fast as water sinking into sand. He felt confidence strangle his desperation. His phone rang again, this time it was Fabel, his accountant. He didn't get the chance to greet Fabel before he was met with a tirade of anger.

"I have just about had enough of you; I hear your latest purchase is a bloody Ferrari?" he barked. "What the hell are you thinking of this time?"

Charles grinned coolly, stood up and walked toward the window. Outside, the daylight was drawing to a close and the outside lamps, previously never turned on by his mother, illuminated the Ferrari's red fire hide.

"I'm thinking of sheer unadulterated pleasure," he answered cockily. He looked over at Hugo who appeared to be mesmerised by something on his Blackberry screen and walked out of the room. "There will be no need for conversations like this anymore," Charles assured. "Don't you realise? A fortune will be heading my way." He laughed. "In another few weeks you will be thinking yourself lucky you have me as a client." He felt his anger rise. "Now, piss off and harass someone else, you boring little shit!" Charles angrily cut off the call.

There was, however, something of benefit that had come from Fabel's call, he decided, it reminded him to call his mother's solicitor about the will.

Hugh Stephenson promptly took Charles' call.

"Hello, Hugh," Charles said. "Hugo and I are especially grateful for the wonderful reading you voiced in church; mother would have been truly delighted."

"That is no problem at all, Charles," Hugh replied curtly. "Being involved in your mother's affairs over the years has been a true honour, it really has."

"Mmmmm, I'm sure, that's another reason for my call to be honest. Hugo, as you know, resides in London and is planning on going back down the day after tomorrow. We wondered, on that basis, if you could shed any light on the will reading? Can we fit it in whilst he's here?"

"No, definitely not," Hugh answered abruptly. "The will reading will take place in six weeks time, by your mother's requests. I have an awful lot of people to try and track down before it can go ahead."

"Six weeks time?" Charles questioned aloud. "That all sounds rather precise, and tracking people down?" Charles' face grew distorted by a frown. "Perhaps I can help you? I have Mother's address book here."

"No, thank you, Charles, that will not be necessary, I can assure you everything is in hand." Hugh paused. "Is that everything, Charles?"

"Who are the people you are trying to locate?" Charles asked, sensing hostility in Hugh's tone.

"I'm afraid I can't say anymore than I already have at this stage."

With the call ended, Charles walked back into the drawing room and heard Hugo talking to one of his girlfriends.

"I feel horny. What are you wearing you saucy little minx?" he laughed as he listened to her reply. "Where's your hand?" Charles heard him whisper down the line.

Charles walked out of the room, he was uneasy. The conversation with Hugh had unnerved him. There was something going on, something untoward being held from him. What could it be?

He poured himself a Jack Daniels and began to pace the floor.

Chapter Fifty Four

"I'M DREAMING of a white Christmas," Bing Crosby sang in the background. Julia thought how lucky Bing Crosby was to only have the weather to worry about, she had so many dreams and wishes but all of them seemed to be so far out of reach.

She was sat in a coffee shop, not far from 'the clinic' and watched as the steam from her latte waved its way through the air. It was a small establishment and not particularly popular, the latter being the reason she had chosen to step inside. She needed quiet and the time to think, two facets when living in a cramped caravan upon a bustling gypsy site – that proved hard to obtain. Tinsel and baubles hung from the ceiling and a lonely Christmas tree stood in one corner. She felt an immediate affinity to its solitude.

"We got burnt down in May," she heard a waitress telling a couple at the far end of the room. The waitress wiped the table next to them, clearly happy to have someone new to talk to. "The old chef, he was a smoker," she shook her head and rolled her eyes. "Didn't put his cigarette out properly, the whole place burnt to the ground. We had to close for six months and now our customers have gone elsewhere, it will take a while to get them back."

May, Julia reflected. It appeared that May had demolished many lives. Her dark brown eyes gazed out of the window and swept the bustling streets for answers to her impractical questions. *What would have happened if I had not gone to the races that day?* she asked herself. There was such a large part of her that wished she hadn't. Meeting Luca had marked both the beginning *and* the end of her life.

Her nervous stomach twisted angrily reminding her that in half an hour she would be involved in a consultation that discussed the finer detail of aborting the baby growing inside her. For Julia, it was the worst thing she could ever have to go through, possibly even on the same par as losing her mother. She had created a baby with a man she loved more than anyone else in the world and the thought of killing it just crucified her.

Since telling him the news, on the odd occasion she had answered his calls, she had initially taken comfort from his voice, but when the facts re-emerged she would rebuff him. His response would always hold the same heartbreaking symmetry.

"Julia, please, please meet me," he begged. "Let's talk, we can be together, I know we can, we can be a family just the three of us."

He was living in a fantasy, a fantasy she so wanted to believe in, but knew could never be. Her plans for abortion were kept to herself, locked within a personal prison from the outside world. But, with aching frequency, she could feel the strength of her lowly secret desperately trying to bulge its way out of the iron wall within.

She took another sip of her latte before pushing it aside. She would make her way to the clinic; it was only there, within the confines of the four cold walls, that she would have the opportunity of being honest with someone.

"I'm sorry, Mr DeMario," Professor Sanderson's secretary told him. "It is the first time the Professor has been absent from work due to illness for fifteen years, it is just unfortunate," she added bluntly.

"Unfortunate? I can't believe it!" Luca bit. He hastily retracted his temper. "When will he be back, then?" he asked forthrightly.

"Hopefully he will be returning within the week or by the end of it. But, he has advised me to tell you that his colleague could help you if the matter is pressing."

"No, No. Definitely not," Luca answered abruptly. He knew he couldn't take any chances on this getting out; Julia had already gone through enough. The words she used, *unfortunate* and *pressing* were now grating hard. "No, I will only deal with Professor Sanderson," he told her.

"As you wish, Mr DeMario," his secretary offered sourly.

"Just tell him it is most urgent that he calls me upon his return to his office."

"I will pass your message on," she said.

Luca ended the call and put his head in his hands. Everywhere he turned the odds were piling high against him. What was wrong with the world? All he wanted to do was to prove to Julia – and to himself – that their bond was not within the DNA of hair, but within their hearts. This was going to be the longest wait of his life, but still, wait he would, and anyway, he consoled himself, even if the results *had* been delayed by one week, what difference would that make? Nothing could happen in that time.

"Julia Smith?" A lady in her mid forties with a kind mothering face called her name.

"Yes," Julia answered quietly, standing up. The lady gave her a comforting smile.

"Come this way dear," she said, beckoning her with an outstretched arm. Timidly Julia made her way toward the open door of the treatment room.

Like cathedral bells, their footsteps pealed merrily against the stone floor of Cedars Hall.

"Thank you so much for coming, Harry. It really has been a pleasure seeing you again." Charles had a grin fixed to his face, one that he found quite impossible to mask.

"It's been my pleasure, Charles. Just such a dratted shame I have come to value the property under these circumstances."

Charles forced his mood to drop. "Yes, quite," he answered soberly.

It had been Hugo that had organised the valuation, but since he was now nowhere to be seen, it had been Charles, who, reluctantly at first, had shown him around. The valuation figure currently sang in his mind.

"But," Harry said taking the chance to spin around and marvel once more at the property from the driveway, "it really is a superbly unique property and I reiterate, I wouldn't hesitate in marketing it at fifteen million."

Charles remained cool and shrugged. "Well, Hugo and I will discuss it. I think if we do put it on the market we will wait until January now." Harry nodded in agreement "And, like I said before, we don't need to sell." Charles broke their stare and looked away. "It's the memories that stifle your daily existence when someone close to you has passed away."

Harry nodded sympathetically. "I understand, Charles." He patted him on his shoulder before climbing into his Range Rover. "Let me know what you decide." He casually saluted, a habit that had proven hard to break from his twenty years at Sandhurst. "All the best, Charles," he called out as he drove away.

Charles watched him leave and allowed Harry's words to hang in his mind.

"All the best," he repeated aloud with a huge smile. "You bet, Harry, you bloody bet. All the best is exactly what I will have."

It was bitterly cold. Charles looked up at the dull grey sky. It stared back at him blankly like the screen of a failing television. *I need sunshine*, he decided, *a change of scenery*. Whenever he thought of sunshine he habitually remembered his childhood days in Barbados. Then it came to him. He wondered if his old friend Sebastian Thompson had sold his luxurious Villa in Barbados that he told him about at the Summer Ball. The place was now a mere snip, he could easily afford it. He reached for his mobile phone and began to search through his address book for his number.

Hugh Stephenson sat at his desk; he only had three more calls to make and then everyone that Kitty had requested to be present at her will-reading would have been informed. He leant back on his leather recliner.

Paris Montford was sitting on the terrace; she replaced the receiver and looked out across the Spanish landscape surrounding her home.

Why the hell would Kitty Lancaster-Baron invite me to the reading of her will?

Frustratingly, she had some weeks to endure before she would discover the answer; *maybe she should go to England sooner,* she questioned, *that way she could find out from her mother what was happening. If there was anything worth knowing, her mother was sure to have all the information.*

Julia lay on her bed looking up at the very same ceiling she had stared at for most of the week. Every part of her body ached to speak to Luca, to tell him what had happened to her today, to hear something from him that prevented her from having to go through with it, and even better, something that proved they were not related. That would never happen, she concluded with pessimism.

She sighed and rolled onto her side, aimlessly fingering the numbers on her phone, daring herself, yet resisting the temptation, to call him. She scratched at the plaster on her arm, a souvenir of the blood samples they had taken at the clinic. "Just a precautionary measure, in case of any problems on the day," the nurse had told her. She had seven days to wait before she could go back to the clinic and 'the procedure,' as they coldly termed it, could be carried out. This was going to be the longest seven days of her life.

She jumped as her phone rang and sat bolt upright, hoping it was Luca. A number she didn't recognise covered her screen. She answered the call and listened to the caller with a perplexed scowl.

"Are you sure she has asked that I am present? Are you sure you have got the right number?"

Two minutes later she cut off the call. *What could that woman possibly want with me at her will-reading?*

Hugh Stephenson took a deep breath and exhaled forcibly. Trust Kitty, he thought, even in her death there was a unique trait to the stir she left behind.

Chapter Fifty Five

A WHITE TEA-STAINED VEST, navy blue underpants, bare feet and a freezing gale blowing directly towards him – Luca looked back at Mr Smith filling the doorway to his caravan, unperturbed once again by his lack of attire and certainly not giving the weather a single thought. Luca hugged his waxed coat around his body.

"No, sorry lad, she's not 'ere again," Julia's father told Luca for the third time in a week.

"I can't believe it; I came early purposely this morning, where could she be at 7.30 a.m?"

"You never know with that girl," he laughed guardedly, "she is like her mother was, God rest her soul, always on the bloody missing list!"

With that comment Luca felt himself recoil internally and simultaneously he could have sworn he saw Julia's bedroom door move and close another inch. He craned his neck slightly to investigate further, the door remained still. He put the movement down to the strength of the wind.

Julia's father recognised the suspicion in his eyes and felt guilty. It was certainly a winter's morning, one that beckoned a cold wind to howl around the sleeping camp. He wished he could invite him in; he liked Luca, not least because he could see how much he loved his daughter. However, orders were orders.

"I'll tell 'er you called again, Luca."

"You must tell her I called, please tell her. I desperately need to see her."

All Mr Smith could do was give a brief nod. Then Luca turned and walked away. Julia's father closed the door on the grave elements outside and once again watched Luca walk away from the caravan.

Slowly Julia's bedroom door inched open. "Has he gone?" she whispered from behind it.

"Yes," he snapped "You can come out."

Skulking in her nightshirt, from the darkness of her bedroom, Julia made her appearance.

"I can't understand you," her father told her. "The catch of the bloody century hot on ya trail and you hide from him." He shook his head in exasperation. "There isn't a girl in the land that wouldn't fall into 'is arms. E's bloody minted, more swag than you could ever imagine *and* a nice lad." He flopped down into his armchair. "What the 'ell did I do wrong; only *my daughter* would let 'im walk free."

"Stop it, Dad," she responded lightly. "Money isn't everything, you know."

Her father laughed. "No, dammed right it 'int, but tell me what you can do without it? And anyway," he continued in Luca's defence, "it's not just money that lad is offering to you. It's love an' all. A combination you'll be lucky to find again."

Julia didn't answer. On the face of it his words were true, what could she say? Only the facts she had recently learnt would make him see her need to hide from him, but to tell her father? That would be unthinkable.

"I'm going back to bed," she announced.

He ignored her and impatiently grappled with the remote control for the television.

Julia lay on her bed. Darkness shrouded the room with a grim silence. Now Luca had gone, she wished he hadn't. She wished he had forced his way into her room and allowed her to pour out her confession of the impending abortion and her deepest fears. Maybe, just maybe, he would have found the right words to alleviate her troubles.

She stroked her flat stomach; still it showed no sign of life beneath. She wondered, with heavy breaths, why this mighty, yet minuscule capsule of nature remained adamant in its quest for life. She felt mortified at how many times she had wished she would miscarry and even more ashamed as to what she was about to undertake to end its short fragile life.

There were only two days to go before her baby would be taken away from her forever, only forty-eight hours in which she had to remain strong. She silenced her martyrdom thoughts with a deep stubborn breath.

Luca sat in his car outside the camp and waited. He couldn't see Julia's caravan from the small clearing he had parked in, but he just couldn't prevent himself from hoping that she would walk around the corner. He rebuked his thought. Why would she do that? He knew exactly where she was; she was already at home and had been the whole time he had stood at her door. It was plainly evident; she didn't want to see him.

He beat his fist hard against the steering wheel in frustration and guilt. Frustrated that he couldn't see her and tell her everything he was doing to try and alleviate their pain, but secondly guilty, guilty because it was, after all, his own family, even if it was just one member, that had caused the whole nightmare of a scenario to transpire. He dialled Professor Sanderson's mobile number and the call immediately went to voicemail. The message he left was simple.

"Professor Sanderson, it's Luca DeMario here, I have changed my mind," he hesitated and cautiously bit his lip. "Ask your colleague to carry out the tests. Please, ask him to do them as soon as he can. I can't stress to you enough how important this is."

Luca hung up. It was his instinct that told him it was urgent, it was also his instinct that told him everything would work out the way he wanted. He rested his head on the steering wheel and hoped that these instincts, which he had relied on throughout his life, would not let him down now. There could never be a more significant time for them to prove accurate.

At eight a.m. Francesca Montford shook. She sat on the edge of the bed and tried to focus upon the bulbous swell of her bedroom whilst a hazy memory of the night before came to light. Only three hours ago she had found herself asleep at the top of the stairs, a carpet burn had torn at her knee and the precious wine bottle that she had tried so carefully to carry had swished its way free and drenched her hair in an ocean of burgundy red. The imprint of the carpet still indented her face, but that, she neither noticed nor cared about. The only focus she had was trying to get through yet another day of hellish suffering. Alone and still clearly inebriated, she staggered from her bed to try to make her way down the stairs. She anchored herself against each spindle of the staircase, clinging onto each one in turn as if her life depended on it in a bid to secure her swaying steps.

As she neared the middle of the stairs her eyes flickered with interest. A half bottle of gin sat on one of the steps. She had no idea why or how it was there, but neither did she care. Like a man dying of thirst, Francesca inched her way down on her rear to the next set of steps and grabbed it. With shaking hands she unscrewed the top then, with uncouth raucous slurps, she began to drain the remainder of its contents.

Piers, Sofia and Emma sat in the cinema room. The three of them had only been in the room for thirty minutes and already their attention to the film had drifted.

"Do you think Mama is depressed?" Sofia asked Piers.

Piers turned down the volume. "Probably, who wouldn't be after what she has had to suffer?" He looked to Emma for her opinion to the question.

"Why do you think Kitty Lancaster-Baron wants us at the will-reading?" Emma asked distantly, completely unaware of Sofia's question.

"God knows," Sofia scoffed coldly.

"Well, if there is a God," Piers responded, resting his hands behind his head, "it will be to give us all some compensation for the fucking torture her son has put us all through. Fucking hell!" he sniggered, "With everyone that bastard has pissed off there won't be a penny left for him."

Emma fell silent and looked back at the screen. She saw the moving pictures upon it but paid no heed to the words. Her mind began to wander, exploring all the times she had shared with 'The Bastard.'

Charles sat at the Santé kitchen table. The morning sun poured through the window and settled upon his face. With James and Victoria sitting opposite him, he watched as Rebecca, with the baby in her arms paced the kitchen floor in agitated steps whilst her hand gave insipid pats, like the hurried flaps of a pigeon's wing, to his back.

"I think he's asleep now," Charles told her, looking back at the baby. "Why don't you put him in his chair now so you can sit down?"

"Because every time you put him down he starts crying again," she answered in frustration. "Anyway, at least it's exercise, I feel like I haven't done any for ages. We've only got seven horses on the yard; even the staff have taken to painting the tack room."

"Where have the horses gone this winter for their holidays?" Charles asked.

"Most have them have gone to their individual owners."

Charles noticed that conversation about the yard increased her enthusiasm.

"I like it when the horses spend time with their owners," she continued, "it gives them an opportunity to get to know each other better." She rolled her eyes. "And, to be honest, for me it couldn't have come at a better time. I don't know what I would have done had he arrived in the thick of flat season. Thank God we don't get involved with the hurdlers."

"What will you do next season with him then when you are busy?" Charles asked.

"Well, we'll probably use the nursery in Chelmsley. Being frank, I have got so sick of his screaming I have badly needed a break, so I have already put him in the nursery for the odd day, they are fantastic. So," she said casually "if he has calmed down by the time the racing starts, I'll get a nanny and take him with me, if not, the nursery is as good a place as any."

"Bloody hell, he's only just been born!" Charles said. "How old are the babies they take in?"

"Six weeks, if you can believe that!" James answered.

Charles continued to watch Rebecca uncomfortably parading up and down the kitchen and felt so surprised how his feelings for her had altered. Sitting at the table today made him realise just how far he had been prepared to compel his feelings and desires to remain at the top of the game. Like a square peg in a round hole, he had tried to force her to fit into his life, all for the sake of social status and money. Now, however, his prayers had been answered. Aided by the worst lovemaking he had ever encountered and the fact that hoards of money was about to plop into his bank account any day, his obsessive compulsion to win Rebecca Santé had ceased. It felt comforting to be freed from yet another mania. Yes that mania, like cubes of jelly in boiling water, had dissolved and, these days, he had much more interesting topics to discuss and dwell upon.

"Did I tell you I have bought the Villa in Barbados we all used to stay in when we were younger?" he announced proudly to the table.

"Really?" Victoria answered. "The one that used to be owned by the Thompsons?" Charles nodded. "Well that's fantastic news, Charles. Kitty, I am sure, would be delighted that you are not only investing the money wisely in property but also somewhere that will hold such fond dear memories of the family times you all shared out there." She turned to her husband, "Wouldn't she James?"

"Yes, yes, she would." he nodded approvingly, sensing his wife's urge for encouragement. "We know from Gerard's death, keeping memories alive are the only thing that will get you through the pain."

Rebecca picked up the baby and kissed him on his head. "That's true."

Charles took a breath. "By the way, talking of Mother, you have been called to the will-reading on the fifteenth of January, have you?"

"Yes, we have," Victoria answered giving, a shifty sideways glance to Rebecca.

Charles felt slightly relieved; they were obviously the ones that Hugh Stephenson had referred to. "Well, that's understandable, you were her great friends. I am sure she will have left you something special to remember her by." Remembering that Hugh Stephenson had spoken in plural as to the people he needed to contact, his mind urged him to probe a little more. "Do you know of any other invitees?" he asked casually, though feeling embarrassed at having to ask.

"No," Victoria answered swiftly. "Not that I know of."

James got up from the table and slid the kettle onto the hot plate of the Aga. His wife was lying; in the last week they had received several calls from old acquaintances, all informing them of their invitation to attend the reading. They had relayed the information with scurrying whispers across the line, having been sworn to secrecy, and risking goodness knows what by repeating their summons.

James Santé listened to the steam beginning to pour from the kettle. Even though he had spent a long time perusing Kitty's reasoning behind the list of attendees, still his varying hypotheses proved doubtful. He felt sorry for Charles, but, as much as he loved him and felt torn, he knew discussing the secret was not possible. He had known Kitty well; there must be a good reason for the confidentiality that was bound to her requests.

He just felt uneasy; one of the most sentimental and private times of Charles' life was about to be invaded.

Chapter Fifty Six

LUCA just couldn't wait any longer. Since issuing instructions for Professor Sanderson's colleague to take over the tests he had heard nothing. Now, two days later, he managed to get through to Dr Carnes' secretary.

"I'm sorry, he is not in his office at the moment, Mr DeMario, but I am sure he has completed the tests and has the results."

In the background, Luca heard the secretary shuffle the papers and thought of the results being somewhere among them; the suspense incensed him.

"Do you have the results?" he asked with eager impatience.

"I'm afraid that, even if I did, I am not in a position to read them out over the telephone, only Dr Carnes can speak to you about the results."

"I asked you if you had the results, not if you could read the bloody thing," Luca snapped furiously. "Have you got those results?" he demanded.

Her voice turned professionally cold. "Yes, Mr DeMario, I believe the results are available. However, until Dr Carnes returns I am unable to help you." Luca heard her take pleasure in delivering the frustrating news. "I will tell Dr Carnes to contact you as soon as he is able upon his return," she added.

Please, please," Luca begged, "tell him it's urgent."

"Yes, Mr DeMario. Goodbye," her angered voice broke off the call.

Luca looked at his watch, it was ten a.m. He would give him half an hour, if he hadn't returned his call by then he would call back. That is what he would do, every half hour and on the hour he would continue to call, *they* would tire of him before *he* tired of calling.

Julia thought she was going collapse from hypertension. She hadn't slept at all. With the dreading and loathing of what the break of day would bring she had found it impossible.

She began to dress, they had told her to wear something comfortable, something that would ease the pressure against her stomach. She pulled on a pair of stretchy black leggings and a long black jumper. She heard her father whistling to the tune of Whitney Huston's *I Will Always Love You* and wondered if he had felt that the day she was born. She couldn't remember another day in her life where she really wanted to have a heart to heart conversation with her father. Today she would have welcomed a conversation with anyone that would ease this gut-wrenching feeling.

She looked back at the opened directory and the large circle that highlighted her one o'clock appointment at the clinic. All the procedures were undertaken in Leeds, so she had to set off in good time in order to catch the train. She pulled her hair back into an untidy French knot, secured it with a clip and glanced at her mobile sitting by the side of her bed. It would stay there for today, the last thing she needed was distractions. Sombrely she walked out into the sitting area.

"Now then, 'ow are you this mornin'?" her father asked.

Shall I tell him the truth or shall I lie? "Fine thanks," she answered with a weak smile.

"What are you up to today then?" he asked.

Julia couldn't bear it; she looked across the room and into his hazel eyes and wished she could tell him. What would he say? Could he help her?

"I'm going to Leeds," she answered quickly. "I will be back around six." She looked away from his stare and bit down hard against her bottom lip.

"You alright?" he asked, his concern plainly evident.

She turned her back and nodded, unable to show her tear filled eyes. She grabbed her coat. "I'll see you later," she shouted over her shoulder.

"Hell fire!" Her father shuffled back into his armchair. "There is nothing queerer than bloody women," he mumbled to himself.

Luca was in his car. He just couldn't bear to be at home anymore. Not long ago his home had been his sanctuary, a safe secure place for him to hide, to cocoon himself away from the pressure and stress of the outside world. Now, though, it was a place that helped to cause it.

He was driving to York, he was adamant that today he would see Julia, even if it meant sitting outside on the steps of her caravan and taking squatters' rights until she showed up.

He looked at the clock on the dashboard, it was ten thirty. If he could get the good news now, he was certain that his happiness would grow wings in order to get to her sooner. Again he dialled the number and this time after repeated rings even the secretary didn't answer the call. He left a message.

"Luca, DeMario here. Obviously I am still awaiting a return call from Dr Carnes regarding my results. I would appreciate a call back as soon as possible."

It would take him approximately forty minutes to get to Julia, in that time he was sure he would have heard some news.

Julia sat on the train. It was the slow train, the one that stopped at every conceivable town and village on the way into Leeds. She had picked this slow train purposefully, thinking that she would appreciate the time for reflection and, if she was honest, delay her arrival into Leeds. She wondered if she had made the wrong choice. She began to feel claustrophobic. This journey was taking too long. She looked at her watch, it was ten fifty-five. In another two hours her procedure would possibly be underway. She felt sick.

"Fucking arsehole!" Luca shouted looking at the clock again and seeing yet another thirty minutes had passed with still no call from Dr Carnes. Without hesitation he called back again, this time the secretary answered.

"Dr Carnes has just called me. I passed on your message but unfortunately he is delayed by heavy traffic at present. He said he would be back in the office in ten minutes. He will call you then, Mr DeMario."

Luca couldn't stand to say goodbye, her voice and her professional smoothness jarred at his agitated mood. He put the phone down. He was on the outskirts of York, surely, next time he saw and spoke to Julia he would have the news that she, just like he, so desperately wanted to hear.

At eleven thirty Julia sat at a table in the station feeling so terribly sick. The journey had been long, bumpy and uncomfortable. All these factors had heightened her pregnancy sickness. She took the tiniest sips of cold mineral water from the bottle and wished she didn't have so much time to waste. She rubbed her tired eyes and, though she knew it was possible to walk to her appointment, she decided to take a taxi. The thought of walking through the crowds of strangers filled her with dread. There was only one person she wished she could see today, but that, she knew, was impossible. Poor Luca, she mused, how it would break his heart if he knew where she was about to go.

He had waited so long for it, Luca almost burst when the call actually came.

The doctor cleared his throat before he began. "Sorry about the delay," he told Luca.

"That's okay," Luca quickly urged, "have you got the results, Dr Carnes?"

"Yes, I have," he answered. Once again as though he too was nervous, Dr Carnes cleared his throat for the second time.

Luca was stationary in his car, already parked at the side of the road with his engine switched off; he closed his eyes and rested his head on the headrest whilst he awaited the news.

"Mr DeMario," the voice declared across the cars speakers. Luca held his breath in complete trepidation. "I can tell you that…"

Julia was an hour early for her appointment, but she decided to make her way to the clinic anyway. The sooner she got there the less likely she was to lose her nerve. She could read the magazines and feel safe that the people around her would at least understand her plight. There, although all reasons would differ, everyone was in the same boat.

As she walked around the corner she felt her legs become heavy and her steps, referred to by many in the past as elegant, now thudded gravely upon the pavement. The glass doors to the clinic were ahead of her, this was her final destination that would include her baby being with her.

She couldn't call it anything else but 'her baby.' The clinic referred to it as an embryo and, yes, maybe medically that was the correct term, but every moment of the day that embryo was gaining strength and growing in *her womb*, a place where it had lodged in the belief it was a safe haven to develop into *her baby*. She imagined the birth and seeing her baby for the first time. In her mind she stroked its thick mass of black hair and pictured herself smiling down at its minute features. A painful gust of memory propelled her body and mind with the recollection of the passionate love making that she and Luca had shared on the night she was sure her baby had been conceived. Her strength began to drain away, causing her to feel too weak to fight back her tears.

She neared the steps to the doorway. With teardrops galloping down her cheeks, she looked up at the building. It was large, large enough for Julia to look like a tiny pea against the mass of tinted privacy glass that encased the outside. She slowed her walk to a standstill and rested herself against the glass front. How had her life come to this? She demanded internally. She searched inside her pocket for her mobile then recalled leaving it behind.

She needed to speak to Luca *now*. He was her friend, her lover, her soul mate. She crouched upon the dirty pavement, oblivious to who saw her or what they thought. Her uncontrollable sobs, along with the pain and regret that surged through her chest, signalled that her heart was breaking.

Freedom! Freedom! Freedom! The word sailed through his head over and over. He drove towards the camp; his eyes wrinkled in joyful creases all the way to his temples whilst his mouth arched with a broad, proud smile. He heard his blackberry beep with an incoming email, written confirmation from Dr Carnes of the results. He couldn't wait to see her, couldn't wait to hear the information spilling from his mouth and couldn't wait to see her reaction as she assimilated the news for herself. It was true; they were now free, free to marry, free to be a family, and free from the controlling reins of his father.

Luca swooped into the clearing next to the camp, pulled his keys out of the engine and ran through the site toward her caravan. Luca was oblivious to the younger inhabitants of the camp staring in disbelief that a Mercedes SL, a shining luxury, stood still, beckoning them to investigate with the driver's door wide open. A recent downpour that had now ceased left the ground slippery with mud; Luca lost his footing several times but his eyes remained firmly fixed on the door of the caravan.

Noisily, with an internal excitement that was almost unbearable to contain he thudded upon the door.

"Julia! Julia!" he shouted

"Oh, not again," her father mumbled inside. He lifted himself from his armchair and ambled toward the door.

"Hi! It's washing day again is it, Mr Smith?" Luca laughed as he looked at the under-pant clad giant in front of him.

"Yep, sure is! You always seem to call when I'm in me undies and Julia is not in."

Luca's face dropped, his disappointment and annoyance rose. "Look. No offence, Mr Smith, but please, cut the bullshit." He pushed through the door and, amazingly, Julia's father stood to one side.

Luca strode forcefully straight toward Julia's room to find that she was indeed not there. Her room was empty, her bed was made, the curtains were drawn and just looking at the evidence of her morning's preparation to leave the caravan made him miss her all the more. He swung round to face her father.

"Where is she today?" he demanded impatiently, his eyes shifting quickly around the caravan at the open doors this time so evidently unguarded.

Her father shrugged. "I dunno," he answered honestly. "She left this morning, she didn't say where."

Luca walked over to him. "Please, if you know, please tell me. I have some news for her, news that will change our lives forever." His eyes begged for information, pleaded for understanding.

"Honestly, Luca lad, I have no idea."

Luca slid his fingers desperately through his hair; he had no idea where to start looking. He pulled his mobile from his pocket and called her number, the ringing of her phone led him back to her room.

"Fucking hell!" he shouted before plunging onto her bed.

Her father's huge frame stood in the doorway and watched Luca's desperation. He felt sorry for him but simultaneously bemused by this week's continual visits.

"What information do you have for 'er, I can pass on the message when she gets back? Or, why don't I get her to call ya?"

Luca jumped in temper from the bed. "I don't have time to wait for her to return, I need to find her now!" he shouted, walking toward the window. Angrily he thumped a closed directory on top of her makeshift desk "I need to talk to her now." He repeated aggressively.

Mr Smith was all too familiar with aggression and tempers, he personally found them hard to contain. However, he recognised instinctively that there was something within Luca's behaviour that spoke more of an all-consuming urgency than anger, he felt duty bound to sympathise.

"Look, Luca," he said, walking over to him "Why don't I put the kettle on, we can 'ave a cup a tea then, me clothes'll be dry and we can go and take a look for 'er together. 'Ow does that sound?"

Luca rubbed his hands together and nervously tapped his foot against the floor. He looked up and gave Mr Smith a weak nod, along with an even weaker smile. As her father walked from the door happy to have made brief appeasement, Luca looked around her room. He noticed that the directory upon her desk had a scrap piece of paper edging out of the middle of its thick wedge of pages. He reached for it.

Opening the directory he pulled out the piece of paper. He read the words upon it,

The clinic, 36 Westergate Road, Leeds, Wednesday 1p.m.

Then with a frown that furrowed his brow like a knarled tree branch, he looked back at the directory. 'The Clinic' was circled in blue biro, beneath the title the description of '*Women's health issues and confidential abortion.*' His emotions plunged to the depths of his feet.

"NO, NO, NO!" he exploded. "Julia, you can't do this!" he boomed. He felt weak; he began to shake and the cold rush of fever seeped through the skin on his forehead. He wrestled with his shirt cuffs to check the time. It was twelve o'clock. He had one hour to get to her, could he make it?

Mr Smith came back with two hot steaming mugs of tea but, like a whippet after a hare, Luca had already gone.

Chapter Fifty Seven

JULIA sat in the waiting room, she sat still, staring blankly ahead and silently wishing there was another option other than the one she faced. She was one of three women sitting within the room, all three of them tried hard not to make eye contact. One of the women moved, Julia looked up, their eyes met, the stranger's eyes were rimmed with fearful tears. Julia immediately looked away, feeling as though she had intruded on her privacy, but realised her heart was not the only one breaking within this room. The radio, playing from discrete speakers within the wall, tried its damndest to break the emotional silence, but all it did was remind each one of them that, regardless of *their* turmoil, life outside went on.

They sat and waited for their names to be called out. *Like lambs to the slaughter,* Julia thought morbidly. She could feel her heart thudding against her chest and a bulging, banging pulse that she could clearly feel swelling within her throat. She was frightened, more frightened than she had ever been in her life, not just about the procedure that was to follow, but about how she would be able to continue with her life once it was over. After today, she knew a large part of her would never be the same again. This experience would change forever the way in which she thought and lived. Julia hated the possibility of becoming resilient and hard.

The conscious throbbing of Julia's pulse continued to aggravate her self-control. The cold bare facts rolled over and over in her mind, she wanted this baby more than she wanted anything, she also wanted its father, but the cruel sadistic actions of Frankie DeMario had taken away her freedom of choice. Her eyes narrowed, she was glad he was dead, she hated him.

Julia's heart leapt in the air like a threatened gazelle as the receptionist walked into the room. She looked around at the three women before smiling briefly and looking down at her list of names. In her mind, Julia begged it not be hers. She called out a name, Julia felt her shoulders slump in relief, it was not her, she had more time. One of the ladies, the one that had made tearful eye contact with Julia, stood up and slowly walked toward the door. Julia felt nothing but commiseration for her; she looked up at the clinical white clock that hung on the wall. The black ticking hands continued to consume the seconds; it was twelve forty, only twenty minutes to go and then she knew, she would also feel that same commiseration for herself *and* her baby.

Luca screamed with a mighty force. His face was angry and his mind was almost fizzing out of control. He had watched every minute on the electronic clock on his dashboard pass by, and now, at twelve forty-five he had hit a tailback of queuing traffic caused by an unrelenting downpour of rain. The automatic wipers on his car began to swipe away the rain in an aggressive attempt to clear his windscreen. The sky darkened to a gloomy sheet of slate grey; cautious motorists began to turn on their headlights, some even put on their hazard lights, warning vehicles behind of impending danger and delay.

"Fuck, Fuck, Fuck!" he screamed banging his fist against the horn. A selection of other frustrated motorists, taking his anger as a personal affront, retaliated with repeated blows of their own and Luca, his fury increasing by their petty outbursts, slammed his hand upon his horn and held it there.

Fifteen minutes and one mile away, he knew he was on the right road. Without traffic it was a five minute journey, but this queue was going nowhere fast. He looked at the hard shoulder and was about to use it, but saw a car with its hazard lights on, blocking the whole lane.

"How the fuck can I make it?" he hissed through gritted teeth.

He couldn't take this any longer and with that decision all his senses disappeared. With a determination like he had never experienced before, he thrust his gearbox into park and grabbed the keys from the ignition. As he opened the door the forceful wind and the driving storm that pounded the rain against his face barely registered. There was one thing he realised; if he didn't try, he would never make it. With an athletic prowess that left the rest of the queuing motorists open mouthed, Luca began to run.

"Julia Smith?" The receptionist asked with the same timid smile as accompanied her last entrance to the room.

Julia stared back at her and then looked back at the clock, she was five minutes early. Those five minutes meant everything to Julia; she wanted to tell her to come back in a moment and that she wasn't ready yet. But, she knew she would never be ready for this. She stood up and reached for her bag and, as she did, her hands began to shake uncontrollably and that pulse thing in her neck returned and almost throbbed her tonsils from her throat. She followed the lady into a small consulting room where a woman sat in a professional white uniform. She looked up.

"Hello, Julia," she greeted.

Julia felt unstoppable tears begin to drain from her eyes and short sharp whimpers burst from her mouth, never had she felt so terrified.

Luca ran, with all his strength, he ran. He could hear his footsteps hammering against the dull pavements. It was a sound he would remember for eternity, his racing footsteps on a frantic mission to stop Julia from doing something they would both regret. He continued to run through the streets, his shoes tramped obliviously through the numerous puddles and rushing gutters. The rainwater, with every one of his strides, took pleasure in soaking his clothes. He was wearing only a shirt and jeans and now he was saturated, the water dripped from his face and the wind battered against his wet body, but he had no care for any of it. He just needed to be with Julia. He only had two more streets to go and then he would be with her.

"Please, Lord." he begged breathlessly, "Please, let there have been a delay, please let her be late." He ran with greater exertion, he needed to get to her before it was too late.

Julia pulled back the curtain and stood uncomfortably still snivelling in a nightshirt she had been requested to bring.

"Look, Julia," the consultant informed her, sympathetically reaching for her hand, "I have decided we will give you a mild sedative today to numb the procedure a little for you. Now then, a nurse is going to be with you the whole time, she will hold your hand and look after you, and I can assure you the pregnancy is so small it will literally take only a few minutes."

Julia nodded, admittedly the consultants kindness was helping. The consultant sat on the edge of a bed and gave her the injection. With a whoosh of comfort a clarifying meltdown began to take place. She felt her emotions begin to calm, she felt her pounding heartbeat begin to slow, and the pulse in her neck stopped its incessant terrified banging. She felt sleepy and closed her eyes, then felt the warmth of a blanket being placed over her torso.

"Julia," the nurse said softly clamping her hand tightly, "we just need you to put your feet inside those stirrups at the edge of the bed, please."

Julia felt herself tense up again as the nurse's words reminded her of her whereabouts. Delirious with trauma and sedation, she lifted her heavy, lifeless legs one after the other into the restraints that hung in mid-air. She heard the cruel clank of metal instruments by the foot of the bed. *This is it now*, she thought. She felt the reassuring squeeze of the nurse's hand in hers and clamped her eyes tightly shut. Like the consultant had said, *in a few moments this will all be over.*

Luca dived through the street and saw the building with the same company name and logo as in the directory. He ran up to the doors, they were locked and intercoms secured the building inside and out along with the menacing stare of mini cameras. He rattled the doors briefly before standing to the side out of view, he had seen a figure approaching from the inside, and she was coming out. As the door opened, Luca dived inside, sending the woman spinning in the doorway.

"Sorry!" he shouted over his shoulder and ran into reception. "JULIA!" he shouted at the top of his voice. He turned round and round in mad circles hoping to connect with her through one of the various doorways and rooms "JULIA, JULIA SMITH!" He bellowed again, "IT'S LUCA!"

"Call security," one of the receptionists ordered to a colleague.

Julia inched her way onto her elbows, "It's Luca," she whispered disbelievingly. She listened again. This time the voice was even louder.

"JULIA, JULIA, PLEASE!" he hollered.

"Please, no," she whimpered, deliriously scraping her legs from the hoists. "It's Luca. I can hear him," she told them. "He's here." She tried to sit. LUCAAAAAAAA.......!" she shouted.

His name ricocheted against every one of the clinic walls.

Chapter Fifty Eight

IT WAS SIX A.M. and Julia's eyes slowly opened. Whilst she listened to Luca's restful, sleeping breaths by her side her large eyes blinked ravenously at the prospect of a brand new day, a brand new life. Her heart flipped and turned as she remembered yesterday's trauma and then allowed her mind to revel in the tender facts. Luca had saved her from it all. She turned onto her side to face him, her wonderful, brave, adorable Luca she appraised, an ecstatic smile adorned her fresh young face.

She leant her elbow on the soft white pillow and stared down at his shadowy face, allowing the delightful memories of the night before to flood her mind. When Luca had told his family of their reconciliation, a look of unquenchable love and adoration had smothered his face, and his hand, so protectively clasped around hers, had gripped tighter as the ecstasy of the news sank into his own mind. Julia, beaming with pride, had watched their faces avidly. Their reactions had been as they expected. His mother had given her blessing with genuine affection. However, acrimonious looks of hostility from his sisters had reigned savagely upon her. Julia had brushed their disdain for her to one side; she had no intention of allowing them to seize her day. After what they had gone through together nothing could ever stand in their way again.

She heard the winter's rain pattering against the window and the wind, so fierce in its fight to enter the room, howled ferociously outside. She wondered for a second if the aggression of its howl was the after-life of his father, still determined to expel her from his home and his son's life, but she fervidly pushed the idea from her mind. There was one thing that Frankie DeMario *didn't* get involved in, and that was wasting time.

Her thoughts slowly drifted away from herself and Luca and towards the conversation she had had with her father. She had telephoned him and informed him of her news, he had been utterly delighted.

"Me? A granddad?" he had confirmed disbelievingly, forgetting to ask where she had been and why Luca has rushed off so quickly.

"Yes!" Julia had responded with relish. He gave out a huge hearty laugh.

"Well done, me' girl! You know 'ow to make ya daddy 'appy. You'd better put Luca on."

Luca had taken the phone.

"You'd better get yerself round 'ere lad and get the baby's 'ed wet with some of me cider, I've got a bloody good batch in, this time I brewed it me'self!"

"Fabulous idea," Luca had answered with a twisted grimace.

After a brief chat between the two men her father had then asked Luca to put Julia back on.

"Ey, by the way, a letter has arrived for you this morning, it looks like som'et posh, it's got a stamp on, and I can tell it's nothin' to do with the coppers."

Julia's mind raced, wondering if it could be anything to do with 'The clinic,' but then her nerves tempered, remembering that she had specifically asked them not to write. Intrigued, she responded.

"Will you open it please, Dad, I don't know when I will be home next," she told him looking over at Luca with a smile.

Julia, lying still in the bed, recalled the contents, it was written confirmation regarding the phone call she had received a week ago. *A summons to witness Kitty Lancaster-Baron's will-reading in three weeks time? Why?* she asked herself again for the hundredth time. She shuffled nervously in the bed at the thought of associating herself with 'those people' again, but yet, ashamedly, she couldn't help but feel that her interest was already captured.

The winter had proved laboriously long with the weather barely breaking from the monotonous descent of darkness and sheer bitter cold. Despite the cruel winter, Charles had found incredible solace in that. He too, had felt 'Lady Luck' on his side.

The Lancaster-Baron family name had spoken volumes in obtaining temporary credit for his newly acquired possessions. He looked across at the ravishing red Ferrari in the drive, he thought of the villa in Barbados, purchased more from the need for sentiment of happier times than the desire to travel and, of course, refusing to be outdone by Hugo, Charles had a brand new helicopter of his every own, and due to be delivered by the end of the week.

Although his recent purchases had managed to offer subtle compensation for the enormous void his mother's death had left in his life, he was nevertheless looking forward to his financial worries coming to a close. The day of the will-reading was nigh, tomorrow in fact, a day when all his purchases and debts could finally be paid. That, at least, was one major problem solved, but he felt strange. This financial freedom was all he had ever yearned for, the reason for his unscrupulous dealings in the past, and yet now, he felt there was something, in fact a large part of him, completely missing and empty.

He sat upon a bale of hay beneath the large canopy of the stable block, surrounded by a new delivery of straw and hay. Wrapping a strand of hay in repeated twists between his thick, experienced fingers, he was happy to rest a while and allow the time to pass in solitary state. His taupe wax jacket was old and worn, it crumpled softly into seamless cracking folds and the faded familiarity of its sandy colour harmonised effortlessly with the choppy lengths of his blonde hair.

Darcy, his mother's black Labrador, sat by his feet licking horse muck from his green wellingtons. The other dogs circled close by, sniffing at the ground and chewing on trimmed horse hooves, remnants of the blacksmith's visit the day before. Ironically, having never done it when his mother was alive, he had mucked out and fed the horses every day since she had died and, rather oddly, had actually begun to enjoy his chores, not least because, whilst he was there, he felt the strength of her presence alongside him.

He looked down at Darcy and clicked his tongue to beckon her attention. She swiped her chubby sausage tail through the air and slid her ears to the side of her head, immediately responding with a deep affectionate smile of respect and a wet-nosed nuzzle of appreciation. He stroked the smooth contours of her head and again, like every other time he paid attention to a dog's presence, thoughts of Paris came to mind.

She had loved those dogs she used to walk, and God; with all his heart he missed her. Her amazingly pretty eyes came into view and their presence was so clear it was as though she was in front of him. He slowly shook his head as a signal of personal disdain. Those eyes, he pondered again with fond remembrance, like priceless sapphires, shining with a trusting loyalty, he knew he would never experience such authentic charm within anyone again. He wondered what she would say if he was to travel to see her in Spain? Then, his sprits wilted. He was not stupid; it was obvious what her reaction would be. He had ruined her life, trampled all over it and then continued with his own life as if none of her pain mattered. Would he ever be lucky enough to see her again? He foraged for an answer and looked back into the eyes of the serving Labrador. After everything he had done to it, he felt saddened and humbled by the loyalty she showed to him. He didn't deserve it. What a fool I have been – to everyone, he concluded.

Paris Montford walked slowly down the steel steps of the plane and inhaled the unmistakable chill of the British air. It had been almost two months since her and her father had left for Spain, and now, she realised, England's winter weather was something she had not missed.

In truth, she hadn't missed a lot about England. They now lived in a modest rustic villa which backed on to an orchard bulging with orange and lemon trees and even the bark on their dainty trunks effervesced with the tang of citrus that swamped the surrounding air with mouth-watering clarity. Every day they woke to the morning sun filtering its way through the wooden shutters; they lunched daily in local tavernas, feasting on traditional helpings of lentil stews and paellas, bursting with fresh seafood and crisp salads with a medley of ingredients that exploded with colour and taste. She had even made a new friend, Sarah, an outgoing English girl who had married Paulo, a kind and handsome Spanish bar owner. The two of them had made her and her father feel very welcome in their new surroundings and had even taken Paris on a few nights out to the local town. Most unexpectedly she had enjoyed herself and, although the burning loss for the son she had given away never left her heart, the Spanish turf and fresh wholesome food had been exactly what she had needed to recharge her body and soul.

Paris was all too aware that it wasn't just Spain she had to thank for her revitalisation. The stray dogs she had rescued to save from a cruel fate had also given her good reason to get up on a morning. She pulled her mobile from her jacket pocket and tried once again to contact her mother, but again, there was no reply. She had tried repeatedly to contact Francesca to inform her of her stay but as yet all her calls and messages had gone unanswered. She would see her soon enough, she thought.

She heard her high heels tap against the makeshift staircase and realised that, with every step, she was one step closer to seeing Charles again. The will-reading was only hours away, and although she still didn't have a clue why she had been invited, her instincts told her that her day with Charles Lancaster-Baron was yet to come. Her smile grew more pronounced.

Revenge, she had heard, was a dish best served cold.

Chapter Fifty Nine

PARIS drove the small hire car toward Goldsborough Crescent. As she drove up the old familiar road it was plainly evident by the way she erratically switched radio stations and impatiently slammed the air vents up and down, that the journey into the Crescent was rekindling many unwanted emotions. Her primary reason twisted her gut. Should she not have been duped into giving away her baby she would still have been here and, for all she enjoyed living in Spain, the thought of being a mother and holding and nurturing her baby son, ran far beyond the preference of location.

She tried to swallow away the lump that had formed so suddenly in her throat, and feeling she needed some reprieve from her anguish, she decided to call her father.

"Are you there yet?" Bill asked.

"Yes, I've just parked at the entrance to the Crescent to call you," she said quietly.

"Have you seen her yet? Are you alright?" Bill had tried so hard to discourage her from returning home for this ridiculous will-reading and had been worried from the minute she had left the house.

"No, I haven't seen *Mum* yet, and yes, *Dad*, I'm fine," she assured. "I wish you had come with me though, you were invited just the same as I was."

"Well, however worried I am about you Paris, I will no sooner accept an invitation from that lot than I would set foot on Chelmsley soil while your mother and that Charles Lancaster-Baron are there."

"Sometimes people can change, you know," Paris answered sadly. "Mum, I mean," she quickly added.

"Those kind of people, your mother *and* the likes of Lancaster-Baron," he spat his name, "will never change, you can be as optimistic as you like, but I know, I have been around them, willing them to change for far too long."

Paris sighed, "Well, I'm just calling to remind you of everything. Don't forget that Slinky needs her antibiotics this afternoon, will you?"

"No," Bill answered, casually reading the 'dog to do list' she had already gone through with him several times before she left.

"And don't forget that Daisy, you know which one Daisy is, don't you? The one with the black patch on her eye, she needs to have the wound on her leg redressed. If you get too squeamish Paulo will help you." She hesitated. "And, Dad…"

"Mmmmmm," Bill answered.

"Will you slyly give Chuck a piece of ham without the others seeing?" She wondered if her father would notice her sentiment and the essence of favouritism in her voice. "It's just that, I feel so guilty at leaving him, he is only just warming to me, it's good to keep to the routine while I'm not there," she added casually.

"How long will you be anyway, when will you be home?" her father asked with concern.

"I won't be long; I'll call you, and don't worry!"

"You really should not have gone," he told her again.

"Bye, Dad." Paris smiled feigning exasperation.

"Bye, Paris," Bill answered, sitting down and wondering how much more trouble and upset the visit would bring to his daughter.

Paris was pleased to get off the phone; every time she spoke about Chuck to her father she expected that the truth would be exhumed as to where the idea of his name had been derived. He had known the reasoning behind the names of the others, but strangely, about the naming of Chuck he had never asked.

Chuck was a golden mongrel, but not a mongrel in the common

sense of the word, just an indistinguishable, yet very handsome breed. He had a feral curly coat which was a mass of golden matted tangles when he had initially arrived. She had found him scavenging on a rubbish tip and, as he turned to face her that day, it was the wild suspicion in his eyes and his stunningly proud face that she had found so irresistible. In that very instant, noticing his alert pricked ears, his strong thick neck ceremoniously arched and his large powerful frame, he had reminded her of one person, Charles.

Slowly she had approached him, rubbing her fingers together soothingly and quite naturally, unprompted by thought, the name Chuck began to be whispered from her lips. Her presumptions had proved to be correct; within days of her taking him back to her home she had also discovered his insatiable habit for delivering the most unpredictable mood swings.

When his mood was compliant he would allow her to bathe him and would stand whilst she patiently brushed out the tangles one by one whilst she fed him treats from her hand. An hour later he would stand with his back against the wall and snarl savagely, threatening definite hurt if she was to come closer. She would do as he asked of her and leave him. Then, a little later, after not being able to get him from her mind she would return with more treats. Gently, given time, he would take it, but the titbit would remain hanging from his mouth, he would stare back at her with eyes that were so distrusting, surprised at her return. Yet, it was so clear in the way he hung his head as if showing shame in the way he had treated her, that he was ever hopeful in his search for love. Paris knew she needed time; time to show him that not everything in this world was as cruel as he imagined. She started the car's engine again and realised once more, Charles and Chuck really were so very much alike.

Reflecting with disappointment on all that had transpired, Paris indicated to turn left and, looking in her rear view mirror, she instantly felt her spirits lift by the repeated surprise of her reflection. Her once dulling blonde hair had been exchanged for a chic baby blonde bob that framed her pretty face. Her previously chubby red cheeks had been banished and in their place high cheekbones protruded from beneath a coating of tanned, flawless skin, and her body ...

"Yes!" she announced appreciatively to the empty car.

That too had been transformed. Her five foot seven frame that had previously gone unnoticed behind baggy oversized clothes had been emphasised by a much slimmer body. Unintentionally she had lost two stone. Her new regime of healthy eating and the urge to walk away the pain of her past along the beach with her dogs had awoken every facet of her physical and mental existence. Even her eyes had responded to her new life. There was a time they had appeared devoid of life, as though they had ruefully accepted the cards her existence had been dealt. Now, they shone like invaluable jewels, as though they had witnessed an internal phenomenon and were now celebrating the awe-inspiring possibilities of life.

She turned into Goldsborough Crescent and the brass sign that greeted the horseshoe gathering of houses forced her whole body to tense. It reminded her of her mother's grandiose demeanour when telling people of their address; she remembered the essence of pride in her voice that overflowed into their home like the sour curdle of milk, and the inhabitants within it, fully aware that her smugness was backed up with nothing but an ever swelling enormity of debt. She was sure that just escaping from these falsities had improved her state of mind; she hated the life her mother had forced upon her. She drove on, chastising herself for dwelling on the negatives. After all, she thought with conviction, just like dogs, people can also change.

"I can't believe you're not coming over tonight," Charles informed Hugo, trying to disguise his insecurities at being alone. Hugo remained silent. "What time will you be arriving in the morning then?" Charles continued sharply.

"Shit!" Hugo answered with a muffled laugh. "Get off!" he muttered, placing his hand over the receiver, clearly trying to prevent Charles from hearing the second of his two way conversation.

"Who have you got there with you?" Charles demanded with rising irritation.

"Amy," Hugo answered truthfully, oblivious to Charles' dark mood. "We'll be arriving at about ten a.m."

"What do you mean, we?"

"Amy is coming too, she says she will be a good girl and sit at the back, didn't you my precious?"

"You can't bring her!" Charles shouted. "This is a private family affair."

Hugo didn't respond again, but Charles heard Amy giggle and it became quite clear that Hugo was as high as a helium balloon on drugs and, no doubt, Charles concluded, having met Amy once over the Christmas period, she would be too.

Charles ended the call, realising there was no point trying to discuss the issue. He sank into his mother's favourite chair in the drawing room and aggressively ran his fingers through his hair. *How the hell had her two sons ended up like this?* he wondered. What a mess. Her eldest son, should she not have died when she did, would most certainly be bankrupt, and the other, a reputed banker in the city, was now heavily addicted to cocaine. His phone beeped, it was a message from Rebecca, it read;

Thinking of you tonight, if you need me, you know where I am. Otherwise see you tomorrow; do you need a lift to the hotel?

Ignoring the message, he reached down to the side of the chair, picked up his bottle of scotch and drank a large slug straight from the neck. He rubbed some of the spillage from his chin and felt the scruffy shabbiness of stubble, stubble that his mother so hated to see on a man. *I have to make an effort*, he told himself, *for her last appearance I must show respect*. Charles began to think, *if she were here, what would Mother most want me to wear tomorrow?*

He stood, walked upstairs and opened the oak wardrobe doors that housed his formal attire. Coincidentally, the first item of clothing he noticed was his navy blue blazer. *She loved to see me wearing this,* he remembered, *it was her favourite*. He pulled it from its hanger and chose a crisp white shirt and a blue and red tie to compliment it. Then he reached for the gift his mother had given to him on his twenty-first birthday – a pair of diamond cufflinks. They had been her father's, she had handed them to him on his birthday morning with such emotion. He sat on the edge of his bed and sentimentally rubbed them between his fingers. It was clear by the way the diamonds sparkled and glistened in the lamp's light that the stones were first class. But what else would have been expected of his mother and his grandfather? The Lancaster-Baron name preceded them; they were exactly that, first class. *Once I get this money, Mother, I promise I will make it into so much more.* He bit his lip hard, hoping she could hear his thoughts.

"What a bloody mess," he whispered aloud, remembering all the opportunities and money he had wasted throughout his life.

Charles began to root around for his dark charcoal trousers, he would wear those. She had approved of those too. He sat back on the bed feeling unable to continue and a regretful solitary tear dropped down his face. Looking back at his attire that lay upon his bed, he made a promise both to himself and to his mother. As of tomorrow he would make her proud.

It would have come as such a startling and loathsome surprise to Charles if he had known how many others were also choosing their outfits for the will-reading the next day. Yet they were, in droves. However, due to the so called secrecy of the summons, the pretentious stench of socialite gossip excreted itself in poisonous whispers through the negating underground of North Yorkshire.

"What are you wearing?" they asked one another with cruel undertones shading their upper-class voices. "What do you think is going on?" "Someone has mentioned it's the end of them and that the Lancaster-Baron name is history."

To the majority of these socialites, so called 'friends' of Charles', tomorrow was viewed with as much excitement as a public hanging would have been centuries before. They planned where they would meet for drinks before the event and where they would dine after the event. To them, it was a circus, the chance for a day out with the added thrill of obtaining authenticated information regarding another family's worth.

One lady in particular would have given her life for an invitation.

"When did you receive the letter?" Francesca hiccupped and stammered searching through her piles of unopened post.

Paris watched her mother's shaking hands, with her knotted hair and her thin, bony body poking from her nightshirt as she drunkenly spread out the piles of letters across the heavily wine-stained carpet.

Paris had been aghast when she had first entered the house. Firstly, not only had her mother's drunken compliments regarding her appearance nearly flawed her, the only compliment she could *ever* remember receiving from her, but the house that had once been so uncomfortably pristine was now in an appalling state. It was clear that her mother was now completely out of control with her drinking habits and verging on a breakdown.

"Just think," Francesca said, trying to heave herself up from the floor whilst sliding upon a mountain of post. "When Charles sees your transformation tomorrow, he might just share the lot with you," she said, standing and trying to focus, "you know, marry you!" Her eyes ignited into life as the dream in her inebriated mind took shape. "We would be back in there with them all, we could really show them all how to go on."

For the first time since her husband and daughter had left home, Francesca felt herself smile. This was her last grasp at the chance for a real life. "Oh please take me with you tomorrow, Paris, please." she begged.

It was the first time her mother had asked her for anything, the first time she had needed her, but as ever, her gluttonous needs were to satisfy a flawed and lonely mind. Paris felt heartbroken and fought the instinct to shake her mother into reality. She could see that Francesca Montford was a broken woman without her husband, a husband that in her eyes had never made the social grade. She was lonely and desperate, yet, her need for acceptance within a false deceptive world drove her blindly, like an addict to drugs, to the same circles that made her retch in misery.

Paris couldn't speak, she felt smothered and gagged by the reminder of a life that had blighted her with unhappiness for so long.

"I'm going to the shop," she managed weakly. "Do you want anything?"

"Gin!" Francesca answered swiftly.

Paris parked up in the lay-by of a nearby country road and sat for several minutes, repetitively sliding her hands around the steering wheel as she trawled through the painful facts. Foolishly, she realised, she had expected her mother to have changed on her return. She had harboured a secret image of walking through the door to the smell of fresh baking, of walking into the kitchen to find her mother's hands appear bleached by the fine powder of self-raising flour and baking a cake. On seeing Paris her mother had rushed over to the kitchen doorway, hugged her with conviction and told her how much she had missed her only daughter.

Paris openly laughed in the car; *how could I have been so ridiculous?* Maybe her father was right, she thought sadly, maybe people really don't realise what is important in life, and maybe people *never* change. But, it was the last question she asked of herself that really hit home.

Are you going to emulate your own mother and have your son grow up to believe you didn't love him either?

The question bore so much pain. She had never looked at her son's life that way; selfishly believing that the pain she was going through since giving him up was all hers. *What will he think of you, the mother that gave him away?* The painful digging continued. She sank her head into her hands. The thought of instilling pain to her own flesh and blood and allowing him to believe she didn't love him reverberated with her own childhood and every facet of her past. She engaged her car into first gear.

She couldn't wait a moment longer; she swiftly pulled away from the roadside. She had all the motivation she needed to visit her son.

Chapter Sixty

REBECCA SANTÉ sat at the kitchen table with a large glass of wine and listened again to the baby screaming itself to sleep. This torture was now a daily and nightly occurrence; only her increasing anger bore any leverage on the monotony.

"This shit doesn't work!" she had shouted ten minutes after bounding back downstairs for the seventh time and throwing the small bottle of supposedly 'miracle colic cure' across the kitchen.

"I'll go to the chemist and buy some more," James had quietly suggested after picking up the bottle from the floor.

"Why are you *both* going?" she had shouted when she noticed her mother following her father outside.

"I'll speak to the pharmacist whilst your father waits in the car, there's never anywhere to park," Victoria had replied softly.

"You must think I am a bloody maniac, I know darn well it's so that you can talk about how bloody crap I am at all this!" she had yelled.

In a fiery rage, Rebecca slammed the door on them so she couldn't hear their response; simultaneously she had wished to God she could do the same to the baby.

So now she was left alone with the baby. She turned up the radio to try and drown out the deafening screams and waited for her mobile to respond with an incoming message from Charles. She wished he was here to take over, moreover she wished he would ask her over to Cedars Hall. That way, when her parents returned, she could just get away from this hell hole.

It was dark outside and, as the electric gates opened to allow James and Victoria onto the road, they were surprised to see a pair of bright headlights facing them. Paris got out of the car and walked to the driver's window.

"Goodness! Hello, Paris, I didn't recognise you then," greeted Victoria. "You are looking so well. Your hair so suits you," she added, feeling humble on remembering their last meeting in the hospital. "What brings you home?" she asked, trying to make general conversation and not thinking for a second it would be for the will-reading. "I believe you're living in Spain now?"

Paris was grateful that Victoria had fired several questions; she didn't want to give an answer as to the reason for her visit.

"Yes, I feel well thank you, Mrs Santé," Paris answered politely. "I just thought I would pop in to see you all, well, and the erm, my erm..."

"Yes, baby," Victoria added swiftly, feeling equally as embarrassed and unprepared in the situation.

"You go on in," James offered warmly. "Rebecca's there, she'll be glad to see you. We're only going to the chemist, we'll be back soon."

Paris smiled. "Thanks." She walked back to her car and made her way up the drive.

"Do you think that Rebecca would have wanted to see Paris?" Victoria asked James unsurely as they drove away.

"What do you mean? Of course she will," James answered looking perplexed. "With a racket like that going on, she needs some help, she won't care where or from whom she gets it."

When Paris got out of the car she could hear her son's screams from the driveway. Without hesitating she rushed to the kitchen door at the side of the house and knocked hard, all the while looking up at the window she thought the crying was blasting from.

Rebecca answered the door with her mobile in her hand and stood silent for a second whilst Paris' new appearance registered. However, when it did, for the second time that evening, the reception Paris received was not quite as she had envisaged.

"How did you get through the gates?" Rebecca asked as if talking to a member of her yard staff.

"Your parents let me in; I passed them as they were leaving for the chemist," Paris answered, feeling her hackles rise by both Rebecca's tone and the fact that the baby was still screaming with no relief or comfort in sight.

Rebecca looked at her watch. "It's nine thirty, Paris. Do you not think of phoning before you descend upon people's homes at this time of night?" Rebecca asked with a condescending frown and a slight shake of her head.

"Do *you* not think of comforting a screaming baby, Rebecca?"

The chill to Paris' words brought both women to an abrupt silence. They stared into each other's eyes; both of their moods blighted by the emotional torment of the day.

Paris broke the silence, unable to restrain the thick etch of sarcasm to her voice. "Look, you said that I could pop in any time to see *my* son Rebecca, can you remember that, the day you *took him* from me?

Rebecca's lips tightened into one fine angry line, she was about to respond but the baby's screams turned into a high pitched ear piercing screech causing them both to react.

Paris' heart began to erratically thump with the need to run to him, and Rebecca, completely incensed with anger, looked up at the ceiling above her head, allowing Paris to witness the look of scorn and infuriation she harboured for her baby. Rebecca turned and looked back at Paris with hatred burning in her eyes.

"Yes, as you have just confirmed Paris , you *gave* your baby away, and may I say," Rebecca's eyebrows arched and her eyes gloated pompously up and down Paris ' body, "I think it is a down right disgrace that you are accusing me of taking your baby from you. If you remember rightly, Paris, it was you who realised you would never cope."

Her words wounded Paris to her core and as the hurt clobbered, Paris made a lunge for the door in retaliation.

"You are not fit to have my baby," Paris shrieked.

Rebecca blocked her entry with a shove to the door and the brief struggle caused Rebecca's mobile to drop at Paris' feet as the door banged shut. As it hit the gravel the phone bleeped and the screen illuminated with an incoming message.

Paris looked down at her feet, the screen read,

'Message received, sender; Charles.'

The knife dug in deeper, they were all in it together, they had broken her heart and stolen her baby and now they refused to release her from their prison. She turned to face the door as she heard it bolt and lock behind her and, unable to control herself, Paris picked up the phone, launched it against the wall and witnessed it smash into smithereens.

She ran to her car with her hands tightly covering her ears, she couldn't bear the heartache of hearing her baby's cries, but there was no reprieve from it, as she released her hands from her ears and yanked open her car door it was clear her son had still not been given any comfort. His shrieks of desperation bit savagely into the cold night air.

Charles re-read the message he had sent Rebecca and wondered if it was too harsh, Rebecca had, after all, only been trying to help with her kind offer of a lift tomorrow.

Concentrate on your little one, he needs someone more than I do.

But, he thought, *it was true.* As the days had rolled on into weeks and the weeks into months he had expected Rebecca long since to come to grips with motherhood. When he had agreed to help her he had genuinely believed that she would have made a fabulous mother, patient, kind, devoted and most of all loving, in fact, everything that a mother should be. Instead he had seen the *real* Rebecca Santé appear, a self-obsessed selfish woman whose only devotion was the yard, her only obsession was the business and her only goal was to win at both.

Charles realised that, under normal circumstances, his observations of her casual, often hostile attitude to motherhood would have gone unnoticed. However, it was his sympathy for Paris, having witnessed the turmoil she had gone through to hand him over and his utter conviction that she would have made the most natural of mothers. That pervaded every dimension of his conscience. He wished beyond hope and reason he had treated her differently.

As she drove down the road Paris felt helpless and hysterical, her mind raved, her breaths were hard to find, and her limbs shook so violently she thought she was going to die. She opened the window to get some air to her face and took some sharp breaths whilst her mind tore across the entirety of the forced adoption. This situation, she concluded, had been born out of two things, the pompous pretence of the so called 'upper classes', "fucking upper classes!" she spat. "They are as common as peasants; the only difference is they can pay their bills on time." And the second reason for her suffering was him, again. "Charles Lancaster-Bastard-Baron. There you are, Sir," the venom in her voice managed to escape her tightened lips, "you have a triple barrelled surname now."

There were times when it infuriated Paris that, at some of the most poignant times in her life, a song would enter her head that she would find it impossible to shake away. Nevertheless, the song that came into her mind now couldn't have been more fitting. Her vision was Eliza Doolittle hitching up her dress in *My Fair Lady* and screaming threats of revenge about Henry Higgins. Paris turned the song on its head,

"Just you wait Lancaster-Baron, just you wait. Just you wait Lancaster…"

As she sang her new improved version, her eyes had narrowed in hatred. This time she really meant it, she would show him. She didn't know how yet, but he was going to pay for what he had done to her and her son.

Charles was alone at Cedars Hall and something, or more eerily, someone was causing him to wander, wander from room to room like a vagrant in the city streets. Cedars Hall, his long treasured lifetime home, had cast a formidable silence in every room, and the vast residence, for the first time in his life made him feel small and inferior. With the darkness outside appearing to close in on the house and the echoes of his footsteps against the stone floors permeating his ears, he began to feel enormously vulnerable.

He stood in the doorway of his bedroom, staring at his clothes for tomorrow's event and wished for something, anything, to break the ghostly spell that seemed to have so suddenly materialised. He didn't have to wait long before his wish was answered; Rebecca called him on his mobile. Tentatively he took the call expecting her to reproach him for the bluntness to his message.

"Charles," Rebecca said tearfully, "I have had a nightmare of a night, Paris has been round."

Charles dropped upon the bed and sat bolt upright. "Paris?" he asked hoping that he had indeed heard correctly.

"Yes, Paris," Rebecca continued. "She wanted to see the baby, demanded in fact, she caused such a scene."

Charles could see her caring eyes bestowing, only in a glance, love to her son as she cradled him in her arms. Then Rebecca's words registered, *why would Paris cause a scene?* "What do you mean a scene? What did she do?"

"She tried to force herself in and tried to insinuate I wasn't looking after him properly." Rebecca let out a huge sniff.

"Would you not let her in?" Charles asked in disbelief, thinking instantly of Paris' heartache.

"No, I was having a nightmare round here when she turned up, why the bloody hell would I have let her in?" Rebecca admitted petulantly.

"And why the bloody hell wouldn't you?" Charles snapped defensively. "She would have a perfect right to come in if she so wished."

Rebecca winced and closed her eyes tightly shut. The sharp severity of his words confirming with a sudden jolt that this baby, the one that kept her up for hours on end with his screams and interfered with every aspect of her life, was indeed not actually hers. She ended the call.

The line went dead and Charles wondered if he should call Rebecca and apologise for his tactless and insensitive comments, but then he cast the thought aside. He had been protecting Paris, and after the way he had treated her, he realised it was the very least he could do.

He lay on his bed with his arms behind his head and looked up at the ceiling. Suddenly and without warning, a question floated through his mind, *are you protecting her because of your guilt or are you truly in love with her?*

The blatancy and the shock of the question eradicated any other thought.

Chapter Sixty One

CHARLES had barely slept. For hours he had rived at his sheets and fought with his mind before eventually, at four thirty, he had drifted into a restless sleep.

He had woken at eight a.m. and the same two questions he had gone to sleep scrutinising leapt back into his mind. Why was his mother's will-reading taking place in a hotel and not in her lawyer's office like every other customary will-reading? And why was Paris home?

He had toyed with the idea of calling her, and had wondered several times in the night if she still had the same mobile number, but the fact that today had weighed so heavily on his mind and the fact he really didn't feel strong enough to accept the verbal abuse he knew he so deserved, he had concluded that, for now at least, he had enough to deal with.

He looked smooth, his carefully chosen attire was stylish, his polished shoes shone like an ebony mirror and his soft, newly shaven face drifted the woody scent of Acqui Di Parma around every room. Every inch of him exuded 'Lancaster-Baron' status and, to anyone observing him, not a soul would have guessed that this eminent male had a stomach that was churning like a Cornish buttery.

He paced around the house, checking the time at every opportunity. He passed a clock and swore in a steely rage as he thought about Hugo's whereabouts. Already it was eleven a.m., they had to be there at twelve and so far there was still no sign of him. He had tried to phone him several times, but his calls had gone unanswered and the ballistic messages he had left his brother had been completely ignored.

It wasn't long before the pacing stopped and Charles, responsive to the deafening noise, stood by the drawing room window and watched Hugo's helicopter descend. For a second, a sense of conceit and arrogance pervaded his thoughts as he watched the magnificent machine land upon the finely manicured lawn of Cedars Hall. The sight was everything one would expect of a house with such stately and dignified splendour. Cedars Hall offered itself as a most befitting host. However, as the doors opened and Charles saw his brother saunter towards the house with one hand in the pocket of his jeans the other casually holding a cigarette whilst he coolly pointed out North Yorkshire landmarks to Amy, Charles felt his contempt foam.

He vividly remembered his mother's opinion of "That dreadful object", and her words reminded him that Cedars had never been acquired out of the need for boasting or as an illustration of their family's wealth.

As he watched Hugo swagger nearer to the house, Charles was introduced to a new emotion. Envy. He felt envious of Hugo's nonchalant attitude to today's events and was aware that the responsibility of what their mother was about to bequeath to them had not registered in Hugo's mind in the slightest. Charles realised he had a heavy burden of responsibility on his shoulders, he was the Lancaster-Baron's eldest son, and with that privilege came the added pressure of becoming accountable, for his own actions, as well as Hugo's.

Charles stood in the doorway with a fixed look on his face and, seeing him, Hugo held out his arms in a hippy type gesture. A broad smile charmed his face, confirming to Charles that Hugo's life was definitely free of worry and concern.

"Hey, Charles, you okay?" Hugo drawled.

Charles threw Hugo's arm away with a hefty shove. "What are you doing dressed like that you disrespectful bastard?" Charles shouted pointing to Hugo's jeans and his casual sweatshirt that hung loosely from his rapidly slimming frame.

"What's the matter with you?" Hugo asked looking astonished.

"Mother is about to hand over her assets to you today and you turn up looking like a fucking burglar."

"Hey! Calm down, Charles, for goodness sake," Hugo answered, still smiling. "It's her will-reading, not her hundredth birthday. Whether she is giving us money or she isn't, what we are dressed in is not going to make a shit of difference at this late stage." He turned to Amy who looked stoned, "Come on in Amy." The pair of them casually walked past Charles leaving him standing in the doorway.

Charles followed them into the house and didn't know whether to be grateful for Hugo's carefree attitude or to begrudge it.

"We need to set off now," Charles told Hugo, tracing his steps.

"Yah, no problem, we'll just have a drink first," Hugo answered, pouring himself and Amy a brandy. "You want one?"

Charles shook his head. "Hugo," Charles insisted, "it's eleven thirty; we have to be there for twelve o 'clock prompt."

"Where are we going again?" Hugo asked casually, quickly taking the opportunity of nipping Amy's bottom as he walked past her. "Nice arse, hey?" Hugo stated, pointing at Amy.

"The Black Swan," Charles replied in exasperation.

"Oh, we've plenty of time; it will only take us five minutes." Hugo pulled a packet of cigarettes from Amy's jean pocket which were so tight she had to wriggle suggestively to set them free. "Chill out, Charles. Have a cigarette."

Charles took one from the packet in the hope it might quell his rising irritation.

Fur coats, designer handbags, shining cufflinks and sharp tailored suits, the room in the hotel was crowded with fifty of the best dressed individuals in North Yorkshire. The room was charged with adrenalin, with every attendee still mystified, some even disbelieving that they should have been summonsed. Some hungrily whispered supposed theories to the people next to them, others, recollecting past indiscretions towards Kitty's sons, sat stiffly, looking down at their feet, guiltily wondering how they were implicated in her dying wish.

A privileged few had been allocated front row seats that perched beneath an adequate stage area, housing a table with a jug of water, three glasses and three chairs. As the final minutes ticked by, all of these front-row seats had been filled.

Julia and Luca sat at two end seats, their fingers were lovingly entwined whilst Julia twiddled and stared at her engagement ring, a large princess cut diamond that sparkled like a shooting star and forced her to fight with the ethics of showing it to everyone in the room. Alas, with a sigh, she appreciated on this occasion the time and the place would be inappropriate.

Emma DeMario sat next to Luca. She had decided late last night to put the detail of the day aside. So, placing her pin striped suit back in the wardrobe, she had instead pulled out a low cut figure-hugging red Versace dress, remembering that Charles had once commented appreciatively upon a dress just like it at a summer garden party the year before.

Sofia, sat next to her sister and was now certain, on seeing all these people, that thanks to the infamous Kitty, whom she had never met, they were about to reap the sweet reward of revenge. Ever her father's daughter, and holding such appreciation for someone getting their just deserts, she sat back in her chair in her black trouser suit with a cunning smile that craftily stirred upon her face. With Piers by her side, who was also finding it hard to disguise his satisfaction, she wished that, like her sister, she had also worn something much more in keeping with what seemed was going to be a celebratory carnival.

For Piers, although satisfaction looked promising, with the Santé's filling the seats next to him, he wouldn't have termed his experience as 'a carnival'. He observed Victoria and James from the corner of his eye, with their awkward stance and their self-important upturned noses, and considered how much he hated them. He then turned purposefully to see Rebecca. Consistent with her character, she wore a stiffly starched white cotton blouse with her collars turned up and a fine string of pearls that dozed boringly beneath. *As dull and as frigid as ever* Piers chided privately. Remembering how James had treated him in their last meeting, he couldn't resist delivering a lasting quip.

"Hello Rebecca." Piers spoke with a glimmering smile and as she looked up, he took Sofia's hand and kissed it. "On your own are we?"

Rebecca gave Piers a disparaging frown that acknowledged her confusion.

Piers moved closer into their circle and spoke in a cold whisper. "I was talking about the baby Rebecca – You know, the one you look after for its *real* mother." His brutal chortle harboured no mercy.

James bit his lip and had to stop himself from standing and hitting him. Instead, determined to exhibit the calibre of his breeding, he took hold of his chair and turned it away from Piers.

"It was a very interesting question, though." Paris kicked in with hatred, one seat away from Rebecca at the very end of the line. "Where is *my* son?"

It was Bill Montford's empty chair that sat in between Rebecca and Paris, and as far as Paris was concerned this was a day where there would be no holds barred. She had been treated like a piece of trash by Rebecca and Charles over the last few months, and now, she was ready to fight back.

"Oh, dear!" Piers sniggered. "It appears I've opened a can of dirty, slimy worms."

Rebecca began to speak but her father swiftly interjected.

"Darling," he said, patting her tenderly on the knee, "do remember where we are. Don't retaliate to these kinds of people on a day like today."

A door at the rear of the room opened and gasps of disbelief from the back row diverted everyone's attention. All the heads turned to witness a number of reporters march into the room. With their Dictaphones at the ready, they took to their seats at the back.

"Shit! This really is like a bloody circus," Sofia grinned.

"What an earth is going on?" Julia whispered to Luca "This is all getting so embarrassing."

Paris hung her head. The feeling that this was a trap for Charles made her want to run and find him and tell him not to come. Her heart began to beat faster, *but surely his mother would never hurt him?* she told herself; *maybe this was one of Charles' jokes? Why are you worried anyway?* another internal voice asked her, *he broke your heart.* She dug her nails into her clenched hand. *Yes,* she allowed another voice to answer, *yes, he did break my heart, but that doesn't stop me loving him.* Paris hated that last voice and did her best to block it from her mind.

Charles rushed up to Hugh who was stood in Reception and held out his hand to shake his. "Hello, Hugh, sorry we are so late." He shot a thunderous look to his brother. "We got a little held up."

Hugh couldn't look Charles in the eye whilst they shook hands, but felt enormous relief that, in this instance, the shaking of his hand was permitted. Passing more pleasantries with Hugo, who seemed as carefree as ever, Hugh turned to Amy.

"Are you coming into the reading?" he asked, obviously embarrassed.

"Yes, she is," Hugo replied for her.

"Erm, when we get into the room it will probably be as well if you were to stand at the back," Hugh informed her.

Hugo laughed, then realised that Hugh was serious. "What do you mean?" Hugo asked.

Hugh, shrinking with embarrassment beneath the professional disguise of his suit and briefcase began to walk toward the room, allowing the three of them to follow. "I am working under your mother's instructions," he told them hurriedly over his shoulder.

Inside the room, the attendees were getting restless and helped themselves to a second cup of tea.

Outside the room, Hugh Stephenson realised that he only had about five steps to go before his hand would be on the door handle and he would be left to open it. He thought of Kitty. "On the day, I do not want my words to be read by anyone but myself," Kitty had insisted to him all those weeks ago. "Everyone, especially my sons have to hear this from me," she had persisted. "Therefore, *I* will record the whole reading."

So, in her sickliest hours, with Hugh by her side, that was exactly what she had done. And now, as he walked towards the door, he remembered the day. Such a strong, brave woman, he recalled, trying desperately to draw strength from his memory of her. Never did he imagine the day would be as hard as it was.

He winced as his hand touched the door handle. This is it, he gasped. He pushed the handle down and felt his stomach flip into oblivion.

Charles looked around the room and felt every cell of his blood drain from his body and then crash, like a cannon ball in water as it plunged to the depths of his bowels. His body began to shake from the calves of his legs to the tips of his fingers and a high pitched whistling, like a radio out of tune, rang in his ears as his brain tried to interpret the scene before him.

The room was ear crushingly silent, and all Charles could see was a blurred ocean of faces turning to watch the three of them, Hugh, Charles and Hugo, walking down the slim aisle that parted the assembly of chairs. And as they walked, the atmosphere in the room lay carpet thick, an atmosphere that activated his instincts and told him horror was about to ensue. His heart thumped like a tribal drum, and the reverberations of its pounding echoed in his ears in giant pulsing waves.

He followed Hugh and from three steps back noticed how the lawyer's head was uncomfortably bowed, even he was anxious, Charles realised. Charles was consumed with a need to escape, to call a halt to the proceedings, demand a meeting with Hugh, or to shout at the top of his voice, "What the fuck is going on?" But, as quickly as those thoughts entered his mind, the misty haze of turning heads became more lucid, making him realise that to react irrationally would be exactly what this audience expected. The only option he had was to disguise his fear, mask his anger and act out this torturous masquerade. They reached the short set of steps that led up to the stage and he saw a table was ready for them to take position, with three seats, a jug of water and three glasses being their hosts.

Charles looked at the three steps before him. As he stood on the first he felt overcome with vulnerability, the second step elevated him, allowing the spectators a clearer view of his humiliation, then, as his foot hit the third and he slowly walked along the stage, it was then he became aware of the ever expanding sense of raw exposure. He could physically feel the hundreds of eyes scrutinising his every move and their stare burnt through his body like firing lasers. He stood on the stage, completely powerless, and allowed Hugh in a hushed formal whisper to delegate him a seat. Charles sat down, grateful to give his shaking legs reprieve.

His nervous eyes shifted quickly to his brother sitting next to him, he needed a hint, just the briefest sign of his reaction, but, Hugo, aided by the drink and drugs, remained expressionless. Charles' eyes, pained with panic and hunting for the offer of salvation, swiftly glanced up and naturally they gravitated toward the front row. He frantically searched the line and looking back at him he saw the DeMario's, Piers, the Santé's, and lastly, Paris; it was there his eyes ceased their search.

For a moment their eyes locked. Her blue eyes, crystallised by her natural inner warmth, poured out sympathy for him and willed him, like a lighthouse to a sinking ship, to maintain his dignity. Then as quickly as the connection had transpired, Paris broke it and looked down to her feet.

Hugh stood up and looked edgily across at Charles and Hugo before addressing the crowded room.

"Good morning. As you are aware," he cleared his throat, "we are here for Kitty Lancaster-Baron's will-reading. You may have already guessed, this is not an ordinary reading. However, for those of you who knew Kitty, I am sure you will join me in agreeing, she was no ordinary type of lady."

Hugh allowed the truth of his words to echo among the room's attendees before turning to face Charles and Hugo.

"To that end, it is *not I* that has been given the opportunity to read your mother's will to you today, in fact your mother insisted that she should read it to you personally." Feeling the scorch of Charles' stare, he turned back to face the rest of the room.

"The result is, you will all listen to her personal recording which was carried out from her home in December."

Hugh grabbed the remote for the system, obscured from view under the table and motioned it to play. Then, glancing once last time at Charles, he put his own nerves to rest. However disconcerting today was for Charles, it would never match the heartbreak that the wonderful Kitty Lancaster-Baron felt when she delivered what he was about to hear.

Hugh sat down in the chair and waited to hear Kitty's voice for the last time. As he did so, he found it impossible not to distance himself from the rest of the room. The day of the recording at Cedars Hall had been so moving; he didn't want a single movement or whisper from anyone in the room to taint his reminiscing.

Chapter Sixty Two

"I, KITTY LANCASTER-BARON, write and record this, my last will and testament on the first of December Two thousand and...."

The refined eloquence of her voice filled both the silent room and the people within it with a sense of privilege. The tall ceilings and the period Georgian walls of this grand hotel appeared to cosset her every word, as if trying to persuade the grandeur of each syllable to linger. The hairs on Charles' arms prickled to attention and stood upright in fond recognition of his mother's voice and a painful lump in his throat began to swell as he wished she could be sat by his side, just one last time.

With complete admiration Hugh listened intently to her every word, still in awe that what she was about to deliver she had done so without the aid of any notes, and that, just like everything else in Kitty's life, it had come from her heart.

....Hello Charles, hello Hugo. To find so many people here today must be a heart thudding surprise for you both, after all, I was never one to enjoy centre stage, but I am glad that, even at my ripe old age, I can still keep you all guessing." She paused "If everyone I have summoned to this reading has attended then I am more than aware the room will now be full with the County's so-called socialites." The room's guests heard the mocking sarcasm in her voice. "To that end, having watched my sons for the past three decades, I know how crammed your diaries can become, so, for your benefit, I will get on with what I have to say." There was momentary silence.

"You know, for you youngsters sitting there today believing, and rightly so, you have so many years ahead of you, I can't tell you how strange and how shocking the feeling when suddenly, out of the blue, you recognise that the years have caught up with you and it is time to give a curtsey to the world you have loved. Yes," she said faintly, "it is time for me to say goodbye to it all and depart." Her voice drowned in emotional sentiment. "But, like any death, there are various formalities one has to deal with before one can truly rest, and for me, the thought of leaving you two boys, my sons, Charles and Hugo, to brave this world alone *and* the matter of distributing my own inherited wealth has played heavily on my mind for some time." Her voice shaded to a much cooler pitch. "I will cut to the chase and tell you all what I feel certain the majority have come to hear."

Her noble voice saturated the room with elegance.

"The Lancaster-Baron property and business portfolio consists of the following. Twenty-five farm cottages, all of them rented out to farm workers around the Chelmsley area and all of them courtesy of my husband Charles Baron Senior. They have a combined worth of five million pounds." With a precise, factual bluntness the list continued to roll "One cottage at Wickruns Bay courtesy of my father, apparently worth five hundred thousand pounds, one hundred and twenty million pounds worth of shares courtesy of my father's company Lancaster Law International, and of course, last but certainly not least, my home, the home I have adored and cherished for a lifetime." She paused again, this time for longer. "Cedars Hall. Apparently," she forced, "various expert valuations have informed me that my home has a market value of fifteen million pounds, but for me, Cedars Hall holds a sentimental value that is, quite honestly," her voice gave out to a tiny whisper, "priceless."

An enchanted hush rolled delicately across the room as each person in it became charmed by the unusual comfort of sincerity.

Conversely, for a second, Charles, digesting the facts and

figures, missed the opportunity for sentiment as the eyebrows above his greedy eyes rose, then fell, in utter delight. In the past, his mother had been insistent on discretion regarding their financial worth, but today she had managed to surprise him for a second time. Suddenly he acquired the strength to face the room and allowed his eyes to gleefully sweep over the sea of envious faces before him.

Kitty's voice returned.

"It is a very impressive portfolio isn't it? And now I am going to tell you why I think it is so impressive. You see, unlike most of you sitting here today, including no doubt my two sons, my admiration far outweighs the monetary value of the family's worth. You see, my admiration is born out of knowing the two people who created it."

The audience heard Kitty take a deep breath before exhaling slowly and Hugh remembered the faint smile that had crept upon her face.

"Goodness, how I adored and loved those two men," Kitty said earnestly. "You must understand, the wealth I have now, I have acquired. Some individuals I know see inheritance as the devilish passport for snobbery, and in their small conceited minds forget that it is due to someone else's hard work that they have acquired it at all. But, I will *never* forget what my father and husband achieved for me. In fact not just for me but myself *and* my two sons. And now," the profundity of facts brought strength to her voice, "I am going to tell you about them so that you are all in no doubt the kind of stock my two sons sitting before you today are bred from. Charles and Hugo," she stated crossly, "for once, I want you two to listen also.

My father, the mastermind of the majority of my acquired wealth was the most courteous man one could ever meet. He was a gentleman, one that felt as comfortable walking with kings as he did with peasants. He was a lawyer, and worked so incredibly hard, with ethics, such strong ethics." She sighed. "Ethics so honourable that the words honesty, trust and respect were almost engraved on his brow. As a result, he succeeded in building one of the most highly regarded law firms in the world.

I witnessed him, on many occasions, defending anyone that he believed had a just cause, from the dusty realms of a travelling circus owner to the stately grandeur of film stars and royalty. And you know what made his appeal so strong?" She stopped, leaving the audience to wonder whether an answer was expected before her voice continued. "Because he dealt with everyone in the same way, showed them the same amount of respect and gave them the same amount of time and attention. There was no room for snobbery and condescension in my father's life." She remained quiet for an instant, "It was his honesty, sheer hard work and his brilliant brain that allowed you two, Charles and Hugo, to enjoy your privileged life, and that privilege stretched across many facets of your life." Her voice was now determined and powerful. "We can speak of the superficial realms, an Eton education, the fact that by the time you had reached eleven you had travelled the world *four times,* and whilst doing so stayed in the world's finest accommodation. There is also the undeniable fact that both of you are incredibly handsome with an equal helping of charm and allure thrown in. But what does all this mean? What attention can those facets warrant at the end of the day?" Kitty's voice drenched the room. "That is why I call it *superficial.*" The word spat from her mouth. "You see, to me, the real privilege is in the very genes you two carry within your bodies, the very genes that enable a person to fight and succeed in the face of adversity and grow stronger as a result of it rearing its head. And indeed, the genes that have given both of you the intelligent brains that rest in mollycoddled silence within your skulls. They are the Lancaster-Baron genes, it is this legacy alone that you should worship." Her voice quietened. "I think that I too, as a result of their teachings, shared the same philanthropic habits as my father and my husband and what I have realised in my hours of reckoning is that, if I pass on their hard earned wealth to persons that would not abide by the same traditions, then in my opinion, it would be an offence and a downright insult to them both." Her voice boomed icily. "Do you hear me, Charles, Hugo? An absolute offence."

As his mother's voice grew cold, Charles felt the instinctive chill of threat run down his spine and return its warning journey all the way back up.

"I have deliberated and considered on all these facts for so long and, in doing so, I was delivered to a place that harboured enormous complications. You see, after a while it became clear, my sons are spoilt, they have no appreciation of the divine laws of nature and what a life filled with *real people* and *genuine love* can bring. The kind of people they mix with, *you lot* out there sitting here today," her voice stated angrily, "the majority of you are *false social climbers.*" Insistence swarmed through her voice. "Now, please, Charles, Hugo, I beg of you, look at the people before you, watch how many squirm and cast their eyes to the floor."

Her rich voice hung ominously throughout the room, and its sheer profundity forced her two sons to feel beholden to fulfil her request. Awkwardly Charles looked up and saw what could have been a million eyes shunning his stare and a sea of heads trying to sink beneath the false camouflage of designer outfits. Only one person could look him in the eye, it was Paris.

"These people are not your friends; they are fair-weather associates, only around you because of what you have. They are as eager as hunting dogs to keep in the loop with the likes of you, it is not that they like or admire you, it is quite simply to ensure that their designer shoes, the shoes that most can probably ill afford, remain on the rung of the social ladder." Another pause. "But, unfortunately, you two boys are by no means innocent in the disgusting bogus world in which you live. In fact I would go as far to say you are most certainly worse. You see, Charles, I know about *everything.*"

As he heard his name, Charles' squirming innards twisted to attention.

"I know this will be a dreadful shock, but I have had a private detective follow you for the past ten months."

In that instant Charles felt a lightening rush of horror strike his body and splash frantically within his blood.

"I know about the sickeningly cruel, selfish tricks you have resorted to in order to get your own way. Yes, I know about your attempts to blackmail those DeMario girls in order to gain the wealth, respect and love of the Santé family by way of splitting up Rebecca's marriage." Sharp breaths sucked away at the room's air and Charles saw from the corner of his eye Victoria Santé throw her hands to her chest.

"I know about your seedy attempts at drugging racehorses in order to try and recoup your enormous gambling debts."

Luca's eyes narrowed in hatred as he glowered at Charles. Then, Kitty's voice lowered to such a degree that everyone within the room witnessed the revulsion within it.

"AND," she paused as if fighting to expel her words, "I know about the way you deceived Paris Montford with false empty promises and forced her to give up her baby son." Her audience heard her groan in heartbreak. "Can you imagine that? In my son's world, because of his crude obsession with money and social ranking, even a mother and her new born baby are unsafe from harm? Can you imagine sinking any lower?"

As her silence ensued, Hugh remembered the tears of regret and shame silently fall down her ageing face. The intensity of her misery had been overbearing, yet somehow Kitty managed to utter a final sentence. "I am ashamed of you, Charles," she told him. "You are my son yet at this moment, you have made me ashamed that you are."

Behind uncontrollable blinks, Charles' eyes began to waver from one place to another. He didn't know where to look within a room that was magnifying maliciously in and out of focus. His panicking pulse sounded like a gushing tide around his ears and the sound of his blood fighting for freedom from his evil body began to close in around his head. He heard her angry voice return.

"And do you know why he has done all this everyone? Because, without some form of money from somewhere, my son is bankrupt. If it weren't so heartbreaking for me it would be laughable, yes, he is bankrupt."

Within the room the atmosphere had grown as sharp as a butcher's blade and Charles felt its evil stabs slice into his flesh.

"And now, I turn to Hugo, the second of my fortunate sons. He, at least, has managed to build a career for himself in the City, and has actually and very surprisingly done rather well. I say surprisingly because I was always under the impression that one night stands, a blasé attitude to everything he has, and the effects of sacks full of cocaine were inappropriate distractions to a good brain." She let out another sarcastic snigger and her words were icy cold. "Yes everyone, my second son is a sex obsessed drug addict."

Hugo's shaking hands rummaged violently through his hair; beads of perspiration began to sprout upon his forehead and his mother's accusatory words of 'drug addict' rang like deafening church bells in his ears.

Hugo stood from his chair. "This is an outrage!" he shouted, "She's off her rocker!"

He didn't know if it was the silent audience staring back at him, the hoard of reporters holding up their Dictaphones at the back of the room, or the fact that his body was screaming for another fix that caused him to slump back upon his chair, but, as he did, he let out a hysterical laugh that jerked with flashes of madness around the room. He slid his hands in his jean pocket and felt the safe harbour of a plastic bag, his fix, a fix his body was now trembling to receive.

"I need the loo," he insisted.

"You will stay where you are until your mother has finished," Hugh ordered frostily, feeling personally offended by his portrayal of disrespect to Kitty. Hugh remembered how at this stage, Kitty's revelations regarding her two sons had forced her to turn off the Dictaphone.

She hadn't sobbed, she hadn't turned to hysteria as a release of her personal pain, she hadn't even looked across at Hugh; she had just sat with her frail ladylike hands placed together on her lap and allowed her agitated fingers to twist and turn, waiting for the outpouring of tears running down her cheeks to cease. Even in her greatest trauma she had behaved with such dignity, there was no doubt about it, Kitty Lancaster-Baron was the only true lady that he had ever met.

Along with Kitty's silence the room smoked with unspoken thoughts as everybody in it silently speculated on what was to come.

Charles shuffled furiously upon his chair and clumsily reached for the water and simultaneously he felt all the eyes in the room watch him shakily pour it. Aggressively he put the glass to his seething lips and threw a large slug to the back of his mouth. For a few seconds, the water remained enclosed within his mouth as he decided whether or not his larynx would allow him to swallow, but a cough he recognised from the audience suddenly freed him.

It was Paris; she was staring back at him and had purposefully vied for his attention. She didn't smile, she didn't move, just silently and without motion she held his gaze. She had wanted him to know she was there. In that second, in that very instant of a world that was apparently leaving him for dead, a connection to the real love his mother had mentioned only minutes before had become apparent. It was a connection that, having never felt so alone before, made him realise he had a companion for life. He swallowed down his water and with his eyes, tried to send waves of undiluted gratefulness toward her.

Then and there, Paris witnessed, for the very first time, there was a lost, weak soul within the deceptive confines of a very strong body.

The click of the Dictaphone could be heard across the room and Kitty's voice returned.

"So, the question I was forced to ask myself repeatedly was: How can I ensure that everything my father and beloved husband have brought into this family is honestly appreciated, devoid of even the smallest trace of conceit, bequeathed with the aid of people being the main priority, and all the while ensuring that the interests of my two sons who have so much to offer the world are also looked after?" She sighed. "I was in fact truly amazed at how quickly the answer materialised. So," she said pointedly, "my attention will now be turned back to my assets.

I would like to begin on a sentimental note. As you have heard, I have been very privileged in life and have been lucky enough to own many pieces of fine jewellery. Being of religious mind, one of my particularly favourite pieces is a large diamond cross, and Mary, my ever faithful trusted housekeeper has always admired the piece. It would give me great pleasure, Mary, for this to be my gift to you along with a heartfelt thank you for everything you have ever done for me. With someone like you, Mary, the Lord will never walk in your shadows, he will always take comfort by resting in your good, clean heart."

Mary's eyes had sunk beneath a grateful sea of tears.

"And that brings me to Sam, our gardener. You have put your heart and soul into the grounds at Cedars since I was a young girl. As a result, I have so many fond memories of walking through your treasure trove of designs and colour. To you also, thank you, Sam. I give to you my father's gold and diamond pocket watch; I hope that your time with the people that you love is long and frequent, whoever those people are, they are indeed eternally blessed."

Charles looked over at Sam and watched him, with a trembling mouth, respectfully tip his hat toward the stage.

"Now, my dogs." Kitty laughed, irony was so clearly present. "They have been true friends to me for many years; to them I bestow my entire art collection and the remainder of my jewels. These possessions when liquidised will see that they, and many others, live in the comfort that they deserve within Chelmsley Dogs' Home. A place where they will be free from being disrespectfully kicked and beaten. So, Charles, for your information I will ensure you are omitted from the visitors' list."

The room witnessed Charles squirm again as the list continued.

"The thirty cottages presently occupied and rented by local farmers will be given to those very farmers and their families, a gift from my husband and I, and of course my two sons," she added sarcastically. "Those families will have struggled financially for a lifetime; it will be the Lancaster-Barons' greatest pleasure to relieve them of that burden. Moreover, this gift is a personal thank you. My heart is filled with gratitude for the labour of love you have shown to the countryside that has surrounded me throughout my life. The land is your master and your servant and there is no doubt, due to your understanding and your dedication to nature, you have served each calling admirably. Thank you."

Charles looked to the back of the room where a small selection of local farmers ignited a flurry of jubilant whispers, their excited red, rosy faces smiled back at him in appreciation. Charles, poker faced, stared back.

"One hundred and twenty million pounds worth of shares within Lancaster-Law international," she continued. "Everything, every last penny will go back into the company in which it originated…." Her words trailed away.

Charles wanted to shout, he wanted to scream. He felt himself about to crack, but as his eyes scavenged across the room with the craze of a madman, allowing the sea of colourful outfits to register in his mind, he forced himself not to surrender. They were emotions, he told himself, and he would conceal them. He held his breath and felt the muscles all over his body clench in a resolute bid to remain strong. His mother's voice persisted.

"There are so many individuals whom, like my father, have worked so hard and earnestly within the company over the years to build it into what it is today; as a result I have given Hugh Stephenson the list of names that I believe should have full autonomy as to the distribution of the funds. Next, Cedars Hall, the place where I, and my sons had the privilege of growing up. Words could never describe what this place means to me. I know that should I leave this to my sons I would not be doing them any favours at all, they would *never* be able to resist the temptation of selling it to alleviate their spiralling debts and fund their drug fuelled lifestyles. Therefore I have no option but to place my home in the hands of the National Trust, allowing a mixture of people from all walks of life the opportunity to love and appreciate it just as I have over the years. It will give me so much pleasure to know that its unique beauty will bring joy to others."

Like the rumble of thunder clouds Charles' eyes darkened then swept angrily across the room as if daring, almost goading anyone to sneer.

Paris watched as the anger within Charles began to inflate and felt her own heart pound with a selfless anxiety. She observed his jaws pulsate as he ground his teeth viciously together and realised that, throughout the reading, she had put herself so close into his shoes that her mouth now watered and grimaced as she imagined her own teeth grating away. His right leg, filled with the poison of loathing, shook and tapped fearfully against the floor. Paris swore she could see his ashen face turn a more distinct shade of green as every nanosecond passed. Paris wished now she had never come to this reading. Of all the plots of revenge she had imagined him receiving, public humiliation to this degree was not one of them.

"So what am I going to leave you two?" Kitty stated. "That again was an obvious answer. Wickruns Bay is a place of marvel, a place of sanctuary at needy times, a place where the beauty and power of nature is forever evident. It seems only right that my two sons each inherit this precious place, I leave this to you both and trust that it will compel you to acquire an appreciation for the very world you find yourself living in, the one that I, so reluctantly have to depart."

Charles felt his innards try to crawl away from his body. Before all these people she had broken him, exposed his whole being and humiliated him in the most unimaginable way. In panic, his eyes staggered in frenzied jolts around the room and rested upon familiar faces, pleading them to show a grain of compassion. In response they looked to the floor. His eyes shot to the front row, he saw the darkness of the DeMario eyes mock him with venom. He quickly passed them and moved on to the Santé's, his trusted friends for a lifetime. He stared back at Rebecca with a pleading hope, Rebecca's face was detached. Her eyes continued to stare at his face but it was as though she no longer recognised him. To him it was clear – she had already quietly 'removed' herself from his life.

He couldn't take any more. He felt terrorised, the air in the room seemed inescapably warm and he felt its malicious grip close in and slowly, like a python with lethal intent, it began to strangle him. Discreetly, his nervous hands twisted at the neck of his tightening collar and it was this movement that made him conscious of his fine cotton shirt. His body had been perspiring so much that it clung coldly like a parasite to his panicking body. Then he realised that her voice, her bloody voice continued.

"I know you both well enough to know that, as a result of my decision, it will leave you feeling physically sick with a burning hatred towards me. But, your feelings towards me are insignificant, not only will I have left the physical realms of life and therefore be impervious to your reactions, but I know I am the only person who can help you. I concluded the only way for you to achieve your destiny, whatever that may be, is to force you into a situation where you have to start again. All your misdemeanours and law breaking pursuits are now out on the table. The press know, your friends know, the world knows. You are now two of the luckiest people alive, there are many *supposed* good people out there, heads of state, politicians and lawyers, all of them have their skeletons barraged inside a closet. From this minute forward you no longer have the burden of secrets and lies to bear.

With these revelations, some people I know will turn their backs on you, others will judge *me*. However, I have not one thought for anyone else. Believe it or not, I care about you two, you are my flesh and blood and contrary to what you may think now, I love you both very much. What is imperative for you now is to use the gifts that your genes will bestow, those genes that are pulsating through your veins and the make up of your skin. Remember, most of all, the heart of a Lancaster-Baron is a strong and determined one, but moreover, it is true.

You need to learn the lessons of life again, and maybe, just maybe, as I have obviously let you down so badly, you will learn those lessons more effectively without *me*, and those lessons will certainly be easier to learn without the money.

My darlings, once the shock has dissipated, I hope it will not take long before you pull yourselves up by your bootstraps and begin your new life. A life with purpose and true, honest intentions and a life with true, honest people around you. I can assure you, within days, hours, possibly even minutes you will find out who those people are. All the while remember this, that when that time comes, whether you want me there or not, I will be with you every single step of your journey."

Her voice positively shook and hovered in various emotional pitches across the room.

"I have tried so hard to remain in this life, and to think of ways to teach you these lessons before my passing. To leave this life gracefully has been the hardest thing I have ever had to do. There have been times in the constrictions of this claustrophobic prison of nearing death that I have wanted to kick, scream and fight with every grain of energy I have left in order to stay longer and finish what I have supposedly started. But, I am sorry." She began to cry. "I just can't do it."

For the first time the audience heard Kitty sob and were immediately swept into the rare, raw, rudiments of human emotion.

"I promise you both," Kitty struggled through the strain of tears, "although I may not be with you physically anymore, my heart will forever live in your own." Her voice pleaded to her sons. "I love you both, and have always loved you, so very, very much."

Despair. With his elbows on the table, his arms upright, Charles threw his head into the flat of his hands. Despair filled his very being.

Chapter Sixty Three

AS CHARLES looked up at Paris, his pain was unguardedly evident, eyes that were accentuated by an ashen, lonely, face were lined by savage red lines, scorch marks of suppressed, burning tears. Her generous tears spilt down her face, but she managed to give him a smile, it was a smile that trembled from her quivering lips and informed him she was proud of the composure he had managed to maintain. He acknowledged only her in the room by way of a faint, appreciative, nod before slowly raising himself from the chair and walking form the stage. As he walked past the room's battalion of people his head surrendered to the deep discomfort of shame and regret as he allowed it to sink to the floor.

Paris sat staring ahead, trying desperately to make some sense of the storm of thoughts that swirled in her mind. Had the masculine form of Medusa managed to captivate her heart once again just with the power of his stare? Or, had the man she had foraged so hard to hate for the past few months really allowed her to see his genuine humanity? She felt so confused. Only hours before, she had wished, planned and seen herself exacting revenge for the hurtful torture he had bestowed on her, yet now, witnessing the pain and vulnerability in his stare, she felt certain that his eyes had informed her, she was his only salvation.

In the background, she heard mobiles beeping as they were reactivated into the land of socialite scandal, followed by galloping gasps of whispers.

"You'll never guess what," they indulged, "he's a broken man."

Paris, disgusted by their shallow, superficial means of amusement thought of Kitty, how right she had been. These people were as false and as meaningless as the designer labels they wore on their backs, and Paris knew she would rather die than be a part of their faction. *Within minutes you will find out who your real friends are* she recalled Kitty telling her sons. Instantly, forgetting the pain he had caused her in the past and pushing to one side the danger that he could cause her more in the future, she picked up her handbag and raced out of the room.

"Charles!" she shouted as he walked down the corridor.

He turned to face her, his hands were sunk in his pockets, his tie had been unknotted and hung loosely around his neck, and his clammy shirt had already been yanked from the restriction of his tailored trousers and hung untidily beneath his jacket. Numbly he stared back at her.

She ran down the corridor toward him.

"Are you okay?" she asked with genuine concern pouring from her eyes. She quickly shrugged and reached out to touch his arm. "Sorry, it's a stupid question, I just don't know what to say," she admitted.

"No, neither do I," he murmured before nonchalantly turning to make his way toward the reception doors.

With a torrent of words still stumbling for order within her mind she walked quietly by Charles' side. Charles broke the silence when they reached his car.

"For the first time in my life, I don't know what to do," he told her, unable to look in her eyes.

Paris was internally drained by the amount of sympathy she felt herself bestowing. Here was a man that within minutes had been transformed in front of her eyes. The once powerful masculinity of broad strong shoulders were now buried somewhere beneath his sharp tailored suit and the mouth that had, on numerous occasions, forcefully magnetised her own to kiss it, now trembled like a day old gosling in a lonely nest. But it was his eyes that stamped upon her the greatest sadness.

His once-magnificent blue eyes that had been seeped in power, persuasion and mysterious prestige, at this moment had a look of weakness and limitation. No longer did they give the slightest hint that they could have once stunned and captivated an individual's attention with the briefest of glances. In fact, on the contrary, at this moment, such was their lack of strength, that they looked to have been ungracefully shoved into the world of ordinary suburbia, as though the outstanding soul that had steered them had now disappeared, abandoning him to face his future alone. The thought panicked Paris, the man she loved to hate appeared to be sailing away and she found herself willing with all her strength for him to return.

"Of course you know what to do, Charles," she assured, grabbing his hand and squeezing it hard. "It's just that today has been an enormous shock. Tomorrow you will feel so much stronger," she explained with her own eternal hope spilling into every syllable. "Like your mother said, you have everything within you, all the tools you need to guide you in the right direction." She searched his eyes, looking for a hint of his attention, but they just stared carelessly, almost unconsciously into the distance. She shook his hand vigorously as if trying to awaken him to her presence and words.

"You can't just give up simply because you don't have money, what difference does that make?"

Her words whistled frantically around his head, she didn't understand, he was a broken man. He wanted to scream at her until the penny dropped as to what this had done to him, but simultaneously he didn't want to drive her away. He wanted her, and needed her to stay.

"What a fucking mess," he mumbled, still looking into the distance. "How could I have made such a mess of it all?"

"Why did you do it, Charles? Why?" She searched his eyes longingly for a plausible explanation. He privately mulled over the answer.

Charles felt utterly consumed by misery, he had spent his whole life naively believing that the love and respect his mother held for her father and her husband had been born out of what they had achieved. Yet, today he realised it had been *his own* shallow beliefs that had wickedly drawn him to believe it. Her respect, he realised, had been instigated by the kind of people they were, a person he knew he could so easily have been.

"Ironically, I did it for her," he answered truthfully, looking back to the ground. "I needed her love and respect."

The frankness of his confession almost made Paris cry, and she would have done were it not for the fact that she knew he needed her strength. She took his hand in both of hers, drew it up to her mouth and kissed it hard. Her voice responded tenderly.

"Well, now, Charles, she has given you the chance to *gain* her *respect*. There is one thing for sure you have *always* had her *love*, she has shown you that today."

For the first time since they had come outside he looked into her eyes, the first sign she had that her words had registered. He squeezed her hand and allowed the silent stare that penetrated deep into her eyes to go unbroken.

"I have been such a bloody fool," he acknowledged guiltily.

Paris looked up and saw that many of the attendees, their ears uncompromisingly glued to mobiles, were beginning to leave the hotel and sprinkle their way across the car park.

"Shall we get in your car?" Paris suggested protectively. "I think it's better you keep out of their way."

Relieved to feel he had someone on his side, Charles unlocked the car and got in. Paris walked to the passenger seat. From the Reception doors she heard Rebecca, just leaving the hotel, call over to her parents.

"I'll see you back at home, I need to pick the baby up from Nursery," she informed them coldly.

The baby? The baby? Paris seethed. *She doesn't even call him by his name, and a nursery? How often does the poor little mite have to go there?* She felt the hatred for Rebecca Santé flare. Simultaneously she was reminded that the man she was now holding out the greatest sympathy for had instigated the whole scenario.

She stormed into the car, slammed the door shut and slumped into the seat next to Charles. Her lips were tight, her breaths fast and heavy as her thoughts were tortured with pain for the loss of her son.

Charles, still consumed with his own pain, continued analysing the situation, utterly oblivious of Paris' change in demeanour.

"Of all the people to exact revenge," Charles uttered in meek reflection, "of all the people who have a right to hate me, and it turns out it is my mother who hated me the most."

Paris immediately fired back in response to his self-pity. "I can assure you that is not true!" Paris snapped, feeling consumed with rage. "There are people that hate you much more; it's just that she had the power to do something about it."

Temporarily surprised by her sudden change in tone, Charles looked at Paris then promptly looked away. He couldn't face another battle, he felt too weak.

"That's true," he confessed faintly.

"Stop that look of self-pity, Charles," Paris snapped bluntly. "Don't expect me to give you any sympathy; I will *never* give you any," she lied. "What about what you did to me? You completely fucking wrecked my life."

"I'm sorry, Paris," he mumbled.

"You're sorry?" She screamed. "You speak those words like a little boy, Charles, as if having thrown a toy from your cot, you just say sorry and then everything will all be forgotten about." She shoved him hard. "In real life, in this cruel bad world, life just does not work like that. How ironic that I am telling *you* this today, when you are the one that taught me the cruel lesson of life in the first place."

Yet again, he didn't retaliate. He just stared out of the windscreen. Paris grabbed the arm of his jacket and pulled him round to face her.

"I gave up my baby for you," she screeched, "I gave up my son, can you imagine the pain that causes me every day of my life? You bastard! I fucking hate you!" Paris flung herself hard against the seat.

"I don't know what to say to you, Paris, I just don't know what to say, apart from," he took a deep breath and looked into her eyes, "I love you."

Paris lurched across and slapped him viciously across his face. "Love? Love?" she bellowed "You don't know the meaning of the word."

"Paris, I can assure you that I do," he answered ignoring the sting that had struck his face. Quietly he held her stare. "I know its meaning because I have felt my love for you grow since the day you left Chelmsley."

There was something in his eyes, something in his words that trapped her to listen. She sat still and felt her angered breaths begin to calm slightly as her contrasting emotions were stirred. Her eyes flickered wildly as she tried to fight her succumbing, but as he grabbed her hands and held them in his, the incomprehensible fact that his confessional words could indeed be authentic, came alive.

"Paris?" he said. "Let me show you how much I love you. I don't expect you to trust me now, just let me prove to you over time how much I *honestly* love you."

His words were like lyrics, and Paris felt her heart beat to their very tune. Like a gas flame in a boiler that had been suddenly ignited to heat a house, she saw his eyes begin to come alive. He squeezed her hand so hard she felt it burn beneath his strong grip.

"I promise, with all my heart, I will never let you down, I will never ever let you down again. Stay with me, let me prove it to you."

She heard her father's words of warning ring alarmingly in her head and fought to take heed of it, yet, she felt herself slipping away from her own flesh and blood as every morsel of her body and mind commanded her to allow Charles the upper hand. His hypnotic charisma that only minutes ago looked to have vanished seemed to have been swiftly resurrected, and as she felt herself losing control, she found herself regretting ever missing it. She was repulsed by her feelings, yet seduced by his tender words and couldn't help herself from becoming entrapped all over again. He sat upright to give her his full attention, his shoulders seemed to inch by inch grow in strength, his mouth, from which his romantic words were oozing, once again became a haven for tender kisses, and his eyes, those electrifying, audacious eyes had been given the breath of life from Cupid's arrow and rooted her, quite literally, to the spot. There was something in his eyes that pleaded his sincerity and worst of all, something in her heart that wanted to hear more.

"How will you prove it to me, Charles?" she asked faintly.

He took her hand and kissed it. "I will marry you," he answered boldly.

His answer took her breath, a flush of thrill travelled at lightening speed from her feet to her face. As she stared back at him, the authenticity and power of his stare made her conclude, this time with great authority, his words were genuine. The hidden love she had disguised for hate for so long began to revivify and froth inside her. Its intensity was such that it commanded and controlled her every thought, and it told her his love was all she needed.

As if reading her thoughts, Charles lovingly smiled back at her. "With you by my side, Paris, I know I can make something of myself, be everything Mother wanted me to be. I may not have anything now, but I will have."

"You have everything I need," Paris answered with sincerity.

"Where do we go from here, then?" he asked her affectionately.

Paris didn't have to think. "I want us to go to the exact place your mother wants you to be, Wickruns Bay. Let's go there and play Monopoly and Scrabble for a lifetime. Personally, I don't know why you are so down, I can't think of a better place, nor can I think of a better gift." Her smile filled the car.

Charles looked into her eyes and realised that her words were as genuine as his mother's had been.

"You really don't give a shit about money do you?" Charles asked her.

"Has it really taken you all this time to work that one out, Charles?" As quickly as the words left her mouth the lyrics of a song jumped into her mind, she sung them lightly "If you don't know me by now..." She looked back at him, giving the hint of a soft smile.

He let out a small laugh, then reached out and touched her face and, as he did, Paris' skin trembled beneath his touch.

"Shall we set off now then?"

Paris looked down to her lap and hesitated, temporary frightened as she listened to the pessimistic thoughts that steered her to fear a repeat in the love torn cycle.

Charles gently lifted her uncertain face to face his. "Don't go back to Spain, Paris; I promise you, I will make you truly happy."

He allowed her to study his face in her search for trust. "Will you come with me to the cottage, just you and I, alone?"

Paris gave a hesitant nod. "I just need to go to Mother's first, pick up my things and let everyone know I'm okay."

Charles nodded. She reached for the door handle but Charles pulled her back. Paris felt his warm hand glide passionately behind the back of her neck and tenderly he pulled her face toward him. She knew he was about to kiss her and the anticipation caused her heart to thump and bang like clattering pans at the very thought of it. His mouth was so close she could feel his breaths upon her lips and she remembered the smell of his naked skin as the scent of his expensive cologne delicately drifted toward her. He allowed her to feast on the glorious suspense of his kiss and for a second he just stared into her eyes, as if he too was basking in the romance of their reunion. Then, in dashing throbs, she heard his voice again.

"I'll tell you something, Paris Montford," he whispered, "I love you more than I have loved anyone in my life. You are going to be my wife and the loving mother to our children. I in return will make you the happiest woman alive."

Paris couldn't speak; the magnetic force that pulled her toward his vision was indescribable, and whilst vivid pictures of Paris Lancaster-Baron's family life caressed her mind, his soft mouth touched hers.

His lips glided with masculine swoops against her open mouth, he ran his fingers through her hair and as the intensity of his kiss grew stronger, she was certain; the pilot of his passion was definitely true love.

As Charles kissed Paris he became very much aware that this was a new world in which he had to find a way to survive in and Paris was the only person he knew who didn't fear it. With her as his wife, they could face this future together, she deserved to be cherished for a lifetime, he told himself, and that, he decided, would be exactly what he would do, cherish her. As they kissed, Charles felt himself genuinely appreciate the priceless gift of loving affection, two facets he knew had been sadly lacking in his life. The sound of a car unlocking nearby and the feminine scrape of stiletto heels against tarmac temporarily distracted his thoughts of gratitude.

Intrigued, he peeped through squinting eyes and saw Emma DeMario getting into her Porsche. With swift, accurate precision, despite his restricted view, he managed to faintly appraise the dress that cosseted her breathtaking figure.

God, she looks fantastic! he concluded.

Chapter Sixty Four

PARIS drove through the car park of the hotel, acutely aware that Charles was watching her from his car. With what felt like giant eagles flapping in her excited stomach, she turned and waved at him, holding up five fingers in gesture as to the number of minutes it would take before she would meet him back at Cedars Hall. Then, glancing one more time at his handsome face, she zipped off in her little hire car toward Goldsborough Crescent.

It was a typically cold and miserable January day, but Paris, fuelled by the satisfaction of knowing Charles loved her, felt dizzily hot and happy. In fact so hot, that even the spots of rain now spitting at her face through the open window couldn't persuade her to close it. She needed the chill of the fresh air to solidify her chaotic thoughts.

Once again, Charles Lancaster-Baron had managed to turn her life upside down, disrupt her thoughts until they were inside out and touch her heart until it melted like butter in the oven. She smiled, feeling strangely content by the sharp twist that had suddenly entered her life and began to think of where and how it would all end.

Without realising, whilst pondering the unpredictability of life *and* her emotions she had already sailed into the centre of Chelmsley. She drove through the pretty meandering streets, past the myriad of colourful shops and sandstone cottages, all of which, she realised, she had missed so much whilst living in Spain. She slowed the car in a bid to re-familiarise herself with the quaint country village in which she had grown up and it was then, quite unexpectedly, that she saw Rebecca Santé.

She was walking from the nursery with 'the baby' as she had termed him, dangling in her arms. His high pitched scream reverberated across the street and the look of exasperation on Rebecca's face was as clear as his cries. Paris' eyes narrowed with an angered frown and, anxious to get a closer glimpse of her son, she swiftly pulled into a nearby parking space.

Rebecca had parked right outside Chelmsley's country clothing store, a haven renowned for high-quality country clothing for ladies and gentlemen. Paris watched as Rebecca placed her screaming son in the baby carrier on the back seat of the car and fought to clip the straps, turning her head away from the shrillness of his deafening screams.

"You poor dear!" The owner from the country clothing shop said, standing in the shop doorway. "Does he ever stop crying? Every time I see you, he's always at it," Paris heard her say.

Rebecca turned to face the lady with a look of annoyance crowding her face. "Honestly," Rebecca replied sullenly "He just never gives it a bloody rest."

"I know what will cheer you up, Rebecca." The woman's eyes grew bright with enthusiasm. "Come and look at my equestrian range, I have some hunting waistcoats that have just arrived this morning, the suppliers have made an enormous faux pas and they have been delivered four months too late, but you will love them, they are just your style."

Rebecca looked round at the woman, then briefly back at the baby. For a split second Paris noticed her hesitation before finding the appeal of waistcoats too much to resist.

"Great, I'd love to," Rebecca replied, seemingly relieved to be offered respite so soon. "There's no point me bringing him in, he'll scream your place down to the ground. I'll leave him. Nothing will happen to him here, and anyway we'll hear if there's a problem."

"It sounds as though we'll hear if there isn't one too!" the woman chuckled, directing Rebecca into the shop with her arm.

"What is she doing?" Paris whined inside the car. "Anyone could take him."

Paris waited until Rebecca was in the shop and out of view, then, leaving the car's engine running, she burst out of the car and rushed toward her baby son.

Chapter Sixty Five

CHARLES walked into Cedars Hall and, just like the night before, felt the place treat him like a stranger, a visitor that had outstayed his welcome. Standing in the grand hallway he felt a cold, haunting atmosphere envelop him which caused his face to twitch with unease, followed by the sinister realisation that his face was already damp. The icy trace of the atmosphere was shouting its message; he was, without doubt, unwelcome inside.

Disbelieving that his lifetime home could turn its back so abruptly, he stood rigidly still, internally begging that his feeling was led by the paranoia of imagination. His eyes wandered anxiously through the air as he tried to decipher the origin of the menacing mood surrounding him. His penetrating stare swept across the panelled walls and the oak beams above until he realised, this perpetrator was invisible, undetectable to the human eye. However, with every frosty breath he inhaled, Charles *felt* its undeniable presence.

Fuelled by irritation, he heard his footsteps boom and ricochet against the walls as he forced himself with indignant strides to survey every room. Intently he began to scrutinise every detail of the numerous hallmarks that had made Cedars Hall the Lancaster-Baron home for so many decades.

He heard the graceful tick of the grandfather clocks, traced the grain of the oak furnishings with his finger, examined the intricate weave of the rich tapestries that hung on the walls and stared reflectively at the clarity of their depictions, as if seeing them for the very first time. His eyes traced the length of the elegant swooping curtains which trailed to the floor and, with appreciation he thoroughly embraced their undeniable class.

He turned to face the door of the drawing room, a room that since his mother's death he had purposely restrained himself from entering. With trepidation, Charles slowly turned the door handle and, as the door swung open, an explosion of memories and the amplification of irrefutable facts hit him hard in the face. Just standing in the doorway made Charles realise exactly why the house had taken back the offer of a lifetime welcome.

A swell of emotion lodged in his throat as his attention became fixed on his mother's beloved armchair. He placed his hands in his suit pockets and walked steadily from the doorway toward it. With regretful strokes of his hand he smoothed it along the arms, allowing the warmth of his masculine fingers to rest upon the faded areas of the material, a souvenir of the loving familiarity of his mother's hands. With instant clarity he saw her sitting serenely in her chair and watched her brilliant blue eyes appreciate the oil paintings that hung around her upon the walls. He too looked up at them and remembered dourly how he had never before thoroughly examined their content. He blew out a breath of dishonour; he had only ever matched each painting with a correlating price tag.

Determined to translate mother and son's opposing views he studied each one and, as he did, he couldn't help but notice the depiction that these portraits held. Just like the tapestries that he had scrutinised only moments before, incorporated in each piece, was the unassuming seal of nature. Be it creature or earth, each one portrayed a vibrant tenderness to all things living. Horses, dogs and the rolling hills of North Yorkshire's countryside that she had so adored, all took centre stage. Although many of these paintings were now considered treasured works of art, it was clear that their purpose and value had never been the motivating factor to their purchaser, instead, like everything else his mother had stood for; her impetus had been her love and gratification for anything that nature kindly bestowed.

He slumped into her chair and felt its comfort surround him, a comfort he realised that only genuine articles could offer. He looked over at the fireplace, and remembered the soft crackle of smoking coals that would have inhabited the grate, should she still be here. But today, without her presence, newly laid newspapers and freshly chopped kindling, courtesy of Mary, seemed to chill the room.

Charles nodded in agreement to the hostile host that hung impenetrably in the atmosphere. For now he understood – without Kitty in the house, he was not worthy of its hospitality. Without his mother's authentic beliefs and morals, her undeniable strength that anchored this house to its foundations, there was no point in him being here, and, for a brief moment, he thought he could feel the house physically shake in revulsion to the fact he was in it.

There was no mistaking it; Cedars Hall was most definitely his mother's home. It depicted an understated class, free from the glaring shout of money, and instead, absolutely crammed with the faint whisper of wealth. So much more made sense to him. He only wished this sense had pervaded him sooner.

The sombre strike of the grandfather clock reminded him of Paris' imminent arrival. He looked at the time and realised that sixty minutes had already passed. She would be here soon, he assured himself. He rested his head against the back of the chair. Thank God he had her, he concluded. Without her he would struggle to find a purpose. He reached for his mobile and tried to call her, but was immediately directed to her voicemail. He frowned; it wasn't like Paris to have her phone turned off. He remembered that there was a dip in the country roads about two miles away and receiving a signal on any phone was nigh on impossible. Yanking off his jacket and pulling his shirt over his head, he took the stairs two at a time. She would soon be here he told himself, he needed to take a shower.

With only one passport but two individuals in the car, Paris looked on as an army of cars, trailing into the recently opened doors of the ferry, sailed past. She looked across at her son, sitting by her side in his car seat and smiled lovingly.

"There, there Gerard," she cooed. "You are safe with mummy now." She stroked his face and stared into his innocent blue eyes with a tender smile.

Her son, for a second stared back at her, his little fingers and his chubby legs ceased their wriggling as his tiny brain registered being in receipt of genuine comfort. She touched his tiny button nose with the tip of her finger and moved her face closer to his and kissed his cheek, taking pleasure from the milky smell of his perfect skin. Beneath her face, his legs and fingers resurrected their zest for life and she felt his stillness disband into a frenzy of lively kicks and jiggles. She looked back at him and was instantly repaid with an enormous gummy smile that filled not only the car but her whole life with a sense of unequalled purpose. Her heart leapt from her body and she laughed away the tears of emotion that swamped her eyes. She was sure it was the first time he had ever smiled.

"I haven't missed much at all, have I?" she asked him behind the suppression of an excited laugh. "And I promise you," she assured, nuzzling her loving face into his tummy, "I will never miss anything in your life again."

With her index finger in the firm grip of her son's tiny fingers, Paris thought about her promise and knew that she had never spoken a truer word. For today's promise meant that to all intents and purposes she was now labelled a criminal. She had stolen her baby and was about to abduct him across the continent. Rapidly replacing the haunting image of a prison cell with the safe confines of Spain and her father, she gave Gerard the last ounce of milk from his bottle and watched his eyes lazily drift into sleep. She moved her head closer to him and marvelled at the perfection of his twitching eyelashes, before quietly unclipping his car seat and placing it into the foot-well of the car. She reached for the crocheted blanket from the back seat, enlarging the holes with the penetration of worried fingers to allow him room to breathe, completely covering the car seat and her sleeping son with it.

She looked ahead at the ferry on which she was about to embark and noticed a brigade of security staff pulling over a car to check its contents, a sight that made her stomach whip itself into frenzy.

"Go on!" she heard Charles' strong voice encourage. "You can do it!"

Bitter sweet torrents of sentiment and longing pummelled her body as she thought of him. The love of her life had almost been within her grasp. They had come so far, she realised, in a journey that had been so bloody hard. She thought about the harshness of Charles' day and worried that he may have been trying to contact her. She should have been at Cedars hours ago and, in the rush to grab her passport, she had forgotten everything else, including the charger for her mobile. She hoped he would be okay, and then chastised her never-ending naivety and concern.

Charles would always be okay, she told herself. Like Kitty had said, Charles was made from powerfully strong stock. She looked down at the parcel of disguise which her son lay beneath, but even if Charles wasn't fine, unless he came to her, there was not a person in the world that would take priority over her son. Not even the delectable Charles Lancaster-Baron.

She smiled fondly, remembering his every irresistible feature, before starting her engine. *And anyway* she asked herself, *who the hell am I kidding? He has probably forgotten about me already.* Her foot shook above the pedals as she wondered fearfully which one to press and watched the security officers ahead open the boot of the car they had pulled over.

"Shit!" she whispered through the apprehension of gritted teeth "What shall I do?"

Suddenly she remembered Charles' words the night they had spent at Wickruns Bay.

"The greatest pleasures are always born from the greatest risk," he had informed her coolly.

He was right, she would take a risk, take a gamble. Although they weren't together, and probably never would be, she wanted to live her life as though they were. Paris thought she knew Charles better then anyone; he was unique, exciting, never afraid to take a chance and always on the look out for an adventure and that, she decided, was the way to live life. She admired him, she realised - for all that he was.

Placing the car into gear she positioned her foot on the accelerator and watched the security guards wave the car they had been searching free from incarceration, through the gates and onto the ferry. They turned to look for a new mission and Paris felt their presence appear all too quickly as she drove toward them. Turning up the radio in an attempt to drown out the sound of her thudding heart she heard Diana Ross singing 'Someday we'll be together.' The melody swam drunkenly around her ears.

"Oh, Charles, I hope we will be," she squealed in fright. "I know for a fact you are the only person who could brazen this one out!"

She became conscious of her leg shaking violently against the accelerator and felt herself become physically faint as three pairs of scrutinising eyes looked directly at her.

Charles had showered and changed hours ago. He sat in the snug; his newly washed hair had dried some time ago. The bag that he had packed appeared to groan in boredom and his attire, a pale blue linen shirt that hung casually against tight black moleskin jeans, had long since lost their appeal.

Charles tried to contact Paris again; it had been five hours since she had left him in the car park. A sense of hope that the five fingers she had held up had in fact signified hours as opposed to minutes temporarily drifted through his mind, but its optimistic visit was brief. For in his heart he knew, Paris had no intention of returning.

Today was a premeditated plan on her part to seek revenge and, he had to say, it had been perfectly executed. Just like his mother, she too had left him in his hour of desperate need. He had so believed that her feelings for him were sincere and had so believed that the sparkling look in her eyes, when he had asked her to be his wife, to be true. But, as he had deceived *her* all those months ago, now *she* had turned the tables on *him*. *It had all been a hoax, and who could blame her?* he concluded.

He glanced down at the bag he had packed and an impulsive thought flashed through his mind. Maybe, if he was to chase after Paris, then she would really understand just how much he truly loved her. *But, what if she wasn't there?* A pessimistic voice in his mind asked. Charles pushed the thought aside, feeling certain that she would be, and anyway, he reminded himself, *I have always been a gambling man; why should today make any difference?*

He walked over to his laptop and fired it into action. If there was a flight available to Spain in the next twelve hours he would most certainly take it. *And if there isn't?* he heard the pessimistic voice return. He snubbed it again; he would cross that bridge when he got to it.

For now, Charles just felt relieved that he had managed to source a new purpose to his life. Life was a game of fate and chance, he told himself. It was just a twist of fate that had encouraged him to speculate on the chance of love instead of money.

Moments later, in a room that was darkened by the early cast of the winter's night, Charles' handsome face was illuminated by the screen of his laptop. He placed his broad masculine hands behind his head, arrogantly lolled upon his chair, then laughed aloud.

For once, Charles Lancaster-Baron had found *exactly* what he had been searching for.